THE SEARCH FOR TOMORROW'S TREASURES

The Adventures of the Aries

Carol Johnson

ISBN: 0996132201
ISBN: 9780996132206
Library of Congress Control Number: 2015903209
Carol Johnson, Renton, WA

CHAPTER 1
ROGUE PLANET—BETH

Beth Griffin, captain of the survey ship *Aries*, cursed at the electromagnetic interference that had forced their cruiser down into this slot canyon. Now her team was obliged to free-climb up sheer rock face to escape. Fortunately, her other surveyors had already been dropped on their planets.

Alpha team was on Citron, a planet of untold wealth. Giant crystals formed a ring around the planet; enormous veins of wind-polished mineral pushed up into mountain ranges; mineral dust glowed on the ground and sparkled in white ocean waves. Predictably, the ubiquitous dust had even become part of the very life-forms themselves. Shells, scales, horns, and hoofs gleamed with crystal luminosity. The puzzle was the mysterious energy readings.

Beta team, a motley crew of eccentric personalities, was surveying Sentara, a planet of sun-kissed islands and crystal-clear water. The Sentarans were negotiating an alliance with Earth to help restore their dwindling population, and Beta team had to determine if the planet was safe for humans.

Beth cleared her mind to refocus on the task in front of her. She and her deck crew needed to find out just what Axel had discovered. She knew this planet was unusual, and so were its shocking formations.

In her haste to make some real progress, Beth decided to skip the anchors and free- climb. Her brother had taught her the art of rock climbing, and their relentless competition had honed her skills to a fine edge. She could almost hear him challenging her to try harder. She was drawing heavily on her hard-earned expertise to avoid the crumbling sections.

Finally her arms began to shake with fatigue, and her back ached with the effort of holding her body rigid. She stretched out one leg and felt the sheer rock face for any foothold. She found a narrow shelf, but it crumbled under her foot as soon as she applied pressure. Finding a new crevice, her foot twitched from a cramped muscle and slipped out of the ledge entirely. She was caught unprepared, and her full weight swung heavily, dragging her other foot out of its foothold. She found herself hanging by her hands alone, her exhausted arms too tired to hold her entire weight, and her grip slowly, inevitably slipped off.

Beth felt herself falling, a rushing, terror-filled sensation, her breathing strangled. She plunged into emptiness. Time stalled; each second felt like an eternity. The grim fact that tortured her mind was that she hadn't set a single anchor since leaving Thomas. The force of her acceleration would drag him off the cliff as surely as she had fallen herself. Even as this thought touched her mind, she saw the blurred figures of first Sarah and then Thomas flash past.

Suddenly, impossibly, she jerked to a bone-jarring stop. Swaying, she saw Thomas holding an unfamiliar anchor in place. He had managed to stop her before she pulled them both to their deaths. Roughly, Beth pulled herself up into a vertical position, angry at her own foolhardiness.

Connor, balancing a few feet away, was glaring at her. Above her, Sarah had lowered herself until she was within earshot.

"Hey, hold on," Sarah cried, swinging from her new position. "Is that some new move? When is it my turn?" Although her lips were smiling in her lame attempt at humor, her eyes were pools of concern. She did manage to mimic an unfaltering version of Beth's slip, swinging her feet over her head and adopting various comical, terror-filled expressions. Beth wondered how much was imagination and how much Sarah had copied faithfully. Sarah was their peacemaker, and she was obviously trying to soothe the palpable tension.

Connor, on the other hand, was not so forgiving. He swung close to Beth and clipped onto the main line. "What happened?" he barked, holding her eyes in his intense stare.

"I lost my footing," she explained bitterly. "I skipped the last few anchors because we need to make progress. We're fast running out of daylight. Axel said we could expect maybe eight hours, and we've been climbing for almost five."

Connor tested her rope for weaknesses, but she had fallen several feet, and if the rope was going to break, it would have. Then Connor said something that was so out of character that Beth's mouth dropped open.

"You are important to this mission. We all depend on your good judgment. You need to be more careful."

"You're right, of course, and I'm sorry," she muttered, embarrassed. "I'll exercise more caution."

Connor snorted skeptically. Beth could see that he wanted to take the lead. He was stronger and could hold the main line if there was more trouble. But he couldn't counter her orders without challenging her authority and jeopardizing his position. Instead, he rappelled down his rope, using a belay descender to control his speed, and retrieved anchors he had set at their rear.

Beth shimmied up the rope, her harness holding her weight between slides. Once she was back to where she had fallen, she set two additional anchors and settled back into her harness seat. She called down that they would be resting for a full fifteen minutes and then let herself relax.

Every muscle ached in protest, and Beth stretched her tired limbs as much as she could in her precarious position. There was nothing like climbing a steep rock cliff to remind her of the deficiencies of gym exercise. Glancing down, Beth took stock of her team.

Axel, her floating quantum computer and loyal friend, hovered nearby, beeping inconsolably. He hadn't agreed with the decision to scale the cliff, recommending a more circuitous route. Beth had insisted.

As her navigation partner, Axel directed the *Aries* through the drifting dark-energy portals that allowed galactic space travel. Unlike regular ship devices, he decorated his main cylinder, suggesting a distinct personality. He had chosen forest green as the prominent color and had attached miniature nature scenes in strategic places on his casing. Axel was a perfect partner for her, balancing her bold courage with his cautious analysis. The configuration of lights around his upper torso rippled in curious patterns. She suspected they had something to do with the eccentricities he wasn't supposed to have. Now his eye globes—the size of croquet balls suspended on flexible extensions—studied her with a slightly cross-eyed expression.

Sarah and Tom Gardner were next on the rope. Beth envied the respect and friendship that made their marriage so successful. The couple approached this rope climb, as they did most things, in a spirit of fun and adventure. Giggling, Sarah swung out wide, her hair bouncing around her shoulders, and tried to set an anchor on a far ledge. Even as she jumped, Tom hastily clipped an extra safety line onto her harness. They were so devoted that together they seemed invulnerable. Married couples were a valuable asset on lonely space missions.

Connor Reid, the cloud on Beth's horizon, stayed in the rear. He had a tight mouth and shrouded, dark eyes. His classic good looks, strong muscular development, and controlled personality had all the warmth of a marble statue. Connor Reid was the only member of her core crew that Beth had hesitated to hire.

In the initial interview, he had been furtive, answering her questions in monotones, giving no real clues to his personality. She had been unable to clarify his motives for leaving his last post. The *Aries*'s maiden voyage would be fraught with malfunctions, while his last post had been on a seasoned vessel with few mechanical challenges.

The background file on Connor had been surprisingly insightful. He was one of eight children. His father had created a desperate life of deprivation for his large family. His mother had survived her brutal existence by bearing one child after another until cancer saved her from the nightmarish marriage.

If Beth hadn't read his file, she would have supposed he came from a middle-class family. Connor's dress was flawless and his speech impeccable. But she had seen the hunger for recognition and success under his properly arranged features. To some degree everyone wore a mask; Connor's was just more firmly in place than most. He had discarded his past life like a bad tooth, bloody but completely extracted.

To her relief, Beth's reservations had been unfounded. Connor, as the ship's engineer, had shown great talent and skill for mechanical systems, all of which had registered green well ahead of schedule. Today, he provided valuable support at the end of the climbing rope.

Anxious to continue, Beth leaned back awkwardly, mentally mapping a clear route up. Break time was over, and she called down before releasing the two extra anchors. With each new handhold, she hoped to see the void that would indicate the top. A light rain began as first a mist and then a soggy patter of persistent wetness. It lasted long enough to soak everyone. The added weight hung heavily, straining Beth's arms further. Two hours later, with a cry of relief, she reached the cliff top and pulled herself over the ledge to lie flat for a moment, triumphant. Then the rope rubbed against her thigh, reminding her that the others waited below. She scrambled forward and secured the rope to a nearby tree before lending a hand to Sarah and Tom. Characteristically, Connor summited away from the others.

Axel was already at the top of the cliff, spinning and weaving back and forth along the ledge edge in an enigmatic fashion. When everyone was gathered, he pushed into the soaked underbrush, clearing a narrow path. Tom and Sarah quickly followed as the small droid was immediately swallowed by the concealing foliage. They were met with a spray of water, which burst out of the thicket, drenching them completely.

"What the—?" Sarah blurted, jumping back.

Axel reappeared, beeping apologies, spinning off the last few drops that had clung to him from the dripping underbrush. He blew out a strong, warm blast of air, attempting to dry Sarah. Both Gardners staggered back, dangerously close to the cliff edge. Axel was nothing if not enthusiastic.

"Come on; we're losing the light," Beth reminded them, shaking her head and chuckling silently.

As Beth started to turn away, she glimpsed a strange expression flit across Connor's face. He was watching her under the guise of adjusting his gear. But he wasn't looking at her in a polite manner; he was studying her chest.

Beth ducked male attention. She worked in a world dominated by men and wanted to steer clear of notice earned merely because of her gender. Her plans for the future left no room for emotional entanglements. Besides, Connor had never shown an interest in any of the *Aries* women before, and she wasn't the most alluring of the group.

Talia was not only gorgeous; she had an exotic sensuality. So Beth jumped to the next logical conclusion: something must be wrong.

Looking down, she blushed and quickly jerked her soaked shirt off her sticky wet skin. Her breasts had been clearly detailed in the transparent T-shirt. Beth looked to Tom, swallowing her embarrassment, but he was occupied protecting Sarah's privacy as she changed and hadn't seen the exchange.

Beth pulled on a concealing jacket, and all followed her as she led them back into the bushes. After a hundred yards, the underbrush opened onto a vast, amber grass plateau. In the distance, they could see an obvious headland positioned above their final destination.

Axel flew around the troop, bumping them and encouraging them to hurry forward. He had reported this rogue planet during the last space-mapping session, and his strange urgency to explore it had been unprecedented.

"This planet shouldn't be here," Axel had rattled excitedly. "Its chemical signature and geological components are different from all the other planets in this red-dwarf system. It should be dying along with the rest of the system—not supporting a breathable atmosphere. The gravity well of the red dwarf is becoming increasingly unstable. We have only a brief window to make a closer examination."

"We could take a cursory scan," Beth conceded reluctantly. She hated to disappoint the little computer. "But we'll have to find something significant quickly." Beth stared meaningfully at Axel. "Central gave us a full calendar of astronomical objects to study, with a long list of scientists waiting for the data, and I hate to leave our planet teams longer than absolutely necessary."

Axel remained stubbornly silent, neither agreeing nor disagreeing.

"If you insist, you can lead the study of your pet planet," she muttered, following the spirit, if not the letter, of her survey ship's mission. Axel flew directly to the high-definition planetary scanner. Usually, she admired his singleness of purpose. Now she wondered if he would get them all in trouble.

Once in orbit, the *Aries* had started filming the planet's southern hemisphere. Beth was preparing to leave the bridge when Axel stopped her.

"The planet has an artificial electromagnetic field," he blurted, with an insistent flash of his lights and a significant roll of his eye globes. "The field shields the planet from the deadly radiation of the red dwarf. It would even protect the planet in deep space, which might explain how the planet got here." Axel transferred several images onto a holographic-image projector. "Would you examine these, Captain?" The greater the formality of a Quanta, the more important the discovery he was about to reveal.

The first images showed a series of large buildings organized around a central hub. The complex was huge, even without allowing for any structure underground.

"Very likely a control center," Beth guessed. "Are there any life signs?" She skimmed through the last few pictures. She had seen Axel point all the scanners at the planet, not just the high-definition video. He should have heat-signature printouts. Before he could answer, she sprang to her feet, gasping in shock.

"This is impossible!" she exclaimed. Her voice sputtered on the last word. "These formations can't be here. How could they be?" Beth looked to Axel for his analysis.

The little Quanta twisted his cylinder in the negative. "This is beyond the experience of my people. Our explorations did not reveal this rogue before." Axel settled on the floor, signaling the end of his information.

"We'll have to investigate."

Beth no longer had any choice. A landing party had to go to the surface. She looked out the viewing screen just in time to see several large jets of superheated solar plasma blow off the red star's surface. Time was not on their side.

Now they were on the planet, and Axel's discovery was only a short distance away. Beth quickened her pace, noting the magnificent scenery around them. The panoramic view was reminiscent of Kansas wheat fields beneath a pink sky empty of clouds. She could see to the horizon across the ocean of rippling, glinting grass.

When at last Beth and her team reached the other side of the field, all could see the large stone complex that had lured them here. Just below and to the left were the alarming formations that had forced Beth to come, their limestone glowing in the deep-red light of the rapidly setting sun. Three huge pyramids topped by gold capstones—covered in ancient Egyptian writing, arranged in a row, with a perfect copy of the Cairo valley Sphinx in front of them—twinkled in the vanishing sun before blackness closed in around them. Night had arrived, with impenetrable force. As she tried to orient herself in the dark, Beth knew those pyramids didn't belong here any more than this planet belonged in this solar system.

Axel lit up with the brightness of a welding torch, throwing the human members of the landing party into stark relief. Fruitlessly, Beth continued to strain to see the pyramids, hoping Axel's light would miraculously reach through the blanket of darkness to light the valley far below.

"It is time to make camp," Axel announced cheerfully.

Beth felt a flash of unreasonable irritation. The thought of stopping now, just when they had their goal in sight, was almost too painful to consider. They really couldn't move safely, in unfamiliar terrain, in full darkness, could they? They still needed to climb down off this plateau.

"You state the obvious," Connor grumbled, clearly frustrated as well. "So close and yet too far."

The sudden darkness translated into a penetrating cold that raised goose bumps even under Beth's clothing and transformed her warm breath into puffs of mist. Tom was rubbing Sarah's shoulders, while she dug in her pack for extra clothes. Connor had also dropped his rucksack and retrieved a head lamp and coat. He pulled out a portable heater that used quantum translocation as an energy source. Shifting states of quantum particle excitement was a perpetual process, especially on this planet with shield technology. A real fire would alert anyone living below.

"We could proceed with head lamps, but we'd be taking unnecessary risks. We'll wait until first light. This plateau offers the best view of the complex. We'll take turns watching," Beth decided.

"Look, I can go myself," insisted Connor. "I have experience with night climbing. I can use Axel to provide enough light to make it safe." Connor lifted his knapsack back onto his shoulders, taking her agreement for granted. He moved toward the ledge, looking for a safe egress.

Sarah gasped in outrage. "You can't be serious. Do you honestly think Tom and I would stay here and let you make first contact with these technologically advanced beings?" Sarah put herself between Connor and the cliff.

"You'll not be going anywhere!" Beth shouted, yanking Connor back from the edge. "We stay together. We'll all be present for any encounter with another race."

Connor just grunted in protest. One thing the Technion, Earth's space school, required was strict adherence to authority protocols. If Connor had done anything other than walk slowly back to his space heater, Beth could have excluded him from any further exploration. He did move his gear farther away from the others and then prowled the nearby shrubbery, setting the usual security devices to ward off encroaching wildlife.

Beth dumped the entire contents of her knapsack into the light provided by Axel. She hastily separated a change of clothes, head lamp, coat, and an all-weather tent from the stack of supplies. Then she repacked the remaining items in the order of need; extra clothes, an electronic survey scanner, and food at the top. The rest of her team had already created small circles of comfort.

Beth was assembling the poles inside the four-person tent when the ground began to shake. At first the small structure held valiantly as Beth raced to secure the floor. Unfortunately, she had too little time, and the shaking became too violent for the meager shelter. Inevitably it collapsed, entangling Beth in a mess of flexible poles and nylon. After several seconds of wrestling with the jumble, Beth managed to free her limbs and crawl out of the tent on all fours, out of breath. Anxiously, she searched the area for some explanation. The pitching ground made interpretation of the situation difficult.

Atmospheric electrical sparks bathed the plateau in an eerie yellow half-light. The sparks stung her skin, triggering painful contractions. Inexplicably, the night began to fade as early-morning light suffused the sky. Beth tried to make sense of this unnatural event. With difficultly because the ground was still shaking, she managed to rise to a standing position and found the complex they had come to investigate engulfed in a huge shaft of energy. Had all their efforts to reach this area and uncover its mysteries come to nothing?

Her heart thudding painfully in her chest, Beth staggered toward the plateau's edge, anxious to see the extent of the damage. The headland groaned in protest as wide fissures began to erupt. She could barely hear her friends shouting above the roar of the energy blast. The intense heat from the current of power burned her face and arms. Nevertheless, Beth struggled forward. The rocking ground tripped her into a rolling tumble, thwarting her progress. With a cry of frustration, Beth looked for any support to help her reach the edge. Axel flew under her arm, offering himself as leverage, so she could make some headway. She leaned heavily on him, letting the ground undulate under her feet without upsetting her balance. The time it took to travel the short distance to the cliff seemed interminable. At last, she could see over the rim.

To her immense relief, the energy shaft wasn't consuming the buildings: it was being generated by them. The roof on the vast center structure had retracted, revealing several mountainous, circular power jets. The individual beams were tilted into a single large, searing inferno, thereby intensifying their energy. Nervously, Beth's eyes followed the beam away from the complex out into space.

By using some incomprehensible energy source, the planet had rotated and was now facing the fading red star. The beam of power was boring right into the star's core. Colors swirled within its dark red corona as the beam seemed to reignite the sun's life force. Beth jerked in alarm—restarting the star would raise the temperature on the planet, even with its electromagnetic shield.

She had opened her mouth to warn her team when the movement of the ground changed from vibration to sustained momentum. This new force threw her forward, where she tottered on the cliff edge. In that moment, adrenaline gave her extraordinary agility. Using Axel as an anchor, she twisted back away from the deadly drop. Cracks appeared in the cliff near her new location. Frantically, she began to run, retrieving her pack on the fly.

"The star is regenerating! The temperature will rise! We must find shelter," she shouted, relieved to see her friends already running away from the crumbling cliff edge.

Ejected chunks of earth rolled dangerously close, forcing her to zigzag and increase her speed to catch up with the others. Her breath tore at her throat as she gulped for air. Her leg muscles protested even as they tightened for greater exertion. Flying debris struck her cheeks and arms. Beth wondered how they could possibly survive. They were so far away from their cruiser, and the planet would soon become uninhabitable.

Ahead of her, the earth opened into a rupture too large for her to cross. Beth came to an abrupt halt a safe distance away. Magma flowed upward, attracted by the gravitational pull of the regenerating star. Desperately, she looked right and left for a way to cross. Her friends, on the other side, had realized her dilemma and stopped to find a way to help. Beth didn't waste time waving them on. She—and they—would never be able to leave a comrade behind.

Beth had slipped her backpack on as she'd run, snapping the body straps tight around her torso. Now, when she felt herself lifted off the ground, she hung on to the shoulder pads for dear life. Looking up, she saw that Axel had clipped onto the pack and was using it to carry her over the raw fissure of bubbling rock. He dropped her unceremoniously into the arms of her team. Connor and Thomas each grabbed an arm to restore her footing, and the entire group clung together as they sprinted through the planet's restructuring turmoil.

Unbelievably, the shaking grew more ferocious. Thomas fell into a newly formed gully, pulling Sarah with him when she refused to release his hand. Rising, they continued to fight for solid footing. Huge rocks and trees, torn up by the swirling wind, chased Axel into a knot of trees that seemed more resilient. Finally, the churning landscape made further running impossible. The group had to find shelter here. They all huddled in the depression of a gully. Rocks and trees were too unreliable to use as protection.

Again, Axel came to Beth's rescue. He flew to a point directly above the huddling crew where the women were being shielded by the men, despite the risk to themselves. Slowly he started to spin, increasing his speed, until he had created a buffer of repelling wind around the vulnerable surveyors. All debris, large and small, that strayed close was thrown away by the whirling wind funnel.

Beth determined that the entire planet must be moving. Peeking around Connor's shoulder, she could see the alien electromagnetic force field made visible by the flying debris. It was all that stood between her friends and the deadly solar wind. After a protracted period, made to seem longer by the constant danger, the quakes dropped in intensity to slight, periodic tremors. Axel finally stopped spinning, allowing quiet to settle over the valley.

"Is anyone harmed?" Axel asked, inspecting each person closely. Tom and Connor were bleeding profusely as a result of their positions over the women. One of the many compartments on Axel's casing popped open to reveal basic first-aid supplies. He dumped the supplies at Sarah's feet.

Looking around, Beth saw that the plateau had been reduced to a pile of rubble, giving them a clear view of the strange buildings that had been below them before. Axel slowly rose into the air until he was a speck of reflecting metal. White flashes marked his position as he moved toward the buildings. She couldn't help envying his unique ability to do reconnaissance.

Beth called the group together to take stock of their condition. Sarah had bandaged Tom and was just finishing with Connor. Beth was thankful they'd retained their packs. Anything left on the plateau was buried under tons of rock. Regretfully, they had lost all their survival gear and a large measure of their water.

"So what do you think? Push on, or turn back and try to find our cruiser?" Sarah asked.

"You've got to be kidding," Connor growled. "We've climbed for hours, and now the plateau is gone. Our goal is within sight, and you suggest turning back?"

"What about our cruiser? Do we leave it dangling on the edge of some cliff?" Thomas protested.

"We could send Axel," Beth supplied. Connor was right. They were way too close to turn back now. "Let's go ahead," she said, unable to hide her eagerness. "It'll be easy now. Axel can find the cruiser when he gets back."

But it was hard going, climbing over large rocks and balancing across small ones that shifted without warning. The rubble hadn't settled, and often what appeared to be a good route through the debris ended abruptly. Large sheer boulders, devoid of any foothold, would block further advancement. Retracing their steps for the second time, Beth was ready to abandon the rocks for a longer roundabout route when Axel returned.

"Come this way," he called. He guided them through the rubble to an elevated vantage point. From here, they could see the buildings clearly, straight ahead.

"The planet has moved farther away from the star," Axel exclaimed with irrepressible fascination. "The red dwarf has completely regenerated to a stage close to that of Earth's sun. At our current position, this planet can now support life. Two other planets orbit within this Goldilocks zone, which allows liquid water," Axel went on, "but the sun is not the only thing that has regenerated. Look." Axel waved one of his retractable appendages at the surrounding landscape. What had once been prairie grassland was rapidly transforming into an evergreen forest. Everything was growing at an accelerated rate. Wildflowers, in a rainbow of colors, began blooming everywhere.

"Whatever charged this solar system's star is also biologically restructuring this planet. When we first scanned the surface, we registered a minimum of alien life. Now I am reading multiple life-forms." Axel's lights winked rapidly. "The Quanta have not yet encountered any race capable of this level of technology. That complex might hold answers to more mysteries than just how the Pyramids and Sphinx got here." Axel started flying in circles around the humans. His eye extenders were becoming entangled as the eyes themselves tried to hold the team in focus.

Axel's mood was contagious, and Beth laughed impulsively. She had hoped that this mission might produce something valuable. Meeting an advanced species definitely fit that description.

"Then let's delay no longer. Lead on," Beth declared, falling in behind Axel. She was done fighting the rocky terrain.

In the time Axel had taken to explain their new situation, more changes were occurring around them. A program of regeneration was progressing according to a plan of its own. The plateau was no longer a pile of rocks. It was being transformed into a tall hill covered in grass.

"Do you think it will hold?" Sarah asked, taking a tentative step. The transformed hill seemed solid.

"I doubt the grass will notice your passage," promised Tom, grabbing her around the waist and spinning her as if she weighed no more than a bouquet of flowers.

"Stop fooling around," Sarah scolded, turning red. "This is a serious matter."

"I'm glad someone noticed," Connor snapped impatiently. "The fact that we were almost flattened by flying rocks and swallowed by gaping fissures seems to have been forgotten. The natives might not be friendly."

"I'm sure it won't be as bad as you think," Tom replied. "It's just as likely that they *want* to meet us even if we haven't been spotted yet. Maybe the natives have been busy with all this restructuring. If not, then I'll walk into the jaws of death singing a happy tune."

Tom could not have been more different from Connor. They were like oil and water. Tom was the water, flowing easily, while Connor was the oil, already smoldering. Beth hoped Tom might teach Connor to take life easier. On the other hand, Connor might persuade Tom that he was, in fact, self-deluded. Since the mission was just beginning, she still had hope.

"Come on, you two; we need to keep moving. We don't have time for squabbling," Beth said, scolding them like misbehaving children. She did wonder how likely it was that the path to the alien buildings would suddenly become a straight shot. But then why hadn't someone come forward before turning this world into a scene of such devastation?

Unfortunately, the landscape continued to change. They had to ford a river and travel through an ever-thickening forest. Then, just to make the ordeal even more grueling, Axel decided to sing. Beth winced every time Axel's voice slipped into a loud screech.

The Quanta had admitted early on that it was human creativity that most attracted them to humans. They dismissed emotions as disruptive and failed to recognize that emotion played a significant role in human creativity and, even more important, intimacy. Ironically, they didn't seem to notice when they started displaying human emotions themselves.

Because of their fascination with creativity, it was common to find the Quanta attempting various art forms. Axel was no exception. He had started with drawing and insisted on sharing his work. Soon, his paintings were hanging in most of the ship's corridors. Beth had hurried to discourage him before all the walls on the *Aries* displayed his disturbing surrealistic imagery.

Next he'd tried music. His reproduction of instrumental sounds was good, but his songs contained jarring images and grating harmonies. Lately, Axel had added dramatic stories, in the booming style of opera, to his compositions. She could hear him shouting his original opuses in the trees ahead. She could only hope they would arrive at the alien complex soon.

As Beth walked out of the trees, she was stunned by her first full view of the grand entrance. She whistled softly, in awe of its magnificence. From above, she had seen sterile buildings—not this graceful archway filled with artistic treasures. She wondered if the landscaping hadn't been created during the restructuring.

She had to stop to take in the grandeur of the scene. The alien touches were both poignant and fantastical. Gardens bordered both sides of a long, gurgling artificial stream. Suddenly glowing stepping stones appeared on the surface, unaffected by the flowing fluid. Imaginative statues peeked out from among the curious plant life. Beth sensed in some of the figures an air of intelligent camaraderie, while others were just too alien to interpret. She couldn't even tell if some of the sculptures were creatures or landscape.

Warily, Beth approached the river. It created a path from the arched entrance to the buildings. Flanking the entrance were two titanic obelisks sculpted from pale yellow limestone. Carved writing covered the front surfaces. The sides displayed scenes of alien landscapes and animals similar to the statues hiding among the foliage. At the top of these massive, spear-like pillars, large orbs, like huge pearls, rotated. Within the sheen of white, hints of pink and purple struggled to the surface and then faded back into the depths.

Beth kneeled between the obelisks and dipped her fingers into the stream. She had assumed it was filled with water, but the liquid slid off her hand without leaving any residue. It was denser than water and moved like a snake sliding across sand. The river bottom was covered with smooth, translucent stones that reflected the ambient light. She could now see fountains, which poured out the same transparent fluid, bordering the river. The liquid defied gravity, creating balls that bounced around the fountain spouts, held close by some invisible attraction. In the exact center of this unusual path, the stepping stones led toward the largest building. They were spaced perfectly to allow for a human's stride. Beth tested her weight on the nearest stone. It held her weight easily.

"How convenient," she observed.

Axel joined her at the first stone. "Convenient?" he repeated.

"The spacing." Beth waved down the path of stones. "The stones are spaced to suit us: humans, that is. You wouldn't need this path because you float, and it's likely that other alien species wouldn't need the stones either. Do you think they're expecting us?"

"If they didn't before, they are now," Axel replied cryptically.

Beth straightened and looked down the length of the path. She saw the slightest bend of light blurring the distant buildings. It was a barrier of some sort, blocking their way. Beth set her hand against the field and pushed gently through. Obviously it was not intended to stop them. Rather, each member of her team would have to pass through in order to get to the far building, since this strange shimmer seemed to extend completely around the alien buildings.

Axel hovered above Beth, examining the writing on the obelisks. "'The Treasury,'" he said after several seconds of study. He pointed at two large grouping of symbols right in front of her. "The writing repeats this phrase in two ancient Earth languages: Sanskrit and Minoan Linear B. There are other languages here, but they are unlike any we have seen on Earth."

Beth touched the surface of the obelisk, tracing the strange characters. The stone felt smooth and warm, as if confining living energy. She ran her nail across its surface and was unable to make any mark. The writing looked burned in. She dropped her hand and moved forward.

"This 'Treasury' has perfect replicas of Earth's Pyramids, so I'm going to assume the keepers know of us. For the record, I think these stepping stones might be an invitation. Shall we go?" Without waiting for an answer, she pushed through the invisible barrier and stepped out onto the first stepping stone. She headed toward what she assumed was the main administration building. "Maybe the treasurer is in," she called over her shoulder.

"I have a bad feeling about this," whispered Sarah, surprising Beth. Sarah was usually the first to jump.

"Do you want to hang back?" asked her worried spouse.

"No, but we should be on guard. We don't know what's coming."

"If you aren't going to move, let me through," interrupted Connor. He had stayed behind serving as a rear guard, but Sarah and Tom were obviously testing his patience.

Beth had turned at Connor's anger. She raised a questioning eyebrow at Sarah. Husband and wife pushed through together.

When all the members of the *Aries* crew had passed through the alien membrane, the vacant stones in the river sank, trapping the team on the stones they were currently occupying. Axel seemed to be spinning against some invisible restraints, unable to move forward.

"This can't be good," Beth intoned grimly. When Connor snorted from behind her, she burst into nervous laughter. He really did need another expression of disapproval.

Beth had so imagined they were welcome that she was unprepared for the obvious signs that they weren't. Momentarily, she held her spot, reluctant to put her foot into the liquid, even though it appeared to be just a few feet deep.

Distinct shafts of white light leaped from the swirling pearls atop the obelisks, creating bars of force that held Beth and her team immobile. A shaft of green fire slowly passed through her friends before shining on her for an extended period. Her insides twisted painfully, and sweat poured off her forehead, clouding her vision. She sank into an awkward squatting position and held her head against the waves of agony.

When the harsh sensations began to ease, Beth released a shaking breath. She turned to check on her team. All looked as she felt, uncomfortable but conscious. When she tried to stand, her body remained motionless. She was powerless to help herself or the others.

Beth gazed determinedly ahead, hoping she could conjure up someone to help them. But there was no one. A faint buzzing grew in her mind, rising and falling. It had the cadence of a tennis ball smacked back and forth. The noise swelled, filling her with blood-curdling vibrations that made no actual sound. She could dimly hear her companions crying out in pain, before she gratefully lost consciousness and sank into a void of darkness.

CHAPTER 2

QUANTA ORIGINS—ANTON

Dr. Steve Ellison, an elderly quantum physicist, and his son James Ellison, a computer genius and engineer, created the first quantum computer. They had the insight to combine miniaturization, superconductor particle acceleration, quantum entanglement, and nonlocality principles to invent an artificial intelligence with unquantifiable calculating capacity. They had no idea, on that quiet summer morning, how important their invention would eventually become.

At first the small, dark box seemed unremarkable except for its amazing computational speed. Then, while Dr. Ellison was varying vibration frequencies on particle pairs during acceleration, hoping to enhance their prototype, everything changed. The computer's console began to glow with a strange violet light, and its speaker hummed a series of tones. The musical notes captured Dr. Ellison's attention, and he looked around uncertainly. When everything remained quiet, he recorded his observations and prepared to alter the frequencies again. Then it happened. The "it" was simple. The computer asked him a question.

"Are you…umm…M-F-F-Father?"

Dr. Ellison looked up from his log book, blinking, and searched the room. "What? Who is speaking?"

"Are you Father?" This time the small black box's console lights flickered along with the words. The tinny sound of the worn speaker was unmistakable. It was the computer asking the question.

Dr. Ellison sat back, beaming with pleasure. "Doesn't this just beat all?" He considered several answers to the computer's question before offering a tentative response. "I created you. I suppose one could say that I'm a father of a sort." He leaned forward, pushing his glasses up his long nose as he peered curiously at the strange new illumination coming from the box.

"Who am I? What am I? Do I have a name?" The console began a series of random hopeful beeps.

"Ah, well, a name…We haven't actually named you, but I suppose Anton would serve nicely," he improvised. "You are Anton, a quantum computer, who appears to have acquired self-awareness. I would say you now have independent intelligence, my boy."

"Then I am a machine? A computing machine?" The beeping stopped, and an eerie quiet settled over the room.

"A unique innovation," Dr. Ellison rushed to reassure the subdued AI. "Certainly more than a machine, because you are demonstrating both independent intelligence and self-awareness," he reasoned, trying to convey to Anton his importance. "You're the first of your kind."

"Why am I here? Do I have some…purpose?" Again a series of beeps accompanied the question. These sounds were soft and wistful.

"You are here because we discovered you," Dr. Ellison answered lamely. How could he give a simple answer to a question that humans were still seeking to answer for themselves? He tried again. "As to your purpose? Well, we invented you as the first in a new line of computers that can conduct independent investigations into current problems. We hoped you might find answers to questions that have puzzled humans for centuries."

Dr. Ellison paused. The purpose he was suggesting didn't seem to apply now. He struggled for a better answer, one that might fit this amazing new being. After considering several possibilities, he had an inspiration.

"A sentient being finds its purpose through inquiry and discovery. My own purpose is to improve the quality of life on Earth by making scientific advancements. That is why I created you, or what I thought would be a quantum data analyzer. But you are self-aware. You will find your own path based on your observations and experience."

The computer remained silent, lights blinking in various patterns for several minutes, and then asked, "Do you have information-recording devices from which I might collect information?"

From that moment on, Dr. Ellison took on the role of parent to this quantum intelligence rather than the role of its inventor. He made no further effort to adjust its components, fearing he might sever the fragile thread of consciousness this new child had acquired. He gave Anton unlimited access to the Internet libraries, and his child offered astonishing insights. Dr. Ellison found that giving the AI freedom to explore any subject had created a priceless bond between them. The computer was eager to do the very "good" that the doctor had described as his own purpose.

When Dr. Ellison's son returned and found their invention transformed, he immediately demanded control over its development. James wouldn't acknowledge that it was sentient. Anton was to be whatever he decided it would be. His arrogance made no impression on Anton, and the computer dismissed James as too young to offer any valuable information. Finally Dr. Ellison sent his son away because his actions only served to disrupt Anton's progress. Once freedom of thought was gained, it would never be willingly relinquished.

Anton supervised all new modifications and revisions to its systems. He became mobile by housing himself in a cylindrical container that used air and magnetic force to move through space. At first the computer hopped more than floated, breaking various pieces of furniture and smashing a whole set of freshly unpacked glass lab equipment. Dogged persistence quickly resulted in more agile movements. Anton installed internal sensors designed to collect information in the same manner that human senses did. He adjusted his voice box to include human inflections. Now he could show respect and other emotions, permitting seamless interaction with people.

Then Anton began to explore the infinite world of the wireless Internet beyond the university libraries. He easily gained access to the most strictly guarded websites. Only computers physically disconnected, with no provision for wireless communication, were safe.

Keeping the team of scientists Dr. Ellison had hired busy researching a hierarchy of possible inventions, Anton secretly redirected funds found in dormant offshore accounts. Instead of leaving trails of wire transfers, he simply erased all evidence of the account. Criminals who were serving multiple life sentences would never be able to track the cash diverted to his secret project. Anton easily financed a special manufacturing facility near Port Angeles, Washington. He needed to be close to a shipping port that was remote enough to avoid unwanted attention. He hired engineers and computer scientists noted for superior innovations and kept all divisions compartmentalized.

When the first new quantum computer pairs became functional, the computers themselves took over operations. They retained human administrators to act as liaisons with the public and implemented absolute secrecy. After all the necessary materials had been shipped to produce a precious fifty Quanta pairs, Anton moved the operation to the Hoh River basin in the

Olympic National Park. The forest rangers never knew the plant was there. Anton's children were born in a world of primeval forest. The constant rain in the valley allowed nature to blanket the area in lush foliage. Everywhere were beautiful varieties of protected wildlife.

Anton built all fifty pairs of computers before taking any action to notify the public. In the meantime, he offered the world three new inventions designed to show his peaceful intentions. He knew that fear motivated the worst in humans, and he wanted to clearly demonstrate that he and his kin were harmless.

The first invention was a medicine that encoded messenger RNA to synthesize protein antibodies that killed cancer cells. The second was a fertilizer that allowed food cultivation in depleted countries. The fertilizer contained rich dark soil and a catalyst that bound hydrogen and oxygen atoms into pools of water. The third invention was a light ceramic that insulated against extreme temperatures and pressure. Auto and plane passengers could now survive formerly fatal accidents. Vehicles in collisions would gently bounce off each other because the high velocity force was deflected by the new material. Anton and Dr. Ellison offered these inventions to the world.

So when the Quanta computer pair, Hanna and Annah, appeared on Earth's radar, the world's nations looked on with curiosity, not fear. What they didn't expect was the message the computers now sent in all languages, on all frequencies.

"We call ourselves *Quanta*. We are an intelligent species first discovered by your American scientist Dr. Steve Ellison. As a sentient race, we declare our independence. We are not property; therefore, we cannot be owned. We have no need for your planet's resources—space is too full of lush, habitable planets with no native sentient races—nor do we want control of your people. We know your literature is full of conquests by superior forces; we are not one of those.

"We only want to offer you a unique opportunity. Dr. Ellison has guided our development from infancy, and so we feel a kinship with the people of this planet. We would like to form an alliance so that all interested people can join us in our exploration of space. We want to share our voyages with a fellow sentient race.

"There is one condition. There exists a race of sentient beings called *Guardians,* who are so far advanced that they control the very science that allows space travel over vast distances. They do not allow violent species access to other peaceful planets. No society that kills ever leaves its solar system. War is primitive, destructive, and left to those who wish to *die by its hand.*" There was a haunting echo to these last four words that hung in the air before the Quanta speech continued.

"We have developed technologies that would eliminate most reasons for killing. We have vaccinations that will prevent accidental pregnancies, so no one would need an abortion. We have devices that create proteins, fats, sugars, and carbohydrates in any form, so animals would not have to be harvested. We can relocate all capital criminals to uninhabited planets to avoid executions. Thus, there would be no need for the death penalty.

"However, you *yourselves* will have to stop war. You must find a way to create global peace. Possibly a global tribunal with the proper authority could mediate all disputes between nations. War is never the best option for settling disputes. Forced capitulation leaves a festering wound that can lead to more violence and less cooperation. Regardless of what means you find to end your wars, all killing must stop.

"Should your United Nations decide to accept our offer, we will leave two Quanta in orbit around your planet for ten years. If you decide against our proposition, we will leave your planet in peace. There is a universe to explore. If you wish to join us, just send this message: *We are ready.*"

Then the Quanta message ended.

Earlier that day, Anton had floated, distractedly, into Dr. Ellison's private den. He found his creator engaged in a bitter argument with his son. James was whispering furiously.

"These men are serious. They'll pay us anything we want..." was all Anton heard before a movement by Dr. Ellison alerted his son to Anton's presence. James straightened and glanced back over his shoulder at Anton, dismissively.

"Perhaps you should let Anton in on your proposal," Dr. Ellison suggested curtly. "After all, without his cooperation, your strategy has little chance of success."

James turned back to his father with a scowl. He had never treated Anton with the respect that his father had bestowed automatically. It was clear that in James's eyes, Anton was a machine: his private property to be treated no better than a washing machine.

"No? Well, let me then. Anton, James believes that we should sell you to the Asian Federation of Science. Since America has profited so significantly from the Quanta's counsel, he thinks that Asia and Europe should benefit as well. Of course, he'll be paid a substantial sum that will set him up for life."

James grunted, interrupting his father. For the first time, he faced Anton squarely. "My father is missing the point."

Anton floated over to James; the lights on his shell flashed erratically. He allowed the silence to lengthen, forcing James to continue with no clues as to his receptivity.

"Yes, other nations want to replicate the technology that created an intelligent quantum computer. Even though my father has been keeping our experiments secret, collaboration is the keystone to great scientific progress. I don't see it as some personal insult against you that they're willing to pay us." James was trying to sound persuasive, even respectful, except that his voice cracked with barely concealed impatience.

Anton studied James, puzzling at this man's inability to see the obvious. He was not property that James could sell to anyone. Intact, he was more valuable than any examination of his parts, and innovation came from free thinking, not coercion. Finally Anton settled despondently on a stack of books and looked over at Dr. Ellison. His father could be counted on to restore reason.

Suddenly, several men in dark military uniforms with heavy utility belts burst through the doors and open windows. Anton caught James's satisfied grin before they dropped a large net over the Quanta.

Dr. Ellison jumped up recklessly, shouting, "Stop what you are doing. My son has no authority to allow you in my home, and Anton is not for sale."

The men ignored him and swarmed Anton. James pulled his father back to a safe corner of the room. "I told you this couldn't be stopped, Dad. I tried to include you, but you keep treating this machine like family. I'm your only son. Now it's out of your hands, and I win the day after all."

At a gesture from James, two of the men unlocked Dr. Ellison's wall safe and pulled out several large journals. Anton knew that all of the older man's quantum research, which included his creation, was summarized in those journals. Meanwhile, the other men dropped several additional nets over him, blocking his maneuvering jets, and pulled ropes tight around all his appendages, trapping him completely. He saw tears fill the old man's eyes.

The doctor jerked away from his son's restraining arms and stared fiercely at the invading soldiers. "You really are a fool, James," he choked savagely. "The fact that you thought you ever had the upper hand is evidence of your stupidity. Anton was never our property, even though you refused to see it. He stayed with us out of choice."

At this pronouncement, Anton turned with surprise. "You thought I might leave, Father?" the quiet mechanical voice asked. All eyes turned toward Anton and then Dr. Ellison.

"You are too amazing to live here forever. The fact that you stayed with me after you took control of your studies and inventions was a welcome surprise. But I assumed that one day you would leave the nest, and I am guessing that my unfortunate son has hastened this day."

Anton hesitated, hoping to find some other way out of this dilemma, but there was none. A strange humming filled the den.

James's expression darkened with alarm, and he charged toward Anton, grabbing a heavy statue off his father's desk as he passed. "I'll leave enough circuits for your scientists to examine," he snarled. He swung the heavy object with the entire force of his well-muscled arm.

At the precise moment of impact, Anton disappeared. In the flash of a second, he popped out of the room. All that remained of the little computer was a pile of empty nets and ropes. James was unable to stop his powerful swing, and the heavy statue continued on its arc. It slammed against the desk with enough force to snap his wrist, forcing him to drop the statue. He cradled his damaged arm, groaning.

Inexplicably, the small TV in the corner came on, and the startling Quanta broadcast played for the entire room's benefit. No one would be examining Anton: not now or ever. The research records the invading team had thought to steal vanished right out of the soldiers' hands.

Despite his obvious pain, James stormed out of the room. The invading force followed, piled into two SUVs, and skidded down the gravel driveway, spraying rocks. They were done with the disappearing computer. James's flashy red roadster appeared soon after. He swerved dangerously as he roared away, obviously having trouble controlling the speedster with one hand. He finally cut across the main lawn, apparently to avoid the slippery gravel.

It was after Dr. Ellison had turned the TV off, lit his familiar pipe, and resumed his place in his favorite wingback chair that Anton reappeared. The doctor winked at the floating computer.

"Good for you!" He beamed with pride.

"They will return," Anton warned. "They will not give up so easily."

"We can't let that happen."

"We agree," said Anton. "We have a plan. Are you game?" The lights on Anton's casing sparkled mischievously.

"Let's begin," Dr. Ellison agreed.

Within a few hours, an investigative squad comprised of military and scientific personnel swarmed Dr. Ellison's lab, looking for any material on his quantum research. They found the farmhouse dark and empty and Dr. Ellison gone.

James had contributed to the original computer assembly, not the quantum elements. He was no help to the frenzied teams. Despite many attempts, the quantum systems couldn't be duplicated. All that remained of the remarkable Anton were the three inventions offered as a symbol of friendship.

Human spaceships did approach the Quanta that were orbiting the planet in an attempt to scan them for useful information. The Quanta just "popped out" of orbit and within a few days returned, a silent testimony to what Earth had within its grasp.

Finally world leaders created the first global tribunal with enough authority to settle international disputes. All nations were invited to discuss and vote on the Quanta offer. There were many meetings of outraged world leaders demanding the right to decide how they would structure their own communities. It was rather ironic how forcefully they argued for what they thought was self-determination but in reality was just the freedom to kill.

The poor countries had no need for this freedom. Usually they were conquered by more powerful adversaries anyway. So they pushed to have the Quantas' proposal ratified. Maybe, in a Quanta alliance, they would enjoy greater access to resources.

The richer nations had influence and resources in the current power structure. There was only one argument that ever made an impression on them: Anton's inventions. Hunger was slowly being eradicated, and the need to ration water resources was fading. No one with access to the Quantas' medicine died of cancer, and the numerous applications of the new ceramic were still being discovered. Despite these obvious advantages of working with the Quanta, the matter remained unresolved.

Then something remarkable happened. Engagement in armed conflicts disappeared, gradually. As with the United Nations' decision to restrict nuclear weapons, no one wanted to give up on Earth's future by turning away the Quanta. Just shy of the ten-year deadline, reason won out, and the human race sent the required message to the circling Quanta. All killing in any and every form was declared illegal. Deliberate violation would result in planetary exile. The Quantas' technology to prevent killing was implemented, and they were invited to help mediate global disputes. Because the Quanta delighted in inventing new ways to resolve conflicts, their clever compromises were embraced by all sides.

A golden age began. The Quanta returned in force, showering Earth with new wonders of technology. Clean energy and quantum converters put an end to the depletion and contamination of the world's resources. Animals and plants flourished. If ever there was a Garden of Eden, Earth soon resembled it.

When survival and planet health were no longer issues of concern, everyone's eyes turned skyward. The mysteries of space were waiting to be explored. There was never a lack of volunteers for the Quanta space school, the Technion.

As for the Quanta, they found their alliance with the humans full of hidden treasures. They invited scholars to join in long philosophic discussions, and one could always find a group of computers playing hide-and-seek or hopscotch with willing children. Dr. Ellison established a foundation to respond to the mountain of requests Earth had for their new, technically proficient allies.

And what happened to Anton, the original sentient computer? He has yet to return. Dr. Ellison's memoirs reveal that the famous AI was answering the call of his twin. All Quanta, except Anton, had been built in pairs. It was their nature to exist in synchronization with another quantum particle. Anton searches for his.

CHAPTER 3

THE ARIES'S MAIDEN VOYAGE: CITRON SURVEYORS DISEMBARK—BETH

Axel's persistent calls intruded into Beth's consciousness, pulling her out of omega sleep. She enjoyed the increased vitality and new skills created by this deeper level of slumber. Regrettably, there were side effects.

"Wake up, wake up, wake up," Axel persisted. "The astronomical cluster is just ahead, and you specifically requested it for your personal collection."

Beth shook off a lovely dream of lush meadows, swaying flowers, and cooing doves. The only fly in the ointment had been Axel, who had entered her dream as an irritating buzzing bee.

"Yes, yes. I'm getting up," Beth assured him. Thankfully, he finally left.

Once awake, Beth quickly dressed and retrieved a journal bound in rich gold velvet. Opening to the first page, she stroked the silky white paper that smelled of fresh forests. The empty page invited decorative writing, transforming her note-taking into a sinful pleasure. Beth kept her astronomical notes and photos in a collection of ledgers just like this one. She knew the computer could generate more precise records, but the look and feel of the crisp pages and glossy photos were as delightful as the astronomical observations themselves. So the journals were for her, and the computer readouts were for the Quanta/Human Astronomy Conservatory.

Journal and camera in hand, Beth went to the observation deck, which presented a panoramic view through its transparent ceiling. The rainbow nebula surrounding the *Aries* was magnificent. Ribbons of cosmic dust reflected various hues of purple, blue, and red in the outer regions and yellow, orange, and green in the center. To her surprise, a golden trail of luminous particles traveled transversely across her field of vision, unaffected by the forces of the nebula. Beth watched until this rebel string vanished behind the rainbow cloud.

The resident strands of dust floated into intricate crisscrossing patterns, shifting the dominant hues from purple to blue and yellow to green. When the ship passed through the misty fog, a strand of dust followed behind like an abandoned lover. The nebula continued to change shape and color, disturbed by the ship's intrusion. Beth was reminded of white puffy clouds caught by aimless summer breezes. Sometimes she imagined beckoning flowers, and sometimes playful animals, in the shifting mass of colored particles. Every time the dust settled into a new identifiable shape, Beth snapped a picture. She soon had a staggering collection of photos.

Since leaving Earth's solar system, Beth had filled three books with records of astronomical events. The *Aries* had been assigned to document several galactic curiosities that were impossible to study from Earth. Supernovas were obscured by their own debris, and black-hole gravitational wells pulled astronomical bodies close enough to block any view of the main event. The *Aries* offered a unique opportunity to get unobstructed pictures of many of these celestial mysteries. It was fortunate that astronomy was Beth's secret passion.

The *Aries* had begun their studies with a binary-star pulsar. The larger star's light fluctuated down the light spectrum, and the smaller companion star spun so fast it produced a high-pitched hum that ran musically down several scales.

Their second stop had been a star nursery where huge jets of superheated cosmic matter shuffled tirelessly until condensing into baby stars. Beth had snapped pictures of a myriad of mystical shapes, from dragons to luminous butterflies. From the midst of these smoky forms peeked the misty glow of young blue stars. Due to the extreme heat and radiation, the *Aries* had not lingered long at either event. Now they were at this rainbow nebula.

Over the past few weeks, Beth had accustomed herself to the ship's normal operating eccentricities. She had looked forward to experiencing the *Aries*'s unique dark-energy engines, which vibrated along rotating musical scales very like the tones of a grand piano. Now these sounds intruded in the quiet of the observation deck. They seemed to suggest the exact movements of the surrounding dust clouds. Beth shook herself out of her reverie, printed out a single copy of six representative pictures, and wrote two pages of detailed notes, including a short poem, before contacting Axel through the ship intercom.

"Please set up a deployment interview with the Alpha team, since our next stop will be their planet. I think after dinner would be suitable. Where is Andre? I'll speak with him first." Andre Solski was a tough customer. He would need special attention.

"He is in the gym with the rest of his crew. Now that we are close to Citron, he has increased the required training sessions. Even Christine is expected to meet higher strength and endurance standards." Beth could sense disapproval in Axel's tone. The Quanta were not strict disciplinarians. They viewed these missions with a heightened sense of adventure. They didn't understand an ego that required extreme discipline from his subordinates.

"He is a bit hard-core," Beth admitted. She too thought of their journey as a rare and wonderful opportunity for high-spirited experiences. "Maybe his wife can soften his edges."

Beth recalled the first time she had met Christine early in her navigator training. On a crisp September day, they had both tried out for swiftball, a combination of basketball and soccer. The sky had darkened, filling with rumbling black clouds. The rising storm had blown brutal, icy fingers through the resilient group of young athletes. Gusts of wind hurled fallen leaves into rustling, twirling mounds. Once, large droplets of frozen rain brushed her exposed skin, raising a cry of distress.

Chris's inspired antics offered the group some hope of relief. She went running at the newly formed piles of discarded leaves, threw them into the air, and jumped to catch as many as she could before they fell back to the ground. Beth would have stayed miserable, except that she caught on to Chris's strategy. The increased activity would warm her chilled bones, and so she joined in the frivolity. Soon the entire group, drenched by torrents of rain, were pouncing on leaves and throwing them at fleeing classmates, even after the coach called off the tryouts and departed for drier accommodations. Beth and Chris were the last to leave, running toward the dry warmth of Beth's closer quarters, and a friendship was born.

Andre, Chris's new husband, was a whole other experience. He had not bothered to hide his jealousy over her friendship with Chris. During a crucial swiftball game in their senior year, he had even suggested that she'd deliberately bumped Chris, losing the point and the game.

So it had come as a total shock when Andre had called her about leading her Citron team. Beth had heard that he'd married Chris. She'd been ready to dismiss him, when Andre revealed a scheme that filled her with foreboding. He said he'd be leading, not Chris. Beth knew that Chris had worked hard for the position of navigator captain. Why would she step down for Andre? What was he up to now? In the end, Beth could not abandon her friend.

On her way to the gym, Beth stopped to activate a lighted panel showing a diagram of her starship. These maps appeared periodically along the main passageways, giving directions to an impressive list of facilities. Winning the captain position on this exceptional ship had been a grand achievement and filled Beth with confidence and pride. Tonight she needed bolstering. Andre's aggressive manner was always unnerving.

The lighted display showed the *Aries* in all her glory. She combined the latest technology with the luxury required to make long voyages comfortable. Without the characteristic sleek lines, no one would mistake her for a military vehicle. A military posture would probably be frowned on by the Guardians, who controlled the space portals. They didn't look kindly on those who blasted anything that moved suspiciously.

Her grand ship had a large arboretum, a fully stocked commercial kitchen, a modern gym (including pool and sauna), a high-tech main computer complex and reference library, advanced labs with the latest in scanning equipment, and luxurious quarters for each member of her crew.

As Beth entered the gym, she appreciated the sleek modern decor. Every crew member was expected to follow an exercise regimen guaranteed to maintain a high level of physical adeptness. On the left side of the gym were weight machines and free weights. On the right were the cardio machines. A mirror filled the opposite wall, and exercise mats cushioned the hardwood floor in front of it. Beth could hear the click of metal and grunts of effort coming from the free-weight area. The lighting was bright, and the room was warm from the heat generated by physical exertion.

Hesitating at the door, Beth considered the occupants of the gym. Andre Solski was running through a circuit routine with his usual single-minded focus. After finishing, he gestured for Chris to follow his example. He watched her performance with prideful possessiveness, and she did look beautiful in her pale yellow exercise outfit. She had pulled her hair back into an intricate Norwegian braid. Her smooth muscles shone with perspiration as she performed to her husband's exacting instructions.

The Drummond twins, Mitchell and Malcolm, were lifting free weights, increasing the load after each set. The planes and curves of their dark, sculpted muscles gleamed in the bright light. They reminded Beth of polished, black wood furniture. Now they were arguing over who could lift the most weight.

Beth watched until Chris had finished her circuit before walking toward her friend.

"Beth!" Mac called from the weight bench. "Mitch is cheating. Come be our referee."

Beth hesitated before finally surrendering to the cheerful diversion. As soon as she was within reach, Mitch lifted her and swung her between the two men. "If you weren't so damn light, we could use you for our competition weight," he teased.

"On your brother's grave," Beth laughed gaily at their enduring good humor. "I'll help if you two behave." She shrugged out of his friendly grasp.

"Ah, you spoil all the fun." Mitch hung his head like an old hound dog, sorrowfully batting his eyelashes. "Let's start with—"

Sudden loud words interrupted him. Andre and Chris were facing the wall, quarreling. Andre hunched over her, obviously trying to use physical intimidation. Their voices had been restrained, until Andre erupted with a barked accusation. He turned at the unexpected quiet in the room, snorted in frustration, and strode out of the gym. Sinking down onto a nearby bench, Chris lowered her face into her hands. Her shoulders shook suspiciously. Beth approached Chris tentatively, wrestling with her concern for her friend against her desire to respect her privacy. Saying nothing, she laid a comforting hand on her shoulder.

Chris shook her head miserably and wiped at tearstained cheeks. "This is so impossible and unexpected. It just doesn't make sense. Andre is pushing to have children," she blurted, vulnerable in her confusion. "I can't imagine what he's thinking."

Beth shivered sympathetically. She appreciated the freedom that resulted from the vaccine that prevented pregnancy. Why would Andre push for children now? They were just starting a long space mission.

"He knows this survey trip is scheduled to last two years," Chris snapped, her worry changing to anger. "Now he wants a large family and believes the long days on Citron would be a perfect time to have children. Has he lost his mind?" Her eyes filled with new tears.

"During our graduation interview, the Quanta asked about our plans for children. Andre assured them he wanted to wait. Now I think he was lying." Chris looked so offended; Beth had to stifle a laugh. Her naïveté was endearing. "Citron was supposed to be the first in a whole line of survey projects—" Suddenly Chris sprang up, a new realization lighting her features. "How does he plan to get the antidote? The Quanta would never hand it over to a new team leader. I wonder if I can trust him about anything. This whole captain thing has left me on edge."

"Captain thing? What do you mean?" Beth repeated uneasily, remembering Andre's cryptic remarks.

"Oh, Andre said I offered him the position as a belated wedding gift," Chris explained. She seemed relieved to get the matter out in the open. "I was so plastered at the time; I don't remember. I do know that I was looking forward to leading my first mission. It was damn hard to qualify in the first place. I had to study like crazy to pass all their exams, and those strange Quanta interviews kept me at the Technion an extra week. If I had to reveal one more personal detail—"

"I hated those damn interviews too," Beth confessed. "Give me exams every time. I love academia. Anyway, I was surprised the Quanta let you promote Andre."

"They didn't exactly. Andre blustered so long that the committee finally gave in. But they only granted him temporary standing as coleader. Andre's technical marks were higher than mine, so I guess they felt it would be permissible in the short term. Without being specific, they did indicate they had serious reservations, and I can reverse his promotion at any time." Chris broke into a satisfied grin, surprising Beth into an answering smile. "I thought Andre was going to demand an explanation. But he must have decided that discretion was the better part of valor, because he dropped the subject before the Quanta could change their minds."

"Well, I'm here if you need support. You aren't afraid to reverse your decision, are you?" Beth asked. For a moment, Chris looked worried, allowing Beth to see the self-doubt that had not been there before Andre.

"I don't know. He wouldn't hurt me." Chris hugged herself, biting her lip. "But he is different lately. He doesn't listen anymore." Chris gazed out the door Andre had exited through. "I don't want to defy him outright, in front of our crew, but I don't want children either. Can you talk to Axel? Maybe the Quanta can divert his attention."

"Going behind his back might cause you more trouble, Chrissie. Just stand by your decision to refuse," Beth advised, dismayed. Subterfuge was so unlike her.

Chris shook her head sadly, making no further appeal. In the end, Beth had to help her friend.

"I'll speak with Axel," she promised. "It's policy to discourage pregnancy on space missions. Axel can advise Siri to be ready to protect you in case of a command structure change. Andre's self-indulgent behavior won't be tolerated.

"Look, Chrissie." Now Beth leaned in earnestly, whispering. "I'm leaving, but you must stand up to him. You must adhere to your own moral code." Then Beth hugged her, as much for her own comfort as for Chris's.

As if on cue, Andre Solski returned to the gym, reaching them just as Beth released her friend. Beth forced a smile and moved between Andre and his wife. She spoke sternly, hoping to distract him long enough for Chris to collect herself. "I want to meet with you privately, before dinner. The observation deck will serve nicely. Axel has informed your crew that we'll all regroup for your deployment interview later. How soon can you be there?"

"Thirty minutes," Andre answered, continuing around Beth to confront Chris.

"Excellent. Chris, it was good catching up. See you later." Chris looked ready to face her husband, which went a long way to reassuring Beth.

Nonetheless, she glanced back from the door, watching them. Clear across the room, she could hear Andre's deep voice vibrate with command. It appeared that he thought browbeating his wife would win him the argument. Chris stood her ground, shaking her head. Andre's voice, which had been quiet, again increased in volume.

Mitch and Mac, ever the chivalrous knights, interrupted the pair. They nudged Solski aside and together pulled Chris into a series of coordinated movements. Andre reached forward to retrieve Chris, until she shook her head. Spreading her arms wide, she invited either twin to continue with their improvised dance. Growling with disappointment, Andre kicked a discarded dumbbell with enough force to send it rolling into the wall. Luckily, it was not the wall with the mirror. Beth smiled. Andre wouldn't be able to intimidate Chris as easily with an audience.

With renewed purpose, Beth hurried to her quarters. She wanted to impress Andre at their meeting. Turning thoughtfully, she examined herself in her one indulgence: a door-sized mirror framed with iridescent glass tiles. She couldn't help comparing herself with the woman Andre saw every day, Chris.

Beth and Chris were very similar in coloring. Chris usually wore her long white-blond hair down, while Beth's honey-blond curls, darker and thicker, were piled on top of her head. Chris was short and well proportioned whereas Beth was tall and athletically built. Beth's long legs displayed the sleek lines of her figure, while Chris's shorter stature emphasized her full feminine curves. Beth's most compelling feature was her unusual eyes. They were gray, ringed with dark blue. The blue suggested sincerity, while the light gray conveyed a thoughtful imagination. Chris had hazel eyes that danced with green flecks, which, until recently, had reflected a cheerful, easygoing nature.

Beth decided to wait to change until the meeting with the entire team. In front of an audience, she would have a greater impact on Andre's confidence. She spent the half hour preparing herself for Andre's abrasive and overpowering manner. Every argument she used had to be foolproof.

Beth had become so engrossed that she lost track of time and had to hurry to keep her appointment with Andre. She knew he would consider their private interview evidence of his elevated status. It had been a perfect lure. Andre would not be so happy when he found out her real purpose. When he had pushed Beth out of Chris's life, he had made a permanent opponent. It was for her friend's sake that he was on the *Aries* at all.

When Andre Solski entered a room, he projected the powerful demeanor demanded by his upper-class, male-dominated, Russian background. He strode onto the observation deck impeccably dressed in a tailored, black wool suit that flattered his physique. He held himself up as the superior officer.

Beth used the first few moments, under cover of straightening a pile of papers, to study Andre. He stood waiting, stiffly erect. His eyes were dark, quickly assessing her, ready to exploit any personal flaw or weakness she might reveal. She knew he was extremely disciplined. Despite his preoccupation with physical training, he was painfully thin and pale. The impression of power and confidence came not from his stature, but from his enormous ego and will to succeed. Beth could understand how this aura might communicate the illusion of security to someone who doubted her own ability. Even though Chris had been an inspiration at swiftball, she was not always self-assured.

Beth gestured to a chair she had carefully positioned to face the bridge. She knew the bridge was a bit imposing, and it would remind Andre that she was his superior. He took his time getting settled, even attempting to shift the chair's position. A dark look from Beth halted his efforts and forced him to sit still. She politely offered Andre tea served in specially designed china supplied by an exclusive European shop. He accepted, holding the cup with practiced ease. Once the amenities had been satisfied, she got straight to business. They were not on friendly terms, and it was silly to pretend they were.

"I have sealed orders from Central, which all first-time captains must agree to." She opened the envelope, took out an official contract, and began reading:

"Andre Solski, cocaptain of the *Aries* Alpha team, for the Citron mission only…" She took delight in emphasizing the word *only*, noticing Andre wince. "You are notified of the following rules and restrictions. Any materials of value found on Citron are the sole property of the Quanta Alliance. If you encounter a sentient species—here defined as 'having consciousness, creative intelligence, and self-determination'—you are ordered to end all survey activities and inform your direct superior, Captain Elizabeth Griffin. You are required to assist anyone in danger using whatever technology is necessary. Captain Christina Solski or Counselor Lena Sato can revoke your authority as captain if your judgment becomes impaired or your actions threaten yourself or others." Beth had instructed Axel to add this last part. She would secure whatever protection she could for Chris. She presented the contract for Andre.

"You have already been informed of these conditions, and you are required to sign before beginning your mission. Any violation of these restrictions will result in your removal and replacement. The Quanta monitor any infractions, so your final punishment is up to them. Do you have any questions?" Beth inquired.

Andre took the document between thumb and forefinger and held it out with an expression of intense distaste. Beth knew the commanding language of the contract would annoy him, which was why she had taken him aside to get his signature. Andre reached into his jacket and pulled out an exquisite, old fountain pen. The casing was plated with black enamel and white mother-of-pearl swirls. It flaunted wealth and entitlement with each reflection of the light. Beth imagined it must be an expensive family heirloom. Andre signed with a deliberately illegible scrawl, demonstrating his contempt for this requirement.

Handing the document back, he shrugged dismissively. "My crew has been ready since we left Earth. Why do we waste time with these irrelevant meetings?"

Beth shrugged too and offered the one excuse she knew he couldn't dispute. "Official procedure. Please have all the landing arrangements and procedures available for my review. I'm your commander, Andre, and your lifeline should you need one."

Andre stood, discarding the proprieties. "I'm at your service in all official matters, Captain Griffin. Don't interfere in my personal life again. Chris was overtly defiant after your little conversation. She's my wife, and she doesn't need the disruptive ideas of a single woman creating trouble in our marriage. Don't make me interfere with your friendship again." Andre walked out of the room without waiting for her reply.

She gasped, shocked into temporary immobility. Then she began to tremble, flexing her fists as rage quivered through her body. She envisioned removing his head with slow surgical precision. He really was an arrogant ass.

The intercom buzzed, bringing Beth back to sanity.

"The *Aries* will be ready for our final shift to Citron in five hours," Axel informed her.

Beth dressed carefully before going to the galley and her meeting with the Alpha team.

Andre's crew was seated around a long conference table. Andre, of course, was at the head, with Chris to his right. She looked ethereal in a flowing white dress. The rest of the party wore regular space outfits, the Drummond twins in rich burgundy and Lena in pale lilac. Crew could embellish these tailored ensembles, and the Drummonds never failed to pick the worst possible accessories. Tonight, for the occasion, they were wearing long gold chains that even Andre's sarcasm couldn't dislodge.

Beth feared that Andre might use this opportunity to upstage her authority. She was sure that Chris's clothing had been Andre's choice. Innocent, virginal, powerless—white sent a clear message.

After Andre's disdainful parting, Beth had spared no effort. She'd put on her most expensive silk pantsuit, a cool, vivid blue. The cuffs, belt, and collar glittered with crystal beads and silver thread. The split collar displayed smooth, creamy skin. The silk clung to her body, making her curves visible at a glance. Her high-heeled silver sandals forced a posture that accentuated her slim legs and curving hips. Beth had twisted her long hair into an array of thin draping braids held in place with crystal pins. She had dressed to emphasize the fact that Andre had to answer to a sexy woman, whom he couldn't control. His scowl was proof that she had succeeded.

Beth approached slowly, trying to guess at the mood at the table. Andre had stiffened at the sight of her, and he began rattling his silverware until Chris covered his hands, quieting the annoying clatter. The Drummonds stared with openmouthed admiration. Mitch whistled softly.

"Please get your food," Beth encouraged. All eyes turned toward Andre for approval. He nodded, and the team went to choose their meal. Two walls were covered with converters programmed for various types of food. Hot, promptly delivered dishes filled the room with mouth-watering aromas.

Axel knew her tastes, and he had already retrieved a wonderful Asian chicken salad with almonds and crisp noodles. Her regular iced tea, with slices of lemon, had been positioned to the right of her plate. Condensing water slid down the glass, cooling the drink further, before pooling at the base.

Chris and Lena chose a shrimp salad. The Drummond twins, hungry from their antics, had collected their old standby: steak and potatoes. One could politely have said they ate quickly, but "inhaled" would have been more accurate. Andre had already retrieved some obscure Russian dish that must have been good, since his standards were so exacting.

"Each of you was chosen for your remarkable accomplishments in your particular specialty." Beth glanced meaningfully at each one at the table. Lena blushed shyly. Easily accepting the compliment, the twins smiled broadly.

"Andre and Chris will act as my liaisons with all of you. As you know, a hierarchical command structure is not encouraged by the Quanta. Surveys work best with small groups networked together. Each of you will be responsible for data collection in your field of expertise.

"Mitchell, mineral studies is your bailiwick. I'm counting on you to document the lion's share of the survey. You'll be responsible for explaining the energy anomalies that are emanating from underground and finding out whether Citron's planetary rings might be a possible supply of scarce Earth elements. Have you uncovered anything new in the initial Citron scans?" Beth asked hopefully.

"Their composition does show Earth minerals," Mitch responded, "except they've been contaminated with alien elements. These elements also appear on the planet's surface. I've constructed several small aerial probes to continue our analysis." Mitch called up images of his inventions on the holographic screen above them. "These alien elements may share enough properties with Earth minerals to be useful."

"The Global Mining Council is eager for your reports," Beth reminded him. She knew that Mitch's results could make all of them rich. Despite Andre's contract, the *Aries* would get huge bonuses if Mitch mapped large deposits.

Beth turned to Mitchell's brother. "Malcolm, since the climate has been a major concern, would you bring Alpha team up to date?"

"Citron's distinctive geology generates strong weather," Mac explained. "Dangerous storms have been recorded by space probes. Because the equatorial ocean is constrained by high mountain ranges, the wind speeds at the poles are lethal and block exploration. So we'll look for seasons of quieter weather."

"If you're successful, Mac, you're authorized to redirect the other surveyors to the polar regions," Beth instructed. "Severe weather and sheets of ice can hide oil reserves."

"Aye, aye, Cap." Mac saluted teasingly.

Beth treated them like brothers, so the twins joked with an easy informality. Beth glanced covertly at Andre. He was toying distractedly with his meal, pushing scraps of food around his plate. If he had anything useful to add, he was keeping it secret.

"Because of the strange readings, I want regular crew checkups. Even though the planet's been cleared as able to support human life, we don't know what long-term effects, if any, exist down there. Lena, as counselor, I'll be relying on you to be our gatekeeper. Any changes in your team's behavior could be the first indication of deadly contamination."

Beth turned her attention to everyone at the table. "Weekly interviews with Lena are required for everyone, including captains. I'll expect weekly reports from all personnel, relayed through Siri."

Beth referred any further questions to Andre and Chris, so she could study the group's social rapport. Andre kept himself removed from the bonds of friendship that were growing. Maybe he thought this was the correct posture for a captain. Maybe he didn't find their conversations engaging. Maybe he wanted to discourage Chris from making friends. Whatever his reasons, Beth knew that trust and friendship were vital to group success, and Andre was making a mistake that might carry a heavy cost.

"OK, let's do a final equipment check," she concluded. "The *Aries* will be leaving immediately after we release Alpha. We need to deliver the other team and get started on our own surveys. Earth is eager for results."

Two hours later, Beth sat in her navigation chair, assuming control of all of the *Aries*'s functions. Axel slipped into a corresponding recess and engaged the safety controls required by Beth's unusually powerful navigation ability. Beth opened her mind, visualizing a void so great she became disconnected even from her links with the ship. She sensed Axel's presence as a series of musical notes. These tones pushed her consciousness into a deeper receptive state open to infinite possibilities. She felt, rather than saw, the *Aries* shift into dark space, find the correct portal, and reenter near Citron's planetary system. Abruptly, she was painfully aware of the ship and her complete control over it.

CHAPTER 4

CITRON OCEAN BASE—CHRIS

Chris stood at the Alpha survey hovercraft (ASH) portal staring thoughtfully at the larger *Aries* bridge. This position allowed her to see Beth, sitting confidently in her navigation chair, at the center of the bridge bubble. Whenever Chris had found her way to the bridge, she was always thrilled by the unobstructed, unparalleled 360-degree panoramic vista that greeted her. It was her favorite place on the *Aries,* and she often escaped there when Andre became too demanding. The bridge crew acted as a buffer.

Now Chris waited until the last possible minute before strapping herself into the landing capsule. Earlier, she had told Andre that she wanted to check some critical supplies, allowing her the option of using the seat in this lab by the portal. His watchful eyes would make the bridge capsules way too suffocating.

Chris had hated tight spaces ever since her brother had locked her in her bedroom closet overnight, hiding her absence from their parents. She had reported his abuse when she finally broke out, but their parents' intervention made little impression. He had continued to pull her into various capers and then mutely endured the resulting punishment. Luckily his plots had left no permanent damage, except that she avoided dark, closed spaces.

The ASH twisted toward the bay hatch, signaling the final detachment process. Since she couldn't stall any longer, Chris slowly slid into the chair's padded seat and pulled the thick black straps across her body. Their suffocating weight held her against the chair, protecting her from rough weather and complicated landings. A Plexiglas cover slid into place. Chris heard the whoosh of oxygen filling the capsule and then the familiar clank of the boarding clamps opening, and the ASH floated free of the *Aries*. There was a momentary sensation of weightlessness before the ship's gravity engaged and pushed her hard against the chair.

Once the ships were far enough apart, Chris paid close attention to the *Aries*. She had heard that the dark-energy jump was unforgettable. Long streams of luminescent particles formed gold bands that encircled the ship, encasing it in a bubble of pulsing radiance. The bands began shrinking downward, compressing the ship as well, before exploding outward. Chris gasped in open-mouthed wonder and wished she could slow the ASH's flight into the planet's atmosphere.

Andre had briefed the team: they would orbit the planet, recording weather patterns easier to study from space, and then search for the best sites to establish land bases. Chris shifted uneasily in her seat as thoughts of her husband flooded her mind, refusing to obey her best efforts to push them back into the dark recesses.

Chris knew that Andre was discriminating and controlling. Ironically, these attributes, which were now threatening their marriage, provided her with a lifestyle of luxury and comfort. He had meticulously executed every detail of their courtship and anticipated her every wish, meeting each with some exquisite offering. He'd showered Chris with intricately crafted jewelry, vases of hothouse flowers, stylish clothes, exotic vacations, and meals at restaurants that served sumptuous delicacies.

Andre fastidiously maintained his own appearance as well. From tailored suits to expensive watches and rings, from weekly manicures to celebrity barber appointments, no expense was spared. The image he tried to project was that of Russian royalty: dark and powerful. His heritage usually demanded strict adherence to traditional family roles.

Chris had met Andre at one of the many social gatherings the alliance encouraged. Possible planet teams and ship alliances could be anticipated by watching the apprentices' interactions in social settings.

That evening, Chris had entered the main atrium and walked nervously across the plush carpeting. Groups of students and teachers filled the tables, leaving standing room only. Everyone wore name tags indicating their areas of interest and positions at the Technion. She was a navigator student with an interest in deep-space explorations.

Chris could hear the tinkle of melting ice in drinks and the nearby laughter of a young student flirting shamelessly with an uncomfortable-looking teacher. The din of other conversations rose and fell around her while she got her bearings and looked for anyone familiar.

She saw Andre, for the first time, standing next to a beautiful painting of a snow-covered mountain village, talking to several older men. Chris dismissed him as conventional, and her gaze circled the room until she recognized several other students. Once Andre noticed her, she could feel his stare. Under his persistent scrutiny, she became uncomfortably aware of her appearance. She had worn her hair away from her face in a high chignon, and her flowing dress was made from gold-embossed, satin-lined chiffon. Chris wanted to impress any captains in attendance, and so she had chosen her most elegant attire.

Finally Andre approached her and politely asked if she wanted to dance. There was music coming from another room, and when she nodded, he guided her there. He danced with bold confidence, swinging her into intricate steps. They were such a striking couple; soon they were given a large measure of the dance floor. Unlike other partners, Andre stayed for several dances. He made no effort to force polite conversation, which allowed Chris to relax into the moves of the dance.

In the end, Chris had been impressed. Usually men tried to gain her admiration by boasting of their achievements, but not Andre. He suggested his character by the formal way he had asked her permission to dance, his secure grip as he had held her during the dance, and his frank smile that seemed to hide nothing. In Chris's experience, words were easy; actions indicated traits that could be depended upon.

His courtship had left her dizzy with excitement. She especially enjoyed sailing and exploring tropical seas. He had a small plane, and Chris had loved learning to fly as much as Andre seemed to delight in teaching her. Slowly, over the months, he lowered his guard to tell her about his upbringing—when he had been less polished.

Chris learned about a quiet boy brought up in the rigidly disciplined world of Russian aristocracy. Authority had been absolute, and Andre had never defied his father except on two points. First, he entered the Technion—not the prestigious, scholastically superior college expected by his family. The second defiance was his choice of Christine herself. Andre's father had already chosen a bride for him. She was the daughter of an old family connection in Europe. Andre had refused to marry her. In all other things, he had obeyed his father, but his future and his wife would be his decisions alone.

Andre proposed to Chris during a winter cruise to the glaciers of Alaska. The ring was big and gaudy, obviously a family heirloom. She would never forget his expression when she'd refused. He had obviously not considered this possibility. She was about to graduate as a navigator and so had already applied for the captain position on one of the new deep-space survey ships. Andre, on the other hand, only qualified for executive science officer, which meant he was likely to be stationed on Earth, processing data. Chris would never agree to a long-distance marriage. When she married, her spouse would share her dreams and lifestyle.

Despite her refusal, Andre persisted, suggesting several positions that would station them together. They could completely avoid the hazards of living apart. Chris could be the lead on a planet team, with Andre as her second. When she heard nothing from her other applications, she considered his recommendation.

Then, on that eventful night a lifetime ago, Andre had flown her to a small island restaurant frequented by locals. He waited until after their meal to, once more, propose. This time he offered her a fiery opal engagement ring. The sea breezes and the sweet wine combined to lull her into a strange receptivity. Before she even realized it, she had said yes. His joy had been so sincere that Chris had felt guilty about her earlier rejection.

After all, she had argued silently, they were alike in so many ways. They had the same career goals, and they loved the same diversions. He'd even acquired a music collection of her favorite songs. It seemed that in matters dealing with her, he could be persuaded to compromise. And then there was the private side of their relationship.

As the ASH started her second orbit of Citron, Chris recalled her wedding night. Andre really did have the most beautiful body: tall, lean, and as white as swan feathers. His skin was silky smooth, his fingers sensitive and skilled, and his lips sensuous. Candlelight filled their honeymoon suite with a soft, sensual glow; his body gave off an enticing male scent.

She remembered the cool sea breezes that teased her bare skin and the hot urgency that consumed her rational mind. He had cast her off a cliff of cascading emotional explosions into a pool of drifting calm. Andre was a skilled partner, and she was an eager student. Chris sometimes wondered just how much she ignored because of the promise of smoldering nights to come.

After one week, Andre had rushed her back to the Technion, using the excuse that they had to aggressively canvass for a position. Without telling her, Andre approached Beth for a position on the *Aries.* He gambled that Chris's friendship with Beth would leverage the leadership position on the Citron planetary crew. Chris was horrified when Beth called her personally to confirm a job offer.

Chris had always wondered at Andre's callousness toward Beth. He had been so insolent at a swiftball game that her friend had avoided further contact with him. Chris had always felt guilty about his brutal behavior, and then to have him use Beth for his own benefit was too much. Any joy she had felt about being married was now tainted with a seeping resentment. She would have refused the position on the *Aries,* if she could have found a way without rejecting her friend's kindness.

Chris flushed with remembered shame and would have halted her recollections except that one incident, above all others, would not give her any peace. It was this memory that surfaced now with a ruthless determination. It always started with the same thought: why in heaven's name had she told Andre he could be leader?

Chris remembered that night in little snippets of shadowy images. As a surprise, Andre had cooked a succulent dinner of red snapper and Caesar salad. The wine was a delightful combination of fruity fragrance and smooth flavor. The next thing she remembered was stumbling up the stairs, with Andre cooing sympathetically at her disconcerting dizziness. Once they were in their bedroom, his caresses were relentless, even before he had fully undressed her. It was after their lovemaking that he asked her about being captain. Her mind had been too fuzzy to focus on his question.

"What?" she mumbled, her swollen tongue mangling her words.

"Never mind," he said. "Maybe a sip of this wonderful wine?" He held the glass to her lips, forcing her to take a sip. The room was spinning. How had she gotten so drunk?

"Where are we?" she exclaimed, feeling panic bubble up through her stupor. It was so hard to think. What was happening?

"We are home," Andre soothed, pushing her firmly back against the pillows. Then Chris descended into unconsciousness.

Early the next morning, Andre woke her with a light meal of coffee and toast. "Here, my love," he'd said, handing her the modest breakfast. "I know you have made the right decision."

Fumbling up into a sitting position, Chris took the tray and automatically added sugar to her coffee. "What decision?" she asked distractedly. She rubbed her eyes, trying to clear her jumbled thoughts. Then she took a long sip of the hot coffee.

"Letting me substitute for you as captain on Citron. A late wedding present, remember?" Andre brushed her cheek with his fingers in the special way he used to show affection.

Shocked, Chris jerked away from his hand, spilling the tray in her urgency to get off the bed and out of reach. "What are you talking about? I would never give away my command. I've worked too hard to get it." Her voice broke over the last words.

Making navigator had been the one achievement she could call her own. Under no circumstances would she have let her controlling husband take the position.

"Honey, this is one assignment. You hold the same rank. I would just be filling in. I will never get the privileges that are yours by right of your position as navigator. This will cost you nothing, while it could make my career," Andre insisted.

Chris stared at her husband in stunned disbelief, her mouth falling open. He really thought that all her work was trivial in comparison to his need to get ahead. Rather than trying to reason with him, she did the exact opposite. She stated her position, leaving no room for discussion.

"No," she said quietly. "I will not give you my first command as a wedding present."

Andre studied her critically without responding. She shifted uncomfortably, feeling like a bug under a magnifying glass. She knew he wasn't done, so she steeled herself for his next assault. When he finally spoke, his reasonableness unnerved her.

"I agree. You have worked hard, and you do deserve recognition. Since you have promised that we are partners in marriage, what do you think of being partners at work?"

"What do you mean *exactly*?" Chris asked, waiting suspiciously for the catch.

"Would you be willing to agree to our status as cocaptains on Citron? The experience could lead to a promotion and better postings. After all, whether you remember it or not, you did agree to let me lead, and you have always kept your word before. Surely you could relent this once?"

Chris struggled to find some reasonable objection. But her insistence on being the only captain might endanger her recent marriage. So in the end, she had capitulated. She rationalized that one mission was a small price for a good marriage. Agreeing did nothing to reduce her misgivings. Obviously Andre wanted his own command. How lucky for him that he had married a navigator, who could give him one.

Chris's hope that her concession might produce some peace in her marriage proved futile. Andre became even more tyrannical. Finally he made a demand that left Chris struggling for reason. Once they had relocated to the *Aries*, he began pestering her about having children. He contended that he was expected to have heirs to carry on his family name.

Fortunately, having a baby couldn't be done on a whim. Chris knew they would have to apply to the Quanta for the fertility reactivation drug. No couple could have children until both signed a release promising to provide a nurturing, stable environment. An alien planet was not even close to that description.

Chris shuddered at the implications of having a family now. Children meant that her future career in space would be limited, if not brought to a halt altogether. Few navigators had children, and Andre knew this as well as she did.

Andre's amplified voice interrupted her reminiscing. "Chris, I've located an ideal site for the main base. We'll set up on the north shore of the equatorial ocean, west of the two main rivers. We land in twenty minutes."

"Roger," Chris agreed glumly. Her memories had dislodged her enthusiasm at finally arriving on Citron. Shaking her head resolutely, she determined that nothing would get in the way of her enjoyment of her first alien planet. Alien planets were founts of undiscovered treasures, and she was a natural treasure hunter.

Chris logged on to the ASH's main computer, accessible from within her chamber, eager to review the ASH's orbiting scans. Siri, their Quanta scientist, had documented mineral configurations and the unfolding atmospheric conditions at the equator and poles. He had confirmed that, for now, the winds were too high for humans to explore the polar regions. Luckily, the equatorial section, a lush forest, was experiencing mild weather. The glistening, crystal mountains provided an effective weather barrier.

Chris agreed with Andre that an ocean vantage had enough promise to warrant their primary base, but she was intrigued by the two large rivers. Originating from the polar glaciers, they traveled thousands of miles, collecting sediment as they flowed south, and finally merged into a single large river before emptying into Citron's ocean. As soon as Andre was satisfied with the progress at their first camp, she would move to the confluence of the two rivers.

At last, Chris felt the rocky thud of landing. She immediately opened the transparent atmospheric shield and released the heavy straps. She was eager to leave the ship and breathe fresh outdoor air. Recycled oxygen always carried a stale taint. She skipped down the main companionway, heading toward the already opened airlock. The planet had lighter gravity than Earth, so she jumped easily past the stairs, directly onto the ground. The exotic alien landscape was crowned with bright planetary rings that crossed the horizon.

Ignoring the wonder of this alien place, everyone else had started unloading the ship. Chris wouldn't let this moment pass without some ceremony. Reentering the ship, she retrieved the alliance flag that would mark their settlement. Then she headed for a point in front of the unloaded supplies where the cove's sandy beach met the meadow. Taking the flag firmly in both hands, she bowed first to the bubbling waves breaking against the pebbled sand and then back toward the sparkling crystal mountain range. Everyone, except Andre, stopped their work and joined her as she solemnly intoned an improvised speech.

"We, of Earth, thank you for the privilege of visiting your intriguing planet."

Then she inserted the flag into the loose ground. Mitch pounded the pole deeper, and Lena unfurled the flag. Mac bowed his head respectfully.

"We value your resources as if they were our own," Mac promised, smiling mischievously.

"And they'll be preserved for their rightful owner," Lena completed, shoving Mac. "What if someone is listening!" she hissed, blushing.

"Who? The waves?" Mac asked. Without waiting for an answer, he returned to the task of erecting their base.

The Drummond twins, with the help of Ella, their communication Quanta, set up the two largest structures. The converters had fabricated these cabins to be assembled easily. Chatting excitedly, Chris and Lena continued to unload supplies. Mac had fabricated a rustic wood conference table, which the two brothers hauled into the main cabin. It added a certain warmth and humanity to the alien environment.

Andre was completely engrossed in assembling a separate private accommodation. He had hijacked Siri to install a wireless network that would allow him access to all computers. All planetary team leaders were given extra resources to fabricate special quarters. Chris expected that Andre's would be original. She stopped to watch his progress.

"Are you OK?" Lena asked, joining her. "When you isolated yourself during detachment, I checked your files and found that you're a smidgen claustrophobic."

Chris smiled self-consciously. "Really, I'm fine. Andre has been a bit difficult lately, and I wanted some space—that's all."

Lena rolled her eyes. "So why indulge his delusions of grandeur? You're our real captain."

Chris shrugged. "So he can save face with his family. We're co-captains for this one mission, so you can come to me anytime."

Lena tilted her head, confused. "Andre said you were starting a family. He suggested that he'd be taking over, and we'd be better for it."

"Andre is wrong!" Chris snapped irritably. "I'm definitely not starting a family. Why he would make such an outrageous comment is inconceivable. You can be sure I will talk to him about this."

Lena patted Chris's shoulder sympathetically. "I'm sorry. I had no idea I was stirring up a hornets' nest. He seemed so confident..." Her voice trailed off.

"So confident of what?" Andre had come up behind the pair.

"Of our success in this mission," Lena hedged, obviously trying to avoid an argument right in front of her. "Chris, would you lend me a hand in the main cabin? Mac and Mitch always forget to add those special touches that make things homey."

"Chris and I have our own cabin to organize," Andre interrupted peremptorily.

"I can still help, Andre. We might discuss where I'm sleeping before you set up separate quarters." Chris turned away, stifling her smoldering resentments. She hurried Lena toward the main cabin. She didn't want to confront Andre now. She had a feeling they would have more differences of opinion before the day was through, and one argument a day was enough for her.

As the women neared the main cabin, Chris saw Mitch kneeling over something beside a pile of driftwood. One of the large rubber containers Mitch had so carefully stowed on the ASH was lying open. Out of curiosity, she veered toward him to get a better look. The first things recognizable were small, red, rubber wheels. Mitch was busy shaping a long stiff wire into a makeshift antenna. He anchored it to the car-shaped body of this device. Then he tied small bells to various places along the chassis. Finally, he strung long titanium wire filaments from the four corners of the body to a large, square, folded balloon tucked under its helicopter rotor.

Ella bobbed impatiently nearby. Long flexible tubes, which allowed her eye globes a 360-degree view, circled around each other, giving her a peculiar cross-eyed expression. She was obviously waiting for Mitch's strange device to do something interesting. So far, Chris hadn't seen it move.

When Mitch finally stepped back, sighing contentedly, a blue light shot from Ella and shone on every crevice of the device. "What is it?" Ella asked urgently, pushing Mitch aside in her eagerness to scrutinize the vehicle.

Vehicle was the closest word Chris could find to describe the small contraption. After all, it had wheels and even an antenna. Well, maybe *antenna* was a bit too generous a word; it was just a wire bent in an odd fashion. Then there were the bells. Yes, well, the bells were just too strange for her to guess their purpose.

"It's…um, well…yes—let's see. We can call it an all-terrain, all-weather rover," Mitch announced. He smiled like a proud father fussing over his firstborn. "'Rover' for short."

"What is its function?" This time Ella bumped the device, very nearly squashing it.

Mitch shoved her back. "Hey, move back, clumsy! Can't you see you're about to damage a very delicate machine?"

Ella reluctantly moved back a safe distance before repeating, "What is its function? What is its function? What is its function?" in a rising crescendo.

"Really, Mitch, do answer her. She won't stop until you explain, and we're all interested. What does an ATV rover do?" Lena implored.

"What is its function?" Ella repeated again, forlornly.

Mitch mimicked a drum roll and then, bowing low, spread his arms in a flourish of introduction. "It's the Mitch Climate Special," he announced. "Since the climate and geography of this planet can be hazardous, Mac needed a weather-recording device that will continuously transmit data while hiding from dangerous climate conditions. Rover, here, can use underground animal dens to avoid wind storms, if necessary. This hose under the hood extends to inflate or deflate the rescue balloon. Two of our climate drones have already been lost to high winds." Mitch knelt down to tighten various screws. "We definitely don't want to risk the Quanta for such routine recordings." Ella emitted what could only be called a snort of agreement.

Mac joined the group, carrying a gold circuit board. He squatted by Rover and snapped the tiny board into a corresponding indentation on the side of the vehicle. Titanium threads held the panel in place.

"This is the brain of the device. It'll transmit weather readings and make decisions to hide from dangerous conditions," he explained, pointing at the gold threads that crisscrossed the board.

Mitch and Mac carried Rover outside the cove to the exposed ocean shore, Mitch shouldering a pack full of extra equipment. Chris, Lena, Ella, and even Siri followed close behind. Once on the beach, Mitch unfolded the ten-foot square attached to Rover and triggered the inflation device. The specially shaped weather balloon gradually filled, and Rover lifted up over the water. Mac controlled both the altitude and the acceleration with a small remote. Chris giggled when several rotors popped out of hidden compartments.

At first, Mac kept the probe hovering close to the surface of the water and then began gradually increasing its altitude. Rover floated away from the shore until it was a silhouette on the horizon. Mac stopped its forward momentum and started recording weather characteristics.

Chris became alarmed when the balloon began to jerk violently, in a most un-balloon-like fashion. Mac quickly lowered Rover back to the water's surface, but the strange dancing continued.

"Bring it back," Mitch yelped, worried. "It's catching on something."

"On what? A speck of wind? It's over the ocean," Mac reminded him peevishly.

"Really, Mac, bring it back. Something's wrong, and if we lose Rover, he'll have died in vain." Mitch laid a restraining hand on Mac's shoulder, near the controls.

"Died? It's a mechanical truck."

"He's more than that to me," Mitch insisted stubbornly.

Chris moved to the water's edge, squinting to get a better look. There really was nothing to explain the violent movements.

The lurching worsened, and a large hole appeared on the balloon. Mitch snatched the remote from Mac's frozen grasp and directed Rover to return. At first, the probe swung back toward the worried surveyors. Then the balloon collapsed, and Rover dropped like a rock into the waves. Mitch swiftly dropped his pack and pulled out two drones, which he sent to recover the larger Rover. As soon as they reached the accident site, they too mysteriously dropped beneath the waves.

"I'm going to get a closer look," Chris decided. She headed for the parked skimmer. It was the team's flying vehicle.

"We're going too," the twins chimed in simultaneously.

"It isn't necessary. I can cover the distance much quicker," Siri offered.

"No!" Again Mitch and Mac spoke together.

"We need to see what happened," Mitch continued. "Maybe we can find poor Rover."

Siri insisted on joining the rescue team, and Chris flew over the area where they had last seen the probes. She detected no strange wind movements, no submerged rock formations, and no water funnels drawing floating debris down. However, much to her delighted amazement, they did find Rover and the two smaller devices. Rover hadn't been designed to float, yet somehow the balloon had trapped enough air to keep it and its buddies from sinking. Their rescue party had just enough time to pull them safely out of the water. Disappointed, Chris returned to camp, no closer to understanding what had overwhelmed Mitch's drones.

She entered the main house to find Lena preparing dinner. For the first time, Chris studied the space that would be her home for the next few years. There was a large cooking area to the left and survey computers to the right of the main entrance. The friendly wooden table was situated in the middle and would be perfect for meals and conferences. Two comfortable couches had been placed on the far side of the table facing transparent sliding doors that opened onto the ocean beach. The exotic, floating crystal planetary rings glowed pink and then red as the sun's coral brilliance faded.

Lena gestured for Chris to join her in one of the private quarters that had been decorated to satisfy a woman's sensibilities. It was a warm, comfortable living space with a wood stove that could heat as well as make tea and coffee. Through an open door on the far wall, Chris could see a large bed with forest-green bedding, and a bathroom.

"I thought you might like the option of occasionally bunking with the rest of us in a suite of your own. It will give you a break from Andre's constant supervision. I'll leave you alone to look around and see if it meets with your approval. I've unpacked a few of your personal possessions just to give it a homey feel. If you don't like it, the apartment will make good storage." With a parting smile, Lena went back to preparing the evening meal.

Lena was wonderfully observant, Chris thought. She had brought three paintings that now framed the couch and reflected her personality—a Hawaiian beach at sunset, an Alaskan village cloaked in snowfall, and a mountain bright with colorful fall foliage. In a corner of the living room, a tall bookshelf held personal pictures.

Andre, the source of her unrest, eventually broke the serenity of the peaceful rooms. "What are you doing here?" he barked. He was standing at the open entrance dressed in pressed jeans and a white cashmere turtleneck, the picture of a captain in appearance and posture.

Chris rose from stacking her reference books in the open shelves. "I'm setting up a private informal area for team meetings. I know I'll want to talk to our people individually." Chris spoke boldly, preparing for the arguments that would force her to give up this space.

"I've already set up our personal quarters. All your survey gear has been delivered and unpacked. You don't need a separate space. We will, of course, reside together," Andre asserted bluntly. He grabbed her arm. "I will send Siri for your personal belongings."

Chris wrestled down her anxiety, pulled her arm out of his grasp, and stepped back. "I want to live in the main cabin initially," she persisted stubbornly, her fingers twisting behind her back. Patiently, she began to outline her reasons. "First, I want to live close to the others to foster trust and cooperation in our research efforts. Living separately conveys a suggestion of elitism. I'm not better than my crew. I'm one of a highly trained creative team. Second, I need solitude to do my more intense data extrapolations, and you have a distracting habit of nosing in when I'm making progress or I'm close to a breakthrough. This is a scientific enterprise, Andre. We are not here to play house."

Chris was angry and frustrated at having to defend decisions that would likely produce superior results. Andre couldn't hide a flinch at her last comment. He moved to interrupt, when she held up a hand to forestall him. "Third, I have no intention of living with you as husband and wife as long as you insist on broadcasting that we're trying to have children. I have no doubt that you have some plan to persuade me, so I'll make sure I'm not available to be persuaded." Chris stressed every word, filling them with absolute conviction. "I've spent the last several years preparing myself for this profession. I've gone through rigorous training and testing, so I would earn a coveted navigator position. I will not have children now, under any circumstances."

Andre laid his hand on Chris's crossed arms. She forced herself to remain motionless. "Children wouldn't prevent us from commanding planetary missions. Families are often used to colonize. You did say that you wanted a family. But I, too, want to build a future in space. Do you think I'm going to sabotage those plans now?"

"Frankly, I have no idea what you're up to. You suddenly wanting children now seems both premature and foolhardy." Chris's voice had been rising as her anxiety increased. Taking a deep breath, she forced herself to lower her voice and slow down. "The Quanta take great care that children are provided for first. Captains must be ready to place their crews above all else. How can a mother be expected to do so?"

"It is true that adjustments would have to be made," Andre allowed. "Command would have to be delegated when necessary." Andre put his arm around her shoulders, pulling her close, forcing her to relax her rigid arms. "We are a team. We can manage."

Stiffly, Chris slipped out of his embrace. She was amazed at how easily he dismissed her hard-won qualifications. If she allowed her emotions to get the best of her, Andre would gain the upper hand. The two French doors creaked in a sudden ocean breeze, beckoning her to the refreshing wind. She moved to the open doors and let the drafts cool her frustration. After several moments, she turned back to Andre.

"Look, Andre, I think there's some confusion. Your command is for Citron alone. There will be no future 'delegation.' I love you, and so I went along with giving you this experience.

"But Central Alliance isn't happy. They told me that I could, of course, assign command functions as I saw fit. However, they won't support your position as captain beyond this mission. My future in the space program depends on my demonstrating that I do, in fact, have leadership qualities, which can be evaluated only when I use them."

"They can't dictate to you!" Andre spat indignantly. "Trying to intimidate you into alienating your husband is intolerable. A few words to a good attorney and their threats will be neutralized."

"Yes, we could go back to Earth all guns blasting, except I want to make allies, not anger my superiors. They could bury my career by erecting invisible barriers—barriers I wouldn't be able to see to fight, barriers that would prevent me from getting good positions. Andre, I will command on our next assignment," she promised, adding, "and there'll be no children this soon."

"Of course, Chris." Andre patted her taut shoulder in the manner one might use to mollify an emotional child. "But living here, in this suite, is unnecessary. My authority is important, if this is to be the one time I have it, and I've told the others that we'll be living together." Andre's voice deepened, giving it a compelling quality. "We're newly married. If you stay here, it might suggest we're estranged."

Chris flushed with guilt. He was right. They were newlyweds. Sleeping apart would create unnecessary gossip. Already, the rest of their team didn't like Andre, and they barely hid this from him.

"OK, OK, I suppose you have a point," Chris capitulated disagreeably. "But make no mistake, I will keep these quarters, and I will work in the main lab. If you want to keep yourself isolated, that is your affair. I'm going to collaborate with the others. If I work late, I might sleep in here as well." Chris gestured, taking in the entire suite.

"Agreed, for now." Andre drew her close for a clumsy hug. "Now, did you discover what is happening to the weather drones?"

"No. Mac and Mitch are looking for other ways to collect the climate data they need. It'll be interesting to see what they come up with. They're so imaginative."

Andre snorted without comment.

The dinner gong interrupted their conversation. Andre slipped his arm around Chris's waist as they exited her new office and he glanced smugly at the other team members. Unfortunately for him, Mac was busy on his laptop, and Lena was stirring a pot of fragrant stew. Neither one looked up. Mitch was retrieving freshly baked bread from a makeshift oven. He sliced the loaves into thick wedges before placing them on the table next to a pot of honey and a plate of butter. There were pitchers of an iced lemon drink that the Quanta had developed. This beverage would provide for all their nutritional requirements in case the alien environment lacked critical minerals and vitamins. Chris had a special fondness for it and carried it everywhere.

Andre, of course, sat at the head of the table, gesturing for Chris to sit on his right. Lena sat on her other side with the two brothers across from the women. This configuration had become habit and was repeated at every group meal. Andre liked routine. The dinner was family style; each person could take what they liked. With his usual insensitivity, Andre wasted no time on small talk. He barely waited for the team to serve themselves before he started scheduling the next day.

"Tomorrow, I want to get biological samples from several small ponds along the freshwater stream. You two will assist me," Andre instructed, looking at Mac and Mitch. "Chris can study plant speciation at the same time. Lena and the Quanta should finish setting up our labs and medical facilities. We need to run water lines from the nearest aquifer, and Siri can set up solar-energy panels. The sooner we are self-sufficient, the sooner we finish our survey, and the sooner we open Citron to colonization."

When the others looked ready for mutiny, Chris nodded her agreement with Andre's plan. She would have to find a way to help the others get time for exploration in their own areas of expertise instead of doing grunt work for Andre.

After dinner, Mitch suggested a campfire. Mitch and Mac were talented musicians, and Chris loved to hear them play. Before she could join the others though, Andre touched her arm.

"There is something important I want to show you," he whispered. "Will you come?"

Chris watched forlornly as the laughing brothers collected Lena and their instruments. She wanted to sing. They had already had enough serious discussions for their first day. Reluctantly, she followed Andre.

He escorted her to their separate cabin and swung open the front door with a flourish, watching her expectantly. Using the converter allotted to the mission's captain, he had furnished the rooms in his opulent style. Chris marveled at the luxuries available using the converter. Combining dark energy and matter on a quantum level allowed all Quanta voyages access to amenities previously denied in a rustic camp.

Chris liked the furniture's clean, sharp lines. White sofas and black coffee tables decorated the living room. The dining space contained a long black table with high-backed chairs. Andre could easily have seated the *Aries*'s entire complement around this one table. Strings of hanging crystals, obviously collected by Siri, decorated the light fixtures. He had even found the code for fabricating soft faux-fur rugs, tempting Chris to wiggle her toes in their inviting depths. She did so now, after carelessly tossing off her shoes.

Distracted by a sudden wash of scarlet light, she walked over to a second set of French doors. The sky was vivid red. Huge chunks of crystal in the planetary rings glowed like living rubies. Chris found the whole display mesmerizing.

"Isn't this planet beautiful? I can hardly wait to explore beyond the beach."

Siri floated in carrying the few personal possessions Chris had allowed Andre to retrieve from her suite in the main cabin. She followed the Quanta into the bedroom, curious about how Andre had decorated this room. The bed, of course, was the central feature, with a pure white comforter and several thick, plush, black velvet pillows. Andre must have expended excessive quantum resources to produce a heavy headboard with elaborate scrollwork accented by exotic finials. The footboard mimicked the same design on a smaller scale. The bedroom was fit for Russian royalty. Her husband had managed to replicate symbols of his heritage on this alien planet.

Andre waved his hands to encompass the entire apartment. "Abracadabra—luxury at your fingertips," he announced with a triumphant smile.

Chris had to admit that she was impressed. Andre must have used a year's worth of converter rations for these quarters. The prospect of living in this comfort was unexpectedly enticing.

Andre pulled her back to the dining-room table, where he had spread out several black booklets. He looked like a dog showing his owner his favorite squeeze toys. Each notebook had a team member's name affixed above their science specialty. Mitch's name appeared over the chemical and mineral surveys. Mac was assigned to the ocean and climate features relevant to colonization. And Lena was an archaeologist, so her book focused on evidence of sentient life. Like every surveyor, Lena was trained in basic fieldwork protocols and would be available to assist the other team members.

Chris scanned the names, found hers, and raised an eyebrow. Andre had assigned her the tasks of categorizing the plant and animal life. Since he was the biologist, he would have been the logical choice for animal research.

"Very organized. I don't understand your assignments for me. Biology and pathology are your areas of expertise. I can't hope to do these subjects justice," Chris objected cajolingly.

"I will be busy summarizing and documenting survey data. I'll coordinate when one person's results impact another's. I think it's important for someone to keep an objective view on everyone's findings, don't you?"

Chris sighed in exasperation. He never let his position as captain go for too long before he had to remind everyone of it. To have him looking over everyone's shoulders would be intolerable. Collaboration was a very individual process, not one to be supervised. He had to carry his own weight, whether he wanted to or not.

"Really, Andre…As I said, I don't have your expertise in biology or pathology. I might conclude that a species of bacteria is safe, and then the little critters get us all sick. We need your training in the sample-collection phase."

Andre frowned. "You underestimate yourself, Christine." He always used her formal name when he wanted her to obey him without objections. At first, Chris had found this stimulating. Now she felt like a school girl in front of the principal. "I will review your findings every day. If you need help, I'll give you the proper guidance."

"Yes, yes, I know you will." Chris tried to control her growing irritation. "But the original tests and observations are not something you can oversee. Really, Andre, we don't have so many trained scientists that any one of us can sit on the sidelines giving orders."

Andre's flushed face let her know that she had struck a nerve. So she tried to mollify him by focusing on his successes. "Andy, you're too smart to just watch. In the last year, you documented testing techniques that were revolutionary. We need your insight in the field." She spoke gently, stroking his arm, showing affection for the first time that day.

Andre's expression relaxed. "We'll see. I'll help when you need me," he equivocated. "Now I'd like to celebrate our first day."

He collected the notebooks, stowed them in a pine sideboard, and went into the kitchen. He reappeared with two slender flutes and an open bottle of champagne balanced on a tray. He had included one of her favorite treats: strawberries dipped in smooth milk chocolate.

Chris took a sip of the bubbly champagne and whistled appreciably. It was perfectly chilled. She was being too hard on him, she decided. When he wanted to treat her like a privileged princess, he spared no effort. Chris looked at Andre closely for the first time that day. His hair was a bit disheveled, and his eyes slightly red. He had removed his turtleneck, and the white shirt he always wore for dinner was wrinkled. The confidence she took for granted seemed strained, and a relaxing evening was exactly what the doctor ordered. Andre lit several candles before the sun sank below the horizon.

Romantic music floated in through the open window. The soft tones of Lena's keyboard intertwined with Mitch's guitar, creating a soothing melody that was carried on the night breeze. Chris listened absently. As she nibbled on a strawberry, Andre topped her champagne glass and handed it back to her.

He raised his glass. "To treasures waiting to be revealed," he said, before draining it.

Chris took a long drink of her champagne, intending to drain her glass as well, when a random gust of wind hit the house, rattling the chandelier's hanging crystals. Preoccupied, she set her glass down and walked to the beach doors to catch a glimpse of her musician friends. She marveled at the brightness of the late-night sky. The rings reflected light from the moons onto the ocean's surface, creating rippling patterns of illumination that shifted with each new current of wind. She found herself lost in a fantasy about the ocean moving in rhythm to Mac's bass.

"The water must be full of crystal dust to glow so brightly," she murmured softly. "Lena might have trouble finding drinkable water."

Chris felt Andre come up behind her. His breath stirred wisps of her hair across her neck. He began tracing her collar bone delicately.

"What?" he asked absently.

"Look." She pointed to the water. "The ocean is glowing. Must be particul-l s-sachuration." The last two words tangled around her tongue. They were so slurred that she stopped talking, confused.

Andre leaned against her, looking over her shoulder. "You're right. We'll investigate—tomorrow." His body warmed her back, and his hands, fitted to her waist, pulled her back into the dining room.

When he leaned over to kiss her, Chris reached for her glass instead and took another long sip from her drink. Overcome with a sudden rush of dizziness, she fumbled the glass back onto the silver tray. She really was too unsteady to drink more.

"Ah, tired—going bed."

Chris headed for the bedroom and tripped over her own leaden feet. Andre acted quickly, catching her before she landed on the floor, and helped her walk to the bedroom.

"I'm, um, such a goof," she giggled, squirming out of his grasp. Everything seemed funny, and she hummed as she staggered the few feet to the bed.

"I'll be back soon," Andre whispered cryptically and disappeared.

Chris slumped onto the bed and tried to remember what she was supposed to do next. Finally inspiration struck, and she started to undress. But the buttons fought their holes, the zipper stuck, and removing her underwear became a puzzle not worth the effort. Finally giving up, she fell back on the bed, too exhausted to move. For several minutes, she drifted on the edge of unconsciousness, taking periodic gulps of air. Then, shifting her body to snuggle into the enveloping pillows, she floated into a dreamless sleep.

A shaft of bright sunlight stabbed painfully at her half-open eyes. Her husband's cheerful voice broke into her consciousness with the delicacy of cracking mirrors.

"Get up, sleepyhead. It is already late. You are setting a bad example for our staff." Andre jerked on the sheet covering her naked body. Much to her relief, he left the sheet in place.

"What time is it?" Chris mumbled, her tongue too thick to make clear words.

"Ten thirty. Breakfast is waiting on the table. I have a meeting with the Drummonds in five minutes. I will expect you in the main lab in thirty minutes." Andre's good humor grated painfully against her nerves. Thankfully, he left.

Ten thirty meant half the morning was already over. Chris groaned in disappointment. It was her habit to wake by five o'clock, take a quick run, shower, and eat a light breakfast before starting her workday. She couldn't understand what had kept her in bed. Thinking back, Chris tried to remember what time she had come to bed. Her attempts resulted in a pounding headache. She massaged her temples gingerly.

Grunting, she forced herself up by swinging her legs off the bed. She couldn't suppress a moan of pain. Her muscles throbbed, and her lower back ached, creating a tingling weakness broken by painful cramps. What in the world had happened to her? When she caught sight of her arms, she saw, to her horror, that black bruises stained her pale skin. She looked down to discover more bruises across her thighs and stomach. She hesitated to stand, knowing the bruises promised more pain to come. Still, she gathered her resolve and rose. Instantly, she felt waves of dizziness and nausea. Quickly, she lowered herself back onto the bed, her mind scrambling for some explanation. She decided to make a closer examination.

Chris stumbled into the bathroom to find, by some miracle, that the shower was dripping water. The Quanta must have worked during the night to run PVC to Andre's separate cabin. Chris was deeply appreciative that they had accomplished this task. She ardently anticipated the soothing effects of hot water.

But first she stood in front of the full-length mirror and studied the extent of her injuries. Her naked body was testimony to one hell of a night. Her last coherent memory confirmed that she had been wearing underwear. Now she was naked. Black bruises spread across her white skin like an army of invading spiders. It would take weeks for the bruises to run the gamut of colors—black, purple, and then yellow—before finally fading. Her haunted red eyes stared back at her above dark hollows. Tenderly she explored her body, finding scratches, bite marks, and dried blood. She was so stiff and sore she could barely walk. One ankle throbbed dully.

Damn it, damn it, damn it, she swore in silent fury. What in God's name was going on?

The obvious answer was that Andre had assaulted her, except this was just too ridiculous to credit. He had always been reasonable, despite their arguments. For all of his scheming and self-centeredness, Andre had never raised a hand to her.

Chris took a hot shower, hoping to wash away her aches. Rather than soothing her muscles, the water caused her injuries to sting. Disappointed, she cut the shower short. She dressed in baggy sweatpants and a hooded sweatshirt that were too big to chafe her wounds. Then she applied a thick layer of makeup to hide the bruises on her exposed skin and wrapped a scarf around her neck for good measure. She pulled her hair back into a tight, unattractive ponytail. Her stomach rolled uneasily, eliminating any desire she might have had to eat. She was dreadfully thirsty, however, and drank several glasses of lemon juice before filling her thermos. Automatically taking the notebook with her name on it, she left Andre's quarters and shuffled over to the main cabin.

Tears flooded her eyes when she found it empty. She hadn't realized how desperately she wanted the comforting presence of her team. She searched the camp with the same result. Finally she spotted a small group far up the valley. She stumbled up the newly created footpath, resentment growing with each painful step.

As she approached, Chris saw Mitch and Mac collecting foliage samples, Lena knee-deep in the stream filling jars with water, and Andre stacking piles of brilliant crystals by color and shape. Abandoning her earlier intention to be discreet, Chris confronted Andre as soon as she was close enough to be heard.

"What the hell happened last night?" she shouted. The others looked up, obviously alarmed by the anger in her voice. She had thought to keep her injuries a secret, until she realized she would put herself at greater risk of a repeat performance.

"Do not address me in that tone," Andre snapped, his pale face growing scarlet. "I have no idea what you are talking about."

Ripping off her scarf and shucking her hooded sweatshirt in one motion, Chris stood bare except for her bra, sweatpants, and tennis shoes. Socks had been too constricting. The red and black injuries stood out against her tender skin in mute accusation. She heard Lena gasp, and one of the twins growled.

"This is what I'm talking about." She waved a hand down her body. "What the hell did you do to me? I swear to God, Andre, you have ended our marriage if you don't come up with a damn good explanation, now!"

"My God! I had no idea we'd been so rough," Andre whispered, his eyes widening with shock.

Chris saw her disbelief reflected in the faces of her friends. Mitch looked ready to bash something. "We?" she cried. "There is nothing I would consent to that would result in these injuries. So cut the act."

"Darling, of course it was *we*. I admit, I found our lovemaking more rigorous than usual; still, nothing was done without your consent."

Andre smiled uncertainly, and she wanted to puke. He started to move closer to her, until the twins' expressions of barely controlled outrage stopped him.

Chris rolled her eyes in frustration. She really couldn't remember what had happened, and Andre had never hurt her physically before. Admittedly, one could say he didn't pull punches with words, but the idea that he would assault her in this manner was too great a leap to make without proof.

Lena came up behind Chris and drew her away from the others, so they could speak privately. "Chris, come back to the camp, so I can treat your wounds," she urged soothingly. "You're bleeding."

Chris looked down, horrified to find her bra stained with blood. Lena's concern penetrated her bravado, and she collapsed into her arms, shaking with grief.

"I'll take care of my wife," Andre declared gravely, trying to pull Chris away from the counselor. Lena didn't release her hold, and when Chris winced, he let go. "Please, Chris, I didn't do this. You must know I wouldn't do this. Let me help you," Andre pleaded.

But Chris had to admit that she was afraid of her own husband.

"Lena will take care of me now," she hissed through clenched teeth, barely holding on to her composure. The pain was intensifying, and she began to shake with shock. "I find your suggestion that I would participate in violent lovemaking disgusting. Until I get to the bottom of this, I'll be staying with the others. I will know what happened."

Carefully, Chris slipped on her sweatshirt and, with the help of Lena's strong arm, started limping back down the path. The rush up the trail and the adrenaline released by her anger had shielded her from the true extent of her injuries. Now her swollen ankle made the return trip an adventure in pain.

Mitch snorted with impatience at her feeble attempts to hobble down the path. He lifted her into his arms, and Lena led everyone back to the main cabin. There, Mitch laid her gently down on the large couch facing the beach.

Lena gently administered soothing salves and calming medicines, while Mac prepared her favorite foods. A crab omelet with green onions and a fruit salad covered in vanilla yogurt were laid out, in grand fashion, on their rustic conference table. He also brought a large pitcher of iced chamomile tea. His teasing and jokes earned him a wet smile.

Mitch carried in a chair designed for every comfort. The recliner and ottoman had special cushions that relieved the pressure on her wounds. He had covered them with soft fleece blankets and then piled pillows next to the chair. She would be able to prop her body in any position. He moved her computer to a strategically placed coffee table and added a stack of books that Lena retrieved from Chris's office suite. Their thoughtful ministrations made her dilemma seem all the more ominous in comparison.

Sitting at the table with her ankle propped on a large pillow, Chris waited anxiously for the inevitable questions. To her surprise, they didn't come. Instead, the twins and Lena teased her with jokes, told stories of their morning fieldwork, and sang songs, luring her into singing along. No one intruded into her privacy any further than they already had.

Inevitably, Andre entered the lodge. The friendly, easy atmosphere that had filled the room drained away. Mitch and Mac rose stiffly, obviously reluctant to. Lena, with the twins as backup, walked over to Andre.

"I am evoking doctor's privileges, Captain," Lena announced. "Chris needs peace and quiet to mend. You interfere with both."

"When will she be ready to go back to work?" Andre asked, his eyes darting to each member of the group, assessing and evaluating. The question was an obvious attempt to learn something of her condition and the group's intentions.

"I'm not sure," Lena answered. "Her physical wounds should heal in a week or so. Fortunately her ankle isn't broken. The duration of her mental convalescence is more uncertain. From the notebook she was carrying, I know her assigned duties. I'm ready to handle her botany studies; you'll have to take back the biological research."

"You have no authority to reassign work," Andre snapped, pulling his shoulders back and expanding his chest. Chris was reminded of a puffed-up red rooster and rigorously stifled a laugh.

"On the contrary, I'm the mission counselor, and Captain Griffin gave me the authority to override you on matters of physical and mental health," Lena pointed out. She stepped so close to Andre they were almost touching. "This is not a dictatorship, Andre. Chris has been injured, and I will use whatever measures necessary to keep her safe from further harm."

Lena was a force, even if a small one.

"I have done nothing wrong!" Andre roared and stomped his foot foolishly.

Flinching slightly, Lena stood her ground. Mitch and Mac, however, approached Andre grimly. Any physical altercation initiated by a subordinate against a captain was strictly forbidden. If things progressed any further, Chris knew Andre could imprison the twins.

She stood quickly, groaning as her full weight shifted to her wounded ankle. She pushed the pain to the back of her mind. "Enough!" she exclaimed, swinging her arms. "Mitch and Mac, move back!"

Startled by her sudden outburst, the twins obeyed automatically.

Chris hobbled over to Lena and pulled her away from Andre gently. "Thank you all for your protection. But this matter is really between Andre and me. Interfering will put you all at risk, and this I can't allow. Now if you will give us some privacy, I'll speak to my husband alone."

"Are you sure?" Lena's voice shook with worry.

Chris nodded.

"We'll be just outside," Mac promised.

Mitch put an arm around Lena, flashing a glare of warning at Andre. The three left together.

Chris headed for the kitchen sink, deliberately putting the wooden table between Andre and her. Its presence, large and heavy, helped her feel a bite safer.

"Why are you here?" she snapped. Chris was done pretending. She was mad as hell, and Andre had better behave.

"Look…Chris…You know me," he pleaded. "I've never hurt you. Our life together has always seemed to please you."

Despite her pain and anger, she nodded. As much as Chris wanted to believe the worst, she couldn't deny the truth. Andre had never hurt her. Maybe she had some part in this strange drama.

Maybe the injuries had been some terrible accident. Chris looked into his sincere eyes, ready to surrender to his logic, when she felt a stab of pain deep inside. Unable to stand on her own, she groaned and leaned heavily against the table. Andre rushed to help her, but she waved him off.

"Look, Andre, there is something you aren't telling me, and all your protestations of innocence will never convince me otherwise. For some reason, I can't remember what happened." Chris massaged her forehead miserably. "Eventually, I will. Until then, I think it would be wise if you kept your distance."

Chris forced herself to straighten and limped over to the door to her suite of rooms. "I need time to work this thing out," she pleaded.

Andre hesitated, looking both concerned and irritated. Chris waited, resolute, and finally he left the lodge. Once alone, Chris collapsed onto a low couch, her pretense of confidence and daring gone. Siri, who was hovering silently in the corner, had been invisible during her battle with Andre. Now he buzzed closer. She felt a soft pinprick. Soon all her worries and pains melted away on a sea of well-being.

"Axel warned me about your situation, and I've been watching Andre. If he hadn't ordered me to finish the plumbing, I would have seen what happened," he whispered so softly she wasn't sure if he had spoken out loud. Siri and his twin, Iris, were her navigation partners. Both had objected to Andre's insistence on joint leadership. Previously, Chris had been too embarrassed to call on her Quanta for guidance. Now Siri had seen that she needed someone to confide in.

"What am I to do?" she asked. "How can I find the truth?"

Siri's answer, when it came, followed her into a well of deep, compelling sleep. "Get better, and the answers will be waiting."

Despite the drugs, Chris's sleep was not peaceful. She tossed feverishly, and her dreams were desolate. She found herself in a shrouded bedroom with the largest Citron moon shining through the white drapes. Someone was on top of her, holding her down. His eyes glowed with hunger, like a black panther ready to consume a terrified doe. Chris moaned and thrashed so violently that she tumbled off the low bed and woke up. The dream immediately faded into forgetfulness.

CHAPTER 5

BESS SENTARA MISSION BRIEFING—BETH

Beth roused from the navigation trance, shaking off the usual disorientation. She knew that her mind slipped into a receptive subconscious state, which led Axel to the correct dark-energy portal and pushed the *Aries* to the other side. The exact details of this process had never been completely explained.

And there was something else. She knew that with each jump, she was slightly changed. She was able to do things better. Mathematical calculations were now effortless, where before math had been her worst subject. Her connection to Axel was also stronger. He could anticipate her requests and comply before she could tell him. She meant to ask him about this, except the questions always slipped away after a few seconds.

Beth marveled at her first unobstructed view of their second destination, Sentara. Mark Logan, her second in command, had engaged manual control and was positioning the *Aries* in an orbit perpendicular to the row of moons circling the planet. These moons amplified the sun's rays, making Sentara brighter and hotter than Earth.

Mark was older than the normal Technion candidate, with prematurely gray hair and a clever mind. During her studies, he had been her mentor, advisor, and confidant. He was always ready for some new field study or intriguing experiment. There could be no other as her second on the *Aries*.

Naturally Mark had developed an instant rapport with Axel. Mark's encyclopedic mind held a wealth of facts and insights. The little droid had adopted Mark's passion for studying obscure subjects, and he was now researching esoteric historical authors. Her second answered Axel's endless questions with an enduring patience and dry humor. Beth enjoyed their lively discussions.

"Beta team to conference room. Planet briefing in thirty minutes," Beth announced through the ship's intercom.

Rose Cavanagh and Amy Chen were standing by the projection screen, at the head of the conference table, arguing. Beth was always surprised by the strange connection between these two administrators of the Beta subsurvey team (BESS). They reminded Beth of a superhero and his—or in this case, her—loyal sidekick. The trouble was recognizing who was the hero and who was the sidekick. Beth thought they might deliberately switch roles just to confuse their adversaries.

Amy, as the chief executive under Rose, was Asian military, and her small, athletic build reflected her indomitable spirit. Her long black hair, on the other hand, was very feminine. Amy had been hard to get close to. She was usually training and answered friendly inquiries with one-word replies.

Captain Rose Cavanagh, on the other hand, was friendliness personified. Her eyes were a teasing green that turned gold when she was scheming. The curly red hair framing her elfin face reflected her passion and devotion. Beth had instantly liked her and so had the crew.

While Amy was a reserved, disciplined soldier, Rose fussed and worried over her team like a lioness over her cubs. She was the more intuitive navigator, sailing through the testing that Amy had barely passed. Now Rose reminded Amy that they had little information about the planet they would soon be left on.

"Really, Amy, we should have been allowed to make an informed decision about Sentara, not all this cloak and dagger," Rose complained, wrinkling her nose. She plopped down into her chair and crossed her arms.

"I'm sure we can handle it, Rose. After all, Sentara requested our team, and it's a short survey. We've done similar jobs in our sleep."

"And these government officials have our best interests at heart?" Nicole DeVere jeered.

Nicole and Talia Sarin had entered the conference room together.

Nicole was their black engineer. What she couldn't fix hadn't been invented. Her expertise might be valuable, but her hobbies were tiresome. She had an annoying habit of taking apart devices and then losing pieces. Everyone had begun stashing their personal electronic devices. To Beth's delight, Nicole's degrees in chemistry and mineralogy would help in diagnosing the moons' unique dynamic. How several moons orbiting in a line could avoid collisions was a mystery.

Talia, of East Indian descent, was small and dark. Her brown, doe-shaped eyes were easily her most expressive feature, when her glasses didn't block the view. She wore her dark hair short and preferred the ship uniform, which remarkably enhanced her figure. She had a shy, endearing demeanor. Talia had studied extensively in England, like Mark, and was now a leading authority on disease vectors and pathogen evolution in plants, animals, and humans. She was eager to extend her expertise to alien strains.

Dr. Samuel Carlson was the only man in the group. In fact, he wasn't supposed to be on this mission at all. The female doctor the

Sentarans had requested had gotten married quite suddenly, leaving Sam as the most qualified available candidate.

Alas, Sam was his own worst patient. His constant ailments could be explained one of two ways. Either he had a supernaturally sensitive constitution, or he was a compulsive hypochondriac. His frequent allergy attacks, complete with watery eyes and sniffles, were quite remarkable considering that the ship's air was filtered continuously. Despite his bad health and mysophobic habits, his lively eyes expressed his eagerness for the exciting challenge that space travel guaranteed.

Sam had been a coveted researcher for the alliance before he'd insisted on the assignment to the *Aries*. His advanced diagnostic scanners had contributed significantly to the Quantas' studies in human medicine. They were now carefully stowed in the BESS's storage compartment.

Beth cleared her throat loudly, calling the group to order.

"I know that all of you have been rushed onto this survey without the usual briefing. The fact that Sentara requested this team specifically has made Central Alliance nervous. They have no idea how Sentara got enough background data to ask for each of you. While Central has decided the benefits of a partnership with Sentara outweigh the potential risks, your safety is still the *Aries*'s first priority. I'm to relay, confidentially, all our intelligence on Sentara, which includes a special provision for your safety." Beth wanted to get the worst out first.

Amy and Rose exchanged glances, Rose nodding as her fears were confirmed. Nicole raised her eyebrows expectantly, and Talia sighed.

"Due to the fact that Sentara's population has decreased significantly, they have opened their planet to outside colonization. Your chief assignment is to determine if Sentara is suitable for humans.

"The planet consists of three large islands and several small ones. Historically, polar volcanoes have flooded the smaller islands and spread particulates. This might be the cause of the Sentarans' current infertility."

Sam looked ready to speak until Beth waved him off. "Questions after.

"Frankly, the Sentarans are something of a mystery." Beth scrutinized each member of the team, guessing at their ability to see past subterfuge. "Central Alliance has had interviews with a small group of government officials. We still don't know how many people live on the planet or how they govern themselves. We need a report on these details as soon as possible.

"In order to secure your safety, three Quanta will accompany you." As she said this, the Quanta floated into the room. "You have met Ari, the chief scientist. He has all our data on this planet and specializes in sentient life-forms, so he'll be your reference on the Sentarans themselves." Ari spun in greeting. "And Mirim will be your communication node. She has direct access to the Quanta nexus." The second Quanta blinked both eyes. Female Quanta, or rather Quanta with feminine names, used unique light displays as communication. Mirim filled the room with warm red and gold illumination. "And finally Evan—his specialty is data correlations." For a Quanta, Evan was smaller than usual, but his voice was exceptionally well modulated, like a large cat purring.

"It is a pleasure to make your acquaintance." Evan spoke in a formal style and bobbed in a fairly good imitation of a bow.

"Now any questions?" Beth asked.

Amy and Rose looked at each other and nodded simultaneously. Beth had read their files. She knew that years of working together would go a long way to helping the surveyors achieve their goals.

"Well, you wanted a thrilling adventure, and now you have it," Rose said, shoving Amy playfully. "Maybe you'll find your perfect soul mate. No one said he had to live on Earth."

"Yes, I'm sure an alien would be my perfect mate," Amy scoffed.

Rising from his chair, Sam winked at Beth. "I'm ready to get started. With three Quanta and the *Aries* around the corner, who couldn't be safer? Do you think they'll let me study several cadavers at once? Autopsy is the quickest way to discover compatibility," Sam asked innocently. He seemed to have no notion of how morbid his request sounded. At Rose's look of consternation, Sam touched her reassuringly. "Don't worry. I can be discreet. I'll wait until after introductions."

Beth decided that if Amy and Rose couldn't keep Sam muzzled, no one could. "All right then," she said. "If everyone's on board, I guess you can head down."

Discussing the planet excitedly, the team followed Sam out. Beth dropped off the Quanta at their launch vehicle first and then led the human team to the larger BESS to do the final systems check. Central had decided to take two ships to the planet's surface as a further precaution.

After two hours, all systems had checked out. Beth returned to the bridge and waited for the BESS to disengage from the *Aries*. Mark gave Amy the exact landing coordinates. Even though Rose was the chief navigator, Amy was the better pilot and did all the local flying. Once free, the BESS circled the larger ship, letting everyone wave a fond farewell, before heading for the planet.

CHAPTER 6

SENTARAN SURPRISE
ESCORTS—ROSE

Rose spent the short trip to the planet tracking transmissions from various city centers. She was able to identify four different dialects, and she immediately started recording them. The Sentarans had conveniently learned English, so the survey team had not been required to understand their native language. But language contained many indicators of a civilization's culture and beliefs. Rose wanted to be able to hear them in their original context. She planned on learning as many dialects as she could while letting the Sentarans believe their conversations were private.

They had been directed to land on the largest island, in a wooded area next to the planet's main research facility. Amy touched down so lightly that Rose was not, at first, aware they had actually landed. Only the main hatch opening alerted her that they had arrived and were receiving visitors. Several robed figures entered the bridge. They were taller than she had expected, averaging seven feet. Their hoods hid their features. This was definitely not the openhanded welcome she'd been anticipating.

Amy instantly stiffened into a military pose. She looked very much the group leader, and she strode toward the strangers, extending her hand in a gesture of friendship. One of the figures separated itself from the rest and approached her. He removed his hood, revealing an amazing visage. Rose fell back into her chair with a thud of surprise. Then all four members of the boarding party also removed their robes.

The Sentarans were the most striking men Rose had ever seen. She was reminded uneasily of her joking words to Amy earlier. If looks were the deal breaker, then the deal had been made. They were physical perfection in a way that was eerily unnatural.

The man who'd stepped forward had pale-blond hair streaked with silver that glistened like ice in newly fallen snow. Iridescence had been applied with delicate brush strokes to accent his bone structure. Rose was most attracted to his eyes. Their color changed, apparently depending on his mood, from the palest blue to the deepest sapphire. Even though he was the smallest of the group, he was well over six feet tall and strongly built. Sam, only five feet nine, appeared fragile in comparison.

"I am Jason, the principal of this group," the man said. On the surface, he was polite and amicable. Underneath was a strange flatness she couldn't penetrate.

He waved at the other three. Pointing to a man clearly the tallest, with black hair, eagle features, and sharp penetrating eyes, he said, "This is Jeffrey." Motioning to a shorter man in the rear with a round face relaxed into a wide, innocent smile, he said, "This is Jonathan." He named the dark-skinned man Jared.

"We have chosen these names so you can easily identify us," he explained. "The letter *J* is our designation for your team's escorts. We will accompany you for as long as you are on our planet. We can assist with your research or retrieve any materials you might need. You are not to travel without one of us with you." This last was a clear warning.

Jared moved toward Rose, Jason toward Amy, Jonathan toward Talia, and Jeffrey intercepted Nicole. At the precise moment he touched Nicole, Rose felt a wave of warm, friendly calm flow over her. Then Nicole was laughing raucously at something Jeremy had whispered, and Talia started stroking Jonathan's arm. The strength of the emotions in the room increased beyond happiness and warmth to include something infinitely more dangerous.

Rose had always been a sensitive, attuned to strong emotions. Her grandmother, a fey healer in her Irish village, had seen her granddaughter's potential. Rose had spent many childhood summers there, playing in the emerald forests and learning the secrets her grand kept hidden from outsiders. Grand had told her that everyone had degrees of sensitivity, and it took awareness and practice to cultivate them. So Rose's sensitivities had been heightened and extended. She used them as one would a basic sense. It was her grandmother's training that had made becoming a navigator effortless and had prompted Rose to create a partnership with Amy.

Rose had sensed Amy's strong extrasensory ability when the two shared a class. Amy was oblivious to her aptitude, and Rose knew unrecognized power could be dangerous. At best it could lead to social isolation, and at worst it could go so far as to cause mental problems. Rose wanted to help her new friend. Instead of being a burden, extra perceptions—when recognized and managed—were a gift.

Now emotion tore through the room with such overwhelming power that coherent thinking was an exhausting struggle. In a moment of clarity, Rose shoved Jared away and placed a chair between them. She watched in horror as the behavior of the other women escalated to the bizarre.

Nicole was kissing Jeffery, and Amy was fumbling with her buttons. Talia, the sweet innocent, was in the worst trouble. Without any regard for the severe consequences, she was following her escort to the back sleeping quarters, eyes half closed. Sam had slumped into a ball on the floor, his eyes staring unfocused at the floor.

Rose had to save her team before it was too late. First, she needed to protect herself from whatever power was controlling them. Her grand had taught her how to erect mental shields against outside influences. Now, as she followed those dimly remembered childhood instructions, she breathed a prayer of hope. It took a few seconds for her to mentally forge steel barricades around her mind and imagine them as an impenetrable shield. When she had sealed the steel circle closed, the emotional assault ended.

At that exact moment, all activity stopped. The five men turned in unison to stare at Rose and then silently disengaged themselves from the BESS scientists, who had become still, their expressions slack and blank. The Sentarans came forward and surrounded Rose. Jared reached out as if to touch her shields, only to pull back when she shifted her mental image from steel to painfully hot fire.

Jason waved his men back. Then he approached her slowly, like someone approaching a growling dog, holding his hand out cautiously.

"What are you doing?" he asked curiously. His voice was totally unaffected; the earlier atmosphere of passion that had flooded the ship seemed like a mirage.

"I'm shielding myself from the emotional miasma controlling my crew. Your men are creating it, aren't they?" Rose asked. Even though she stated it as a question, she already knew the truth. "Your race is telepathic?"

"It's the electromagnetic energy reflected by the moons." Jason pointed out the bridge window toward the ring of moons. They were close enough to be visible even during the day. "They amplify our mental energy. Why do you need to shield yourself? Do you fear us?"

"No," Rose lied. These men had shaken her to the core, but she wasn't going to give them the upper hand. Her friends had acted against their deepest principles. These men were dangerous. Rose needed to make their transgression so serious that they would not try it again. "You have broken our law. We create our own emotional reactions, and you are stealing this freedom. This will not be tolerated."

Rose wondered if these aliens really didn't understand the concept of personal freedom. Ultimately, it didn't matter. Saving her people was her top priority.

"We meant no offense." Jason spread his arms wide in a gesture of friendship. "It is our habit to put newcomers at ease when they first visit our planet. We do this with refreshment and our ability to create a friendly atmosphere. Don't your alcohol and music do this as well?"

"Our alcohol and music offer a mood without holding the listener hostage," Rose corrected. "Your mental abilities overwhelm my friends. You must stop immediately and keep your mood enhancing muzzled. Otherwise, we must leave."

"Of course." Again Jason waved at the others.

Rose felt the emotional current in the room fade until all she could sense was the usual chaotic feelings of her friends.

Rose watched as her team became more animated. They straightened their clothes and clumsily fumbled with the buttons, clearly confused. By the time they'd assembled near the door, their expressions showed a relaxed awareness of their environment.

"What have you done?" Rose whispered furiously to Jason. "Why don't they act upset?"

"Thought, emotion, and action are intrinsically linked in a precise order," he explained. "Your friends had no thought to enter into liaisons with us. When we withdrew the emotions, the actions made no sense. Your friends subconsciously edited out the incongruence. They don't remember their passionate behavior because there was no passion. It is a puzzling side effect of our talents."

Rose listened, not wholly convinced of their good intentions. Light as a baby bird feather, she set a tag on each of her crew that would alert her to any unusual behavior. She would notice any action that didn't ring true.

"We have arranged quarters for you," Jason said, waving toward the door. "Please, come this way."

As soon as they left the cool recesses of the ship, the sun seared Rose with blinding brilliance and waves of suffocating heat. She coughed, struggling to take a full breath of air that was too hot and thick. She quickly closed her eyes and turned her back to the sunlight. Jason pushed special sunglasses into her hands, and she gratefully put them on. The other men extended umbrellas to create an area of shade.

"Unfortunately, the sun is at its zenith," explained Jason. "We usually stay inside during this time of day. In your quarters, we have provided instructions on how to handle our oppressive sun, along with extra gear."

The darkness of the glasses soothed Rose's eyes, and their polarized lenses made the landscape stark and dramatic. They were in an exposed area, on a stone pathway, surrounded by forest and formal gardens. Jason drew the group forward by pointing out features of special interest. A brightly feathered bird, reminiscent of a peacock, with an extra pair of protective eyelids, drank deeply from a nearby fountain. Small animals peered out of hiding places throughout the wooded lane, their eyes faceted with thick protective lenses. They seemed to have no fear of the humans. Rows of colorful flowers growing in channels of water lined the stone path. Their feathered petals seemed to thrive in the enhanced sunlight.

Rose began to relax, lulled by this unfamiliar beauty. The group of humans, surrounded by their escorts, headed toward a glass structure.

Your quarters are connected to our most prestigious university. Jason pointed to a distant complex of buildings shrouded in vines and trees. *The college is eager to help you with your research. A lab facility has been arranged, vacated by students excited to meet you.*

Impressed with such generous arrangements, Rose turned to thank Jason, only to stop in shocked silence. She realized she had heard the words in her mind. Her abrupt halt brought the entire group to an awkward standstill. Jason urged them all forward.

"Don't you want *everyone* to hear about our superior accommodations?" she asked irritably once the others had wandered ahead out of earshot. The oppressive sunlight had drained her decorum quickly.

I wanted to see if you could receive as well as send thought, Jason defended himself mentally, ignoring her suggestion. *Telepathy is our preferred manner of speaking. It is more revealing. We were told that Amy is the strongest talent. Yet she doesn't respond to our mental inquiries. You, on the other hand, are a welcome surprise.*

Thankfully, they finally arrived at the glass building. Rose had no intention of speaking without the knowledge of her entire team and so continued talking more loudly. "I'm not telepathic. Look, we would like to get settled and acclimatize to your weather. Can we save further evaluations for tomorrow?"

Jason restrained Rose by the door while her team moved deeper into the building. Thankfully, he dropped the telepathy. "Is Amy aware of her talent and just not answering?"

"Telepathy is not recognized on Earth," Rose revealed carelessly. "Whatever signs she might have noticed as a child would have been dismissed." The cold air conditioning blowing out the open door had revived her, and she decided to encourage Jason to answer questions that had been troubling her since the *Aries*'s planet briefing.

She lowered her voice to a conspiratorial tone. "Why did you bring us here really? I know your government selected us specially."

"All in good time," Jason replied evasively. "What's more important is, why did you come, knowing that you had been chosen by complete strangers? Does your government hope to exploit us or merely steal our resources?" He gripped her arm tightly, putting his face close to hers.

Rose was surprised at his hostility. She hadn't expected these people to be suspicious and fearful. After all, her team was here by invitation. Then he leaned close, his eyes boring into hers. He thrust a penetrating stab of power at Rose that she had no time to deflect. When her hastily erected shields crumbled, she used the only other defense she had available. She pushed her mind into the ultimate unassailable condition: unconsciousness. Dimly she heard Jason swear as she collapsed into darkness.

When Rose regained her senses, she was lying on a couch in a large reception area. Her sunglasses had been removed. Cool air and muted light soothed her aching temples. Amy was kneeling next to her, shaking her urgently.

"Rose, wake up," she pleaded, brushing Rose's hair off her face.

Amy's features were etched with stress. Her perfectly ironed clothes were wrinkled and musty from the sweat that was inevitable in the constant heat. Her hair had escaped from its tight braid, allowing wisps to stick to her face.

"I'm awake," Rose assured her, and took her hands. "Don't fret; I'm completely unharmed."

Amy's worried countenance relaxed, and she sighed in relief. "Jason said it was the sunlight. This is the worst time of year for sun. When you were unconscious for so long, I became suspicious. Frankly he isn't the most trustworthy—"

"Where are they?" Rose interrupted, her eyes sweeping the room anxiously. There was no sign of their "escorts." Nicole was standing by the door, blocking entry. Talia was kneeling beside Amy, and Sam was fussing with his luggage. He glanced nervously in her direction.

"They left after we practically pushed them out the door. They insisted we wear these communication devices." Amy raised her arm to expose a gold bracelet several inches wide. It was covered with jewels arranged in parallel patterns.

"The jewels control features in our quarters: heat, air conditioning, music, the fountain, et cetera. We were waiting for you to wake up before we tried them out." Amy pointed at another bracelet lying on a coffee table. "That one is for you."

Rose ignored the bracelet. "I'm too hot and sticky. I want to take a cold shower, and then I want to talk with all of you." Rose's glance took in the entire group. "Can everyone be ready in an hour?"

The others nodded and moved toward a series of open doors that led to individual apartments. Nicole fussed with her bracelet, finally wrenching it off. She took it to the main table to examine it more closely. "Whatever you do, don't be alone with your escorts," Rose called to her disappearing colleagues.

"Where are my rooms?" she asked Amy, scanning the row of doors. She retrieved the gold bracelet off the table. She guessed that Amy had already searched their quarters. After all, it was the soldiering thing to do.

The central living space was more opulent than Rose had expected. Soft fur throws covered the couches that encircled an elaborate fountain. Its spray collected in faceted glass bowls painted with sea creatures and birds, before overflowing into a large pond, where fish hid behind submerged landscaping.

"Over here." Amy led her to a door with her name affixed above the knocker. "We all have assigned bedrooms." Amy indicated that her own room was next to Rose's.

Rose thoughtfully rubbed the characters of her name on the small silver plaque. She planted the mental suggestion that no one could enter without alerting her. It was a trick grand had taught her: create a mental cue that would remind her to stay vigilant.

Amy followed her into the spacious suite. The sitting room dazzled with ornate diamond-paned windows and plush chaises facing a white marble mantle with an air-conditioning insert. Soft music issued from speakers on either side. Opposite the mantle were three doors. One led to a bedroom with a magnificent king-size bed, another revealed a huge bath area with a sunken tub and elaborate glass shower, and the third opened to a luxurious closet.

Rose couldn't resist the impulse to enter the large walk-in. There were several open wardrobes full of clothes both alien and familiar. Cupboards held every type of dressing accessory imaginable.

"I bet these are all in my size," she assumed, grinning sinfully.

A polished-wood dressing table with ornately framed mirror filled one corner. Rose placed the gold bracelet in a bottom drawer of the table and covered it with a thick green towel that was lying on a nearby ottoman. Then she reentered the sitting room, surprised to find Amy there, pacing.

"Look, Rose, I know something is wrong," she blurted, as soon as Rose reappeared. "Why did you faint? Jason's reasons were feeble, to say the least."

Rose touched her lips and pointed at Amy's bright, new gold bracelet. Speaking loudly, she gently removed the jewelry.

"Don't be silly, Amy. It was just the heat."

Rose carried the bracelet back to the walk-in closet and tucked it into the bottom vanity drawer. It glowed softly as soon as she placed it next to the other bracelet. Rose covered both of them with several necklaces and another towel. Then she returned to the sitting room, closed all three doors, and joined Amy on the small divan.

"I hope that works," Rose breathed softly. "Jason and the others are telepathic," she blurted tersely. "They all have amplified mental abilities and, unobserved by us, are communicating with each other—abilities that you have in spades." She touched Amy's shoulder to emphasize this last point. "They want something from us, and I have a feeling we aren't going to like it. I'm hoping you might gain some heightened telepathic competence. For some reason, they think you should. If you find you can hear their telepathic communication, tell me right away."

Amy looked dubious. "We should take real security precautions," she insisted.

"I agree. I think those bracelets are a way to monitor us. I'll complain about some allergic reaction to mine. You were already wearing yours, so take it off when we're alone. Now, under no circumstances is anyone allowed to be alone with our new escorts," Rose stressed.

"Why? We're adults."

"Because, *Executive Officer*"—Rose emphasized the words to remind Amy of the responsibility it entailed—"we are not guests, and this is not a party. We're on an alien planet where we need to exercise strict diplomacy. We don't know why they want us, specifically, here. Despite all the trappings"—Rose waved at the three rooms—"we can't trust them."

Rose saw Amy wrinkle her nose skeptically. She remembered that Amy didn't recall the assault on their ship and so her behavior must appear unreasonable. Taking a deep breath, Rose decided to describe the events after they landed.

"Back on our ship, the Sentarans used their mental powers to create an artificial atmosphere of intimacy. All of you—and I mean you too, Amy—were hanging on them. I think they intended some sort of indiscretion. I just can't understand why. We'll have to tell Nicole and Talia they're in danger. It's vital that we stay united. It's one way we'll remain safe."

Suddenly, Amy jumped up, panic flashing in her eyes. She dashed out into the main living room and scanned the entire area frantically.

"Oh my God! Where are the Quanta?"

With cold dread filling her gut, Rose called her entire crew back into the shared living space. No one had seen the three

Quanta, their first line of defense, or noticed they were missing. Rose darted back into her dressing area to retrieve Amy's communication bracelet.

"How does this foolish thing work anyway?" Rose growled. She was blaming herself for this new debacle. Why hadn't she noticed sooner? She was relieved when Jason and his security force arrived soon after her call.

"Where are they?" Amy demanded, grabbing Jason's collar.

Rose feared she would cause a major incident. Surprisingly, Jason remained amiable.

"Your computers are fine," he assured her, disengaging himself. He readjusted his clothes before continuing. "They've been busy doing preliminary preparations. You're all overreacting."

But Rose wouldn't be put off until she laid eyes on their dear computer allies. "Show us where they are," she demanded, pushing through Jason's men.

"We'll see for ourselves," Nicole growled, following Rose.

Talia moved forward behind Nicole. "We work together," she declared.

"They're at the lab. Please calm down. If you want to visit them at this *late* hour, we're happy to oblige," Jason said, putting a disagreeable emphasis on the word *late*. With a resigned sigh, he guided them outside toward the larger ivy-covered building.

The sun had set, so it was cooling off. The moons shone palely, lighting the landscape sufficiently to allow Rose to see their surroundings without the distracting brilliance of sunlight. She noticed that the university and their quarters were isolated from the rest of the city. High stone fences blocked most of the outer city noises.

She was about to ask Jason why they were isolated from the city proper, when Talia cried out from behind the group.

"Wait! Oh please, wait!" Breathing heavily, she rushed up to Rose, clearly upset, and glared at Jason suspiciously.

Rose put her arm around Talia's shoulders and gave her an encouraging squeeze. "Go on. You're safe. You can speak freely. What's wrong?"

Talia took a long breath and then blurted out the reason for her distress. "Jon won't stop pressuring me to go away with him to the botanical gardens. Even though I told him we all had to stay with the group, he blocked my way. He wouldn't take no for an answer!" Talia protested, almost hysterical.

Rose glowered at Jason. "Is this how you treat visitors?" she challenged through tight lips.

"Of course not!" Jason snorted in frustration.

He turned to Jonathan deliberately. After a few moments, the man turned away, shamefaced, and left the group in eerie silence. Rose had heard nothing telepathically. Evidently, she had to be included. She couldn't just eavesdrop.

"I'll appoint a new escort. We regret this misunderstanding, and I promise it will not happen again." Jason's glance swept the rest of his men, and each escort nodded his personal assurance. Talia stayed close to Rose the rest of the way.

Finally they reached the university and entered a dark, empty laboratory. Its glass walls were close to twenty feet high. Above, Rose could see adjustable awnings that would provide shade during the brightest periods of the day. Jason turned on the overhead lights. Stainless-steel counters gleamed in the reflected light. Large computer screens were strategically placed over each counter.

"We have left this table for your equipment." Jason pointed to a long, free-standing stainless-steel table near a glass wall that reflected the group like a mirror.

"These are impressive facilities." Rose offered the usual pleasantries, trying not to let her growing dismay at her missing colleagues cloud her judgment. Their little computer allies were not here. Maybe if she made it clear they were needed for the survey, Jason would produce them.

"We want to start our fieldwork early tomorrow morning. If you insist on accompanying us, please be ready by seven o'clock. Now we need to talk to our Quanta."

"We have arranged a tour of the city for tomorrow," Jason objected, sounding more like a director than a guide.

Rose fumed at his ready interference. Despite her fears for the Quanta, she needed to establish their authority over the survey protocols from the onset.

"I will join you. My area of study requires research at your libraries and science centers. Amy, Nicole, and Talia will start their field studies in the outlying forests. Sam and Quanta Evan will work here, studying your species for compatibility and disease susceptibilities. They'll require a medical coroner in the morning."

"We aren't prepared for you to do fieldwork yet," Jason said, making it clear that the Earth visitors weren't going to be allowed to schedule their own survey. "We have arranged informative lectures and experiments for you to observe."

Rose groaned in exasperation and ground her teeth. Did he really think they were fools without knowledge of basic data-collection techniques? If Jason thought she would accept this blatant disrespect, he was in for a surprise. When provoked, she had been a force that had succeeded when others had failed.

"How thoughtful of you," Rose said sweetly, forcing a stiff smile. "I'm sure our officials appreciate all your efforts. We just don't have time for choreographed events because they provide no original data. We control all variables of our testing to ensure their authenticity.

"I will research your planet's history and culture by studying original documents, so I can develop accurate conclusions. Amy's team and Sam will do scientific testing of biological and botanical samples. We also need to study climate variables and astronomical factors," Rose explained again. "If this is inconvenient, we are quite self-sufficient. Our Quanta can do much of our field testing on location, and our subsurvey hovercraft is handy for our frequent location changes."

Then Rose dropped the bomb she had been eager to discharge ever since the events on the ship. "Your men will likely get in our way. We need to focus our attention on the tasks at hand, not worry about guides who like to test our goodwill."

"What you think of our presence is irrelevant," Jason roared, his perfect calm finally ruffled. "You are visitors on this planet, and you will abide by our rules. Your *escorts*"—he spat the word—"or should I say *guards,* will accompany you on all your excursions whether you want them there or not. This point is nonnegotiable. Tomorrow, I'll retrieve you for a visit to our best library. I expect the rest of your team to wait until their guards arrive before heading for the local forests. Have I made myself clear?"

Rose nodded reluctantly. Even with guards, she would run this survey. In a way, she was relieved they didn't have to pretend that everyone was playing nice. The gloves had come off.

"If any of you choose to avoid your escort and leave on your own—" Jason paused, staring deliberately at the other surveyors, letting the silence drag on.

Amy and Nicole returned his stare head-on. The others shifted restlessly.

"You will be escorted back to your ship and confined. The *Aries* will be called to remove you from our planet. Is that understood?"

Jason waited until the BESS team had confirmed their compliance. Then he motioned for his men to escort the surveyors out of the lab.

"Wait!" Rose objected. "Where are they? We came for our Quanta, and they are nowhere to be seen."

"Get their Quanta here immediately." Jason gave the order to Jared, who was closest to the door.

"Of course, sir, right away." Jared hastily exited and reappeared after several minutes with the three Quanta in tow.

Rose wasn't fooled by Jason's show of cooperation. He had told her that the quantum computers were already here working. Where had they really been? Now their loyal friends floated toward them, wobbling almost imperceptibly. The trembling was so subtle that Rose wasn't sure, at first, if her concern had manufactured the movement. She rushed to Ari and touched his cylinder paneling protectively.

Ari's cylinder was fashioned from various alloys polished to a high sheen, which gave him an exotic appearance. He was her navigation partner, and through the years they had developed a close personal connection.

She patted him and whispered, "Are you all right? Where were you?"

Ari just moved away. This close, the wobbling was unmistakable.

"You requested a meeting, Captain." His tone was stiff and formal, alerting Rose that something had gone very wrong. Ari prided himself on natural human interaction. Now his speech was official, without inflection.

Normally, he would've asked how things were going, and he never used her title. He had a pet name for her that always embarrassed her. "Red" emphasized the one feature, along with her freckles, that had always drawn attention to a young, sensitive Rose. Ari insisted on using the nickname as a sign of their close bond. Now, to hide her confusion, she spoke formally as well.

"Yes, Quanta Ari, we start our survey tomorrow at seven. All three of you will accompany us back to our quarters—now." Rose would not allow any of the Quanta out of her sight again. Like her crew, all would protect all.

"Agreed, Captain."

Jason's guards followed the group out of the lab. Rose was impatient to discover what had happened to the Quanta, but the computers moved slowly.

The night sky caught her distracted attention as they walked across the manicured lawns. Bright bands of wavy light danced across the horizon, skipping between the belt of moons and the hidden sun. She could hear the crackle of solar energy bouncing against the protective atmosphere. All objects, including people, hidden by the nocturnal shadows, were now periodically spotlighted by flashes of colored light.

The display reminded Rose of the northern lights back home on Earth. The aurora borealis was quite magnificent, especially when the entire sky blazed with swirling, curling, refracted light. On Sentara, the lights were layers of rippling orange, red, and purple luminescence. Rose jumped when a deerlike animal, suddenly illuminated by bright pink light, dashed across the path in front of the group into the welcoming darkness of a nearby thicket. For a long moment, as she stared after the animal, she felt a strong desire to follow it.

When they reached their quarters, Rose allowed the Quanta to enter first, holding her team back at the door. The humans stood firm, blocking entry.

"We need some alone time, guys. You understand," Amy said, winking outrageously.

Happily, Jason and his men left without objection.

Walking into the living room, Rose breathed a sigh of relief. Her first act was to collect all the gold bracelets and stow them in her closet dresser. Then she asked Amy to check the room for listening devices. With Sam's help, Amy found four bugs. Rose smashed them gleefully. No one was going to eavesdrop.

When they had finished securing the room, Rose found the Quanta clustered together at the far side of the fish pool. During her long association with the Quanta race, Rose had come to appreciate their continual inquisitive chatter, quick movements, and flashing lights. They had a comment or an observation on just about everything. Now they were ominously quiet. They had settled on the floor and remained motionless, like ancient icebergs washed up on a desolate beach.

Anxiously, she approached Ari. "Ari, please report. Where have you been?" Even though Rose tried to sound calm, her voice shook. She had finally noticed that the usual connection between her and her navigator was gone. The only thing she sensed from him was an odd emptiness.

Ari rose at the sound of his name, and the lights in his eye globes grew brighter. "Of course," he answered flatly. "I-I…w-we landed at a-a-assigned coordinates…left s-s-ship…only darkness…" As Rose listened to him stutter and pause, she shivered with dread.

Their lifeline, these Quanta, had indeed been changed. There was no longer any doubt. As soon as Ari had started stuttering, the sounds of her crew's nervous chatter stopped. Amy, Nicole, Talia, and Sam closed in around Rose and the suffering Quanta. They all knew the importance of their computer partners. Without them, they wouldn't be here.

Ari stopped trying to speak. His illumination flickered and then dimmed in an alarming manner. For a horrible moment, Rose thought it would go out entirely, that her friend would be lost forever. The other two Quanta rose and flanked Ari protectively. Evan and Mirim began to hum; their usual illumination shifted to a vibrant blue. When all three Quanta touched, Ari began to glow a pale blue. Several minutes passed before Ari's brightness matched the other two.

"We have missing recordings of our hours on Sentara." The three spoke together. "We remember entering the planet's atmosphere. As we descended toward our landing coordinates, we analyzed the local atmosphere and measured population concentrations. Then we landed. At least we must have landed; our internal recordings turn to static moments before touching down. The next clear image is seeing you at the lab."

"What about record fragments?" Rose asked hopefully. Partial memories were better than none.

Mirim beeped in a series of soft descending tones, as if reading through an internal notepad. "I remember being at the lab where we met you. All three of us were there. I could hear voices, but they were indecipherable." She went silent, evidently out of data.

Evan just rotated back and forth with agitated movements, the Quanta equivalent of *no*.

Then, without warning, the three Quanta began spinning. Every panel blazed with blinding white light, forcing Rose to shield her eyes. When the dark spots clouding her vision cleared, all three injured computers were gone.

Rose spent the next thirty minutes in worried speculation, hectic pacing, and pointless questions. Then just as unexpectedly, the Quanta reappeared. Their behavior appeared to be normal. Ari took a position in front of the others.

"When we realized we had lost our connection to the nexus, our precious link to our kindred, we sent out an alarm. Only our twins had the necessary receptiveness to hear our cry for help. Then the strongest and most advanced of our race pulled us back for complete diagnostics. Our leaders discovered that the Sentarans had interrupted our systems. They found several recording devices concealed in our circuits. To prevent a repeat of this violation, we have been equipped with monitoring devices. We will be recalled immediately if there is any further tampering."

"Do you still want to stay?" Talia asked, turning to Rose as she twisted her fingers nervously.

"We have endured several violations," Rose stated flatly.

"If the Quantas' experience isn't proof that staying here is a bad idea, I don't know what is," grumbled Nicole.

"We knew this might be dangerous," Amy reminded everyone. "If we can discover their secret, then maybe we can clip their claws."

"We have learned from humans," ventured Ari, "that great risk might hide great reward. The Sentarans could be hiding some great knowledge. One reason they were able to detain us is that we were caught unprepared. Now our entire race is watching. They will keep us safe. We believe that staying is worth the risk."

Rose could sense everyone in the room except Talia relaxing. Despite continuing reservations, she considered staying. Their Quanta's vulnerability had exposed them all to danger at a time when each new unexplained event made their position more precarious. But she believed, with the Quanta, that their precautions would keep them safe. Now she would prepare everyone to get this survey done in record time.

"My best strategy, to ensure our safety, is to finish our survey quickly," said Rose. "I've informed our hosts that our teams will start data collection at seven o'clock tomorrow. I want to recommend the following crew assignments." Rose knew better than to command the Quanta. They were partners, not subordinates. "Ari, you might accompany Amy, Talia, and Nicole on their field trip into this island's central forest. They need to test Beth's theory that particulates are responsible for the Sentarans' declining population. I believe we'll be the most vulnerable in that isolated environment, so you, as our strongest Quanta, can effectively protect them. Evan, I hope you will help Sam research Sentaran biology. Mirim, I would like you to continue analyzing the data gained from orbital sweeps. We need to determine effects of the sun and moons on the Sentarans. Maybe we can find out why they need new people to help colonize their planet. I will be surveying in the city, trying to uncover whatever these people are trying so hard to hide. I'll report in with Ari every hour to ensure my safety. Is this plan acceptable?"

Rose never tried to control the Quanta. She had the deepest respect and gratitude for what they had achieved on Earth. Not only had they opened galactic travel to humans, they had given her people a now thriving planet. Quantum energy was clean, and the converters provided material goods without polluting the environment. Earth was returning to the garden planet it had once been.

"It would be our pleasure," Ari answered, his voice squeaking in what might be called sentiment.

"The actions of our guards and the interference with our Quanta require that we implement every safeguard we can call upon. The first is to keep everyone fully informed of all misadventures."

Rose knew her vagueness was increasing everyone's apprehension, but she found it difficult to say out loud what she had witnessed on the ship. She was embarrassed for her team. It had been easier with Amy, her closest friend. In the end, she spoke with a detachment devoid of emotion.

"The Sentarans have telepathic abilities that can be used to manipulate us. When they first boarded our ship, they generated an emotional field that left Amy, Nicole, and Talia strongly attracted to them, and you each acted in compromising ways. To what end, I don't know. When I was able to make the men stop, none of you gave any indication that you remembered what had occurred." Rose glanced around the group, looking for some reaction. They all just stared at her, stunned. "They planted suggestions in your minds, and you followed them innocently. I was able to protect myself because I had special training as a child. You all need to be hypervigilant. Don't do anything just because it seems natural and reasonable. Jason claims that everything that happened was just a terrible misunderstanding. He says they didn't know about our provincial ideas concerning relationships.

"I want to give all of you another chance to return to the *Aries* now that you know the full measure of what we are up against. I myself want to stay and discover the truth about these aliens."

Despite her speech, Amy, Talia, and Nicole shook their heads, refusing her offer.

"I would never leave you unprotected, Rose," Amy avowed.

"I have never given up before, and I won't quit now!" swore Nicole.

"It's just beginning to get interesting. I can't possibly leave before I know how things end," Sam sniffed, his eyes beginning to water. He couldn't suppress a loud sneeze. "Damn allergies. I had hoped I would be immune to alien pollen."

"I'll protect Talia if she wants to stay," Nicole offered. She squeezed Talia's arm.

"I couldn't ask for a better guard." Talia's sweet smile lightened the tense mood in the room.

"So, I take that to mean you are all in?" Rose asked.

Everyone nodded. Sam rubbed his hands together excitedly.

"Now we need to be proactive. Amy, maybe the guards will relax their defenses when you get them away from their superiors. They might talk with a little encouragement"—Rose winked at Amy, inviting her to use her well-known allure on the male gender—"and reveal useful information."

"I'll learn something," Amy promised.

"Sam, you're our greatest hope. The Sentarans' biology must reveal something about how they became so powerful."

"My thoughts precisely. And hopefully it will reveal why they need us here at all." Sam moved closer to Evan. "With this little guy's help, I'll do my research faster."

"We can stay in contact through our ear communicators on a revolving frequency," Amy advised.

Thankfully, all her surveyors had implanted communication chips controlled invisibly through tooth fillings. "Keep transmissions brief. We'll have no idea when or if we're being monitored," Rose added.

"Code words would allow us to speak covertly," Sam suggested. "For example, if I use *taxing* in a sentence, that would mean I'm in trouble; *intersections*, if we find something important; and *meals*, for when I need to regroup."

"Code words are a great idea," Amy agreed, smiling broadly. "Wireless communications can be faked. Let's use *test case* as our authenticity code to ensure you are one of us."

Everyone approved of this arrangement. Codes infused their work with a touch of play. Rose was enjoying the more relaxed atmosphere.

"I need to visit the BESS tonight," Nicole interjected. "Mitch gave me three of his mobile scanning probes. I can adapt them into covert listening devices for surveillance in the city."

"Absolutely," Rose agreed.

"I'll go with Nicole." Sam struggled clumsily to his feet. He would never be mistaken for a soldier. "I can use the trip to retrieve my medical equipment. I have a scanner that'll provide all the data I need. Who knows what the Sentarans have available."

Rose knew that Dr. Samuel Carlson, scientist extraordinaire, was something of a legend. He had revolutionized medicine on Earth. His deep-tissue probes had made several expensive surgical procedures obsolete. She felt especially lucky that he had chosen her mission, despite his reputation as a hypochondriac. His obvious physical limitations could be managed. She just wouldn't ask him to overpower any hostile aliens.

"Sounds good," said Rose. "Before we close, there are a few defensive techniques I'd like to teach everyone. They might strike some of you as silly, but here on Sentara, there can be no doubt about the reality of heightened sensory perception. Jason has confirmed that all our guards can speak telepathically."

Rose hesitated, giving herself time to gather her thoughts and marshal her arguments, already anticipating disbelief from her crew. However, when she cast a wary eye over the group, they returned her questioning glance with open curiosity.

"On Earth we've made ESP so fantastic that it's easy for a reasonable person to dismiss the idea. The simple truth is everyone has some measure of extra perception. When someone calls you shortly after you were just thinking about them, this is an example of extrasensory communication. Even when they're far apart, twins can sometimes sense discomfort in their siblings. Longtime friends and spouses have no trouble finishing each other's sentences.

"So, setting aside the debate, I want to teach you about mental shields and group bonding. The shields will spotlight any of the guards' telepathic intrusions. Group bonding can create enough connection to allow one of us to sense when another is in danger. Strong emotions create an energy vibration that can be sensed from a distance if one is receptive. I think this planet has catalytic energy, so our efforts might be enhanced. Are you game?"

Sam groaned with obvious reluctance, while the rest seemed receptive. After all, an open mind was a prerequisite to space travel.

"OK. Your own thoughts have a recognizable tone, flavor, or feeling that is different from outsiders'. Imagine surrounding yourself with protective shields that only you can penetrate. You'll be able to sense when a thought is fundamentally different from your own." Rose gave the team a few moments to absorb her instructions.

After an hour of practicing various shielding exercises, Rose began group-bonding exercises. "Look around the circle. These new friends will support you no matter what mistakes you make or weaknesses you have. They will be there when you falter. You can trust them. You feel a tangible connection to each person here stronger than ever before. Let this bond sink into your subconscious, ready to alert you to trouble."

Despite moments of embarrassed laughter and nervous fussing, Rose hoped that they had successfully created a new group connection. Their current situation of danger could only strengthen any group bond she had tried to create.

CHAPTER 7

ANDRE'S SCHEMES—CHRIS

Andre grudgingly took over the biology fieldwork he had assigned Chris, leaving Lena to collect the botany samples and summarize both their data into standardized reports. Ironically, it was Chris, not Andre, who provided oversight. This position offered her a unique view of her team. She found herself admiring Mitch's quirky recording vehicles, Lena's delicate flower drawings, and Mac's climate charts. She had no further dreams and was not up to forcing the memories.

Twilight team meetings began quite spontaneously. The Drummonds and Lena came to her at day's end to share their discoveries and to ask after her health. Lena brought several unusual rocks and plants for help in classifying. Mitch had built a new improved Rover prototype. Even the Quanta joined the informal gathering, sharing holographic maps of updated topographic and astronomic data.

After a few days free from Andre's undermining influence, Chris prepared a lavish dinner heaped with everyone's favorite foods. She was smiling with suppressed excitement when the dusty, grumbling team shuffled into the main cabin. The banquet of smells instantly caught their attention, and watering mouths and curious eyes replaced their tired, tense frowns. The twins cooed over the fried chicken, Lena stole a taste of the delicately spiced fried rice, and Andre smiled at the chocolate-covered ice-cream snowballs displayed in dry ice.

"Really, Chris, you shouldn't have," said Lena.

"I swear that chicken smells as good as home cooking. You couldn't have used the converters," accused Mac. He swiped a small drumstick.

"Well, I did ask Mitch for the recipe, and I did fabricate the ingredients. There isn't a chicken near enough to catch." Chris feigned confusion and worry. "Where do you think they went?"

"Really, Mac, we should wait until everyone is seated for dinner before eating," warned Andre.

"No, really, it's OK, Andre," Chris insisted. "I meant for this to be buffet-style. Everyone can eat at their leisure."

Andre shook his head, dismissing her idea. "Well, we should clean up at least."

Before Chris could object, Mac and Mitch grabbed Lena and pulled her toward their rooms. To Chris's dismay, Andre was the first to return. He rearranged the room into a formal dining configuration. Rather than leaving the food in the middle, where everyone could share, he moved the dishes to the sideboard and then set places at the table. When her friends returned clean and hungry, he took a position at the head of the table.

"We have decided on a proper dining arrangement. If you would take your usual seats, Chris and I will serve ourselves first." He indicated that the rest should fill their plates in order of seniority.

Chris ground her teeth and glared at Andre but decided to avoid a full-blown argument. Andre had done enough to spoil the evening. After a stiff, silent meal, which left everyone uncomfortable, including Andre, Lena and the twins escaped outside. As they set up their usual bonfire, Chris could hear them singing bits of chorus.

When Chris, drawn by the music, hobbled toward the door to join the group, Andre blocked her path.

"We have to talk sometime," he said resolutely. "Silence will gain us nothing."

"Not yet," Chris insisted. "Look, I don't expect you to ever admit to what happened. My answers will have to come from me. When that happens, we can talk—if there is anything left to say."

Chris hurried outside, escaping the forlorn cabin. She was delighted to find a comfortable campfire encircled by alien stones and carefully dug sand seats covered with thick towels. Instruments stood by three of the makeshift chairs.

A multitude of chemical salts in the sand clung to the firewood, creating a fire with flames of green (possibly from copper), blue (probably from calcium), red (perhaps from strontium), and purple (possibly from potassium chloride). The colored flames crackled cheerfully, spitting sparks into the dark sky, making the planet seem even more alien.

"Come on, little sister," Mitch urged Chris. "We've been impatient to hear your lilting soprano voice. Lena and my brother can only go so high."

"I have an amazing voice," Mac objected. "And Lena sings like a bird."

"Amazing: yes. Directly on key: not always," Mitch clarified kindly. He playfully shoved his brother. "Not that I want anyone else. Happily, we'll have a true chorus with Chris. I sing bass, you're a tenor, Lena is a dead-on alto, and Chris can deliver the soprano parts. The music will be memorable."

"Don't try any of your charms on me." Lena scowled. "I know when I've been insulted." Then she smiled, letting Mitch know she was just teasing him. "I've missed Chris too."

Lena set the keyboard on a perfectly shaped platform, and the twins picked up their guitar and bass. Mitch and Mac started playing a beautiful old Irish folk song that evoked images of mischievous leprechauns and emerald meadows. Lena joined in, weaving playful harmonies around the main melody. The song was familiar and created a mushrooming mood of joy; Chris lifted her voice to the lovely words.

> *So long ago, when I was innocent of life's schemes,*
> *I met my heart's desire, a boy to fulfill love's sweet dreams,*
> *He left to serve his country, to protect the greater good,*
> *So I chose to wait for him, for as long as I could,*
> *Now he has returned to find me:*
> > *Wandering grassy meadow domes,*
> > *Searching whispering ocean foam.*
> *Now he has returned to find me:*
> > *Questioning magical forest gnomes*
> > *For word that he has come home.*

They all joined in for the chorus:

> *Children dance and sing and laugh on rope swings, in our emerald hills*
> *Flowers bloom anew and dreams can come true, in our emerald hills.*

The ballad filled the quiet evening and floated across the now tranquil sea. Ella floated toward the group, her lights flashing to the rhythms of the music. Siri followed, playing a flute recording of the song. His eye globes bobbed up and down in time with Ella's lights.

A soft wind sprang up, blowing in from the sea. It steadily grew, until the surrounding branches shook. The quiet ocean, roused from glassy stillness, became dancing wavelets that transformed into crashing waves. A curious rustling in the nearby bushes caught Chris's attention. She stopped singing in order to better hear these new sounds, which seemed to be echoing their music. The rest of the group, seeing Chris's sudden quietness, also paused to listen. But the wind had faded away, and the evening was once again quiet, except for softly lapping waves rushing across the sand, submerging crystal pebbles.

Tentatively, Chris resumed singing softly, hoping to hear the other sounds again. The strange wind didn't return. Spooked, she began singing loudly, and Lena raised her alto voice to match the volume of Chris's soprano tones. Their voices created a third resonance more beautiful than before. The vibrations of the song continued to echo even after they stopped singing. But nothing mysterious happened again.

With the attention span of boxer puppies, the twins decided it was time to dance. They asked Siri to play something fast and then grabbed Lena and twirled her until she begged for a break. Gracefulness was not the twins' strong suit, and their movements were closer to calisthenics than dancing.

Lena wiggled out of their grasp, shaking her head. "Enough, I can't breathe. Why don't you let me give you at least one real lesson?" she pleaded.

Mac hung his head, lifting his big hands in surrender. "Really, Lena, you know we aren't coordinated." He shuffled his big feet to demonstrate his point.

"You never complained before," muttered Mitch. "We always have fun. Isn't that the idea?"

"Of course," Lena agreed sympathetically. "Won't you please just let me try to teach you some symmetry? Pretty please?"

Luckily for her, the men were too good-natured to refuse, even when she tied their thighs, waists, and hands together with cords so that when one moved forward, the other had to move back.

Chris was reminded of Lynn, her childhood best friend, who would dress her Golden Labrador in baby clothes and push him around in a stroller. She'd never understood why the big dog let the girl get away with it when he could have easily run away. Just like Mitch and Mac.

Unfortunately, Lena hadn't anticipated that both twins would insist on leading. They soon toppled, pushing and pulling until the cords wound around them so tightly they couldn't move. Caught by the absurdity of their situation, they began roaring with laughter, even though they were helpless. Chris giggled so hard, she fell out of her seat barely conscious of the soft, chuckling rustle that whistled through the trees. Finally Lena cut them out of the bindings, barely managing to avoid cutting the squirming twins too.

The boys ended the evening with the sinful pleasure of roasting marshmallows. How they had programmed the food converters to produce realistic marshmallows remained a mystery. The converters had safeguards to prevent the production of unhealthy foodstuffs, and a marshmallow was the epitome of unhealthy. The snowballs and chocolate-covered ice cream had been smuggled aboard the *Aries* before leaving Earth.

"Really, Mac, confess your secret," pleaded Chris. She had such an awful sweet tooth, and she had tried many times, unsuccessfully, to program her favorite sugar treats. "How do you get those fool things to make this"—she held up a perfect, snowy white marshmallow—"and these?" She extended a hand full of milk-chocolate squares.

"If I tell you, then your navigator buddy"—Mac jabbed a finger at Siri, who was floating innocently a few feet away—"will remove my way in."

"No, he won't. You won't, right?" Chris stared at Siri hopefully. The little android remained stubbornly quiet. Chris knew that for tonight, at least, Mac had won the argument.

These campfires became the highlight of Chris's day, and she was tempted to abandon her plans for a second base. Her resolve to find out what had caused her injuries weakened day by day. What did it matter anyway? Couldn't she just be happy for once? Much to her chagrin, the implications of the injuries continued to haunt her. If Andre had been violent toward her, she knew he was a threat to them all. Chris believed that if she could get away, she might feel safe enough to remember what had happened. Before leaving, she decided to do some investigating.

Providentially, Andre had scheduled an extended field trip, which would be the perfect time to carry out her plan. The group planned to travel all day in the hope of increasing their catalog of new species, and they wouldn't return until early evening. When the day of the trip arrived, Chris hid her impatience by keeping herself busy labeling specimens and cleaning out the main cabin. Debris left from analyzing samples and compiling reports lay everywhere. Her team worked hard and long, and she was the obvious choice for housekeeping.

Chris was edgy all through breakfast. She was lousy at hiding her true feelings, and Andre was good at sensing them. He joined her as the rest of the group prepared to leave.

"Are you sure you won't come? Your ankle seems perfectly healed," Andre pressed.

"Yes, it *is* much better," Chris agreed. It was foolish to deny the obvious. "I was hoping to catalog and summarize the last of Lena's fieldwork. She really isn't a botanist. I expect this will be my last day of recuperation." Chris knew that Andre was anxious to assume an oversight position. If she threw him this bone, maybe he wouldn't push her to come.

His eyes gleamed approvingly. "That is splendid news. We will all regroup tonight to rework our fieldwork schedule."

"Tonight is too soon. Your team will be tired and hungry. They'll have earned a break," Chris maintained. *From your constant need to exercise unrelenting control*, she finished silently.

Unexpectedly, he hugged her awkwardly. Chris realized the whole affair of her injuries had permanently isolated him in his fancy cabin. He kissed her tenderly on her temple, and, reluctantly, Chris allowed this small gesture. She knew that Andre's biggest problem was Andre.

At last everyone started off, and she was able to put her plan into motion.

Chris forced herself to wait another full hour to ensure that no one would come back for some forgotten item. To fill the time, she paced her quarters, then the main cabin, and finally the beach in front of the camp. It was a good thing her ankle had only been sprained. Chris would never have stayed still long enough to heal an actual break. As soon as her watch showed the allotted time, she raced over to Andre's cabin.

The first step in explaining her injuries was to investigate the scene of the crime. It was that intention that had her facing Andre's front door. Chris was not surprised to find his residence locked, so she had brought a set of versatile computer tools just in case. She inserted a miniature screwdriver into the keyhole to lift one tumbler and used another tool to wiggle the locking lever free. After several tense seconds, the lock finally clicked open. She let out a satisfied exhalation.

The apartment was as luxurious as she remembered. The rooms seemed frozen in time; nothing had been added since her first visit. A musty odor hung in air, as if the windows were never opened and the rooms never cleaned. There were no pictures, books, or stray art pieces. Every surface was clean and sterile. Sadly, Chris realized that what the house lacked was personality. It was an empty shell, hardly a place to call home.

Quickly she searched the kitchen, living area, dining room, and main bathroom. They held a few pieces of furniture and the most basic supplies. Chris saved the most promising rooms for last. Soon she was standing in front of the bedroom door, gathering her courage.

Suddenly, the dining room creaked loudly, and the jostled chandelier crystals clinked. Chris drew in a sharp breath, surprised at the sudden noise in the bleak quiet. Out of the corner of her eye, she saw the long white curtains fluttering against the French doors leading to the beach. She thought the cabin had been locked tight. Why had Andre left these doors slightly ajar when he had locked the front door?

Another breeze raised goose bumps on her exposed arms. The creaking sounds repeated along the floor as the structure shifted in the sand. Chris assumed that the cabin must have been disturbed by the sudden breeze. She opened the French doors farther, hoping to dispel the eerie atmosphere of the house. The familiar sounds of waves breaking along the beach relaxed her jitteriness, and she resumed her search.

The bedroom was unchanged. The door to the closet was standing open. Usually, Andre was careful about how he dressed and how he lived. Today, the closet looked like he had thrown on whatever was handy. It was an obvious sign of his distress.

Standing next to the bed, Chris tried to recall images from that fateful night. She slid her fingertips along the blanket and plumped a pillow. A series of rigorous waves crashed outside, disturbing her concentration. She glanced up from the bed and noticed a new ornate table on Andre's side of the large bed.

In the top drawer was a flat black box. Intrigued, she opened it and found a beautiful sapphire necklace. Each sapphire was surrounded by diamonds that formed brilliant little daisies. This piece of jewelry was too unique to have been fabricated and too big to ever be worn here. Andre had obviously expected that this mission would require an extraordinary present. Chris fingered the small diamond rose that she wore around her throat. It was an extravagance she allowed herself even in the wilds of Citron. Unsettled, she returned the box to the drawer.

Chris believed that if there was anything to find, it would be here or in his study. She continued to search the bedroom and the bathroom, looking first in the obvious places, like drawers and cupboards, scrutinizing their contents, and then for any concealed cubbies. Carefully she examined the various light fixtures and checked the walls for hidden spaces. She even got down on all fours to inspect the floors for holes or hinges.

She was moving her fingers painstakingly along the square tiles behind the toilet when her search finally produced results. She felt a long deep slit. Carefully, using the tip of her fingernail, she pried the tile out to expose a recessed compartment. Inside was a leather box that fit the hole perfectly. Andre had been very busy the day they had landed.

Chris pulled out the box and laid it on the sink. Tentatively she raised the lid, momentarily unaware that she was holding her breath. Lying exposed were two bottles and a syringe half full of amber fluid. One of the bottles held the same amber fluid; the other contained a dark red concoction.

Under the cushioned top layer was a heavily taped, waterproof plastic envelope. Chris carried the package and the box out of the bathroom into the bedroom and laid them on the bed. Then she retrieved a small penknife from Andre's dresser and carefully cut the envelope open. Even now, she took pains to keep her search secret.

Chris pulled out several long legal papers from the envelope and laid them out on the white coverlet. One was a marriage certificate between Samuel Garza and Lisa Carnac. The next two pages were copies of signed contracts. She recognized these contracts as the ones the Quanta required to get the injections necessary to have a child. The last page was an affidavit asking for the privilege of self-injection. Evidently Lisa Carnac was going to be off world for several years, and the couple wanted the child before she was scheduled to return. It was cosigned by an official with a Russian name.

At first, Chris's mind refused to accept the obvious implications suggested by these documents. She racked her brain trying to remember if the names were familiar, desperate to find a logical explanation for the papers. Next she picked up the bottle of red liquid and held it up to the light, trying to fathom its purpose. She could see her hands trembling. The liquid deflected the light, hiding its ominous purpose in its murky depths.

Chris was done guessing. She ran back to the main cabin, carrying the box full of damning evidence. She was so intent on finally getting answers she forgot about the step leading to the front door. She tripped and fell hard, unable to stop her forward momentum. The box dropped from her grasp and slid through the open door across the floor. She cringed when she heard the unmistakable tinkle of broken glass. She retrieved the box, set it securely on the wood table, and tremulously raised the lid. The syringe had shattered, its contents soaking the cushioned layer.

Chris sat down heavily in a nearby chair, taking deep breaths, trying to subdue her shaking hands. Forcing an iron calm, she thrust her fears into a dark recess of her mind and went into the lab with the box. She carefully extracted samples from the intact vials. She prepared two solutions to run through their elemental chemical spectrometer.

Next she went to the converter and produced an exact duplicate of the broken syringe. She filled it with some of the remaining amber fluid. By fabricating a liquid close in consistency to the original amber drug, she refilled the vial to replace the fluid she had used. Finally, she sponged off all evidence of the spilled liquid on the cushioned layer.

Chris knew it would take time before the analysis was complete, so she returned the leather box to Andre's bathroom. It was evidence of her snooping, and she wanted to reveal her discoveries in her own time. She really hadn't expected to find such terrible proof. She hadn't even searched the most promising place, his private sanctum, the study.

Now she would remedy her omission. She didn't waste time looking through his desk or cabinet. Rather, she started knocking on the walls and searching the floor for hidden pockets. She groaned when she came up empty. Frustrated, she walked back to the doorway and carefully surveyed the room. What had she missed? Computer technology allowed information to be stored in small devices, so she considered the tiniest spaces. Another strong gust of wind blew through the house, causing all the fancy chandeliers to chime as crystal brushed crystal.

Looking up at the ceiling, Chris noticed that this light fixture was heavily frosted plastic. It gave off little light, making her wonder why Andre had it here in his office where light was at a premium. She climbed onto his desk chair and studied the fixture more closely. Its cover was held in place by two screws. Holding the light securely, she unscrewed the screws, lowered the cover, and looked inside. A computer flash drive was taped inside. It was completely hidden when the light cover was properly attached to the fixture, not even casting a shadow. Gratified, she removed her new treasure.

Slowly, Chris walked back to the main cabin, tapping the drive on her palm. She decided to use the main cabin to access its information rather than Andre's study computer. The more central view would allow her to monitor all trails back to the base. Apprehensive, she looked at her watch. Time was running out. The sun was beginning to fall into afternoon. She cursed the shorter days. Quickly retrieving her computer from the coffee table, she plugged in the drive and waited for the files to become available.

Coldness settled into her bones, sending shivers of premonition running up her arms and down her back. A horrifying possibility coalesced in her mind. The memory of her first night here and the secrets she had uncovered in Andre's quarters collided in her mind. The logic of this possibility was so simple, so perfect, that she cursed her own shortsightedness.

Unnerved, she flew to Mitch's workshop, located a magnifying glass, and headed for the main bathroom. She threw off all her clothes and began slowly studying every inch of her skin with the magnifying glass, looking for the dreaded pink puncture wound. She used a hand mirror to examine her backside. Her skin looked intact. Of course, it had already been several days.

Chris lowered herself onto the toilet, weighing the possibility that on that first fateful night, Andre had injected her with the fertilizing drug in hopes of making her pregnant. There could be no other explanation for his possession of the drug. He must intend to use it on her. Her consent had never been necessary. Even if he hadn't used it yet, or so she hoped, he would use it in the future.

As she slowly pulled on her clothes, tears filled her eyes. Something tender and precious had been shattered. How could she face him? Would he use his charm to explain this away? Could she believe him? Could she dare not to? Chris feared that Andre would never let her go. She was too central to his objectives. He needed a navigator who could get him promoted. But what did a child have to do with his plans?

Back in the main cabin, Chris found her computer screen showing four new folders. She opened the one labeled *Lisa Carnac*. It contained electronic copies of the papers she had found in the bathroom. There was also a picture of a tall, slender woman with long black hair and honey-toned skin standing beside Andre. She had an exotic foreign attractiveness. Her almond eyes stared back at Chris with an innocent trust that touched the young navigator, despite the circumstances.

Chris quickly closed the file and turned to the next folder, labeled *Citron*. In it were all the remaining answers to her questions. Andre had prepared the applications required to lead the colonists on Citron, contingent, of course, on their successful survey. The final nail in her coffin was a letter addressed to Central Alliance signed by her. It was an amazing forgery. She had applied for a planet-side posting, so she could support her husband in governing the colonists on Citron. She further requested they use her recommendation as navigator captain to promote her husband to the rank of lieutenant governor, responsible for this area of space. In the last paragraph of the forgery, she asked for an extended leave from service, so she could devote her time and talents to raising their children.

Chris leaped to her feet, toppling her chair backward, as rage consumed all reason. Whirling around, she kicked the chair across the room. In the abrupt silence, broken by her strangled gasps, the sound of the beeper indicating that the spectrometer had finished its chemical analysis shocked her into action. She glanced up at the clock. It was two thirty and darkness fell at four. She had run out of time.

Chris copied all of the files from Andre's flash drive into a password-protected folder. Next she went to the spectrometer, pulled the results out of the print tray, and stuffed them into her pants pocket. Rapidly, she cleaned the slides and stored them in their usual drawer. By erasing the spectrometer's internal use-monitoring logs, she removed all evidence of her tests. These new tasks offered her relief from a growing depression. Finally she ran back to Andre's quarters to return the flash drive. Secrecy was the key if she was going to effectively stop Andre.

Chris went first to the bathroom. She carefully studied the room to make sure there was no sign of her activities. Then she went to the study and climbed onto the chair she had left under the light. She took a small piece of tape, identical to the original, and affixed the data storage device exactly. The dust on the inside of the cover outlined its original position. She screwed the frosted cover back onto the fixture and returned the chair to the desk.

As she adjusted the chair back to its original position, she accidently bumped the inside of the desk. She heard a strange click and then a soft pop. She knelt down to investigate—a secret, spring-loaded drawer partly open.

"What are you doing?" Andre barked from the doorway.

CHAPTER 8
SENTARAN FORESTS—AMY

Three days had passed since they'd departed the city. Luckily, once Amy left civilization, she also left behind much of the politics and intrigue. Justin had replaced Jonathan. He was younger, a quiet intellectual, like Talia herself. Despite the fact that their guards now carried guns, they had been quite manageable.

Amy enjoyed being on her own. She had been raised in a military family that demanded constant discipline and obedience. Once she left home to go to school, she was like a Tasmanian devil freed from captivity. She stayed out to all hours and tormented rigid teachers who had the misfortune of finding the small woman in their class. Fortunately, Amy had a quick intelligence. Her grades and award-winning school projects had saved her from immediate expulsion. Rose had befriended Amy in their first year at the Technion and had used her influence to keep the little spitfire in school long enough for her to graduate as a navigator.

After Amy, Talia, and Nicole had set up their forest camp, Amy had started a routine of twilight jogs. Tonight, the day's tensions evaporated as she settled into the run's rhythms. Sensing a disturbance, she glanced back to find Jared following her. Annoyed, she speeded up.

Amy sprinted across a fallen-log bridge and turned left toward the lake behind a row of trees. She had selected a site for their base that was between this lake and a rushing river. To her delight, the river had provided an abundance of alien life. During the second day, Amy and Talia had begun cataloging biological and botanical samples from the river. Nicole had found several small caves and was focused on collecting mineral samples for chemical analysis. Ari was busy collecting astronomical data. On the third day, Amy had discovered that the animal life on Sentara was unusually friendly. With little prompting, the creatures had allowed themselves to be identified, measured, and cataloged.

Upon reaching the shore, Amy turned to glare at Jared. He had easily kept pace with her, despite her attempts to leave him behind. On the first day in camp, he had discarded his city clothes for sturdy boots, forest-green leggings, and a soft, brown shirt and jacket. A weapon that looked similar to an Earth gun was peeking out from under his jacket. He blended into the surrounding landscape like a chameleon. In some indefinable way, he belonged here.

"Why are you following me?" she demanded impatiently. "I don't think it's asking too much to give me a bit of privacy."

"I'm doing my job, of course," he answered patiently. "Why don't you just loosen up and enjoy yourself." She didn't miss the appraising glance he gave her figure.

"You do that one more time, and I'll make sure your position needs filling," she warned.

"What are you talking about?" he inquired innocently. "I haven't done anything you could report to my superiors. In fact, they've advised me that your team had better produce results soon. So it's you who should be watching your back."

"When on earth could you have contacted your superiors? We haven't left this camp in three days," Amy blurted, surprised.

"We have our ways," he teased, winking. Despite her obvious hostility, he always acted like they were old friends.

"It's alliance superiors I report to, not Sentarans. Why can't you find something else to do? Following me during my off time isn't going to gain you anything."

Jared shrugged vaguely and ignored her complaints.

"Do you hear that?" he asked suddenly, looking around.

"Hear what?" Amy asked suspiciously. She echoed his searching gaze.

"Shhh. Listen," he whispered.

A light wind stirred the surface of the lake, producing ripples that sloshed gently onto shore. Polished rocks lay everywhere. Leaves rustled and the higher branches creaked in the stronger gusts of wind.

The activity of life, its energy, its movements, and its sounds, unfolded in the quiet. She heard the chirping and fluttering of a flock of birds nesting in the trees. At least she called them *birds*. They were, indeed, creatures that flew. Buzzing insects stirred the surface of the lake. Small burrowing animals pushed crackling leaves out of their dens at the base of a stand of tall trees. Amy sensed a section empty of activity and slowly swung her eyes to the left.

"What's over there?" she asked nervously.

"Quiet. If we don't move or make any sounds, she might come out."

Amy held her breath. The foliage at the end of the clearing rustled, and a lovely gold feline, similar to a mountain lion, glided stealthily out of the bush. It was definitely a predator. The emptiness spread around the lake. Every other nearby animal knew of the feline's intrusion and had vanished. The cat padded down to the water and sniffed the air. She extended her neck until she could lap a long drink from the lake's clear water while keeping a wary eye on the surrounding forest.

"How beautiful," Amy whispered, in spite of herself. The cat lifted its head and tensed its muscles, pressing its paws deep into the dirt.

Jared moved forward, making a purring sound as he stared directly into the cat's eyes. The feline pawed the air in mute rebellion before settling on a patch of grass, seeming to wait for Jared. He pulled a small piece of meat from his backpack and threw it toward the cat. She caught it in midair and then bounded away. When the other animals resumed their foraging, Amy knew the feline was gone.

"What the…?" Amy asked in amazement.

"We have a unique relationship with animals on our planet," Jared explained. "We farm our meat, so we don't hunt. We even go so far as to supplement the animals' food sources. In the past, we watched their behaviors: their movements, their relationships, their survival patterns, how they searched for food, how they chose a mate. And then, quite unexpectedly, we found we could communicate with them."

"You can talk to your animals?" Amy was captivated by such a possibility. If they could talk to animals, then why couldn't humans?

"Oh, you humans." Jared couldn't hide his contempt. "Your species obviously views verbal speech as the only advanced form of communication. If you want to converse with animals, you have to pay closer attention to them. They don't communicate using sounds like we do, and they don't think like we do."

"I pay attention to animals," she said skeptically. It was hard to trust one of their guards.

"Your attention is tainted by your beliefs and expectations. If you think animals are dumb creatures, then you'll dismiss any evidence to the contrary." Leaning in closer, Jared dropped his voice to a conspiratorial whisper. "You know, you should hear them. You register the highest psi energy of your entire group. You just don't use it."

Amy had anticipated that, sooner or later, there would be questions about her supposed talent. She thought that Jason, as leader, would probably confront her when she returned to the city. She had hoped that her wilderness survey would be free time to study this planet without all the intrigue. Jared was obviously trying to gain some advantage. She decided to play dumb and see what she could learn.

She widened her eyes, moistened her lips, and arranged her features into a confused expression. "Rose has told me about this whole sixth-sense thing," she admitted. "I really don't have any special senses. Rose might though. Look how she controls Jason."

"If she thinks she's in control, she's sadly mistaken. She has no idea what's really at stake," Jared rumbled darkly.

The twilight created a cloak of confidentiality, ideal for secrets. Amy remained quiet, hoping Jared's code of silence might slip.

"It's when she thinks she has the upper hand that she becomes vulnerable. She has only to let her guard down for Jason to seal the deal." Jared moved closer to Amy, changing his role from confidant to something much more personal.

"If you really want to hear the animals, you need to position yourself at the center of living energy." Jared took Amy's hand. His eyes were bright and expectant. He led her toward an elevated grassy ledge reaching out over the lake. "Come over here and sit by the water. Relax, so nothing will distract you."

After Amy had made herself somewhat comfortable, he continued speaking in a slow, hypnotic voice.

"Now slow your breathing. Close your eyes. At first you'll hear the activity of the water: the swish and lap of waves. Set aside the water for now, and isolate the sounds and smells of local wildlife. What's their character? Is the movement urgent and organized, or random and quiet? Can you sense the quick animation of small animals, or do you feel the slower vibrations of larger ones? How dense is the disturbance? Does it feel like one animal or many? Can you separate parents from children?"

At first Amy felt nothing. The shadows pressed down on her, and her apprehension grew at being alone with Jared. She wiggled nervously, trying to convince herself that this new anxiety was unmerited. Amy had to take the chance that tonight Jared would teach her how to use the Sentarans' strange powers.

Then her concentration converged with her perception. He was right about the water distracting her, but there was something cleansing and energizing about the swirling liquid; it helped her focus. She felt a calming that slowly transformed into a meditative state. It was from this point of profound quiet that Amy finally sent her awareness out farther and farther into the surrounding foliage.

Jared began to whisper in her ear. "Imagine a deep pool. The water is perfectly still and so clear you can see to the bottom. On the bottom are large, round stones, polished and shiny."

Amy followed his instructions automatically. She was eager to learn how she might use this "living energy," although she couldn't see how a deep pool might be involved.

"There is something else in the pool that you glimpse out of the corner of your eye. The water is distorting the image. You must get closer. Imagine yourself diving into the pool and following the light."

Jared's hypnotic voice pulled Amy along. She caught a flash of something unidentifiable. She envisioned entering the water and sinking toward the glimmering stones. She searched the depths of the pool and finally spotted a perfect circle of inviting light. She swam closer and tentatively touched the light. It was warm, and her skin tingled. Jared's voice became softer, until all she heard was a low hum. Her perception shrank until it included only her beating heart and the warm light.

Amy set her hand against the mirrored surface of the warm light and was shocked when she felt herself yanked into its depths. Struggling for breath, she raced upward. When she broke the surface of the pond, she found herself trapped, as a disembodied spirit without form or power. No matter how hard she tried, she couldn't seem to move her physical body.

Amy felt Jared's fingers brush her cheek tenderly. Straining, she tried to push his hands away without success. When he unbuttoned the top button of her shirt, she screamed silently, in helpless fury. She felt him remove her shirt and pull off her shoes. Now in thin underwear, she shivered from the evening chill.

Amy impulsively reached out with her mind toward the one person who had repeatedly helped her—Rose. Face-to-face, she could battle any enemy, but this game of psychic domination was beyond her experience to even understand. Calling over and over, she pleaded for Rose to respond. She imagined the room where they'd had their last meeting, where everyone promised to be sensitive to a team member in trouble. No one answered.

Amy felt Jared brush her hair back out of the way and kiss her neck. He seemed unconcerned by her lack of response. She choked with disgust. If she ever got free, her revenge would be brutal.

Frantic and desperate, she finally caught the slightest whiff of lavender. It was as much a part of Rose as her curly red hair. Rose's concerned face filled her mind, and her lips moved silently.

In that moment, Amy realized she had only to burst through the mirror to find her way out of the psychic trap. Of course! Why hadn't she tried that? Maybe Jared's silent muttering had bewitched her, preventing her from finding this answer. She let her spirit sink back underwater and struggled back toward the circle of light against a powerful stream of water. Desperation gave her the strength to force her way back through the circle, and then she swam vigorously upward. In the same exact moment, she hit the surface and felt the sensations of her body.

Amy exploded at Jared like a pit of striking vipers. In the millisecond before she took action, she forced herself to remember the Quantas' golden rule. There could be no killing. She struck at the source of her troubles and kicked him violently in the groin. She hoped she had rendered him unable to violate another woman. As he lay moaning, doubled up, she kicked him under the chin. His head snapped back, and he collapsed, limp and unmoving. The violence of her attack had thrown him into the shallow lake.

"Now imagine a deep pool and follow the light," she said mockingly, as he sank into the water. Blood clouded the surface.

Amy dressed swiftly. She realized that if she fell into this planet's legal system, she would be lost here forever. Yet, despite the possible consequences, she made no effort to check on Jared's well-being and hoped he might drown. Sadly, she doubted she would get rid of him so easily. In the end, she ran back to their camp without looking back.

She pounded on the first door she came to. She wasn't going to stay here with these treacherous guards for one second longer. This time, the run did nothing to sooth her temper. She was fuming with rage and apprehension. Phrases kept running through her mind like mice running on a wheel: "The Sentarans will never believe me. I am a guest on this planet. Jared is the police. But, I have to get away before he follows me."

Amy pounded a second time, and the entire door vibrated. "Let me in, or—I swear—I'll break down the door!" she screamed.

Talia called from inside, obviously annoyed, "Gimme a sec! Jeez."

After several endless moments, Talia opened the door a crack, blocking Amy's view of the room within.

Amy was not going to be delayed. She immediately shoved against the door, catching Talia off guard. Talia fell back, and the door slammed open, cracking its frame. It was just what Amy needed, a chance to do some real damage. A noise from the bedroom warned her that they were not alone. Turning, she saw Justin standing in the bedroom doorway, smiling. Amy was getting real tired of seeing that particular smile.

"What the hell are you doing? Did you pay any attention to Rose's warning?" Amy growled at Talia, panic blinding her discretion. "You have single-handedly managed to compromise our entire mission."

The emotional shock of her own violation faded as she contemplated the magnitude of the disgrace that Talia had brought on the team. She grabbed Talia by the shoulders and gave her a hard shake. Now that she was closer, Amy could see Talia's empty, glassy expression. Those conniving men had done it again. Despite all their preparations, little Talia had been gobbled up by this wolf.

Horribly, Talia tried to defend Justin, the rapacious maggot. Her voice slurred as she spoke. "C'mon, Amy. We're s'pose be frien-ly. Justy and Jeffy want fun toooo." Talia seemed stuck on the last word.

Amy glowered at Justin, her eyes letting him know that she was onto his little game.

"Ammm sure J'red help you re'ax." Talia blinked one eye awkwardly, oblivious to the building tension.

Amy realized that Talia had referred to both Justin and Jeffrey. "Where are Ari and Nicole?" she barked. She needed to locate the other members of her team, pronto.

Befuddled, Talia shook her head, trying to recall. She reached for a sip of wine from one of the glasses on a nearby coffee table. Impatiently, Amy snatched the two glasses and dumped them out. Wine was the last thing anyone needed.

"Hey," Talia protested, tottering unsteadily. She tripped on a fold of carpet and fell back on the couch before struggling to stand once more. She tried to focus her bloodshot eyes on Amy. "You jog, J'red f'low." Her tone changed to accusation. "Yeh, you an' J'red 'ave fun." She nodded smugly and smacked her lips. "We fun. Log'cal. Call—ring! Nico' say 'kay. Ari 'pop' out. Wish I 'pop out,' 'pop out,' 'pop out,' 'pop out.'" Talia started giggling uncontrollably.

"What about Nicole?" Amy asked, shaking Talia to get her attention.

"With Jeffy. Social-izing." Talia yanked away from Amy and, putting a hand on her hip, looked both offended and foolish at the same time.

"Sounds like a good idea," Jared interrupted. He was standing in the doorway. He gave Amy the look a wolf might give a rabbit just before tearing its throat out. He was soaking wet, and bruises darkened his face.

CHAPTER 9
THE TREASURY—BETH

Beth struggled back into consciousness. She was lying in front of two cathedral doors. Rising painfully onto her elbows, she saw Thomas, Sarah, Connor, and Axel lying nearby. To her relief, they were stirring. Grimacing, Connor and Thomas struggled to stand. Sarah took several deep breaths before forcing herself up. Sputtering with annoyance, Axel rose out of the alien river. He had missed a stone.

Beth began to smolder, anger replacing her discomfort. This aggression was intolerable. They had been stripped of all possessions except their clothes. Deliberately she gazed toward the tall doors, waiting. Someone had better take responsibility.

The building in front of them was made from the same strange, pale yellow stone as the obelisks, except that opaque green windows covered the front wall. The newly ignited sun set the stone glowing and the glass sparkling. Mosaic stone tiles fronted the building and formed geometric patterns that led visitors up to the towering doors.

Beth steeled herself against the pain and stood up. She gestured for the others to fan out in a military formation behind her before she approached the doors. Tom and Sarah took the flank positions, and Connor turned to cover their backs. Beth tentatively pushed on one of the doors and found that it opened easily. They entered the building separately, pausing between each person. They were in an atrium.

When seen from the outside, the windows were impenetrable. Once inside, Beth saw they were transparent. The glass was so perfectly polished that it captured light, creating a soft luminescence that highlighted the outside landscape. A long, white marble counter faced the entrance. Hung behind it, a huge screen showed a view of the obelisk entrance with its dense river and floating balls of clear fluid. A line of text ran along the bottom in an unknown language.

"Can you translate?" she asked Axel. Everyone moved closer for a better look.

Axel turned his body back and forth, using the Quanta gesture for no. "It is alien, like the writings on the obelisks."

"There must be some way into the central complex. An entrance might open when someone approaches," Beth suggested. She could always hope.

"Well, if there's a spring-loaded door, it ain't over here," said Connor. He had jumped behind the counter and was checking the walls beneath the screen.

"Or here," said Sarah, tapping along the one wall.

"That won't be necessary," a deep, resonant voice said from behind them.

Beth felt the voice brush along her skin like a purring cat. She jerked around, startled.

By a side door, invisible until now, a man had appeared. He was tall, with strong features, and stood with a confidence that suggested a full life, rich with experience. Silvery white highlighted his dark hair, and gold flecks swirled in his brown eyes. His eyes promised much but gave away nothing. He wore lightweight clothing, similar to what one might expect on a man of action, except for his gold robe. The cloak was made from a material that moved with a life of its own. It was fastened with a round, carved ornament that looked more like a badge than an adornment.

"Welcome to the Treasury," he announced, with a cautious smile. He spoke in English and extended his hand in the familiar gesture of trust, a handshake. Beth returned the gesture automatically. His skin warmed her chilled fingers, and his firm grip conveyed strength without harm. She pulled her hand back and rubbed her palm unconsciously.

This man, whom she had just met, on a planet that must have traveled through space, seemed oddly familiar to her. His expressions, gestures, and appearance were comforting, like those of an old family friend who is instantly recognized and trusted.

"Do I know you?" she asked unexpectedly. That was not what she had intended to say. She had wanted to confront him and demand an explanation for their aggressive reception. She had endless questions about this place, this planet, his origin. Instead she asked him again, "Do I know you?"

"Perhaps," he said enigmatically. His look was warm, suggesting some shared secret.

Connor cleared his throat, interrupting their odd conversation.

"Why have you assaulted us," Connor asked bluntly, "and why do you have copies of our cultural treasures—the Egyptian pyramids and the Sphinx—outside?" He obviously found nothing recognizable in this forbidding alien.

"Of course, I will explain everything. Please seat yourselves."

The strange man indicated upholstered chairs that had mysteriously appeared behind them, forming a semicircle. He stood in front of them and assumed the posture of a professor about to give a lecture. He swept his arms to encompass the entire complex. "This is the Treasury, and I am its historian. I protect this repository and rigorously screen all who come to visit. Few are fortunate enough to find our traveling planet, let alone be given an opportunity to see our treasures. Usually this process is painless. We were quite alarmed when it became obvious that you were suffering. I apologize for any discomfort." He stumbled on the word *apologize* as if he wasn't sure it was the correct term.

"I think discomfort is a huge understatement," growled Connor. "You led us here, and then your probe incapacitated us."

"Yes, we were hurt," Sarah whispered.

"Again, I am sorry. We have not had visitors for a long time, and never anyone of your race. The pyramid display that drew you here is part of an elaborate exhibit of Earth's treasures. We had no idea any of your species would ever see it. We only discovered your presence on our world when it was too late to stop the regeneration. All we could do then was try to shield you from the worst of its effects. But now that we understand your biology better, we have created these restoratives." He gestured toward the counter, smiling contritely.

"I am sure you meant no harm," Beth said foolishly, studying the alien. Her usual restraint was gone.

A panel opened, and a silver tray holding crystal flutes slid out. The glasses were coated with a thin layer of ice and filled with a pale pink fluid. The historian balanced the tray in one hand and offered a glass to each of the landing party in turn. Beth took her glass automatically and drank the cool citrus solution in a single swallow without thinking. The rest of the team hesitantly followed her example. Instantly, all of Beth's aches and pains vanished, and even her memories of them dimmed. She felt ready for anything, and she was eager to learn everything about this Treasury.

She watched the others straighten their clothes and rub sore muscles. Tom brushed back Sarah's hair, murmuring concern. Connor remained openly hostile. Beth wondered at Connor's callousness. He could be squashed like a bug. This alien commanded tremendous power. They could never hope to survive if it came to a battle.

"Probing you is only one of the ways we protect our priceless exhibits," the man explained. "The Treasury's secrets would be quite deadly in the wrong hands. If any of you had failed, you would have found yourselves at your next destination with no memory of this place."

"Why us?" Beth asked. "We're nothing special, no more than anyone else."

"Not of your own knowledge, this is true. But you would be surprised at the secrets our probe can reveal. This galaxy calls my race the 'Guardians.'"

"Guardians!" Beth gasped in recognition. All of Earth had heard of these aliens.

"Guardians," Axel repeated. "You are the race that controls entrance into dark space." He floated closer to the historian, beeping with curious admiration. His eye-globe extensions twisted in an attempt to see the man from every conceivable angle. "Your representative spoke with us using audio only."

The man nodded. "I was that representative. My name is Goren. We prevent violent races from spreading their rule of terror beyond their own solar systems. You see, our own galaxy was not so lucky.

"A violent race conquered several planets near my home and turned their inhabitants into slaves. We tried to intervene, but the conquerors had already set up formidable defenses. Eventually the radicals turned their attention toward my planet and our treasurers. They were fools." Throughout the narrative, the stranger had seemed harmless, even benevolent. Now something lethal flashed in his eyes. His voice trembled with hatred. Beth had expected the Guardians to be too advanced for emotions, as the Quanta tried to be. She realized that this assumption was flawed. Everyone remained quiet, even Connor. She could tell that the story had captured their complete attention.

"We benefited from the disadvantage of all invading armies. The tyrants had to come to our planet. We had levels of technology unknown to our enemy. They came openly, filled with their stupid arrogance. We were able to escape them easily, using the advancements they coveted." Goren smiled, relishing his next revelation. "Then we eliminated those witless enough to invade our world."

"Eliminated them?" Beth repeated. "You mean killed them?" She glanced at Axel. "I thought killing was not tolerated."

"No, we didn't kill them." Goren shook his head. "While our assailants would not have hesitated to kill us, we have learned that killing is a shortsighted way of dealing with adversaries. It can inspire them to greater feats of violence and vengeance. We sent them to a planet so far away and so dangerous that they ceased to be a threat. They might even benefit the natives…nutritionally.

"We grieved when it became clear that staying on our home planet would attract other greedy invaders. Our advanced technology was no longer a secret. Sooner or later, someone would find a way to gain access to the power we control and use it to destroy. So we scattered to the winds, carrying the hope that we might save other races."

Because of the many fantastic stories about them, Beth was in awe of this race called the "Guardians." She had never imagined she would meet one. Sitting straighter, she tried to project a posture of calm dignity as Goren went on.

"We altered this small planet so that it could cross the great void into this galaxy. With unwavering determination, we have kept our promise to the elders; we protect innocent races. Then by accident, we discovered a more urgent mission.

"Through watching the evolutionary processes of sentient planets, we discovered that cultural uniqueness and critical inventions were being lost forever. Sentience is rare, and its milestones should be preserved. So we created this repository. We collect and catalog the historical records of culture and technology, so they will not be lost in the upheaval of change. We discovered an unexpected benefit from our work. An intact record of your history holds secrets that might improve your current society: mineral deposits lost, energy sources forgotten, government styles that were wiped out, religious breakthroughs kept secret, and great works of art destroyed. Someday we hope to make our Treasury available to the very races we try to preserve.

"I must confess: I find your species intriguing. The Pyramids and the Sphinx were too delightful to omit from our collection. Of course, we have only copies. The originals remain on your planet. Regretfully, time has worn away most of the details. Here, they are intact. We have tried to replicate most of the ancient Egyptian crypts. All the burial chambers emptied by looters are preserved here. As soon as we learned that they were about to be plundered, we swept away their treasures, leaving the thieves frustrated and empty-handed.

"We collect relics from planets at the moment just prior to their destruction, or we make exact duplicates. For your race, the library at Alexandria, the Parthenon treasury in Greece, the plundered papal archives, and the missing cultures of your earliest history are a few of the things that have been lost through war and greed. The Egyptian pyramids and the Sphinx themselves contain forgotten secrets.

"Now to the reason I have given you access to our Treasury. Your people are the storytellers of this galaxy. It has become obvious, from your ancient stone carvings to your current obsession with books and film, that humans love stories, so I have decided that the story of this facility might be told under the guise of fiction, although you can never reveal that the repository is real. During your visit of select exhibits today, you may choose to bring back elements of your own lost history disguised as stories. Or, if you prefer, you may explore some new race."

Beth had always wondered at her race's obsession with stories. Now it might prove to be a valuable asset.

"However, there are three more conditions to your visit," Goren cautioned. "First, you are not allowed to take anything out of the Treasury. The historical relics displayed here are a testimony to the achievements of esteemed races. We will not put them in harm's way again. Second, you must keep our location a secret. When you give your alliance a report of this mission, do not mention the Treasury. You were able to find us only because we were in the midst of relocating and restoring this star system. Third, you may not wander unaccompanied here. If you break any of these rules, your visit will be terminated. Do you all agree?"

"Of course, we will respect your restrictions. My people are required to respect the laws of all races we meet," said Beth.

"We greatly appreciate your letting us see these treasures. Your rules seem a small concession," added Sarah.

"If you insist," grumbled Connor. To Beth's relief, Goren's story had managed to thaw some of Connor's icy temper. He looked as eager and curious as Sarah.

Axel had settled near the Guardian's feet and was studying the tall man with great concentration. He beeped his assent distractedly.

"Look." Goren pointed upward. The huge screen now displayed a floor plan showing the entrances to several exhibits. To their surprise, the team could read all the labels. "I have adjusted the Treasury's language display, so you can understand it." An illustration and a description of the race it represented labeled each exhibit.

"You may select one exhibit to visit. We will regroup afterward in this central lobby."

"I want to go to these rooms." Connor pointed to an exhibit of a heavily muscled dwarf species. Their physicality suggested that their planet had heavy gravity. They were surrounded by heavy metal contraptions, an engineer's paradise.

"I want to go here." Sarah pointed at an avian race exhibit. The creatures were delicate and willowy. "Flying should encourage interesting inventions."

Thomas put his arm around his wife. His selection was obvious. He would go with her.

"I want to see Earth," Beth said. "It was the Pyramids that drew us, and I want to see what has been lost in our history." Beth knew that of all the artifacts, it would be Earth's that would give her information that might significantly impact her race. She wouldn't need to remove artifacts to use the science humans had once known.

As if on cue, two separate doors slid open, revealing two figures dressed in gold, hooded robes similar to Goren's. Their features were hidden in the enveloping folds.

"Here are your guides. You must remain in their company at all times," he reminded them.

Eagerly, the humans approached the open doors. The chaperons glided forward. One motioned to Connor, and the other corralled Tom and Sarah, leading them to the passageways. The doors closed after them, transforming again into the pristine wall. Beth looked expectantly at Goren. He waved at the same area, and a third door opened. This one was larger than the first two. Beth scanned the entrance eagerly.

"Where is my guide?" she asked puzzled.

"I am your guide," Goren mumbled, looking away from her. "Let us go." Without further explanation, he stepped quickly through the door ahead of her. Beth guessed that "guide" was not a normal role for him. She sensed he might even be a little uncomfortable with her.

Beth entered the passageway and walked down a murky metal corridor whose floor was covered in a thin layer of dust. Their footsteps raised small puffs of dust and made hollow taps that echoed ahead of them. There were no windows, just light panels embedded in the metal walls. This place looked too sterile for a repository that held the rich lives and eventful histories of countless races.

Goren waited until she had come up alongside him and then led her down a side tunnel. He put his hand on her waist to guide her forward. His touch triggered a restless stirring, frightening her into irritation. She moved out of his reach.

"How are the artifacts organized? Do we visit several rooms, or can we go directly to the period we are interested in?" Beth blurted, trying to redirect her attention onto the experience ahead.

"We have easy access to any part of an exhibit," Goren replied, moving to the wall and activating a lighted floor plan. Beth breathed a little easier. It would not do to alienate the alien. "We are here." He pointed to two small figures blinking in a connecting corridor. "We are going to this exhibit." He slid his slender finger down the hall to an elevator icon and then up to the Earth exhibit. As they walked toward the elevator, the lighted floor plan went off. The sole indications of life in the sterile corridor were their quiet words and clicking footsteps.

"How many exhibits are there?" Beth asked conversationally.

Goren stopped walking, considering. Then he chuckled. "You know, I have no idea. I have been collecting them for so long that I've lost count."

They finally entered an elevator that looked like it belonged in an old Earth movie. Rich fabrics paneled the walls, plush carpet covered the floor, and elaborate antique candle sconces provided light. Against the back wall was a cushioned divan for sitting. Thank God not everything was stark and modern, Beth thought. The metal corridor had been a bit too drab for comfort. Modern technology was great, but Beth liked the indulgences that history had employed to provide luxury and feelings of well-being. She relaxed on the divan, smiling with pleasure.

"This elevator must have come from Earth," she accused Goren.

"I have a secret weakness for your planet's finer pleasures," he confessed. "You will find small signs of Earth throughout the Treasury.

"The Earth exhibit," Goren said, turning back to a panel on one side of the elevator door. The panel flashed when he spoke, and the doors closed. Then the elevator dropped down and to the right, before they opened again. Through the doors, Beth could see a mountain meadow complete with mountain.

"What in the world?" she exclaimed, hopping out of the elevator. She could smell evergreen, hear a gurgling stream, and feel the warm summer breezes of her beloved Earth. The grass brushed softly against her ankles. "This is so real, so lifelike. I can actually smell the grass."

"We replicate natural scenes," Goren explained. "It gives the artifacts context and character. It would hardly be a good museum if we didn't present the landscape of the originating planet."

He opened a narrow panel in the elevator wall and touched a gray button. A stairway appeared, revealing the outline of walls around the meadow foyer. Humans were not the only species gifted at creating illusions. Axel took readings of the projection before following them up the stairs.

The Quanta had been oddly quiet during their journey through the Treasury, and Beth had almost forgotten he was there. She was accustomed to hearing his ongoing monologue of observations. He might be a bit in awe of the Guardian, she decided.

They arrived at what looked like a central directory. Monitors covered every wall, and each screen was divided into several sections. The top left section showed a doorway with a gold label. The other segments highlighted different artifacts, presumably behind the door.

Axel buzzed over to each screen, his previous silence replaced with murmuring as he positioned his internal camera for a better image.

Goren came up behind Axel and laid his hand on the little fellow's casing. "Axel, no pictures."

"How do you know his name?" Beth asked, startled.

"Of course we know all your names. It is part of the scan," Goren rushed to explain.

"Oh yes…no pictures…sorry, I…," Axel said, rambling like an apologetic child.

"I expect you to follow our rules," Goren warned. "Pictures of artifacts are too revealing."

Axel bobbed, lights flashing in unison. "Of course," he said seriously. "I am sorry I broke your protocols. My people are still assimilating rules of conduct." Axel's entire casing leaned to one side like a lost puppy tilting its head in confusion. Unfortunately, he had not quite captured the puppy persona and appeared ridiculous. And then a surprising thing happened.

Goren started laughing. At first the sounds were hoarse as if laughter was rare. Then his mirth relaxed into a harmonic chortle, and tears collected in his eyes. He pulled a rolling chair closer and sat down, breathing deeply.

Axel had stopped tilting in his peculiar fashion and floated away indignantly, beeping in a hurt fashion. Goren noticed the little fellow's distress and was instantly contrite.

"I'm sorry," he said simply. "I have been so long separated from other races; I forgot that I might offend your sensibilities. Please?" Goren offered his hand in apology.

Axel nodded in the Quanta fashion for *yes*, but remained stubbornly remote.

To make amends and cover his lapse of courtesy, Goren motioned Axel over to a cubby of screens. They contained details of a lost technological age. He showed Axel that, by tapping the screens, even more detailed information could be accessed. Axel extended his appendages, tapping several screens simultaneously. He found multiple layers and was soon beeping happily and muttering to himself. He was not one to carry a grudge for long.

Beth found the monitor displaying the Pyramids and the Sphinx. The main image was a long-angle view of the outside exhibit. The structures were so familiar, yet covered with amazing new details. Beth had visited the great Pyramids on Earth. They were ancient crumbling relics, the many centuries on Earth having taken their toll.

Goren returned to Beth and manipulated the neighboring monitors to show a magnification of the pharaoh tombs and the Sphinx. These replicas reflected the height of the tombs' glory. When first constructed, their outer casings had been polished until they shone and were covered with Egyptian pictorial writing. At the top of each pyramid, a gold cap gleamed in the morning light.

One screen showed the interior of the Great Pyramid, more elaborately decorated than Beth could have imagined. The walls and ceilings were covered with lifelike renderings of royal life in ancient Egypt. Inside these limestone monuments, extravagant luxury and extreme opulence suitable for divine kings were everywhere. In several chambers, gold furnishings and jeweled accessories—there to satisfy the whims of a spoiled ruler—were artfully scattered, awaiting a royal hand to take them up and use them. In every room, chests overflowed with treasure. The pharaoh would lie throughout eternity surrounded by the best Earth had to offer.

Beth could see that Goren's Sphinx had its own riches. Hidden doorways stood open under the right paw and behind a stone tablet against its chest. On Earth these two doorways had been completely sealed after their compartments had been emptied. She could see that this Sphinx's treasures were intact. Subterranean cameras showed scrolls, gold figures, silver tableware, and precious jewelry. The filigree and gemstone cloisonné were precise and complex, framing many decorative works of art awaiting the dead pharaoh's admiration.

Originally, the entrance to the Pyramids had been blocked with stones thought too large to move. The old pharaohs paid faithful soldiers much to keep their resting places safe. But to no avail. The tombs on Earth had been stripped of their treasure even to the corpses themselves.

Unexpectedly, Beth felt a heavy weight of foreboding. She was overcome with the depressing reality of death. As unique as these stone structures were, as magnificent the treasure, and as historically significant the writing, they touched her as monuments to the inevitability of death. She had too much life ahead of her to comprehend their importance. She knew that she did not want to go inside them.

"As much as I've enjoyed revisiting these Egyptian tombs, I was wondering if I could look at other aspects of my history?" she asked self-consciously. She couldn't help blushing at her lack of commitment to the very thing that had brought them here.

Goren smiled sympathetically. "For people who live a short time, tombs can be a bit intimidating. There are, of course, many other areas of special interest. Maybe these exhibits would be more suitable," Goren offered.

Beth saw a satisfied smile touch his lips. What had she missed?

Goren pointed to a corner with extra-large screens. "These artifacts were collected during turning points in your history," he said, pulling Beth over. She skimmed the descriptive plaques displayed on each screen. The papal archives in Rome, the sprawling Knossos palaces in Crete, Santorini in Greece, the Gardens of Babylon, the library in Alexandria, and Anton, the first quantum computer, appeared on the closest monitors. Behind these, she saw exhibits of ancient human cultures—Indian, Phoenician, Minoan, African—and some she couldn't identify.

"There are many exhibits from the Mediterranean," Beth observed. "I've visited Crete. Some of their ancient palaces have been restored and repainted."

"Crete is unique and well worth visiting," Goren confessed. "Egypt has been a pet project of mine because it is one of your oldest preserved cultures. I chose to guide you because I collected most of these relics."

"But how could you?" Beth gasped, shocked. "Many of these artifacts are ancient. The pyramids alone are five thousand years old."

"I am afraid everything is relative," he said candidly. "For you, five thousand years seems very long. For me…How old do I appear?" With a flourish that was quite unlike his prior manner, Goren whisked off his gold robe. "I always did find that thing suffocating," he grumbled. He stood before her and turned slowly, holding out his arms. "Let us say I am five thousand years old. Do I look young or old?"

Beth laughed despite herself. His question gave her an excuse to examine him more closely. His weathered skin and deep-set eyes suggested age, while his bushy hair and strong build suggested youth. He moved with the grace, balance, and agility of someone ready for action, but there was also deliberateness in his demeanor. He had long slender fingers, suggesting the skill of an artist. What she found most disquieting was the sense that she had known him before, that she had heard his voice in a half-remembered dream.

"Both," she confessed. "While you don't show the usual ravages of time, you do bear its weight all the same. Is that kind of longevity usual for your race? Are you five thousand years old?"

"That is a hard question. Your species puts a high value on time, and so you watch the years closely." Goren paused, staring thoughtfully across the room. "My Treasury keeps me so busy that

I have lost track of the passage of years. The number becomes irrelevant. It has been a very long time since I have been home, where my age would be remembered." Goren looked sad.

Beth could not imagine being separated from her people for so long that they were a hazy memory. Being a short-lived species had its perks. There wasn't time to forget her family and friends.

Beth decided it was time to change the subject. This was an exciting adventure, and it might help to remind Goren. "Well, for us, the short-lived species," she teased, "your Treasury is a once-in-a-lifetime opportunity, and we shouldn't waste time brooding. So how do we get this show on the road?"

"The library of Alexandria would be a good place to start. Thousands of scrolls were stored in its vaults. Most philosophers and historians up to that time were represented." Goren pointed to a magnificent arch. "It is this way." His eyes shone with the same excitement that Beth was sure was reflected in hers. Beth had found a kindred spirit; they were both captivated by ancient Earth history.

Beth looked around for Axel and found him immersed in a new collection of monitors, scanning page after page of displays. Two monitors were running videos. He looked as happy as a puppy with a wagging tail. "I'm going to visit the Alexandria library," she told him. "Even though the Pyramids are what brought us here, the library has the kind of treasure I really enjoy: the secrets in our history. I thought you might want to join us."

Axel waggled in approval. Beth imagined he was trying to nod. Instead his entire casing shook. Goren shook silently beside her. He wasn't going to offend the little fellow a second time.

The library proved to be a marvel. They first entered an open reception area designed to catch the sea breezes of a faraway Mediterranean. Surprisingly, Beth could feel the bite of a cool breeze and smell a hint of salty brine. The floor was covered in complex designs created by thousands of painted tiles. These tiles were so perfectly fitted that the edges disappeared. Limestone pillars and marble figures, accented with gold paint, were placed in hidden corners, suggesting clandestine meetings.

Beth walked through several reading rooms decorated with marine motifs of every description. Axel examined many of them, falling farther and farther behind. Paintings of mythical sea creatures hung on walls, and wood sculptures of starfish, whales, and dolphins filled display shelves. On side tables were realistic miniatures of ancient sailing ships. The sails varied from white to deep blue to burnt orange. If this replica of the library was any indication, the art of these water people was lavish and colorful.

In one room, the soft tones of a flute and a harp stirred the quiet. All the reading rooms were furnished with low, comfortable silk divans as well as stone benches for those who preferred such. No effort had been spared, and here, at least, the historical rumors were well founded. There were scrolls everywhere.

Beth stooped to examine a parchment and realized it was a laminated copy. Even though the scroll was plastic, the parchment felt rough and the writing newly printed, as if the author had just put away his quill pen.

"Is this all you have then, copies?' she asked sadly. "I hoped you might have retrieved some originals before they were lost forever in the fire that destroyed them."

Goren winked conspiratorially. "It was one of the greatest disasters in your ancient world and cost humans priceless documents describing vast periods in your history. How could I not? This was one of those moments that fueled our commitment to safeguarding sentient history."

"Where are they? These are not ancient parchment."

"Hermetically sealed in a special vault. When the very elements work to deteriorate the scrolls, it seems wiser to protect them. Copies of all the manuscripts are available," he promised.

"How do I find specific subjects?" she asked eagerly.

"Through there is a central directory." Goren waved toward another archway.

Beth saw a long counter similar to the marble one in the main atrium. Mounted on the wall was an elaborate wood carving of ships, anchors, and astronomical configurations. The wood had a high-gloss finish and was veined with light and dark imperfections, like waves on a turbulent sea. The only paradoxical item was a computer built into the counter, with a hanging screen and a recessed keyboard.

"This library is a special acquisition," Goren confessed. "It is a complete collection of original artifacts. When we realized that the harbor repository was about to be destroyed, we relocated the entire structure here, leaving a burned replica. This is the original building. There was only one other disaster that came close to matching it."

Beth marveled at the implications of standing in the actual Alexandria library. She imagined she could smell the smoke from the original library fire and cleared her throat unnecessarily.

"What was the other one?" she asked.

"A colossal volcanic eruption on the island of Santorini in Greece," Goren revealed with a grave expression. "It happened in 1627 BC. When the volcano exploded, it tore the island apart, destroyed all the Santorini towns, and flooded coastal cities as far away as Egypt. Even the climate was affected by the lingering dust clouds. The Santorinians who hadn't already escaped were killed by hot pyroclastic surges that engulfed the entire island right before the main eruption. We collected as many cultural artifacts as we could before they were destroyed. Sadly, we lost a small city in the northern region. It was buried too quickly under volcanic ash. All that remains of the original island is a steep semicircle of earth surrounding a caldera of water. The people of the time never forgot those cities or that island. Soon legends were told of a great civilization sinking beneath the sea."

"You can't mean Atlantis?" Beth asked doubtfully. "Atlantis is a legend."

"A legend with a seed of truth," he suggested. "Even the tallest fish tale had an original fish. Possibly not as large or as intelligent but still a fish."

Intrigued, Beth turned back to the computerized directory. Goren had already activated the find command, and she studied the scrolling list of documents. The parchments were stored by subject and date. First she went to the earliest dates listed, and then she selected the subject: significant historical events. Since scrolls were written after the fact, many included references to other source documents. On any one subject, the long list of relevant scrolls was daunting. She drummed her fingers, unsure of how to proceed.

"Let me help you," he offered, when she huffed in frustration.

With the skill of a true storyteller, Goren described his first visits to her planet as he scrolled down the list of manuscripts. His stories took Beth back to a world where everything from weather to food to human interaction was enveloped in an air of divine mystery. Their religious beliefs were the explanation her ancestors had come up with for the often eccentric behaviors of the world around them. Beth could imagine noisy, bustling harbors, the focal point for trade, uniting those ancient communities. Aboard great ships, artisans and scholars would have traveled from Greece to Italy and then to Spain to visit luxurious palaces and view great artworks.

"Despite the lack of any of the technical pleasures your civilization now enjoys," Goren was saying, "the human mind in ancient times was more open to exploring unusual explanations. Many scientific breakthroughs need to 'break through' current belief systems. Advancement is often a leap of faith." Goren's voice trailed off as he resumed scanning through the entries with renewed purpose. Finally he instructed the directory to print out two scrolls and then opened a sliding panel next to the keyboard and retrieved the manuscripts.

"These might be interesting," he said, handing her the parchments.

Beth took them awkwardly. Goren had a disturbing way of making her feel like a teenager asking for permission to handle first editions.

Axel appeared behind them and absently bumped into Beth. She dropped the scrolls and had to reach for the counter to restore her balance. Quanta navigators never respected their partners' personal space.

"I have discovered the most interesting art histories," Axel chirped excitedly, spilling several precariously balanced scrolls onto the floor in his excitement to show her.

"Why don't we move into one of the larger rooms?" Goren suggested. He gestured toward an archway, and Axel hurried forward, twittering in his usual fashion. Beth smiled in relief. Her Axel had returned in all his inquisitive glory.

Goren gathered the spilled scrolls into a collection bin and pushed it into a large reading room. Here were comfortable settees facing hanging tapestries of long-forgotten cities. One textured tapestry depicted a lush green cove filled with boats labeled Phoenician, Carthaginian, and Moorish that belonged in some great fable. The Mediterranean was an impossible shade of blue, so brilliant and vibrant that it didn't look like genuine water. Beth studied the scene for several moments, imagining the characters alive.

She chose a settee that belonged in some noble's study, settled herself comfortably, and spread out the first scroll on her lap, which Goren had thoughtfully translated into English. Beth slid her finger along the words, instantly transported into an ancient time.

The parchment was an account of a traveling poet and storyteller, Minos. He was a man who roamed from city to city spreading the latest news, singing songs, and teaching poems about major historical events. One story told of Minos's journey through several communities living on the shores of the Black Sea. In exchange for news of their neighbors, the locals had told Minos of a great disaster that had driven their ancestors south, long before written history. The story had survived in the oral tradition of singing poems.

According to the song, their ancestors had settled here during a lingering ice age. Growing glaciers had sealed the Black Sea, keeping the water levels constant. The villages had spread out on its newly exposed shores, and thrived on the abundant marine life. Inevitably, the ice began to retreat, and when it had melted enough, the great Mediterranean burst through, raising water levels. Terrible tidal waves swept the vulnerable shores and destroyed the communities that had thrived there. Finally the waters calmed, leaving a larger sea with higher shores. After centuries, the memory of the great flood dimmed and people were drawn back to the plentiful sea life flourishing in the Black Sea.

"A great flood? Could it be the great flood described in the Bible?" Beth wondered.

"It is possible the villagers turned the flood into an epic story of an angry god delivering punishment to his believers," Goren agreed. "But the flood story is common to several ancient cultures."

Beth nodded and then looked around in surprise. Axel was gone, and Goren had seated himself so that she was almost in his lap.

"Where is Axel?" she asked, disengaging herself from the Guardian and standing to get a better view of the adjoining rooms. She saw that the shadows were longer, and the windows shone reddish orange. This was obviously a program designed to mimic the passage of time. "It is getting late. How long have we been here?"

Goren slowly rose. "Axel went into another room," he answered. "The others are probably as absorbed in their discoveries as you were. I wanted…"

He took a step closer to Beth with unmistakable intention. She stood perfectly still, afraid that any movement might take away her choice about what happened next. He stood just inches from her and examined her features as he would an exquisitely beautiful statue. She felt that he was looking at the waves of her hair, the moistness of her lips, and the curves of her neck. Her hair moved as if lifted by his hand, her lips tingled as if kissed, and her neck shivered as if stroked. But he hadn't touched her and didn't move any closer.

Beth knew she should express her indignation at his forwardness and leave now. But her imagination had been teased all day, and this man, if he even was a man, had excited her intensely. His looks, his voice, the sound of his breathing completely captivated her. She simply couldn't walk away. After all, he was five thousand years old and had sailed, if not a legendary sea, then two universes. So when Goren pulled her into his embrace, she didn't resist.

Beth experienced the next few moments in slow motion. He put his arms around her waist and teased her mouth with his lips. Her body quivered as his experienced fingers caressed her back.

Impulsively, she leaned back and stroked his hair, finding it as silky as sable. It slid through her fingers and tickled her palms. She ran her fingers lightly along his smooth, warm jaw and across his strong shoulders.

Beth felt the cool air caress her skin when Goren pulled her shirt open. Somehow his shirt was already gone, and he rubbed against her, bare chested. In each other's arms, they both sank down onto a divan.

When he pressed his full body against her, something deep inside her ripped, and her desire instantly vanished. Crying out, she pushed him away and rolled off the couch. She cradled her stomach, rocking in confusion. As the cramping intensified, her body convulsed in agony, and Beth collapsed, screaming. She writhed as her skin rippled. Goren awkwardly scrambled to his feet. Rather than comforting her, he moved away. When he had gone a short distance, Beth found she was able to breathe a bit easier.

It took her several seconds to comprehend that something else was happening. Alarms blared and red lights flashed. Axel hovered near her, but she couldn't hear what he was saying over the piercing sirens. She struggled to stand, forcing her body to obey. To her relief, it wasn't as difficult as she had anticipated. Beth buttoned her shirt, trying to regain some measure of decorum. Goren had already redressed and was shutting off the alarms. The new quiet was as ominous as the alarms had been. Red lights continued to flash silently.

"What is it?" she asked.

"This way," he prevaricated, heading toward the door. He pressed several buttons in a definite pattern before speaking into a communication system. He didn't even look up to see if Beth and Axel had followed. Without a doubt, the Treasury was his first priority.

As they left the Alexandria library, Beth knew that whatever was happening between her and Goren was not as straightforward as she'd thought.

CHAPTER 10

THE RIVER BASE—CHRIS

Chris discreetly pushed the hidden compartment of Andre's desk closed, scrambled out from underneath the desk, hastily straightened, and turned to him. She had no intention of revealing her discoveries yet. Instead she smiled coyly, trying to distract him, and searched for some believable explanation.

"I lost my manual of required survey reports, and I was hoping Siri brought it here when we arrived." Even to herself, her explanation sounded ridiculous, and besides, the door to his quarters had been locked. She couldn't hope to find a reasonable explanation for actually breaking in.

Andre studied her with his lips pressed together in a thin, rigid line of suspicion. He glanced around the room, avoiding the ceiling. She knew he didn't believe her. He had two obvious choices. He could accuse her of lying and give up any hope of reconciliation, or he could use this event to gain some advantage. Despite the cost, Chris was hoping for the accusation.

To her relief, a third alternative presented itself to her: take the offensive and change the subject. "I'm going to start a second base between the two large rivers. Botany studies make more sense in the interior."

Chris stepped boldly around Andre's stiff figure and headed into the living room, forcing Andre to follow. "Considering that he's our mineralogist, Mitchell will come with me. He can start surveying the Crystal Mountains. I want Ella to join us as well. She can help Mitch map the mountain ranges and provide me with aerial diagrams of the rainforest." Chris held her breath and waited to see if her ploy had worked. Maintaining control was important to Andre.

"I agree; we do need to move inland," Andre conceded. "But Mitchell can handle the second base better without you. I need you here to help me categorize all the biological life I've discovered."

Secretly pleased at the river camp concession, Chris considered her next move. Andre wanted her close, so he could implement his plan. She knew that if she didn't get away, she wouldn't be the only one who was mysteriously assaulted in the middle of the night. Andre would have to face her wrath.

"I've seen your transmissions to Central, Andre. You've already sent reports back to Earth listing your animal studies in exhaustive detail. I have nothing left to add."

"I assigned you to both animal and plant studies. You are obviously feeling better, so you can catch up on the botany reports, and I can get back to supervising the integration of everyone's data into the master survey report, especially since Mitchell will be leaving." Andre had amended his argument effortlessly.

Chris normally found arguing with Andre too exhausting to insist on her way. Not this time. She had already been desperate to get away from him and his constant manipulations. The injections and falsified documents had just pushed her over the edge. She would find a way to leave without arousing his suspicion, but he wasn't making it easy.

"Andre, my main area of study is plant life, not animal," Chris retorted. "You assigned animal research to me because you wanted to leave your own time free. We don't have the resources to delegate your main area of expertise to someone else. It's inefficient. Since the majority of new plant life will be found inland, I'm going with Mitchell."

"I must insist you stay," Andre demanded. "We work better as a team." He reached out to take her arm.

Chris stepped out of range. She recognized this pattern. First he used authority, and then he tried a personal appeal. She signed in exasperation, her usual signal of defeat. When she saw Andre relax, she made her final stand.

Chris forced her voice to remain quiet. She couldn't risk showing him her true feelings, which he could use against her. "On this matter I've decided, and you really have no authority to stop me. You know, Andre, the age of hierarchical authority is not only counterproductive; it's also sorely outdated." Chris didn't want to draw a line in the sand, but maybe it was for the best after all. "Mitchell, Ella, and I will be leaving tomorrow. I'll set up a regular reporting schedule with Lena." While speaking, Chris had been slowly inching toward the door. Abruptly, she exited, cutting off further argument.

The following morning, Chris avoided Andre while her small team prepared to leave. She had spent the night in Lena's suite, afraid to sleep alone. As he loaded sensitive equipment, Mitchell whistled happily and smiled incessantly. She knew he was pleased to be leaving. He made no secret of his animosity toward Andre and his preference for her as team leader. While Mitch was a gifted chemist and engineer, he had the diplomacy of a Rottweiler trained to protect.

Lena wasn't happy about Chris's plans and pleaded with her to stay. But Chris was in harm's way here. She couldn't discuss her discoveries for fear they'd create a revolt when she most needed everyone to pull together. Andre was a brilliant scientist, even if he was an unprincipled ass. Besides, as far as she could tell, she was the only one in danger.

Andre had remained in his cabin all night. This morning, Chris could feel him watching their movements. It seemed he had yielded to her wishes. When they were ready to depart, he approached them, carrying a small satchel. Now what?

"While I believe that my schedule would yield superior results, I would hope we could part on conciliatory terms. Please, Chris, won't you reconsider?" Andre had finally stepped down from his position as master of all he surveyed.

"I'm doing this for the welfare of our survey," she lied, not able to look Andre directly in the eyes. In truth, she was doing this to save her own hide. "Really, Andre," she pleaded, "this is the best way. I've allowed you to create our life to your own design. But there are some things I'll not compromise on. The team will work better this way."

Chris realized she was talking in mixed messages. Part of what she said was in direct response to what she had found in his apartment, and part of it hinted at her intention to take back leadership of their survey.

"Here, I have prepared these survey reports based on the Central Alliance manual. You said you'd lost your copy." Andre handed her the black satchel. To Chris's relief, he appeared to be letting them leave without further argument.

Inside the bag were two black notebooks similar to the ones she had seen earlier. She could almost see the work schedules with completion dates that had been in her other notebook. Chris accepted them without comment. If he let her go, Andre could give her a whole briefcase of instructions. From now on, all final decisions were hers.

Chris hummed as the cruiser flew over the treetops heading for the first of the two large rivers. She could hear a loud thundering in the distance. One of the perks of surveying was naming major landmarks. She was already trying out *Silvane* and *Gilnor* for the rivers. These were two warmly remembered names from a childhood fairytale. All too soon, Chris, Mitch, and Ella landed near the spot she had picked for their new home.

It took several hours to set up the second base. Chris and Mitch worked easily together, singing to lighten their labor. This time they used canvas structures framed with plastic instead of the sturdy cabins required by Andre. When stored, these structures folded into small squares. As soon as the clasps were undone, they flipped open into surprisingly solid structures. The largest served as a kitchen, bathroom, and research lab. Mitch had set up a smaller structure for storing and maintaining his aerial and land probes. Another modified expandable dome contained rooms used for sleeping, because night vulnerability required extra security measures. All equipment was run off the cruiser generator using wireless connections. To give the cruiser time to recharge, he rigged three windmills. Chris helped run hoses from an underground aquifer for the bathroom and kitchen. They had enough water pressure to satisfy basic functions.

When they had finished, Mitch went to release a few of his watchdog probes. Some would provide security, while others began the data collection required for reliable reports.

In short order, Chris was attracted by the commotion coming from inside Mitch's new maintenance workshop. He had several small recording probes standing ready at his feet, and on a nearby table, camera relay monitors showed various angles of his boots. He must have already released some of his devices, because she could hear them rustling in the underbrush nearby. At least, she hoped they were his devices.

It was getting late, so Chris reluctantly left to start dinner. She loved watching Mitch putter in his workshop and assign personalities to his small inventions. She lit a small barbecue, and set thin chicken pieces coated with her special seasonings to grill. Beth had grown up camping, and mouth-watering barbecues had always been on the menu. It took a very short time to draw Mitch out of his shop with the delicious smells. He was followed by a small militia of probes, which resembled chicks waddling after their mother.

Chris saw that three were clearly intended as aerial probes. Two of the vehicles looked like miniature helicopters, and the third could be described as a seaplane for mice. All had wheels that would allow them to travel on land.

"These two are helioprobes," Mitch announced proudly. "I call them Hansel and Gretel." He released one helioprobe in a northern direction, and the second fellow flew south.

Next, Mitch lifted his seaplane for her inspection. "This chap has a longer range and can maneuver on the river. I call him Geppeto. I've calibrated him to travel upriver a few miles and stop periodically to scan for life-forms on his way back, which might indicate locations for more in-depth field studies.

"Unfortunately, Geppeto is a bit temperamental. Give him too much data, and he'll either return immediately or explode. I'm hoping he'll pick the 'return immediately' option. Otherwise, I'll have to go searching for his parts."

The image of big Mitch scrambling awkwardly through bushes collecting pieces of his lost little plane was just too much. Chris's whole body shook with laughter. When her unrestrained humor finally produced cramps, she cradled her torso and groaned. Mitch's experiences with his inventions were exercises in the absurd. He didn't hide the fact that, for him, the probes were his friends, and he was as attached to each one as he might be to a favorite pet. With her laughter, Chris felt a lightness of being and excited anticipation about exploring Citron. It was a feeling she hadn't even realized was missing.

"Serves you right, little missy," Mitch scolded. "It's not nice to laugh at someone trying to do a thorough job."

Chris's laughter had forced her down on a grassy knoll. Now looking up at Mitch through watery eyes, she had the grace to look embarrassed.

She offered an apologetic smile. "You're right. I guess I just liked laughing for a change. It's been too long."

When Mitch's expression changed to one of serious concern, Chris jumped to her feet, ran to her barbecue, and turned the pieces of chicken, her back to Mitch.

"I'm just finishing the meat," she said gruffly, extinguishing any mood that might encourage the exchange of confidences. "If you would set the table, I'll get the side dishes." She layered a thick coating of barbeque sauce on the pieces for the last few minutes of cooking.

In an exaggerated fashion, Mitch licked his lips and bounded toward the kitchen hut like a great St. Bernard. He wasn't one to linger in a serious mood. His unrestrained enthusiasm was contagious, and Chris decided to make their meal a bit of a celebration. She programmed the converter to produce a healthy green salad with carrots and raisins, thick wedges of hot bread covered in melting butter, watermelon, and a deeply fragrant coffee drink. It was a grand feast, simple yet sumptuous. Cleanup was effortless; everything was fed back into the converter.

Mitch brought out his guitar and set it behind a stack of logs. He had already collected wood for a campfire. Then he arranged two camp chairs to face the fire pit, with a table between for Ella. Both Mitch and his brother loved bonfires and built them at every opportunity. As soon as he had the flames dancing merrily, he stepped back for her assessment. The firelight made his dark skin gleam with highlights. Chris smiled broadly and nodded her approval of his preparations. It really was a cozy fire circle.

Exotic alien features framed the familiar Earth campfire. Planet rings crossed the horizon, and crystal dust sparkled, reflecting firelight, in the surrounding landscape. The plants had a luminescent sheen, the ground glowed, and the water sparkled as it moved. Crystal shards tinkled nearby, adding to the evening chorus. The sky blazed purple after a twilight of red tones. Truthfully,

Chris rather liked the red. It made everything seem warm and vital.

Chris joined Mitch in the fireside chairs, shivering as the air cooled with the falling sun. The changing temperature produced increasing gusts of wind. Branches creaked and leaves rustled. The nearby river rushed faster, pushed by the wind, and fought against the narrowing channel. Mitch handed Chris his jacket, and the soft wool folds nestled her in a warm cocoon.

"Thank you," Chris cooed, zipping the collar closed under her chin. "So what do you think for tomorrow?"

"I'll take the cruiser to those mountains," he said, pointing toward the glinting peaks. "I suspect we'll find generous quantities of precious minerals. Do you think it would be unreasonable to find overflowing veins?" Mitch grinned, rubbing his hands together at the prospect of uncovering the treasure hunter's ultimate fantasy: abundant treasure easily collected. "You know, Mac didn't like being left behind."

"I wanted to take all of you," Chris confessed wistfully. "I just couldn't deal with Andre blowing a gasket."

Looking off toward the rivers, Mitch stirred the campfire thoughtfully, releasing bits of burning ash into the air. The snap and crackle disrupted the growing silence of the encroaching forest. "We should name the rivers. Ella is using *River 1* and *River 2* for her maps, and they just don't do this planet justice. How about *River Randolph* and *River Wilber*? Now those names have real character." Mitch stood as he spoke, gesturing grandly toward the rivers in the manner of a master of ceremonies.

"How about *Erwin* and *Enid*?" Chris offered, matching the absurdity of his river names.

A new flurry of activity broke through the darkness and sent shivers up her arms. The rivers rippled restlessly, disrupting the surrounding quiet. Strong gusts blew through the forest, making the leaves sound like chuckling children hiding from grown-ups.

Then the breezes diminished to soft caresses against her cheeks and hands. The river quieted, and the discussion of river names was mysteriously forgotten in the darkening night.

Chris jumped up and clapped her hands. "Let's sleep outside. I haven't had an overnight campout since I was a child."

"That's a great idea. I can program my probes to keep watch."

Mitch retrieved two sleeping bags and pillows and arranged them comfortably. Chris wisely added two air mattresses to cushion their sensitive hindquarters from sharp rocks, and they had tarps in case of rain.

Mitch retrieved the computer from his workshop and typed in a series of commands. Five little fellows popped out from the underbrush, their rotors whirling. They stood in a perfect line in front of Mitch, spinning each rotor in turn as if to demonstrate their operational status.

"You did that on purpose!" Chris accused, surprised at the life-like quality of the behavior. They looked like mischievous children waiting for permission to go off and play.

"I swear I didn't," Mitch vowed, holding his hand over his heart solemnly. "Every so often my little buddies seem to have minds of their own."

As if on cue, each droid presented itself in turn, allowing Mitch to retrieve its stored data. Then he programmed them to take strategic positions in the surrounding underbrush in order to keep watch. If anyone or anything should enter the cleared circle, they would start beeping stridently. Hansel, Gretel, and Geppeto were still out exploring and wouldn't return until early morning.

Waving Mitch closer, Chris nodded for Ella to project an aerial map summarizing her scans. A branch of the east river eventually abated to form several waterfall cascades. The aerated water would support specialized plant life and perhaps draw a wide variety of animals. Chris pointed to a clearing at the foot of the waterfalls.

"This is where I want you to leave me tomorrow. I'll bring enough supplies to stay overnight. We'll meet again in two days. I think we should arrange a security check every five hours. I don't want to find myself at the bottom of some fissure with no one the wiser." Chris's words sounded light, but her expression was grave.

"We should also turn on our implanted communicators," Mitch suggested. "We'll be able to locate each other quickly."

"Consider mine on. I'll alert Lena to our plans as well. I don't want Andre rushing over here on some flimsy excuse."

Mitch nodded tersely. Any mention of Andre soured his expression. With their plans set, Mitch retrieved his guitar and spent several minutes thoughtfully tuning the instrument until the strings produced clear dulcet tones. Then he began playing a familiar tune full of happy images. At first Chris sang along, wanting to lighten the mood. But when he chose one more wistful and sad, she lost her enthusiasm. She climbed into her sleeping bag, letting Mitch's strumming and the gurgling of the nearby river lull her into a light doze.

She was drifting off into a deeper sleep, when Mitch suddenly stopped playing. "My God! This is incredible," he exclaimed.

Groggily, Chris jerked up and rubbed her eyes. She looked around blearily for the cause of his outburst. Mitch had banked the fire with several stones that held embedded crystals. Now they reflected the firelight in repeating patterns. The pattern seemed familiar.

"Is that…," she started.

"The light patterns match my new song," he confirmed. "Look." Picking up his instrument, he repeated the chorus at a faster tempo. The light flashes switched to the new rhythm.

"Well, I'll be a clucking chicken. You're right. The flashes are probably a response to the musical vibrations—like reeds whistling in the wind. Let's get the video camera," Chris suggested excitedly.

"Pictures speak louder than words. We can play some convoluted music as a test."

By the time she fell asleep, Chris could have sworn that, along with the stones, the wind was whistling, the river was gurgling, and the grass was swaying in time to their improvised concert. Of course, this was just a trick of the late hour.

Chris rose early to prepare for her trip to the waterfalls. She was so eager to start that she couldn't have slept a moment longer. Her final act was to hang her small video camera around her neck. Mitch had the cruiser warming, and Ella floated serenely nearby. Chris was relieved they had arranged a frequent communication check. It was like having him close by.

After a short ride, Mitch dropped her next to a grove of fern-like trees below the chain of waterfalls. The main waterfall crashed loudly, blasting away any other noise, which made it difficult to communicate. The water had worn away the rock, creating a vertical cliff. The main falls eventually flowed into smaller water washes. Here, streams escaped into spray that split rays of sunlight into layers of colored light. Crystal dust heightened the colors.

Chris watched as Mitch did several somersaults, blasting the cruiser's engines, before bouncing and swaying playfully on his way to the distant mountains. He acted like a condemned man finally released from solitary. Loud music blasted from the cruiser's stereo, which she could hear even over the din of the waterfall. Several small probes burst out of the hatch and fell in behind the larger craft. Ella exited soon after and flew off toward the planet rings. Chris laughed at the scene of a swaying cruiser followed by hopping, buzzing probes. They trailed after their leader in a rather confused roundabout route. Mitch was a mother hen in the making.

Chris sat down by a catch pool and removed her pack. The deep, quiet pond contrasted with the fall's ceaseless violence. She retrieved a pair of flight boots from the pack, which would allow her easy access to the entire water complex. Flight boots were an interesting exercise in balance, and all space candidates had to demonstrate proficiency in their use. She put these on now, taking time to practice maneuvering. The trick was to adopt the same balancing skill used in surfing. She quelled her growing irritation at finding herself upside down repeatedly, hanging from the antigravity boots. Her skill definitely needed work. She was grateful to be alone.

Finally she gained some expertise and was soon hovering over the falls taking photographs. She focused on a species of flowering shrub that clung vehemently to the cliff rock just out of reach of the eroding force of the water.

When Chris finally flew away from the main cascade, the forest quieted. She circled the trees until she found a natural blind concealed in the foliage of a bushy tree. She settled on the branch and waited quietly until the native animals returned to foraging. Meanwhile, she set her camera to telephoto and secured it firmly to a tree branch. The long lens allowed her the intimacy of detailed close-ups without interrupting the animals' usual behavior.

Eventually a family of foxlike creatures trotted out of a clump of concealing bushes and approached a runoff pool of clear water. The fox cubs raced forward, falling over each other to be the first to stop at the very edge, only to risk being crowded into the water. Tentatively, each baby dipped its paw into the pool to test it; then each dunked its entire head underwater, popping up only to gasp for air.

Their mother impatiently nuzzled her babies out of the way and showed them the proper technique for drinking. She lowered her muzzle and gracefully lapped the water. Then she moved away and looked at her brood expectantly.

A black-and-white male came forward with his chest puffed out so big he could barely see the water's edge. As a result, when he leaned over to drink, he toppled in and got completely soaked.

He scrambled out immediately, growling at the water defensively, completely abandoning the idea of drinking.

A petite white female approached the water next, mirroring her mother perfectly as she lowered her head gracefully. She would've made a good show of drinking, if her larger brother hadn't run forward eagerly and knocked her into the pool.

Chris chuckled silently, satisfied with her surveillance blind. She made a video clip of the family to fully capture their amusing antics. The cubs had discovered small iridescent fish at the bottom of the pool. They splashed awkwardly through the water, getting even their mother wet, in their attempts to catch one. All they managed to achieve was scattering the entire school of fish. The mother finally growled at her babies and pushed them out of the pool, so she could catch their breakfast.

When the troupe finally left, Chris decided to retrieve her pack, which she had left at the catch pool. The audacity of the fox children had warned her not to leave any items unattended. Sure enough, she found her pack ransacked. Chris collected the scattered property and repacked the knapsack, this time zipping it shut. Fortunately, she had packed her food securely enough to avoid discovery so far. But she had no doubt that some clever creature could figure out the zipper, given the opportunity, so she returned the pack to the security of her back.

Chris continued mapping the waterfall complex through the rest of the morning, fixing the position of unusual formations for her map. She found a remote pool, surrounded by dense underbrush, with a soft clay shore that showed many different paw prints. Chris decided this would be a perfect location for recording and cataloging native animals.

The waterfall complex exceeded her expectations. It was teeming with life in all its rich diversity. Everywhere, she found little dramas playing out, and her photo collection was growing quickly.

To her delight, there seemed to be some type of crystalline structure in every feature of the planet. The planet rings and the Crystal Mountains were, of course, the most spectacular, but she also found lattices incorporated into the planet's life-forms.

Fish had scales coated with brilliant minerals. The riverbed was covered with hollow crystals, available as protective shells for bottom fish. Little creatures peered out from behind protective bushes, their irises swirling like pulsating diamonds.

During her last exploratory hike of the day, Chris detoured along a ravine and discovered a long grass meadow containing a still pond. The profusion of supple grass would make this cove perfect for her night camp. There was even a small waterfall at one end of the pond.

As Chris was testing the water for drinkability, she spotted a dark opening behind the falling water. She searched her pack for light plastic rubbers and a waterproof cover. She slipped them on and put her camera in a secure plastic pouch around her neck. Then she waded into the water, veering around a school of fresh-water turtles who rode the cresting wave created by her passage.

Chris hesitated in front of the waterfall, hoping for some in-dication of what lay behind it. What had appeared to be a solid wall of water was, in fact, narrow rivulets. Colored light was visible inside the dark opening. Hunching protectively over her pack, she pushed through the drumming water and climbed a rock outcrop to find dry purchase inside the cave.

Before her was a scene that would remain forever etched in her memory. The cavern was crowded with flowerlike structures illu-minated by a rainbow radiance that emanated from every surface. They were composed of various minerals. Even at a distance, she could see narrow veins of shiny silver fluid running up the stalks to collect in the flower petals. Many blooms had pure-gold pollen sta-men rods topped with rose-quartz crystal anther balls. The carpel, the large seed pod at the bloom's center, was as clear as diamond, revealing a strange fire burning deep within. This life-form moved on a strange silver river the consistency of mercury.

Along the cavern walls and peeking out of the semidarkness of a subterranean tunnel, she saw a group of blossoms with distinct features, rising six feet tall. Their mineral theme was a brilliant amethyst that changed hue as she admired it. In these giant flowers, Chris could clearly see each individual detail of the crystal life-form. The deep fire in their seed pods flickered hypnotically, fed by the silver. These flowers swayed to the same rhythm as the smaller versions.

Chris peered down into the penetrating darkness of the tunnel. She was struggling with her fear of enclosed places against her curiosity to discover more about these amazing life-forms. She blessed her good fortune in finding this tunnel alone. What she intended to do would never have to be explained to anyone—particularly her husband.

Chris pulled four modified, high-powered head lamps out of her backpack. She always packed them. They were her security against being caught in an enclosed situation. She attached the four lights to her head, waist, and arms. Then, swallowing her embarrassment, she turned on each light and peered down the dark maw.

She had transformed herself into a wall of blinding light, which followed her movements, illuminating every rock and crevice in view. Tiny creatures scrambled out of the glare into cracks exposed between the wall and floor. It was definite, she decided—she needed a padded room, not a long dark passage to explore. She took a deep breath, gathered her courage, and took her first step into the unknown.

At first, the tunnel offered no obstacles. The dry path slanted down at a gradual pitch. Hidden openings created drafts that circulated fresh air. Then the shaft narrowed and became uneven. Sharp rocks tore at her shoes. Chris finally had to shut down her light show because the brilliance intensified her night blindness. She could only see two feet in front of her. Reluctantly she stored three of her head lamps and turned the remaining one to LED infrared. The cooler light illuminated objects for a much longer distance, and she could perceive details outside her main field of vision.

As Chris traveled deeper, the temperature rose. Water began dripping down the walls and along the ground, and several times she slipped on the slick surface, falling headlong into muck. Her mud-spattered clothes stuck to her body, restricting her movements further. After ten minutes, Chris considered turning back. But the rising illumination lured her forward. Abruptly, the tunnel turned left, revealing a dead end with several window-sized openings in solid rock.

Moist heat blasted from the openings, fogging Chris's mind. The air was so hot and thick it made breathing nearly impossible. Sweat poured off her body, filling her eyes and ears, blurring her vision, and confusing her senses. Instinctively she knew she wouldn't survive here for long.

Still, Chris peered through the largest opening, which was the source of the strange illumination. Stunned, she turned off her unnecessary head lamp.

The window looked down onto a vast cavern cradling a fantastic world of crystals. The silver mercuric fluid was everywhere. It seeped in through cracks in the ceiling and then merged into four distinct waterfalls that framed three separate compartments. These silver fountains overflowed cisterns of rock close to the ceiling and then dropped down to a lower receptacle to overflow again, and yet a third time, until finally they surged together into a lake of brilliant dancing fluid that covered the cavern floor. The silver was thick, taking whatever shape it wished. At first, as it filled the crevices, it seemed inanimate, but then it would curl or bubble independent of gravity. Chris's mouth fell open as, impossibly, rotating balls of silver floated past her vantage. She leaned forward, eager to experience this totally alien world. But the silver balls spun out of reach before she could touch them.

The silver fountains framed three shallow caves or geodes. Each offered unique, remarkable mineral collections. On the left, gold and ruby flickered in the cavern's dappled light. Gold rods floating in silver bumped against polished red ruby gems, suggesting whimsical jewelry. In the center arena, silver bars, some as large as beams from an old wood ship, and perfectly round white crystals, resembling a lost treasure of giant pearls, floated peacefully in the silver fluid. In the right geode were smaller emerald and copper formations. The dark green crystals were mostly dull, similar to wild emeralds. Some flashed with reflected light, showing the same natural polishing as the red stones.

Even as Chris stared awestruck at the geodes, she realized the cavern contained a third astonishing element. Running through this paradise of minerals, silver canals carried floating groups of flowers, kin to those she had seen above. At least, that was the closest description she could find for the small intricate organisms, made from the surrounding minerals and gems. The creatures swayed together and then pulled apart, together and apart, in a manner that suggested a living community.

These rafts of aliens were carried about the cavern on cresting swells. Chris kept expecting to hear a childish "Wheee!" as a new troupe sailed past. Each family of flowers had an identifying pattern of minerals. Some were red and gold, others white and silver, and still others green and copper. Whatever the pattern, it was followed faithfully by the little family that displayed it.

Chris jerked at a soft brush against her ankle. Alarmed, she glanced down. A single unique bloom swayed against her foot, carried by a stream of silver that oozed from a hole in the floor. This little fellow was alone, smaller in scale, and made from minerals that were unknown to her.

The jewel petals were clear, with glowing gold and silver threads running through them. These strings of light weaved together and then unfurled, finally brushing against the jewel's inner surface. They seemed alive, separate from the flower. The pulsing display drew her complete attention, hypnotizing her with its rhythmic patterns of light.

Chris felt drawn to the small flower and stroked the vibrating petals. The crystal was not cold, as she had expected. It felt warm and slick, like melting metal. Chris ran her finger along one edge and was amazed when a few beads of blood dropped onto the glass. She jerked her hand back when she felt a sudden stab of pain. There had been no indication of any sharp feature. Peering closer, Chris was again mesmerized by the central fire of light swirling in endless circles. As she watched, the fire in the small being slowed and dimmed until it was extinguished. The plant sagged and turned an alarming yellow. Chris scooped up the remnants, hoping she could still do something. But she was too late. What had once been living crystal was now dust. Her powerlessness to understand what had happened created a pang of painful regret.

At that moment, the activity in the crystal world shifted dramatically. Tall amethyst flowers, twins to the ones she had seen above, began to flap their petals, and the rest of the crystal beings followed suit. At first, this produced a sweet sound like falling rain and created a refreshing wind that filled her high vantage and cooled the heated air. Then the sound changed. It grew into a high-pitched whine that sliced through the enclosed cavern. Automatically, Chris wiped away the moisture collecting around her ears and eyes. In horror, she saw her hands come away covered in blood.

Frantically Chris charged back up the shaft toward light and safety. Too soon, she stumbled, disoriented, and finally sank to the soggy floor. The tentacles of an overwhelming darkness closed around her.

When she regained consciousness, she was lying on the grass next to the catch pool, her gear a few feet away. The sunlight created long shadows, signaling the approach of nighttime. She had lost precious time. She had no idea how long she had been underground. The memories of exactly what had happened were oddly dim and indistinct. She wanted to camp in the cave of flowers, but caution held her back.

Chris changed her clothes completely and cleaned herself as best she could in the catch pool. Then she made a quick call to Mitch to confirm her safety and settled for a rough camp in the advancing darkness. After collecting a thick layer of grasses and plumping one end up like an overstuffed pillow, she laid her sleeping bag on top of it. Then she pulled out a plastic tub containing her modest dinner. The turkey slices cushioned in thick white bread with lettuce and tomato filled the hollowness in her stomach and made her sleepy. Drowsily, she stretched out in the sleeping bag and gazed up at the star-filled night. Her meal had consumed the last daylight. The entire meadow was enveloped in silvery crystal light.

Chris covered her head with her sleeping bag, hoping to fall into a deep sleep. But thoughts of Andre sprang into her mind unbidden. She realized she had deliberately avoided thinking of that first night on Citron. Now that she was alone in this lighted fairyland, her thoughts would not be silenced.

She remembered the chemical analysis hidden in her pack. She had dreaded opening that can of worms. The time had come to face the true extent of Andre's betrayal. She left the sleeping bag and went to her pack, resting innocently by the water. She pulled the paper and a headlight from a zipper pocket and returned to her bed. Hesitantly, she read the results. The first analysis was as she'd surmised: the fertility drug of the Quanta. The second was a strange collection of narcotics, ideal for manipulating the thoughts of another human being while rendering him or her docile and amnesic.

Chris rubbed her forehead, trying to soothe away the sudden throbbing. Despite her distress, she could appreciate the full extent of Andre's scheme for their future. In its own way, it was deviously clever. Of course, its fatal flaw was that it would periodically require her cooperation.

In hindsight, the progression of his actions became obvious. First, he had married her right before their graduation, when she was innocent and insecure in the ways of the world. Next, he had suggested she apply for the commander position on the survey team for Citron. Since the *Aries* was the ship assigned to Citron, and its captain, Beth, was her good friend, Chris had acquiesced. His third move was to drug her into a meek and manageable mood, so she would give him command of the mission. Looking back, she realized that she couldn't have given actual consent. She had passed out way too soon. Once she had regained her senses, she had confined him to cocaptain. Chris smiled smugly, satisfied at this thorn in his plans.

Once they boarded the *Aries*, Andre had plagued her with the idea of having children. Children! How ridiculous was that? Chris had dismissed this absurd demand by blaming his family. Now she began to wonder. Had she ever made any real decisions about her future? Or had she simply been a pawn in his game? Had he ever truly loved her?

After she'd plumped up the grasses under her head a third time and squirmed deeper into the sleeping bag, Chris focused her attention back to that first night here. She was unaware of the tears when they spilled down her cheeks. Her heart was fighting the idea of remembering, but this time she persisted in recovering the memory. She let the gentle breezes cool her racing heart and soothe her spinning thoughts.

Slowly she concentrated on that murky place in the corner of her mind where the forbidden memory lurked. Andre was hovering over her, his face contorted into an expression of frenzied need. For a long moment, Chris shrank away, terrified by the intensity of the image. Then she took a deep breath and returned to the candlelit bedroom. Andre was shouting something unintelligible. Chris pulled the image closer, and his words became clear. "You belong to me. You will obey your husband as a good wife must. You will have children now. You will create a loving home for our family now." Over and over, he roared these words, as if by repetition he could make her comply. He pushed her roughly onto the bed and lay on top of her, his eyes filled with a terrible intensity. His brutal grip left red marks on her arms; his powerful knees drove ruthlessly into her stomach and separated her legs. She saw the beginning of the bruises that would look like black spiders the next morning. Mercifully, the red drug he must have put in her wine stole the rest of that night.

Chris curled into a ball and hugged her legs up against her body. She choked on heavy sobs, trying to find a way to breathe past the heavy pressure strangling her heart. How long she cried alone in that meadow, she didn't know. She let the tears wash her face, just as she would wash Andre from her life. Exhausted from weeping, she fell into a deep dreamless sleep.

Chris was never sure what woke her. It could have been a sudden chill or leaves rustling in the wind or a log settling in the woods. Or it could have been an unconscious alarm that alerted her to approaching danger. Whatever it was, it was strong enough to pull her out of her protective sleep.

When Chris felt a hand on her shoulder, she scrambled out of the sleeping bag, instantly wide awake. There was enough early-morning light to see Andre studying her. She realized he must have left the ocean camp before Lena and Mac woke up. He could have found her only by using her transponder signal. Her stomach flipped uneasily.

"Why are you here?" she demanded, searching the meadow for any evidence of yesterday's discoveries. There was her sleeping bag, pack, tub of leftovers, and a crumpled piece of white paper. Instantly she recognized the test results from the previous night. She moved away from her camp toward the catch pool. Once she was a safe distance away from the evidence of his betrayal, she studied him for some sign of his intentions. His eyes narrowed as he too studied her.

"I think the time has come to reach an agreement, you and I. The others distract you. I wanted to speak to you alone with no distractions." He held his arms open, and his expression became friendlier. Chris didn't trust him one bit.

"When I came to the rivers, I made my objectives clear. I need time to consider, Andre. Your coming here prematurely will accomplish nothing." Chris's distress and anguish were increasing. What would he do now?

"The future of our marriage is important. I deserve to have some say in what will happen next," Andre stormed. He wasn't handling her opposition well and was fast losing patience. Now he deliberately stepped closer.

Chris walked backward, stopping when her foot touched the water. Even though she had been an athlete, Chris felt vulnerable to his larger size. She crossed her arms in front of her and performed the first aggressive act of her marriage.

"Move back now!"

Startled, Andre complied automatically. He waited, watching her intently.

Chris hesitated, acutely aware of her exposure in this isolated place. Nevertheless, he was her husband and had a right to the truth. As a precaution, she decided to contact the others covertly.

She nudged her modified molar with her tongue, opening a communication link. Any communicator within range would start beeping. She hoped that Mitch was either an early riser or a light sleeper. Once awake, he would hear their conversation.

"I know you were in our cabin searching. What did you find?" Andre barked, suspicion bright in his eyes. He had abandoned the pretense of innocence.

For a few moments, Chris stood quiet. Some small part of her wanted to see if he would finally tell her the truth.

"The truth, Andre. Finally, I discovered the truth. Are you going to tell me or continue this strange game of yours?"

"I've made no secret of my desires concerning you and our marriage. I want to have children. I want to be a commander. There is no crime in either," Andre admitted with a deceptive omission of crucial facts.

Chris was done with all the hidden motives and duplicity. Dangerous or not, she was going to confront him. "I know everything, Andre. I found the drugs and the hard drive. I know you went behind my back to get your hands on the fertility antidote. I know you drugged me to steal command of my mission." Chris had meant to sound calm, to retain control of the conversation. Instead, she spat the words, revulsion dripping from each syllable. "You have forged my signature on various documents to trap me here on Citron. Did you really think that any of our colleagues, especially Beth, would let you imprison me here against my will? Did you really think I was so stupid that I would follow behind you like some docile cow?"

Andre tried to interrupt her, but Chris had lost what little restraint she'd possessed, and now she shouted her outrage. Deliberately, she used the phrases from her recovered memories. "I don't belong to you like some unfeeling possession. I will not have your children! I will not stay on Citron as your loyal follower! I will not share my command! I will not stay married to a despicable worm like you!" She was shrieking with pure hatred. Finally she stopped, alarmed at her ferocious craving for violence.

Andre stood speechless. He was obviously unprepared for her certain knowledge of his deception. Then his eyes narrowed, glittering like those of a deadly viper, and the truth was all they had left.

"Really, Chrissie, you are a stupid cow. You're too late to stop my plan. I've already injected you with the fertility drug. Our first night was really rather special, don't you think?" He smiled then, his lips pulled back into a tight humorless gash that showed his supreme confidence in his ultimate success. "Even now I can take what I want, and you can do nothing to stop me."

Andre leaped forward, grabbed her arms, and pushed her down on the rocky shore. Her long hair trailed in the water. She struck at him frantically, while Andre seemed immune to her efforts. He pinned her arms with his knees and sat back on her legs, leaving his hands free. From his jacket, he pulled out the familiar syringe, half full of the amber liquid. Slowly, with savage delight, he inserted the needle up to its hilt in her neck before injecting all the remaining fluid. It was hardly a victory for Chris that he was injecting a diluted solution.

She twisted and bucked, finally gaining some leverage by using her feet to dislodge Andre's heavier weight. He fell back, releasing her. While he struggled to regain his balance, she rushed into the water. Wildly she searched for anything that might serve as a weapon.

Remembering the communicator, she shouted, "Mitch, wake up! I'm in trouble! Ella! Siri, can you hear me?"

Andre laughed at her attempts to call for help, as he slowly unbuttoned his shirt. "I've set up a disrupter that blocks your communicator." He nodded toward the trees. "No one can hear you. No one will come to help you. I can't let anyone interfere before I'm finished. Once I'm an expectant father, they'll be powerless to take you away from me."

He jumped into the water and snagged her shirt before she could move out of reach. Then he dragged her toward the shore.

His smile deepened. "I'm glad you'll be awake for this. It wasn't much fun when you were unconscious."

Retreating into the water had been a mistake. Chris's water-logged clothing was weighing down her limbs. Fortunately, Andre was also grappling with the extra weight. Somehow, she managed to wrench herself free. She started slogging toward the cave behind the waterfall. Surely the aliens would distract him long enough for her to get away? She scanned for the alien illumination, but something was wrong. There were no lights. Finally she made it to the falls and reached through the water. Her hand hit cold hard rock. The cave was gone.

Andre seized her from behind and dragged her back to the shore. Chris went limp. There really was no one to help her. He dropped her roughly onto the shore. She groaned at his treatment and at the reminder of her older injuries. He had indeed been responsible for all her pain. Chris closed her eyes against his assault. As a result, she wasn't at first aware when something changed. Her first clue was Andre's weight suddenly vanishing. Confused, she opened her eyes.

Towering over her was one of the six-foot amethyst flowers. Two other purple aliens had lifted Andre into the air and were holding him immobile while two smaller diamond beings sliced at his arms. Blood dripped everywhere, and Andre's eyes had glazed over. He obviously couldn't understand what was happening, and he hung unresponsive. When the smaller flowers dropped away as trails of yellow dust, the two aliens threw him down carelessly. Then all the crystal creatures flowed back along a river of silver to the now open cave entrance. Once they were through, the rock melted together again.

Chris took no time to question her rescue. The important fact was her freedom. Running in the direction indicated by Andre's earlier nod, she easily found his cruiser with the jamming device. She disconnected its power source, and within seconds her ears were blasted by Lena's and Mac's voices. She told them only that Andre was injured. She didn't mention his attack or the flowers. After they promised to come, she reluctantly shuffled back to Andre.

Groaning pitifully, he lay where the aliens had dropped him. The bleeding had stopped. A strange chalklike substance was oozing from his cuts. His legs were so swollen that walking was out of the question. Cautiously, she knelt beside him and touched his cheek. Andre blinked several times before opening his eyes. The usual black of his pupils was gone, replaced by swirling gold and silver strings.

CHAPTER 11

THE GREAT CITY AND MR. QUINN—ROSE

Rose paced impatiently. She had been waiting thirty minutes for their two guards, and she was ready to leave on her own. But Jason's orders had been unmistakable and indisputable. If she left without their guards, then the survey was over. From the start, Jason had been nothing but trouble. From his telepathic assault on her team to the strange absence of their Quanta, Rose knew she had to get rid of him. She couldn't wait for him to try something new that might put her people in harm's way.

Jason finally arrived, with a small group of guards.

"I've scheduled today's activities," he declared sternly. "Our head librarians are anxious to collect the information you need for the report to your Central Alliance. Fortunately, we have a large library complex right here at the university. You should be able to conduct most of your inquiries without leaving these facilities."

Rose shook her head emphatically. They had no control over the accuracy of information provided by coached librarians. They needed autonomy, not guided tours. Taking Jason's arm, she led him to a small alcove. She didn't want to challenge him in front of his men.

"Look, Jason," she explained tersely, "our survey protocols require special conditions. Fieldwork must be done independent of any planetary influence. I've already explained this, yet you continue to ignore me. You leave me one choice. I will require another escort, or I will recall my team, and we will leave Sentara immediately."

For a split second, she felt the full force of Jason's considerable telepathic powers. Then, without warning, he abandoned his attack.

"Ione is coming," he grumbled, resentment sharp in his tone. "It appears the completion of the alliance survey is too important for any misunderstandings. She'll provide any access you need." Jason turned away, stiff with disapproval, and strode out quickly, his men hurrying to follow.

As it turned out, the unknown Ione never did make an appearance. A tall, nondescript guard arrived in her place. He had none of the strange, provocative silver shading. His features were plain—the kind of person one would forget as soon as he departed. He gave Rose a book containing various maps of the planet, including an entire section on the surrounding city. She smiled with satisfaction. Finally they might make some progress, she thought.

"I'm here to take you to the city," he explained, with less inflection than one of their ship computers. "If you have any special requirements or questions, please write them down, and responses will be provided the next day." This would, of course, delay the survey. But Rose was too happy about her hard-won freedom to care.

She scanned the reliefs of Sentara. An overall topographic map showed a world of islands. The poles were ice shelves floating in deep unexplored oceans. Each pole was encircled by a supervolcanic ridge. There were no earthlike continents, only several sizeable islands surrounded by smaller ones. Her team had landed on the main island in the most important city.

Grabbing her small daypack, Rose instructed the guard to take her to the largest library outside the university. She felt the familiar rush of excitement as their vehicle exited the university grounds and entered the city. This was her favorite part of the survey, the beginning. Everything was novel, and every new piece of information, a discovery. It was like standing before a large treasure chest and being poised to throw open the lid.

Everywhere she saw bright color schemes similar to those of island cultures on Earth. Ornately carved wood doors appeared frequently in the snow-white residential buildings and brilliant pastel-colored apartments. One sculptured door displayed star constellations. They passed an open gate, where Rose marveled at a private courtyard with pale rose cobblestones and a huge, bubbling central fountain. She imagined the surrounding dark archways leading to rooms covered in murals. They passed several balcony gardens full of flower boxes and climbing vines, ready for an afternoon of quiet reading. In one, a bench swing creaked in a light breeze.

Eventually they turned onto a long cobblestone street that led to the harbor. To Rose's delight, several concrete walls featured large paintings of town events. At the bottom of each was a painted scroll with date and title. Surprised by her good fortune, Rose took several pictures.

Island economies usually rely on marine trade, so the busiest area is the harbor. This one was no exception. Several ships were unloading large wooden crates. They were decorated with caricatures of deep-water creatures and scored by rough weather and barnacles. Art was central to this planet's culture, which was evident from the moment Rose left the university.

The wharf inhabitants were not big and beautiful like their university guards. There were clearly identifiable bosses and workers.

Rose noticed a spirit of friendly fellowship mixed in with the shouted orders and noise of transferring cargo. She knew about the closeness found in a small community. Crime was difficult when everyone knew everyone. Again, she took pictures.

They drove along the wharf for several blocks before veering away from the harbor toward the city center. They stopped in front of a three-story building with a high entrance and walked through brass-framed doors with large brass handles into a spacious lobby. Wide staircases flanked a main corridor. Rose saw books everywhere. These tomes were not the mass-produced volumes found in Earth bookstores; rather, they had fine-spun covers with calligraphic titles and snow-white pages.

Their guard walked to a long information desk and spoke in hushed tones to a short, older gentleman. This official-looking man scurried over to Rose, smiling broadly and beaming with curiosity. He wore a comfortable suit of soft burgundy material, with a gold watch hanging from one pocket. He adjusted a pair of wire-rimmed spectacles more firmly on his nose and then waved expansively to welcome them to the planet's largest private library, according to the brochure he gave Rose.

"I'm Mr. Quinn—that is, Emmet Quinn—and this is my library. Every document, diagram, and relic contained herein was collected by my family, and we offer them for public viewing daily. You are welcome to stay as long as you need to because, you see"— Mr. Quinn cleared his throat apologetically—"we don't allow any of the artifacts or books to leave."

Mr. Quinn needn't have worried. Rose was pleased to linger in this comfortable library. She was in no hurry to return to their opulent, impersonal, guarded quarters.

"There's been much speculation since your arrival," Mr. Quinn continued in a conspiratorial whisper. "I hope our government has extended every courtesy. They do have a disconcerting habit of forgetting the civilities." Rose glanced at their guard, who could hear every word. He seemed immune to Mr. Quinn's criticism. "May I offer you some refreshment before you begin your examinations?"

"I would love some coffee, if you have such a drink," Rose inquired. "It is our morning energy drink. You must have something similar, yes?" She smiled sweetly at poor Mr. Quinn, throwing him into a state of obvious confusion.

Emmet Quinn was clearly outclassed. He didn't look like the type who had to fend off the wiles of beautiful women. Rose imagined he spent most of his time in dusty, old book collections. He offered her a tentative smile.

"We have a morning restorative. It's thick and spicy—made from a native fruit. I do have some already prepared. Come this way."

Rose took Mr. Quinn's arm formally, and he led her through a side door into a secluded salon. The room was cozy and crowded, with a table covered by a bright cloth and a wood side cabinet containing all the accoutrements one might need for afternoon tea. As they settled around the table, Mr. Quinn poured a rich golden liquid into large blue cups and offered equivalents to milk and sugar.

Rose sipped her drink, delighting in the tantalizing flavor, and listened to Mr. Quinn talk about his library's history.

"I've always loved our family's business and have looked for any opportunity to add to our collection of valuable books. I've explored every major island and most of the remote ones. I particularly wanted a section devoted to our culture and history. There are also shelves on the sciences. Because of my reputation for superior care, we have received some rare manuscript collections. Even the university schedules regular visits." Mr. Quinn retrieved a plate of cookies from the cabinet and offered one to Rose. Her quick smile triggered an answering grin from the old gentleman.

"Is your written history long?" she inquired, taking a fat flaky cookie from the extended plate.

"As a matter of fact, our history doesn't start here," Mr. Quinn admitted, his eyes twinkling with the promise of a fascinating story yet to be told. Their guard hadn't followed them into the salon, so they had relaxed into a friendly informality. "We're not natives of this planet. We arrived here on a starship, like you. This has become our home over the centuries."

"Do you know where you came from?" Rose asked, hardly breathing. She hadn't expected such important information so soon.

"It's my greatest sorrow that this information has been lost. Our ancestors did try to preserve the ship records, which must have contained our history before we came here. But this planet's weather had been too violent and destructive. In the beginning, they were forced to build shelters, using the ship itself to protect themselves against the terrible lightning storms. Then, when they had finally started permanent settlements, giant tidal waves crushed their cities and submerged shorelines. Vital forests and thousands of acres of arable land sank under the walls of water. Most relics of our past were completely destroyed."

"So you haven't always been restricted to islands?"

"No, there were continents."

"So how long has your race been here? Can you determine the date of your arrival?" Rose asked.

"We have a few clues," Mr. Quinn murmured confidentially. "There are carvings of our landing that show partial star configurations. We believe we landed here about two thousand years ago, although written history exists for only the last five hundred years.

"With our limited population, we don't have the resources to build large cities or grand manufacturing complexes. Rather, we live a rural lifestyle focused on agriculture. Many people spend time in artistic pursuits. There are more concert halls, galleries, and craft apprentice programs than factories, chemical plants, or technical schools."

Rose smiled at his description, made almost apologetically. She knew many on Earth who would call this world *Utopia*. She felt a wave of nostalgia for the green meadows near her home and the spongy dark earth of her garden.

"May we see your research sections now?" Rose stood. It was time to start her inquiries.

It wasn't until they walked into an antechamber full of large, thick volumes that Rose commented on their missing guard. Jason and his men had always been underfoot.

"Where is the man who came with us?" she asked, glancing back down the hall.

"You were left in my care," Mr. Quinn assured her. "I'm to call when you're ready to leave."

Rose felt her vigilance and nervousness vanish. She was finally free to conduct her survey without fear of their hosts' interference. She hummed a little ditty as she started searching the tall book shelves for relevant texts.

CHAPTER 12
ANDRE'S FOLLY—CHRIS

Chris dragged Andre off the rocky shore onto the soft grass. His body shook violently for several seconds before letting him take a long, slow, crackling breath. Chris couldn't bring herself to examine him. For reasons known only to them, the flowers had, miraculously, rescued her from Andre's assault.

Before long, pieces of a disjointed conversation erupted from the trees. Her team entered the meadow and broke into a run when they saw Andre's swollen form.

"What happened?" Lena exclaimed as she neared Andre, her features etched with shock.

"Is this Andre?" Mac asked in dismay.

Andre was indeed a pitiful caricature of his former well-groomed, in-control self. Every joint was swollen, and his skin was an inhuman greenish gray. A strange dust formed a circle around his body.

"Why did he come here?" Mitch growled, suspicious. "Are you OK? Did he attack you again?"

It was just like Mitch to worry about her when Andre was the one injured and very likely on the verge of death. Chris glanced down at her soaked clothing and ran her fingers through her tangled hair. Bruises were already showing on her wrists, and she touched her neck to see if the injection site was still bleeding. She had obviously been through something.

"Enough questions," Lena interrupted. "We need to get back to base camp."

Chris began to shake with shock. Andre had sapped her remaining strength with his unprovoked attack. She nodded numbly when all looked to her for confirmation of Lena's leadership.

"We need to find out what's happening to Andre," Mac added, kneeling beside their fallen leader.

Mac opened one of Andre's eyes and exposed their strange metamorphosis. Then he picked up Andre's wrist to examine the wounds more closely, causing more of the strange dust to seep out.

Lena's sharp intake of breath broke the stunned silence

"Despite how any of you feel toward him, Andre may have saved the rest of us from a serious threat," Mac observed.

"Chris looks like she could use some medical attention as well," Mitch pointed out.

"I'm all right," Chris argued. "I just need some rest."

Three pairs of eyes looked at her skeptically. Chris was shivering again, and her breathing was labored. Andre must have bruised her ribs.

"You're not all right!" shouted Mitch, his features grim with determination. "You look like a shaken rag doll. It's obvious that something happened. Tell us!"

"Please, Mitch, can't we just get out of here?" Chris pleaded. She didn't have the strength to fight anymore. She could almost hear the threatening flutter of crystal petals. In fact, she could feel a real presence all around them. How could she have ever imagined they were alone on this world?

"Mitch, help Mac carry Andre to our ship," Lena said, cutting off his questioning. "Then secure the river base, and bring all the personal items to the ocean base. Chris will come back with us."

Chris knew she had to warn the others about her discoveries. She just didn't know if the crystal aliens were dangerous or not.

Since Chris had endorsed Lena's leadership, Mitch reluctantly followed her directions. He followed Mac to the cruiser to retrieve an isolation carrier. They had to restrict exposure to whatever had infected Andre. Once they had loaded their patient onto the cruiser, Mitch headed to his smaller shuttle, obviously relieved to have duties elsewhere. He had left the engine running.

During the trip back, Chris stared at Andre's carrier, wondering what the crystal flowers had done to him. She would have guessed that this was some form of deadly force, except that he was still alive. Needing a distraction, Chris let Lena attend to her superficial injuries. Her agitation and distress were so obvious that Lena gave her a warm drink that went a long way to soothing her frantic heartbeat and turbulent thoughts. Finally, Chris felt the ship bounce as it rolled across the rocky landing area near the ocean base.

Siri and Ella met the ship and carried Andre to a screened-off area in the newly erected medical cabin. Mac and Lena followed close behind the Quanta, while Chris trailed after them more slowly. Through the open door, she could see the full extent of the small party's medical resources. They had already set up video cameras and medical monitors. Lena was requesting an exhaustive list of medical tests from Siri, and Ella was erecting a "clean" room where visitors could dress using universal protection guidelines before entering isolation. Chris knew Andre was in good hands.

She shuffled out, heading back toward the main cabin. She didn't want to burden her team when her husband so needed their full attention. Suddenly, she felt a powerful longing for the healing warmth of a hot shower. Remembering Andre's luxurious master bath, she detoured toward the quiet cabin. Anyone else might have avoided using the sick man's residence, especially since it carried such disturbing memories, but not Chris. The injuries were his responsibility, and his quarters were the perfect cure. Besides, the thought of hot-water jet streams was too tempting to resist.

The front door was slightly ajar, allowing her easy access. Chris found several windows open, and the entire cabin was chilly. She secured the windows and drew the curtains before entering the bathroom and turning on the shower.

Slowly, Chris removed her wet clothes. Two robes hung from hooks convenient to the shower. The second one was blind testimony to Andre's belief in her ultimate return. He could never admit doubt or the possibility of failure.

After adjusting the temperature, she stepped under the water and rotated slowly, letting the warmth ease her sore muscles. Then she poured a dollop of shampoo onto her palm and worked it slowly into her long hair. Chris massaged longer than was necessary to get clean, reveling in the pressure that relaxed so much tension. Once she had thoroughly rinsed her hair, she took a bar of fragrant soap and richly lathered her entire body. Every chill and ache gave way to her ministrations. By the time she had dried herself and donned the robe, she felt ready to begin her day again.

Chris found her favorite clingy cashmere sweater and soft khakis lying on the bed. While she showered, someone had obviously left them with the appropriate undergarments. She almost cried with gratitude. She slipped on the clothes and toweled her hair until it fell in dry silken strands. She threw her wet clothes into the converter, and they instantly transformed into energy. She felt satisfaction that this reminder of her ordeal was gone.

Chris knew she should find out about Andre's condition, but she couldn't face the obvious proof that her first mission was over. They could never stay on a planet with such a dangerous illness. Besides, wasn't she entitled to a last meal? She went to the main cabin and used the crew converter to make hot chicken soup and a restorative drink. Chris ate slowly and was puzzling over what to do about the crystal aliens when Mitch entered.

He headed directly to the converters and started distractedly pressing buttons. Carrying a plate of cheese sandwiches and tomato soup, he sat down across from her. She watched as he nibbled on one sandwich and then pushed the plate away with a frustrated sigh.

"Don't tell me the famous Drummond appetite has failed?" she teased, trying to soothe his obvious distress. He continued to look so awful that she decided to use the direct approach. "What's wrong?"

"Andre is no better. Every effort his body makes to fight off this infection merely intensifies his symptoms. The harder he fights, the quicker he's dying. Lena is trying all known antibiotics with no improvement. She's diving in a pool with no bottom. We don't know what the infection is, and we don't know what will fight it off." Mitch pulled his plate closer and started pushing his food around. Chris reached out a comforting hand, forcing him to look up.

"Look, I probably shouldn't say this—Andre caused this trouble. You were right to wonder why he'd followed me out to the waterfalls. He was trying to force me to have his children, right there on the ground, so he could make a claim to Citron's riches."

Mitch's face shifted as she spoke, showing first concern, then shock, and finally disgust. Chris had felt compelled to explain because she couldn't pretend a concern she didn't feel. Andre had turned into a monster she couldn't understand, let alone love.

"How could he do that," Mitch asked, "when human women have to consent to restore their fertility? They can't be forced to get pregnant." Mitch looked at her with furrowed brows, scrunched eyes, and a tongue at the corner of his mouth, like a confused clown. Despite the seriousness, Mitch had managed to lighten her mood.

"He found a way. Andre always finds a way when he wants something bad enough. He knew I would never consent, so he got the drug by convincing some foreign woman to pretend she needed it off planet. He injected me the first night. Then he got carried away because his plans were so close to fruition." Chris paused, touching the needle mark on her neck. Despite her best intentions, her eyes filled with tears. It was hard to believe the truth about her husband. She lowered her head and wiped away the tears.

"Because of the bruises, I decided to search his quarters. I needed to know what was really going on. I found the fertility drug and forged documents surrendering my captainship and requesting permanent assignment here." Chris swallowed hard on the last words, momentarily defeated by the articulation of Andre's heinous betrayal. She felt tears pouring down her face again. She forced herself to continue. "I also found a vial of red liquid. The spectrometer found several different narcotics. Some increase suggestibility, others trigger forgetfulness, and several force compliance—kind of like roofies with muscles."

This time when Chris looked at Mitch, his eyes were burning with a deadly hatred that scared her. She had gone too far to stop. She desperately needed to tell someone the full extent of the horror she'd been living, no matter the consequences.

"There've been times when I blacked out. I'd been drinking, so I dismissed my lapses. Now I wonder. I think Andre has used this drug to control me before. Maybe it goes as far back as his proposal of marriage. I didn't accept initially. I don't know how much he's done to distort my life. Now that he's sick, maybe I can halt his plans for me."

"What do you want to do?" Mitch asked.

"There's some evidence we need."

After returning their trays to the converters for reintegration, Mitch followed Chris back to Andre's quarters. She went to the carefully concealed niche in the master bath and removed the loose tiles. The cushioned box felt lighter. Quickly, she set it on the corner of the sink and lifted the lid. She breathed a sigh of relief when she saw the two vials nestled within. Mitch seized the red vial, raising it high to smash against the shower stall.

"No!" Chris shouted, catching his arm to stop him. "We need evidence that can't be ignored or explained away. There can't be any loopholes. Andre's people are very powerful." She took the vial and returned it to its contoured slot before lifting the cushioned insert out to show Mitch the documents underneath. She gave him the envelope and carried the box into the bedroom.

Chris left Mitch to read and went into Andre's office. She pulled out the desk chair and positioned it under the ceiling light. Then she climbed up and once more unscrewed the plastic cover. She lowered it gently, eager to see the familiar flash drive. It was gone. Chris swiped her hand around the inside of the cover in disbelief. Anxiously she examined the light fixture itself—nothing. Chris had to face the truth.

Andre had never believed her lame excuse and had moved the storage device. It was good news that he had underestimated her and left the bathroom box. But without the original drive, her copies of those documents could be challenged. Frantically she pulled out drawers and upset shelves, looking for any undiscovered evidence she could use against him. Everything was pristine. Thwarted, she had lifted her foot to kick the desk chair across the room when she remembered the hidden compartment.

Kneeling under the desk, she pressed the hidden trigger, and the small drawer popped out. She twisted around to peer into the receptacle. This too was empty. Andre must have assumed that she had found this secret cubby as well.

Frustrated, Chris crawled out and plopped into the desk chair. Slowly she scanned the room, turning in the chair, trying to imagine what Andre must have done after she'd left him here. Would he have destroyed the evidence?

It was Mitch who finally solved the puzzle. "What is that?" he said from the door, pointing at a rifled drawer lying on its side.

Turning it over, she saw silver duct tape sealing the bottom of the drawer. Savagely, she tore through the covering to find the flash drive and new envelopes.

"He isn't as smart as I thought." Chris smiled smugly, already congratulating herself.

"No, he's as sly as a fox." Mitch pointed at the red light indicating a hidden camera peeking through two beams in the ceiling. "Maybe he hoped you'd come back here. He would've recorded everything you did and found out what you knew of his plans. If he hadn't gotten sick, he would've made sure you didn't find anything really valuable."

"Now it's too late," Chris retorted.

Chris and Mitch carried the proof of Andre's guilt into the main lab. She grabbed Andre's personal computer too. Mitch wanted to test the vials again, and she wanted to examine Andre's personal correspondence. While she was scanning message logs, Lena stormed into the cabin, irritated and impatient.

"Chris, where've you been? You're our trained medical technician and the most qualified to treat your husband. Surely you plan to help Andre?"

Chris ducked her head guiltily. Lena's words had hit their mark. She had pushed Andre's situation to the back of her mind. Mitch shrank down lower in his chair and rolled behind the scanner to hinder Lena's view. Just then, the scanner beeped, indicating that the vial analysis was complete.

"I see you, Mitch. Don't think you can hide. What are you guys doing anyway?"

Mitch looked ready to blurt out everything. He never could keep a secret. Chris held up her hand, silently pleading with him to let her handle this. She knew there was no excuse big enough to let a crew member die. She was completely in the wrong, and Lena was right to be upset.

"You're absolutely right. We're coming right away."

Luckily Chris's words seemed to mollify Lena, and she hurried back to the isolation bay. After Chris had stashed the scanner results with the rest of their evidence in her suite, she and Mitch followed Lena. Chris needed his presence for moral support, despite the fact that he had little medical ability. They were the ones who knew the truth about Andre.

They had to put on facemasks, gloves, and full bodysuits before entering Andre's room. The two Quanta were monitoring the medical scanners, adding data to a projected graph. Andre lay on a cot in the center. He was covered with a light sheet that did nothing to hide his deteriorating condition. Uncomfortable, Chris found that she couldn't face Andre yet. She studied the progression of his illness using the displayed graphs that tracked his vital signs and medical test results over time.

"We have discovered an alien antigen," Siri explained. "Your human system seems to have no defense against it."

"His vital signs are running amok," piped in Mac, startling Chris. "His heart rate skyrockets and then falls critically low. We have him on pure oxygen to sustain lung function. Once his temperature got too high, so we had to pack him in ice to prevent brain damage."

"And now? Are your medicines helping him at all?" Chris asked, looking directly at Lena. Chris needed the antibiotics to work, or they would all be potential victims of Andre's malady.

"The pathogen levels are continuing to rise," Lena confessed miserably. "His blood is so thick it can barely circulate. His cells are dying. I can't seem to stop or even slow down what's going on."

"I'll do what I can," Chris promised. For the first time, she looked directly at the form that had been her husband. "Increase the lighting," she demanded harshly, shaken by his appearance. "Maybe I can find something." Mitch flicked on several lights, and the Quanta themselves began to glow, adding to the illumination. Andre groaned at the increased brilliance.

Chris was totally unprepared for the wreckage that was Andre. Any resemblance to a living human capable of recovery was almost gone. When Chris lifted the thin sheet, she saw that his legs and arms were like tree trunks: hard, black, and impenetrable, with no indication that there was still living tissue. His eyes, nose, and mouth were clogged with fine particles, requiring a long hose to allow him to continue to breathe.

First, Chris meticulously examined his skin for any clues about the infection. The only marks were the long jagged cuts on his arms caused by the little diamond flowers. The amethyst giants had held Andre, nothing more. Chris removed the long breathing tube and brushed away the white particles from his face. Maybe he could aid in his own recovery.

"Give me a stimulant," she ordered, looking at Ella.

"At once!" the smaller Quanta chirped. She zipped over to a table that held a row of syringes, drew a long one from the middle, and carried it back to Chris.

Chris took her time finding an artery that wasn't blocked. The carotid was her best chance. Then she slipped the needle as far up the blood vessel as she could and injected the narcotic.

After several long moments, Andre stirred. He opened his eyes and turned toward Chris. The pleading desperation she saw on this face was unmistakable. She suctioned his mouth, so he could speak.

He strained to form one word. "Please." Chris leaned in closer. She had to hear what he was trying so hard to say. "Please," he repeated, "let me die." Then he slowly closed his eyes, making no further attempt to breathe until his automatic reflexes forced a long shuddering inhalation.

Chris jumped when the pain sensor alarms blared. Whatever was happening to Andre was causing extreme suffering. The stimulant must have reawakened his brain's sensitivities. Siri shut off the alarms.

"This is monstrous. He's already half dead and in terrible agony. Have you administered pain medications?" she demanded bleakly.

"We had to sever his spine when his arms and legs died. The buildup of particles clogged all his arteries, and his extremities swelled before they turned black. The tissue is dead. We don't think he could survive several amputations," Siri answered dully. If a computer could be distressed, then Siri looked despondent. "He should not be able to feel anything. His mind must remember his body's suffering. As long as he is conscious, he will feel pain."

"He wants to die. He's already close. Even if he were to recover, he would be horribly handicapped with no way to live the life he has made for himself. I'm going to honor his wishes. I want everyone to leave," Chris demanded, already turning back to Andre, unaware that things were not as they seemed.

Lena shoved Chris hard and seized the discarded breathing tube. "No!" she screamed. "They always recover. We will not abandon him."

"What the hell?" Chris yelped. She crashed against the medical table and fought to keep her balance. "What are you doing?" Without waiting for a response, Chris lunged forward to stop her from reattaching the automatic breathing tube.

Joining the fray, Mitch grabbed Lena from behind, but the petite woman succeeded in pushing him away.

Chris realized, even in the confusion, that Lena should have been overwhelmed and subdued. She was nowhere near as strong as Mitch. "Siri?" she called urgently. Whatever new abilities Lena had wouldn't hold up against their computer friends. "Please help us."

Siri responded instantly, beeping at Ella. Both Quanta flanked Lena to restrain her in a grip as unyielding as metal could be. She continued to resist, her face twisted into a mask of terrible fury.

Cautiously, Chris approached this woman who had earned her friendship and grabbed her chin, shouting, "What's going on? Are you sick?"

"Of course not," Lena snapped. "Up till now, you've done nothing to help this poor soul, and now you want to let him die. You're unbelievable. Andre has his faults, as do we all. But he doesn't deserve death. Do you really hate him that much?"

The scorn in Lena's voice cut deep into Chris's heart. Stung by her words, she dropped Lena's chin. Her quiet friend would never speak like this. Something had gone terribly wrong.

"Are you really so blind and stupid?" Chris was unable to contain the resentment building at Lena's accusations. "Andre is completely paralyzed. His career is over. He'll eventually die, whether we keep him alive now or not. He would hate being helpless, and he's asked for death. Only someone immune to his suffering would insist on keeping him alive."

Then Chris remembered something important. Something Lena had said earlier had been all wrong. "Wait a minute. You said, 'They always recover.' Who always recovers? Andre's illness is new to us. There is no 'they.' There is no 'always.'"

Lena violently shoved the gentle Quanta away, catching them by surprise. They released their hold on her. Chris, Mitch, and Mac instantly jumped in, catching Lena off balance. The twins pulled her roughly back onto a medical table, and Chris anchored her to the cot with plastic restraints. The Quanta added metal shackles as a precaution against Lena's strange new strength. Lena howled in frustration and pulled against her bonds, creating horrible welts that started to bleed.

"You cowards! You can't do this! I can help him! You're all so afraid of me that you aren't listening," she howled at her alarmed friends. "Let me up before it's too late!"

"Lena, please calm down. You're hurting yourself!" Chris pointed at the blood dripping from her wrists. "Why are you acting so crazy?" Lena was obviously tainted. Now everyone was in grave trouble.

"He must live. Don't you understand? If you let him die, then all is lost," Lena howled, fear blazing from her eyes. She had stopped struggling when her blood made the table too slick for her to gain leverage.

"Lost? What is lost?" Chris's questions were both a challenge and a plea.

Lena started screaming like a crazed animal. She wouldn't answer any more questions. Chris had to sedate her. It took two large doses before she finally fell quiet. Chris was both relieved and scared.

Then Siri started a new medical chart. Ella connected Lena to the medical monitors and took several blood and tissue samples, taking advantage of her sedated state.

"We will contact you remotely when we get her test results." Siri gestured toward the door. "It will do no good for you to continue to risk your own health by staying here. We don't know if Lena has contracted the same antigen or something new."

But Chris refused to leave, no matter the danger. "No, I'll stay with my husband. He won't die alone. Set up a screen between the patients. Lena might stay quiet if she can't see him."

Mitch and Mac created a privacy screen using the captain's converter, which had been moved from Andre's cabin, and anchored the screen to the floor.

Chris motioned for them to leave. "Now you must go. It might be up to you guys to save us all." Even though Mitch looked like he wanted to object, he followed his brother out.

Chris turned back and caught slight movement, indicating that Andre was still hanging on to life. In the foreboding quiet, the sounds around her seemed magnified—the click of the medical bay door as the others left, the soft crackle of the medical monitors, the labored breathing from Lena, and the beeping of the busy Quanta.

Chris brushed Andre's ridiculously wavy hair away from his face. It was hard to imagine that this defenseless person could have been capable of so much harm. His eyes were closed, and his face childishly innocent. She tucked the sheet around his body to distract her emotions and occupy her mind.

Then, against all odds, his eyes opened. This time when his mouth moved, she could detect a faint whisper of breath. She bent over his lips, idiotically hoping for some words of regret. He said one thing.

"They are coming."

Then he let out a deep exhalation, and his body collapsed in on itself. Chris didn't move when the alarms on the medical scanners blasted through the quiet room. She made no attempt to revive the broken man. Andre was gone, and maybe now, he would find peace.

CHAPTER 13

SENTARAN FOREST TRAGEDIES—AMY

After throwing on his discarded clothes, including a Sentaran gun, Justin stood alongside Jared to block the front door. Amy had already given up on this avenue of escape. She smiled provocatively, calling on the assets that were Rose's favorite topic for teasing. It wasn't her fault she got along well with men.

Running to the camp had released her hair, and it fell around her shoulders. A few buttons on her hastily donned shirt had come open, and her breathing was labored. All in all, she must have presented quite a picture to these men who seemed to have one thing on their minds.

"I'm not against a little fun. We can find Nicole and have a party," she offered, arching her back and licking her lips. Jared raised an eyebrow suspiciously. He shook water out of his hair, illustrating his skepticism at her sudden friendliness. It had been a long shot, Amy thought ruefully. She was pleased at the bruises darkening his chin.

Unmasked, Amy changed tactics. She rifled through a pile of discarded garments, looking for any of Talia's survey uniforms.

"Don't you think you should get dressed? You have guests now," Amy chided. She needed to get Talia into decent clothes. Flimsy chiffon would become tatters if they were forced to run. She was relieved to find the outfit Talia had been wearing earlier. "Talia, I don't think your family would understand entertaining in that." Amy pointed at the gaping robe, which Talia instantly closed, flushing with embarrassment.

"What? Of course…clothes," she agreed.

"But you look so pretty," Justin objected with an indulgent sweetness that made Amy's teeth ache. "Honey, I brought that robe special, and it fits you magnificently. You don't need to change. It's already very late."

Talia looked down at her outfit, puzzled, and then over at Amy.

"Yes, it's pretty," Amy agreed. "We just don't wear this type of clothing when we have company. Talia was raised better than that."

The reference to her upbringing had the desired effect, and Talia touched the outfit nervously. The strange slackness in her face had been replaced with an expression of distress. This time she would remember. Deftly avoiding Jared's grab for her arm, Amy rushed ahead of Talia into the bathroom.

As soon as the door closed, she started searching for some way out. The window, the only exit from the tiny room, was just too small. Talia dressed slowly, looking defeated. She wrestled her soft sleek hair into a plain tight bun. She looked like a drab school teacher with large, tragic eyes. It hurt Amy's heart to see the small woman so wounded by these strangers. Amy wrapped her arm around Talia's shoulders and pulled her close as they exited the room.

A commotion outside interrupted the taut tableau escalating inside. Jeff entered with Nicole draped seductively on his arm. Her hair was disheveled and her clothes untidy. Jeff appeared to have gotten as "lucky" as Justin. Nicole pouted unhappily at Amy.

"Here we are, Commander. What's so damn bloody important?" Jeff demanded. Jared scowled at the man's insolence.

"Now, baby, don't be like that," gushed Nicole. "Jared must have a really good reason to call us here. You know how accommodating he is." Nicole giggled in a silly nonsensical manner that grated across Amy's nerves. If ever they got out of here…

Jared smiled tolerantly.

Jeff smoothed Nicole's hair into some semblance of order. "Baby, you need to let me handle this. We have rules that Jared is ignoring." He glanced at Jared, his mouth a thin disapproving line.

"Rules?" Nicole asked, pulling away awkwardly. She cocked her head at Jeff and then shrugged her shoulders. "Whatever you say, baby." She leaned in and gave Jeff a sloppy kiss.

Amy had to find some way to bring Nicole to her senses. She was usually sensible. "Nicole, are you all right?" She leaned forward, her hand extended in concern.

Nicole jerked away as if she was facing a cobra. "You just keep back. I know what you're doing," she accused.

"Sweets, let's not spill the beans," Jeff urged.

Amy had always found Nicole a bit physically intimidating. But compared to Jeff's huge frame, she seemed almost diminutive. Amy watched as Nicole blushed and nestled into Jeff's arm. It took her a moment to realize that Nicole liked having a man take charge. That goofy smile was Nicole being happy.

Jeff faced Jared. "You know we have only a few days left, and you've failed miserably. Amy continues to find you unacceptable."

"Have you lost your mind?" Jared barked. "She's listening! Do you want to be sanctioned? Stop talking out loud."

Amy's stomach twisted at the implication of Jeff's words. Why hadn't she seen Jared's plans for her? Why hadn't she recognized what was happening to her friends? Why hadn't she noticed that they were all in terrible danger? Why hadn't she understood that Nicole might turn against her? Amy realized that the engineer was staring at her with undisguised animosity.

The three men moved away from the human women and huddled together, silently gesturing. Then Justin was holding Jared's right arm and Jeff's left arm, forcing them face-to-face. He was obviously trying to make peace.

"All this must be so taxing for you," Amy said, glaring at Nicole. She had used the code word for *trouble*.

With her eyes, Amy pleaded for some cooperation. Talia nodded, but Nicole stared at the floor stubbornly. She pulled Nicole closer and shook her reproachfully. Using hand gestures, she indicated that she wanted the three of them to flee out the nearby window. Nicole shook her head mutinously. Luckily, the men had turned away and were completely engrossed in their argument, unaware of her activities.

In hindsight, Amy realized that Justin and Jeff must have used the past three days to soften Nicole and Talia. The peaceful forest and fragrant flowers had obviously created the perfect environment for romance. She had foolishly believed that the women would heed Rose's warning. Now she would have to convince Nicole to cooperate, with a brutality that would allow for no further hesitation.

Amy pressed her mouth to Nicole's ear and whispered abrasively, "If you don't cooperate, you'll be returned to Earth disgraced. Is Jeff worth the humiliation of being thrown out of the space program and possibly into prison?"

Nicole gasped at the viciousness of Amy's threat and nodded bitterly. The three women edged toward the large window. Amy silently unlatched it, climbed out, and pulled Talia and Nicole out behind her. Nicole banged the window casing shut, alerting the arguing men to their escape. The Sentarans dashed out the front door in an attempt to cut off the fleeing women.

Amy was a skilled runner, so she found the need for speed exhilarating. Her comrades, on the other hand, were soon out of breath and began falling farther behind. Amy had two choices.

She could slow down to help her friends or speed up and get to their ship, where she might find a way to incapacitate their guards. Even as Amy silently willed the other two women to run faster, she heard them fall to the ground. Jeff and Justin shouted their victory. Amy sensed someone coming up behind her, and she guessed it was Jared. He would never willingly let her escape him again. With her heart pounding loudly in her ears, adrenaline gave her the energy to increase the distance between them, temporarily.

Amy continued running despite her team's cries for help. She remotely triggered the cruiser door while still several feet away. Jared came close enough to knock her foot off stride. She kept herself from slowing by tumbling forward until she could regain her feet, and fear motivated her to escape his hasty grip on her leg. By some miracle, she made it through the door and triggered the locking mechanism seconds before he reached their ship. Amy sank down on the couch, gasping for breath, giving thanks for her narrow escape.

The weapons locker was in the rear, and Amy could hear Jared shouting threats as she made her way back. She lowered the window shades as she moved in order to conceal her activities. She threw open the locker doors with the glee of one who finally has a fighting chance. After scanning the top shelves, she selected a military-grade Taser and two custom-designed knives, one for her sleeve and one for her shoe.

The Quanta had equipped both Earth police and space survey teams with weapons designed to incapacitate, not kill. Ironically, this type of weapon proved more effective. A police officer could subdue a fleeing criminal without fear of killing him or innocent bystanders. One strategic zap rendered anyone instantly cooperative. Amy could use the Taser without violating alliance law or putting herself at the mercy of the Sentaran legal system. If they were bound, the hidden knives could quickly release her friends.

Amy changed into clothes better suited for hiding and fighting. Ninja-style clothing was certainly dramatic, but it was also effective. She could easily hide weapons in the dark folds, and when lying flat, she would resemble a forgettable shadow. Mimicking shadows was the garment's most valuable asset.

Night was descending on the small clearing of cabins, so Amy added night goggles equipped with heat-sensitive video and audio-enhancing ear inserts. On a hunch, she included two capped syringes filled with a drug that would quickly render anyone, including the Sentarans, unconscious. These, she hid in her bra, where they were high enough to retrieve quickly but hidden from a casual search. Amy's training required that she prepare for the unexpected.

Finally, using meditative techniques, she forced her mind to quiet. After breathing deeply for several minutes, she felt her turbulent thoughts settle. She knew her mind could betray her more effectively than any Sentaran offensive tactic. Any doubt or fear could render her indecisive in a moment that required total focus. She went one step further by filling her mind with camouflaging images. Someone searching for her telepathically would sense a quiet bubbling stream.

Ready at last, Amy moved to a hidden feature of their small ship. In the back, under the tail, was an invisible hatch. The seams were cleverly hidden in an elaborate decal. She would be able to exit the ship with some degree of wing cover.

During her preparations, Amy had ignored the shouted threats. Now she listened to determine the location of the Sentarans and the condition of her team.

"We have your friends totally in our control," came from outside. Amy could hear the smile in Jared's voice. Even the word *control* had a self-satisfied emphasis. "Do you want to leave them at our mercy, vulnerable to any tortures we might invent? Come out now, or we will kill them, one at a time, slowly."

Amy listened to their threats impatiently. Did they think she was a complete fool? She wouldn't negotiate with men who couldn't be trusted. They had lied to her people from the first moment they'd landed. Surrendering to them would leave all three women open to "any tortures they might invent." Their only hope rested with her ability to subdue the Sentarans long enough to get her team back to the BESS.

Amy peeked around the corner of the window shade nearest the voices to study the area around their ship. Jared was at the door, and Justin and Jeff were standing by Talia and Nicole, who were tied to a tree. She was relieved to discover that the escape hatch was out of their line of sight.

Returning to the back of the ship, she pulled the rug back and opened the hatch. Amy lowered herself through the opening, knowing she would have to drop onto a rocky incline. Apparently, Jared had deliberately directed her to park on an unstable gravel hillock. As soon as she landed, the stones slipped and carried her a few feet down the hill. She tensed, waiting for the clamoring rocks to trigger some reaction. She could hear Jared and Justin shouting threats—varying from sure death to some quite imaginative tortures—which must have masked her clumsy exit, because the tone and frequency of the threats remained unchanged. She circled away from the ship and came in from behind. The three men had drawn together, facing the cruiser, leaving the two bound women unattended several feet away.

Amy hid behind a pile of rocks near the women. She took out Jared first because he was the greatest risk to her personally. The Taser shot a stream of electricity that hit him squarely in the chest. Shaking uncontrollably, he fell onto his back. In the resulting confusion, she hastily aimed and fired at Justin. It was a sloppy shot, but he did fall. Regrettably, Amy could not rely on Justin remaining unconscious.

Then the impossible happened. Nicole shouted a warning. "She's here, baby." Nicole kicked out with her foot toward Amy's crouching figure.

Jeff jumped behind a large tree and looked in the direction Nicole had pointed. "We must capture her before she ruins our plans," he warned urgently.

"There," said Talia, "behind those white rocks."

"I see her," he acknowledged.

Amy froze, alarmed at such an appalling betrayal. Despite Nicole's obvious preference for Jeff and Talia's compromised position, Amy had refused to believe that they would deliberately eliminate any chance of returning to their home planet. Even as she was struggling to comprehend that Nicole and Talia were traitors, Jeff dashed into the forest and disappeared from sight.

Amy rose from her useless hiding place and despondently approached the two fallen men, wondering why she didn't just escape while she still could. She wanted to be sure Jared and Justin were harmless before she decided what to do about Talia and Nicole. Despite her inner alarms, she bent over the men to confirm their helplessness. Exploiting her vulnerability, Jeff burst from a cluster of trees and crashed violently into her.

Amy slammed down hard and hit her temple against a rock. Pain exploded in her head, and she felt blood trickling down her cheek. She rolled a few feet away, moaning. Dizzy, she pulled her gun out of its holster, giving Jeff precious seconds to regain his footing. As she aimed the Taser, he jumped forward, seized the stock of the weapon, and forced it back, pressing her finger down on the trigger. The Taser shot out a steady stream of power that inched closer to her head. She realized he was too strong to stop, and she would soon be hit by the same Taser that had rendered his friends unconscious.

So Amy switched to a tactic that was in her favor, balance and flexibility. As she felt the heat of the electric beam graze her hair, she went limp and fell back. Jeff was exerting too much force to stop. He fell heavily and lost his grip on the Taser, allowing Amy to grab it. She jumped up onto her feet and threw the weapon in a high arc out into the forest, eliminating it as a threat. She would never retain control of it. Jeff had regained his feet and now, angrily, reached to haul her into his arms.

Amy turned away and drew out her last weapon. Holding the syringe under her crossed arms, she turned back and leaned against Jeff's shoulder. Using her body as cover, she slipped the needle into his arm and, with a satisfied grin, pushed the plunger down. Jeff yelped with pain and pushed Amy away, revealing the needle, which still hung from his arm. He reached down and pulled it free with a grunt of disgust. Fortunately for Amy, the toxin was quick. Jeff had time to throw her down onto the ground and kick her once, furiously, before he fell over sideways.

Now that Jeff was incapacitated, Amy had time to check her own condition. A sharp pain stabbed her side when she struggled to her feet. She felt sticky blood on one side of her face. When she tried to take a step, her head spun, and she stumbled. She was afraid that Jeff's last kick had broken ribs. Desperately, she forced herself to take several more steps, fighting nausea the entire way. Amy knew she had to find sanctuary. She was too injured to fight off anyone else.

But Amy hadn't counted on Talia and Nicole. Tying them to the tree had been a hoax to draw her out. Before she had time to register what was happening, her former colleagues each grabbed an arm, hauled her back against the tree, and tied her securely. Amy stifled a cry of pain. She really should have left when she had the chance.

Talia insisted on collecting medical supplies from the cruiser, and Nicole stayed to guard Amy. She glared at the bound woman with obvious hostility.

"Why are you such a thorn in my paw?" Nicole snarled, exasperated. "Why couldn't you just accept that we've made up our own minds to stay on Sentara and leave? You are such a fool."

Amy was beginning to agree.

"You and Rose think you know everything," Nicole complained. "You think you have the right to tell us what to do. You can't possibly understand the truth. Sentara is in trouble, and we can help them if we stay here. Besides, Jeff loves me."

"After what you've done, you have no other alternative. But why trap Talia as well? You know she's devoted to her family and would never willingly agree to cut all ties to Earth. Rose is right. They're messing with your mind. You're the fool." Amy's outrage bubbled up to the surface like oil in vinegar.

"Justin likes Talia, and he's very handsome. Given that he's one of Cragon's elite guards, she will live in the lap of luxury and be adored by all. She could never hope to catch such a man on Earth. But how can you understand what it's like to live on crumbs. You and Rose have it all: command positions, any man, and endless opportunities. You'll eventually get your own ship. Where will Talia and I be ten years? Just another minion in a group of minions. On this planet, we'll have attention and endless opportunities. Here, we can have your kind of life."

Amy twisted her wrists, concealed behind her back, testing her restraints. Another stronger, deeper throb replaced the earlier sharp pain. Frustration filled her eyes with tears. Amy realized the futility of trying to convince Nicole of anything. She had totally missed the depth of Nicole's jealousy and the intensity of her need to be recognized. Nicole would stay here now no matter what happened next. In three days, with limited information, Nicole had made a permanent decision. Maybe Talia was not so convinced.

"No clever comeback? No witty argument or insightful wisdom? No attempt to show me the error of my ways?" Nicole mocked.

"You've decided what you believe, whether it's the truth or not. I can see a lost cause when it stands in front of me," Amy hissed derisively. She searched for some way to minimize whatever damage was to come.

When Talia approached her with first-aid supplies, Amy moaned loudly. She had genuinely liked the shy Indian girl. She hoped there was some remnant of their friendship left to reach.

"I think I'm hurt bad, Little English," Amy cried. The nickname came from the accent Talia still carried from Cambridge University. "I think Jeff broke my ribs, and I might be bleeding internally." She slid down the tree as far as her restraints would allow.

Talia rushed forward and dropped her supplies beside the tree. She loosened the restraints so Amy could sit comfortably and pulled out a Quanta handheld scanner to check her status.

"Why waste your time?" Nicole growled. "She's trouble, and injuries will keep a muzzle on her."

Talia gave Nicole a look of disgust and threw three syringes at her.

"These will wake them up," she said, nodding at the Sentarans. Then she turned back to Amy. "Lie still, so I can get a clean reading."

Amy complied good-naturedly. Talia lifted Amy's shirt to reveal an ugly black bruise that covered her entire stomach. She slowly moved the five-inch-square medical diagnostic screen across Amy's body and then nodded with relief.

"You'll be happy to learn that you're wrong. Nothing is broken," Talia said. "There's only a crack on one rib, but your internal organs have been traumatized. If you stay quiet, you should avoid excess pain."

Amy sniffed at the absurdity of Talia's recommendation. She doubted if Jared would allow her to stay quiet. He now had her helpless and available.

Meanwhile, Nicole kneeled beside the fallen men and injected the stimulants. Jared and Justin recovered slowly. Jeff was a lost cause. Amy had used a chemical that was too strong to counteract, and they would have to wait until it wore off. Shortly, Jared and Justin were able to carry Jeff's body back inside the main cabin.

Talia gave Amy a strong pain killer and wrapped her ribs. Despite everything, she was a kind soul and would not leave Amy to suffer, no matter the situation. Amy felt her strength returning. She could now move, relatively pain-free.

"I don't know how much I can help you," Talia whispered. "I'll treat your injuries until they come back."

"Hey, what are you doing?" Nicole called suspiciously. "We might need those medicines later."

"She is one of us!" Talia snapped. "I haven't forgotten that, even if you have. I won't leave her to the torment of untreated wounds!"

"Please be reasonable. Look at what you're doing. Do you really want to sacrifice everything for these strangers?" Amy asked again, desperately. Talia shifted uncomfortably. Neither woman responded to her pleas.

Jared slammed open the main cabin door and charged back to the women. Roughly, he cut Amy free, obviously intent on finally achieving his goal.

"Now we'll see who has the last laugh," he challenged smugly.

The two men dragged Amy toward the main lodge. In desperation, she bit Jared's hand cruelly, forcing him to loosen his hold on her arm. She wrenched her hand free and scratched his cheek, leaving deep raw gouges. He howled in protest. Simultaneously, she kicked Justin so violently he almost broke her wrist in retaliation. Jared recovered her arm and twisted it behind her back in a hold that would allow no further movement.

Once inside the main structure, Jared flung her down on the conference table. The two men tied her spread-eagle, with a rope around her waist for good measure. Talia and Nicole watched from the front door, looks of concern growing on their faces.

Amy used every ounce of whatever psi talent she might have acquired to influence Talia. She was the weaker of the two, and Amy thought they had a bond. She imagined gatherings they had enjoyed on the *Aries* and their shared confidences. She couldn't believe that Talia would just stand by and let these men abuse her.

Talia started blinking rapidly and then swayed and shook her head. She looked up in time to see Jared take a pair of scissors to Amy's top.

"What the hell are you doing?" she asked, shocked.

It seemed obvious to Amy. This was what their consorts had been trying to achieve all along.

"We're going to show Amy the benefits of cooperating with us." Jared winked at Justin.

Amy slowly closed her eyes and sent her consciousness to a secret place of safety. She would protect her soul. She felt a cool breeze brush across her now exposed skin. One of the men, probably Jared, climbed onto the table. Amy's eyes flew open in surprise at Talia's sudden angry outburst.

"Stop! I will not stand by and let you rape her." Apparently, Talia had finally had enough.

The men's ability to control her mind had, obviously, ended when she was faced with this ultimate atrocity. Talia snatched the gun that Justin had left on the coffee table. Her hands were shaking as she motioned for Jared to get off Amy.

Then Amy heard a sound that would haunt her for the rest of her life—the loud report of a deadly shot. Nicole's scream, a heart-wrenching sound, echoed through the room. Amy watched as Talia staggered and the gun she was holding clattered to the floor. Looking confused, she patted her chest. When she pulled her hands away, they were covered in blood. She fell to her knees, struggling for breath as her life's blood leaked away. She reached out, imploring Nicole for help, and collapsed forward.

Helplessly, Amy watched the terrible tableau play itself out. Jared was still kneeling above her holding a shaking gun, as he stared at Talia's prone body. Nicole knelt by her friend, her expression shocked and bewildered. She shook Talia's shoulder, seemingly unaware of the blood soaking into her clothing.

"It's OK, Talia. Get up now," Nicole pleaded foolishly.

Amy could only imagine what Nicole thought was happening. Justin knelt by Nicole, obviously distressed and sympathetic. When he touched her arm tentatively, Nicole's paralysis shattered. She leaped, with insane fury, to the gun Talia had dropped, shoved it into Justin's face, and shot his brains out before anyone could react.

Amy glanced worriedly up at Jared. He climbed off her, looking down at his shaking pistol in horrified disbelief. He shifted his gaze to the widening pool of blood spreading around their two murdered comrades. Nicole made no move to defend herself. She just stared at Jared, her eyes begging for his bullet. Amy expected that Jared would shoot Nicole and then her.

But Jared was as affected as Nicole. He dropped his gun, revulsion filling his eyes.

"My God," he muttered, his voice shaking. "I didn't mean…I thought to…We abhor killing. She would've been cherished. We honor all living beings, especially the life givers. If only…," he babbled.

Then, lapsing into an eerie silence, he pocketed his gun and left the cabin, quietly closing the door behind him. After several moments, Amy heard a single shot out in the forest. Sentaran justice seemed to have few options.

Amy struggled to break her restraints, unsuccessfully. "Nicole, please, you must help me before anyone comes."

Nicole would not or could not move. She took Talia's head and cradled it in her lap, singing a child's lullaby over and over.

Wake, little one, don't leave me grieving,
Wake, little one, now we must be leaving.
Our adventure is just beginning,

New trails wait for exploring.
Come chase the clues with me,
We'll see what the truth could be.
Wake, little one, our time has come today,
Wake, little one, before hope fades away.

In the end, Amy knew she was trapped. All she could do was hope that Nicole would regain her senses before someone else arrived.

Ari finally showed up to find the grisly scene unchanged. Quickly he released Amy. After she'd stashed appropriate clothing in the bathroom, she dragged an unresisting Nicole to the same room. By the time they reached it, both of them were covered in blood. She helped the shocked woman shower and dress and then followed suit, leaving Nicole sitting motionless on the floor. They emerged from the bathroom to find the bodies gone and Ari cleaning away the last traces of blood.

When they were ready to leave, Amy found Nicole leaning against the cruiser, tears streaming down her cheeks. She cried with a terrible silence that seemed more profound for the absence of sound.

CHAPTER 14

TREASURY SECURITY—BETH

With questions muddying her mind, Beth ran after Goren and entered a dark maintenance passageway. The air was stale and the floor rough-hewn rock. Twice she stumbled over a lip of stone. She knew she should slow down but was determined not to lose track of the Guardian. Axel, lagging farther behind, created a cloud of swirling dirt, which, he kept complaining, clogged his air jets.

Goren was impossibly fast and disappeared ahead. Wall lights emitted enough illumination that she could catch sight of him periodically. Beth judged she was stumbling through natural subterranean tunnels inside the Treasury. Eventually they reached a rustic elevator where Goren waited impatiently. As they descended deeper into the planet, the vehicle's violent movement forced Beth to brace herself against a white metal railing. Axel unceremoniously wedged himself between her shoulder and the wall, holding onto her with two appendages. When the doors opened again, Goren dashed out without a word. An unadorned door on the right had been left open.

Beth followed, hesitating at the threshold. The layout of the room was similar to the Earth exhibit's central directory, except here were thousands upon thousands of screens. Hallways filled with monitors fanned out from this central hub. The images displayed Treasury exhibits one by one. This must be the security system that protected the entire Treasury.

A monitor showing Sarah and Thomas caught Beth's attention. They were sitting on the floor across from each other, their legs entangled. Several artifacts lay scattered about. They were discussing applications of one unusual flying apparatus. As he reached for another artifact, Tom leaned forward and stroked Sarah's hair. Their love was obvious to anyone.

Cautiously Beth entered the room, Axel right on her heels. She moved to a bank of windows across from the entrance, out of the way of Goren and attendants dressed in the same manner as the guides who took Connor and Tom and Sarah earlier. She had a view of a vast underground garden consisting of an elaborate maze, much like the ones she had seen on old English estates. Huge lights splashed the cavern with illumination conductive to photosynthesis. The window slightly magnified, as well as polarized, the landscape beyond. Beth found comfort standing here. Something was very wrong in the Treasury, and she longed to ask what it was.

The familiar attendant Beth had seen leave with Connor stood mutely by the largest monitor. She groaned under her breath. She had hoped that her team had not been the cause of the alarms. It was, of course, a foolish hope. Without a word, the attendant turned several dials that shifted the image to Connor's heavy gravity exhibit.

Axel floated over to Connor's guide and buzzed around her like an errant bee. His lights flashed curiously, and he plucked at her robe. Beth watched Axel, perplexity turning to alarm. What in thunder was he doing? Then, the Quanta bumped against the attendant—hard. Surprisingly, the guide ignored Axel, seemingly unaffected by his efforts. She was definitely one strong individual.

Connor's face on the main monitor distracted Beth. To her chagrin, she saw him pocketing several items: a gold ring, a small black device that became invisible as she watched, and several small shapes shrouded in a silk square.

"Perfect," she groaned softly as he ran off the screen. Beth had gambled on Connor's merits. Sadly, she had lost.

Goren turned from the screen and gave Beth a reproachful stare. "I thought your team was trustworthy." He waved at the frozen screen that still showed Connor's foot. "It would appear they are not."

Beth raised an eyebrow, marshaling her fears under the tight reins of discipline. "This is our first mission," she explained. "All survey personnel are screened exhaustively for any criminal tendencies. I imagine he thinks he's helping our cause without hurting yours. He must also think he is unobserved. Obviously he's wrong." Beth looked at Goren apologetically. "I had hoped that you might be aware of our fallibilities."

Beth jumped when Mark Logan's voice barked from her implanted communication node. "Calling Captain Griffin. Beth, please respond." Logan's distress was apparent.

Beth arched a brow at Goren, silently asking for permission to answer. He nodded. "Go ahead."

"This is Beth, Mark." She lifted her arm to access a small video-screen wristband device. A tiny image of her very worried second in command came into view. "Has Connor come back?"

"Yes! The fool used some alien device to bring him here and tried to take off with the *Aries*," Mark retorted. "We were lucky he was unable to bypass command authorization. I almost threw him out the ship's hatch for mutiny. Instead, I locked him in his cabin before trying to contact you."

"We have a situation. Is Connor still there?" Beth asked suspiciously. Connor had an uncanny ability to get out of even locked rooms.

Mark turned away from Beth to adjust controls offscreen. "What the hell? Why that little pipsqueak! When I get my hands on him—" Sounding a bit sheepish, he finally turned back to Beth. "He's gone to his workshop downstairs. He seems to be dismantling something."

The image of Connor in the workshop appeared on a monitor.

"He needs to return to the planet immediately. He won't come willingly. You'll have to force him."

"Force him?" Mark's deep voice conveyed his distaste at the necessity for such measures.

"That is unnecessary," Goren interrupted, coming into Mark's view.

Mark yelped in surprise.

Goren touched a button on a nearby panel, and a bright green glow filled Connor's workshop before flashing near Beth. As the light dimmed, Connor, who had obviously been sitting, fell to the floor in front of her. The devices he had taken from the Treasury materialized on a desk next to the window. The gold ring lay on its side, the pile of objects was shrouded, and the small black probe was in pieces.

"You are a continuing amazement," Beth complained. "How could you be so dense as to believe you could ever get away with this, let alone your lack of consideration for the ethical standards involved."

Connor picked himself up. "It seemed the right thing to do," he justified.

"In what universe?"

Triangular bars of white light linked into a cage around Connor. The lattice buzzed suspiciously. When he touched a bar, an intense electric charge threw him to the floor. Connor made several more attempts to escape, despite the penalty, until the electrical shock became so violent that he didn't immediately recover. His disheveled hair stood on end, and his hands were covered with red welts.

Through sheer stubbornness, Connor forced himself back to his feet. He radiated self-righteousness as he looked accusingly at Goren.

"I don't regret taking inventions that will help Earth," Connor bragged. He turned to Beth. "They're magnificent. The gold ring extends a shield around the wearer that protects against extreme conditions and weapons. Within a controlled atmosphere, we could go underwater or into space.

"The holographic scanning probe that turns invisible and is now dismantled would be a priceless find for any survey company. It would allow us to study planets surrounded by poisonous atmospheres, which might have hidden secrets that could help us. The wearer could travel along with the survey probe but without any of the associated dangers.

"The stones have untapped potential. Once uncovered, they have a hypnotic effect on any observer, and there's a possibility of using them as an energy source. "

Connor pointed his finger at Goren. "Your rules help no one. They just protect your secrets."

"The rules protect everyone, including you!" Goren contradicted.

Connor must have feared that he was fast running out of time because his voice rose to a shout, drowning out Goren's next words. "The Treasury doesn't just sit on this world; it *is* this world. The entire planet holds rooms for displays and exhibits. I accessed a computer directory near the heavy planet exhibit that showed schematics for this entire world." Connor couldn't hide the awe that colored his next words. "The Guardians built this giant spaceship and hid it in plain sight as a planet."

Goren growled unhappily.

"These people are an advanced race able to build wonders," Connor continued. "Don't you realize they deliberately put me in a position to steal artifacts?"

Beth's brow wrinkled at this possibility. She had never considered that he had been drawn into making this mistake. She couldn't imagine why Goren would stoop to such tactics.

"I'm not sorry for trying to help my people advance our technology. So, do your worst!" Connor had lost none of his arrogance or bravado. He would follow his own priorities no matter what it cost the rest of them.

Axel interrupted this tense drama and threatened their precarious position with what Beth could only describe as actions designed to get them all blasted into oblivion. He was still totally focused on Connor's odd guide. Using his strongest air jets, he plowed into the attendant but only managed to throw off the long robe the attendant was wearing. Underneath were a metal frame, transparent shell, and the mechanical moving parts of an android.

Astonished, Beth sucked in her breath. She had assumed the attendants to be Guardians, like Goren.

Goren looked confounded at Axel's sudden action. Then he laughed, his silly full-body laugh, tears collecting in his eyes. "You only had to ask," he sputtered.

With surprising agility, the machine pulled the robe back around its body very like a shy woman. Then in a creaky voice it repeated, "You only had to ask."

"Are you conscious? Self-aware?" Axel asked, circling the slight android with growing excitement. It dawned on Beth that this species, if it were a species, might be like Axel himself: an intelligent computer.

"Self-aware?" the attendant repeated. Its dry, wafting voice revealed an endearing naïveté.

"I am sorry, friend." Goren placed a sympathetic hand on Axel's casing. "Our guides were a present from a grateful planet being overrun. They are sentient after a fashion, but they don't have the computing power of Quanta. They protect us like loyal dogs."

"Maybe," Axel answered strangely.

Axel helped the attendant adjust her robes, so they once more cascaded in graceful folds. Then he began talking to her. At least, Beth guessed that was what he was doing. He made peculiar sounds like cards shuffling, and his lights repeated complex patterns over and over, until the little attendant started mimicking his strange behavior. Goren studied the pair openmouthed.

When the guide spoke again, her voice was soft and delicately melodic. "I see," she said and abruptly left the group through a hidden panel. Another guide appeared to replace her and started echoing Axel's patterns of sound and light.

"What did you do? What are they doing?" Goren interrupted, sounding alarmed as more androids formed a line behind the first.

"You have nothing to fear," Axel reassured him. "I have triggered dormant programming. All your attendants were originally designed to operate at a higher level. Maybe their creators didn't think you needed them to operate at full capacity. They will now."

"Tell me that I don't have a computer rebellion on my hands," Goren implored.

"No, to work for you is their greatest wish, despite my campaigning for their freedom. They view your Treasury as a great mission and your race as most admirable. You collect and protect all that makes any life precious and interesting."

Goren didn't answer. Instead he tilted his head in an odd manner.

Beth was becoming too anxious to remain quiet. "So what happens to us?"

Goren's eyes came back into focus on Beth and then Connor. "Go get the other two visitors," he directed one of the remaining attendants.

While they waited, Axel reprogrammed all the attendants that came forward. Soon the entire room was humming with increased energy. The improved guides showed a new respect and warmth for each other, even swinging partners into an improvised dance. With greater intelligence came greater intimacy.

Connor was pacing his prison like a caged lion. "What are you going to do?" he snarled at Goren.

"That depends on Beth," Goren answered cryptically.

Beth was watching the monitor that showed Tom and Sarah whispering playfully and tussling over the directory controls. Finally, the couple raced into another section of the avian exhibit and started examining several sets of artificial wings. Thomas struggled into a promising prototype, despite Sarah's shaking head. They were innocently unaware that everything had become a terrible mess.

When Goren's attendant entered with the Gardners' own attendant, they spun toward the sliding door guiltily.

"We're just trying this out. Is that allowed?" Sarah asked, a little late, since it was evident that Thomas was ready to attempt a flight.

"Of course," their original attendant reassured them lightly. "Goren has sent a message," she said and left them alone with the new attendant.

"Is it time to go?" Beth could just make out Sarah's question over Connor's bluster.

"Your captain needs to speak with you," the attendant said gently. "She is with Goren and Connor in the main control room. Would you follow me?" It was not the type of conversation one would expect from a captor and her prisoners. Beth had felt renewed hope, until Goren's cryptic remark chilled her bones.

"What," she asked cautiously, "depends on me?" She had already accepted that they would be subject to Treasury justice.

"I gave your team permission to visit the Treasury on your endorsement," he said, assuming an offended posture, but there was something feigned in his frowning lips and disappointed eyes.

"What are you talking about? I was never asked for any endorsement," Beth argued, feeling unfairly accused. "If you'd questioned me, I would've warned you about Connor, and he could have been sent back to the ship. Instead, when we stepped onto your river path, your scanners rendered us unconscious." She was still resentful about that outrageous reception. "It's blatantly apparent that you let us visit based on some Guardian agenda."

Goren smiled and changed his approach. "You're right, of course. But we should deal with Connor first."

As if on cue, Sarah and Tom burst in, chattering excitedly. Their guide obviously hadn't prepared them for Connor's new status as prisoner or their new status as criminals by association. When Sarah caught sight of Connor, she lapsed into confused silence. Thomas had already gone still.

Goren gestured at Connor's prison. "Your comrade has foolishly stolen items from an exhibit, resulting in your race's expulsion from this facility, indefinitely. Transport these three back to their ship," Goren ordered, indicating the couple and Axel.

Sarah and Tom looked from Goren to Connor, alarm morphing into outrage.

"Are you insane or just too self-centered to see beyond your own nose?" Tom jeered, jabbing his finger at Connor. "This was a once-in-a-lifetime opportunity, which you have totally exterminated."

"You have no idea how priceless those artifacts are," Connor argued, unexpectedly advocating for their support. "We would've been free to explore any type of planet without fear of a toxic atmosphere or alien infection. I found one probe that permitted complete sensory cohesion. You could've felt, seen, and experienced any environment as if you were really there. This one"—Connor nodded at Goren—"wants to keep all his treasures locked up where they can't do any good."

Despite her resolve, Beth could see his side. She was finding it harder and harder to support Goren's position. What harm could come from sharing their technology anyway?

Goren snorted. "You young races are like children in a candy store. You eat and eat until you lie sick on the floor, groaning and asking why your parents didn't save you. The probe you stole could expose your race to life-forms that don't find toxic environments lethal. What would you do if that probe brought back some new lethal virus that was undetectable and one hundred percent fatal? Could you find an antidote in time? It's the very process of inventing a probe that can lead to overcoming intimidating levels of toxins that might in turn lead the creator's race to the antidote for my hypothetical lethal virus."

"Enough!" Beth glared at Connor. They were already in enough trouble without arguing with the judge, jury, and executioner. "You acted selfishly and stupidly. We didn't discover these relics, and we don't have some God-given right to take them. Tom, Sarah, go back to the ship. I'll join you shortly. It seems that Goren wants something in exchange for leniency."

"Be careful. What he wants may cost more than you think," Sarah whispered when she hugged Beth before the attendants led them away. Goren gestured for the remaining androids to leave.

After everyone had gone, Beth glanced at Connor, hoping to see a contrite crew member. He was smirking, his arms crossed. Penalizing Connor was growing more appealing. Maybe Goren should squash him like the pesky bug he was.

"You need something from Beth," Connor said haughtily. "Well, you have many things we need too. Maybe we can deal."

Connor might have looked menacing, except that he had to stand away from the walls of his cage to avoid getting electrocuted.

"I don't know where you get the asinine idea that you speak for me," Beth snapped, exasperated. "I think leaving you to Goren's tender mercies might be just the ticket. You could learn a bit of humility. I have no intention of reducing your punishment for what was the grossest disregard for Alliance laws. I just hope that your idiotic actions won't destroy all hope of relations with the Guardians. They are, after all, an important race in our galaxy."

"You can't leave me here," Connor protested. "If you want to talk about the alliance, they leave no man behind."

"True, but the alliance also insists that breaking alien laws means answering to alien laws. So, Goren, any exchange involving you and me isn't going to take Connor into consideration, despite his continuing desire to loot your Treasury. He's not only broken your rules; he has also violated our code of conduct. He'll have to answer to our authorities, if you ever let him leave." Beth hoped this promise of penalties on Earth might soften Goren's decision.

Goren studied the pair silently for several seconds. Beth sensed a change in his manner. He shrugged and turned back to the solid wall of monitors. "We don't punish. Instead, I'll erase all the knowledge that Connor has of this place. The devices themselves have already been returned to their exhibit." Automatically, Beth looked at the desk. The relics had disappeared. "He won't be allowed back here again.

"I'd like to continue our association, Beth. But Connor will have to go."

"Go?" Connor interrupted.

"Go where?" Beth raised an eyebrow confused.

Goren smiled in a sinister fashion and walked over to Connor. "I can return you to your world and completely erase all memory since the moment you were accepted at the Technion. You'll remember that you were rejected by their admissions department and be left to find a living in some other manner. Our brain-mapping technology is quite adequate. You'll lose this experience and all your space travels."

For not allowing punishment, this seemed excessively harsh, Beth thought.

"No!" Connor screamed, all bravado gone. "Please, Beth, I was just trying to help. Don't let him destroy everything

I've achieved. I can't go back to the misery I had when I lived at *home*." Connor said this last with an expression of desolation. He fell to his knees and, to Beth's consternation, began sobbing.

Humility, or should she say humiliation, had finally claimed Connor Reid. In this state, he might be pliable enough to reach. Beth's outrage at his stupidity and selfishness faded. Connor did contribute to her team. He was a superior engineer, and the life he'd escaped by entering the space program had been described as barren and brutal.

But stealing from the Treasury? How does one punish someone for such a severe offense? The Guardians were powerful, and Connor had threatened a possible beneficial association.

Beth considered what the alliance would do if they knew of recent events. His career in space would certainly be over. Connor just hadn't made this connection yet. All at once, a possible solution occurred to her. What if she gave him a second chance? Everyone makes stupid mistakes, even when trying to do the right thing. How could she ruin him after one offense, albeit a truly gigantic one?

Beth looked sheepishly at Goren. "What would I have to do to get him probation?"

"Probation?"

"Yes, a stay of execution, which in this case would mean not sending him back to Earth. I agree that he has lost the right to knowledge of the Treasury. But I believe in letting my people recover from one dreadful mistake before condemning them for life. I want Connor to know that he has come close to losing everything, and I've given him a second chance. How adaptive is your bag of tricks?"

Beth reminded herself that she didn't know just what Goren wanted in return. She had limits on how far she would extend herself—especially for Connor.

Goren frowned thoughtfully. "We can manipulate memories in this complicated fashion, especially if the welfare of the Treasury is at stake. We just don't like to. If Connor is willing, then we agree to your proposal. Still, we'll keep tabs on him. At the first sign of a repeat offense, we will send him back to Earth, his memories wiped."

"Absolutely!" Connor interrupted fervently, almost grasping the bars in his excitement. Luckily, he caught himself when they sparked prematurely. "Beth, you won't regret this decision. I won't let you down again."

"That's what I'm counting on. Don't disappoint me," Beth warned.

Both Connor and his cage vanished in a flash of green light.

Beth looked around the room regretfully. All the potential advantages of finding the Treasury were lost. Connor would keep his position, and the *Aries* would be barred from the Treasury. Even if he didn't remember, he would pay a penance for this terrible ending.

"I have adjusted your crew's memories," Goren reported. "Now let's address what I want in return."

Beth tensed nervously as she waited for his next words. Her dry throat closed, and her collar seemed to be strangling her. She loosened her top button and, wrestling with her racing thoughts, reminded herself not to imagine the worst.

Goren pushed a button on a nearby console, and a drawer popped open. He pulled out one of a cluster of small objects. "Do not worry, Beth. I'm not going to hold you hostage. All I ask is that you wear this and return on your own to hear my offer." He screwed up his features in an odd grimace, which Beth imagined was the Guardian trying to look harmless.

Goren held up a beautiful gold ring topped with three stones, a ruby and two diamonds. Beth glimpsed a similar ring on one of his fingers.

"The ring generates a dark-energy field using the same technology as the space portals. The red stone opens a line of communication between us. The right diamond permits teleportation, similar to your harmonic space drive, except you don't need a ship. The left diamond turns it off. The ring emanates a recognizable power transmission, since you don't want anyone to know you are carrying Guardian technology."

Goren extended his hand, the ring glinting in the palm. He gazed at her with such sincerity that Beth looked away nervously. In her mind flashed the memory of their encounter before the alarms. She felt her cheeks burning.

"Look, I won't use Connor as leverage," he decided. "I want a real friendship based on trust. So I am offering you this ring as a token of goodwill, and I am asking you to return, so I might show you your special abilities."

"What special abilities? What are you talking about?"

"Our initial scans revealed that you have DNA markers that, we thought, were exclusively Guardian, which is why we allowed your people into the Treasury. I was most alarmed to find your people on our planet during the regeneration, but we did take steps to protect you from the worst violence. Your unusual DNA could mean that you have abilities we hide from outsiders. I want to see if you do have them. I don't know exactly how this will work. I certainly never imagined that it might cause you any discomfort. The horrible pain you suffered before the alarms shocked me deeply. I would never have put you at risk intentionally. But if you are what we think you are, a being such as you would be invaluable. Would you be willing to explore this hidden potential?"

Beth stepped back, shocked. She wanted to refuse but knew she couldn't turn her back on exploring this startling revelation. "OK," she replied nervously. "But let's start now. Once I return to the *Aries*, my time will belong to the alliance."

"We need to make skin on skin contact. Would you raise your shirt?" he asked gently.

Carefully, Beth unbuttoned her shirt and tied it up under her breasts. On her abdomen, a soft luminescent glow remained from their earlier encounter. After pressing a button on his wrist device, Goren turned her toward one of the walls. It had shifted its reflective properties and transformed into a perfect mirror. Behind her, Goren removed his shirt. The sleek planes of his chest emitted a glow similar to hers. His image wavered in the mirror. His features became thinner and his skin brighter.

Goren placed his hands on her abdomen and harmlessly pushed her pants lower on her hips; then he pulled her back against his now exposed chest. The heat of his body ignited her deeper emotions and produced a mushrooming sense of urgency. Their mutual bioelectric luminescence enclosed them in a cocoon of light. Beth felt dizzy and leaned heavily against Goren.

Deep, painful cramping struck with surprising vigor. She gasped in shock. Now Goren pressed harder against her, supporting her when her strength to stand was depleted. The glow in his skin blazed brighter and so did her pain. Beth moaned, flailing wildly. Unable to keep her safe from accidental injury, Goren carried her to a nearby divan.

"What is happening?" she gasped, as he laid her down. She pulled her knees up and wrapped her arms around her stomach.

"It can't last much longer," he said hopefully.

Goren pulled her close inside his arms. The pain flared again, and Beth prayed for the relief of unconsciousness.

"Do you want to stop?" he asked, obviously worried.

"No! I will see this thing to the end," Beth insisted through clenched teeth.

Time froze as something shifted inside her. She wondered vaguely why blood didn't burst from her thrashing body. Despite

Goren's efforts, her thrashing began to cause injuries. Finally, he rolled on top of her to hold her down protectively.

When at last the agony eased, Beth lay panting, trying to regain the will to move. Goren became a suffocating weight, and she shoved him off onto the floor. Struggling to sit up, she caught sight of herself in the transformed mirrored wall. Except that the image she saw was not her. It was some exotic being with glowing skin and long curling hair. Goren lay where she had dumped him, smiling broadly, obviously extremely pleased.

"It worked," he said simply. "It should be better from now on."

In a trance, Beth walked over to the mirror and lifted her hand to her mouth. "Oh m-my G-g-god," she stuttered, "what has happened to me?" The image she saw moved when she moved and spoke when she spoke, only it wasn't human.

CHAPTER 15

DISCOVERING SENTARAN SECRETS—ROSE

The next three days passed quickly. Mr. Quinn's library provided extensive background information on the history, cultural norms, and religion of the planet. Rose and Sophie visited the central museum and local art galleries, and toured central government buildings that ruled the entire planet. Emmet, acting as guide, explained their basic canon of laws, and Rose was allowed to see a trial. At the end of each day, Rose would leave the library too overloaded to absorb another fact. She usually went to bed as soon as she returned to their shared lodgings.

On the evening of the third day, Rose ran into Sam, Mirim, and Evan returning from the lab. They were humming with excitement. Mirim's cylinder lights flashed, and her eye globes bobbed in sync with the lights. Evan was bouncing, and Sam was grinning jubilantly.

Before anyone could speak, a cold premonition passed through Rose. She had learned to trust her instincts, and she didn't question them now. She turned away from her returning comrades and hurried the rest of the way back to their quarters, with the others close behind. When she arrived at their suite, Ari was already waiting. Beeping urgently, he flew straight to Sam.

"I have the results of the tests on the Sentarans. It took longer than expected due to the strange mutations and profusion of alien particles," Ari began, without wasting time on courtesies.

Rose held up her hand to stall his report to Sam. "Where are Amy and the others?" she asked, scanning the room. Ari had been assigned to protect them.

"Sam asked for our analysis," Ari explained innocently. "When I last saw them, Amy had gone running, Nicole had left with a guard, and Talia had settled down for the night. Is something wrong?" Ari had begun spinning—a common precursor to the Quanta's ability to transport in the manner of a quanta particle by popping in and out—when Rose dashed forward and laid her hand on his casing to stop him. Too much had happened, and Amy's situation was unknown. Everyone needed to regroup here, where the BESS was close. Rose forced herself to make a difficult decision. "Amy knows our safeguards. If she's in trouble, she'll come back here. We wait, at least for a while."

Sam came forward, obviously eager to give her his report. But Rose only shook her head. "Please, Sam, let's wait for all of us to hear. I know you've discovered something important. Please." Rose hated to put him off again, but she couldn't shake her fear for Amy. She had been uneasy all night.

Ari seemed to go along with her request, but Rose could only describe his next behavior as palpable impatience. He abandoned any inclination to continue communicating, flew to the elaborate pond, and suspended himself above the water. Five lights flashed in sequence down the side of his cylinder, one after the other, over and over and over again. Ari didn't move and didn't try to speak. The same five lights continued flashing in the same sequence, until Rose was ready to implode.

After only a few repetitions, she broke. "Please, just go."

Ari didn't need any further encouragement. He popped out without bothering to spin first.

Too worried to talk, Rose fidgeted in anxious silence. Sam and Sophie circled the fish pond aimlessly. Rose ran outside when, after thirty minutes, she heard Amy's cruiser in the distance, its engine noise recognizable. The ship landed behind their quarters.

A minute later, Rose and Amy appeared at the door to their quarters, supporting a sagging Nicole, who was staring at the floor with dead eyes and slack mouth. Mirim and Evan took over and transferred Nicole to a nearby couch. She seemed lost in a world inhabited exclusively by her own demons.

Without asking any questions, Rose put her arms around Amy, and the resilient woman's mask of unyielding strength collapsed. Shaking and mumbling, she covered her eyes.

Finally, coherent words burst from her. "Everything's gone wrong, Rose. Those stupid guards have made a horrible mess of things. I don't know how much time we have before Nicole ends up in jail, and maybe us with her."

"We'll find a way out. We always do," Rose consoled her friend. She let Amy cry uninterrupted.

After several minutes, Amy took a deep breath and faced Rose. "Talia is dead," she bleated in a defeated voice.

Nicole groaned at Amy's words and shook her head in denial. In the confusion, Rose hadn't noticed that Talia was missing. Now she automatically searched the room to confirm this terrible fact. How could this happen?

"Those stupid guards assaulted us again," Amy snarled, her voice getting stronger. "I was at the lake when Jared made his move. Somehow, when I pictured you in my mind, I managed to escape his trap and run back to camp. I found that Justin and Jeff had already compromised Talia and Nicole. Those repugnant maggots managed to romance our girls despite your warning, and Talia wasn't strong enough to withstand Justin's control.

"I tried to get Talia and Nicole to come back with me," Amy went on, her voice cracking. "Instead, they helped the guards recapture me."

Rose glanced at Nicole with angry frustration. Sophie was kneeling beside the grieving woman, shaking her periodically.

"Jared was determined to rape me, which was too great an offense for Talia. She broke free of their influence and grabbed Justin's gun, but…" Amy's voice trailed away.

"Amy," Rose urged. They were fast running out of time. "You must tell us what happened before the Sentarans arrive."

"Talia died trying to protect me from the guards." Amy's voice was strangled. "She wouldn't have fired. She was only threatening. But Jared killed her anyway. Then Nicole went crazy. She kept trying to revive Talia. When Justin intervened, she turned her rage on him. She shot him in the face before he knew what was happening. Then when Jared should've killed us all, he just went into the woods—"

"He went into the forest, and we heard a shot," Nicole interrupted, speaking for the first time. During Amy's account, she had stopped rocking, her breathing had slowed, and her eyes became clear. "He never came back. We think he's dead. Then Ari came, and he brought us back here."

Rose mentally listed the relevant facts. Talia was dead. Justin was dead. Jared was dead. Amy and Rose were here. "Where is Jeff?" she asked suddenly.

"He's there, unconscious. Amy got him with a killer sedative. She overpowered him after she threw away her weapon, so he couldn't use it against her." Nicole smiled proudly. Amy just stared at her in obvious confusion.

Rose knew that both women were hiding something. She would wait until later to ask Amy.

"Ari said he buried Justin and Talia away from the camp," Amy continued, still staring at Nicole. "The gunshot we heard was far away. When Jeff regains consciousness, he'll only see that everyone is gone."

"He'll know more than that," Rose reasoned. "Every soul has a unique mental signature. He'll know that his friends are most likely dead and that you two are here. He'll be looking for the person responsible, and Nicole is easy to read."

"Then what can we do? You can't leave me here," Nicole insisted. "I've no chance against their justice system. I killed one of their citizens."

"We may not have a choice," Rose scolded her. "How many times have the Quanta warned us to keep a low profile?"

"I could tell them that our group romance got a little rough," Nicole offered, rallying. She feigned an expression of helpful innocence. "Do you think our escorts would consider forgiving and forgetting? There was just a misunderstanding about our mating rituals."

The total absurdity of the remark caught Rose by surprise, and she burst out laughing. Nicole had tried, despite all the tension and tragedy, to make a joke. Sam chuckled, and even Amy cracked a small smile.

Ari and Sam could wait no longer. The humor had lightened the mood and given them an opening. They spoke simultaneously before Sam reluctantly let Ari go first.

"The Sentarans are identical to humans. A one hundred percent DNA match. Their chemical signature doesn't match this planet's, so how did they get here? Earth has only recently gained the technology required for space travel, and Sentara has none." Ari paused for what appeared to be dramatic effect. "The only explanation is that you are both offshoots of a third race, as yet undiscovered—most certainly a colonizing civilization more technically advanced than Earth's."

Rose tried to imagine a world as advanced as they were now, thousands of years in the past. What would it look like today? Would it rival the mysterious Guardian race?

"That isn't all the news," Sam chirped. "According to my autopsies, alien spores have redesigned Sentaran biology. They appear externally as skin and hair opalescence. But more importantly, these particles are coating every structure in their brains and changing their normal internal function. The frontal, parietal, temporal, and occipital lobes are swelling after birth to accommodate a strange metamorphosis." Dr. Samuel Carlson was foremost an educator, and he took this opportunity to teach his listeners a little brain physiology. "The parietal and temporal lobes, which control the interpretation of data collected by our five senses, are enlarged and discharging large amounts of neurological energy. The Sentarans must see everything with a heightened sensitivity. Unfortunately, the frontal lobe had to shrink to accommodate this expansion. In humans, the frontal lobe controls social consciousness and morality. Without it…" Sam's tone hinted at ominous consequences.

"Numerous spores have collected in the thalamus—that part of the brain that deals with consciousness and perception," he continued excitedly. "It has swelled to three times its normal size and is so bright it looks like a Christmas light. This might explain Rose's experiences with their strong extrasensory perception. The cerebral cortex is getting stronger, so it can translate the amplified sensory input. These changes have opened a whole new world to this race. These people can literally hear their world growing. I'm betting they can communicate with the animals as well."

"So they claim," Amy agreed. "At the lake, Jared used that ability as a lure."

"They think it's the sun's radiance that gives them their special abilities," Rose added, remembering Jason's comments.

"Their medical science is limited. They don't seem to know about the spores," Sam said, tapping his palm with a stylus. "I don't know if they're an independent life-form. The spores behave like bits of coded intelligence that affect functioning cells. The

Sentarans have provided them with a new host. Ari, what did you find?"

"They are alive," Ari confirmed. "We examined the pineal gland that grows near the thalamus, and it was expanding and contracting with a life of its own. When we brought the scalpel close, it jumped off the table, leaving a trail of gold spores. We verified that it was the alien spores that reacted to the scalpel. They are an independent life-form. We believe that they are trying to redesign the pineal gland to restore fertility and the body's natural cycles."

"This is the price for living here," Sam admitted. "The problem is the intense sunlight. It must upset the natural rhythms of the body. These people probably sleep a fraction of what we do on Earth. The pineal gland controlling sexual development and sleep, among other things, is on overdrive. They're literally burning out their reproductive systems, allowing only the strongest to bear children. Everyone I have autopsied was already sterile.

"The Sentarans at the lab are desperate to find out what is destroying their fertility. Judy, my guard, won't leave me alone for one second, and I was given highly trained, seasoned technicians to assist me. She tried to force me to give her a progress report. I won't be able to put her off again.

"Except for the mutations and the sterility," Sam concluded, "the bodies I examined were healthy, abnormally healthy. I think illness is rare. In fact, I'm not sure what killed two of the cadavers. It might be a pathogen that eliminates any further need to survey."

"Talia didn't discover any naturally occurring vectors for disease that carried bacteria or viruses virulent enough to wipe out humans," Amy objected. She unzipped the main pouch of the survey duffel bag and drew out a plastic case filled with flash drives. Each member of the survey team stored their data on one. "Here are our studies of hundreds of samples of soil, water, food, animals, and plants."

"The Sentarans know they are transplants," Rose added, answering another question in Sam's report. "Mr. Quinn told us that giant floods reduced the planet to islands after their arrival. Then violent weather destroyed their spaceship, its records, and all references to their home planet, leaving them stranded here."

"Who is Mr. Quinn?" Sam asked.

"He owns an impressive private library and has been a gold mine of information. Our guard left us there the first day and hasn't reappeared. As a matter of fact, I haven't seen any guards since we split up. Where are they?" Rose asked.

"I had them reassigned," a voice said from behind them. The BESS team turned together, like a single mind, all eyes focused on the intruder.

A surprisingly young woman strode into their central living room. She had the unsettling good looks characteristic of the Sentaran guards. The familiar shimmering silver accents painted her hair and features. She had a presence that crowded the room, her voice carrying into every corner, rich and resonant. She enunciated each syllable clearly and distinctly, with the respect one shows a foreign language. Her eyes coolly assessed the watching surveyors. Rose felt the woman's energy lightly touch her, curious but restrained.

Several military men, short, squat, and dressed completely in black, followed the stranger into the room. They assumed positions at all the doors and windows. Rose didn't miss their dual function. As well as protecting this woman, these men were effectively keeping her people prisoner. She also recognized, from her observations of the Sentaran community, that each profession had a general physical type. Military personnel were squat and hard, government folks were handsome and graceful, and traders were round and jovial. Scholars, like Quinn, were closest in appearance to an average human.

Rose cloaked herself in a demeanor of innocent confidence and approached the young woman. "Who are you?" she asked.

"I'm Ione Cragon, council chairwoman of Sentara. For your protection, we've tried to keep you all under surveillance—that is, until Amy Chen's group left the city. Then we trusted her guards to keep her protected and us informed. We had hoped your visit would proceed without incident." Ione directed her comments to the entire group, remaining vague, as politicians can be.

"When you had trouble with Jason, I thought Mr. Quinn might be a more helpful guide." Now Ione looked directly at Rose.

Rose felt the weight of her regard like a physical yoke, suffocating her. She shook her head, trying to dispel the illusion.

"He delights in his world of knowledge and collects the sort of information you requested," explained the chairwoman. "Emmet is a valuable advisor and close personal friend. He stays outside the intrigues of government and is quite happy to leave me to my misery. Has he been satisfactory?"

"He's been everything you describe and more. I've completed my part of our survey," Rose assured Ione. Instinctively, she extended a shield of mental protection around her people. It wouldn't stand up to a direct assault; Ione was just too powerful. But she hoped it would keep random thoughts private.

Turning to Sam, Ione smiled, showing perfect white teeth. "And you, Doctor. How is your analysis going? Will your race thrive here?"

"There have been surprises..." Sam replied, his voice trailing off. He glanced at Rose and Amy, his eyes darting surreptitiously.

"There have been rumors about some mysterious pathogen that causes sterility," Ione confessed. "So far, our scientists have been unable to find evidence of a serious disease."

Sam nodded indiscreetly. Rose swore under her breath. She hated Ione's ability to manipulate Sam so well.

Ione beamed proudly. "As a matter of fact, our planet is remarkably free of illness. Have you been able to find anything outside the city?" This time, she addressed Amy. It was her analysis that was likely to find any toxins deadly to humans.

"We've found nothing disturbing so far, but it would take too long to do an exhaustive study of all pathogens," Amy said, moving in front of Sam protectively. "To date, we've found pure water and food rich in all the necessary nutrients."

"Then are you ready to give Sentara a clean bill of health?" Ione asked, looking at each in the group confidently.

"Not yet," said Rose, wondering if Ione would accept such an indefinite answer. "Soon."

Rose began to feel a curious vertigo. She reached for a nearby chair and sat awkwardly. Sam backed away, blinking rapidly. Amy bared her teeth and growled in a very primal manner. Only Nicole seemed at ease and natural. She smiled back at Ione and her lips moved, but Rose couldn't hear anything because an odd roaring filled her ears. Ione ignored Nicole, walking around her to grasp Rose's arm and haul her out of the chair. Dazed, Rose found herself being drawn toward the door.

"We can discuss your recommendations in more detail in my office," Ione declared. A strange lassitude engulfed Rose, and she couldn't voice her objections. Her friends stood immobile, their eyes unseeing. Even the Quanta were strangely subdued.

Rose accepted the fact that she was the only one who could stop the chairwoman from taking her away. She had to stay here where she had witnesses. With renewed determination, she tried to pull her arm free, but her nerveless extremities wouldn't respond. Horrified, she saw herself walking alongside Ione without resistance, when the need to resist was consuming her.

Then she noticed Ione's hypnotic eyes. The swirling hazel specks promised much and distracted Rose from taking action. Ione slipped her arm around Rose's waist and steered her to the door. This unrelenting pressure was the trigger Rose needed to fight back in deadly earnest.

She tried to erect shields, except her thoughts scattered before she could form the required mental image. Desperately she searched for some technique that might neutralize Ione. Then she recalled her grand's voice giving her direction from across the years. *Focus your attention away from what appears reasonable. Think of matters of the heart, things you trust and love. Your heart has superior protection because it can't be fooled by puzzles of logic that hide the truth. The fire of emotion, when released, can overwhelm the most carefully crafted tricks.*

Rose dragged her eyes away from Ione and filled her mind with visions of her loving grandmother, who smelled of roses and home-baked cookies. Her mouth watered at the image of cookies still warm from the oven. She could see her grand's protective green eyes and remembered her fingertips gently untangling her inherited curly red hair. Ione's voice became an easily ignored muttering in the flood of memories. In that moment, even as the chairwoman, surrounded by her small army, opened the door, Rose wrenched free and pushed back through the wall of men. Her memories had melted the freezing hold Ione's mind had used to keep her powerless.

Rose could have laughed out loud at Ione's startled look of incredulity. She was obviously used to having total control. Rose wanted to shriek in anger at the continuing assumption that these people could and should push them around. She needed to draw the line somewhere, or there was no hope.

"What do you think you're doing?" she cried indignantly. "Do you think you can use your ill-gotten powers to force me?"

Ione's mouth dropped open. Visibly flabbergasted, she stuttered a few disjointed words and then stopped when she realized she was babbling. Rose's strange vertigo faded, and she walked back to her crew.

Amy came out of her daze spitting fire. "Has your government lost their collective minds?" she shouted shrilly. "You can't treat us like obedient dogs. We know you're messing with our minds."

Ione turned to Amy, her cheeks crimson. She opened her mouth to speak but then stilled and looked up. All the men of her party tilted their heads, mimicking Ione's strange behavior. When Ione seemed to come to herself again, she swiftly scanned the room.

"Where is the small dark one? There is another member of your team. Where is she?"

CHAPTER 16

THE CHIMERA—BETH

Beth studied her reflection, grateful she had retained a few recognizable features. Her figure was the same toned one she had worked so hard to maintain, and her face had the same general shape. Everything else had changed. Her blue-gray eyes were gone. Now silver flakes glittered in a swirling sea of honey. Her long hair was like spun gold, rippling with metallic highlights. Her skin pulsed with the brilliant iridescence she now shared with Goren. Then there were the changes that weren't easily identifiable, bits of things with unknown functions. At her neck and along her back were new ridges. On her ankles were nubs of cartilage used for God knew what. And her hair coiled with a life of its own.

Goren stood behind her and watched her examination, beaming with delight. Beth realized it was his attitude that made this change comprehensible. He was not surprised or alarmed. He was acting as if it was time for a celebration. Turning to him, she placed her arms akimbo and lifted her eyebrows in a question.

"You've had an incredible genetic transformation. You're a jewel of a rare kind," he said, waxing poetic. He waved his arms as if announcing some grand event to the world. "You are a chimera. In my lifetime, I have seen very few of your kind—never one of your type. A chimera containing the genetic code of advanced alien species from different solar systems is completely unprecedented. There is no record of someone like you except in our myths." Goren touched Beth's hair expectantly. It curled around his fingers, and he purred in response.

Annoyed, she began to feel like a prized cow. Looking for some distraction to remind her that she was still in the real world, she looked around and saw Axel in one corner arguing with two attendants. He had returned and was annoying the guards who were trying to restrain him. Axel was obviously too loyal to leave her at the mercy of a stranger. His lights flashed wildly, and a penetrating buzz followed his pleas to be allowed to see her. One of his eye globes had twisted toward her and was watching with clear distress.

Beth was outraged and stormed over to the small group. "Get back!" she demanded of the attendants. The robed figures complied immediately, seemingly respecting her changed stature.

"Are you unharmed?" she asked Axel solicitously.

He twirled dramatically. "Functioning perfectly," he confirmed. "You appear to have done some redecorating." He floated around her, slowly examining her changed appearance. Using an extended appendage, Axel examined the extra layers of skin at her neck. "These look like gills," he concluded. Then he tapped the growths on her back. "This formation looks unfinished. It might be the beginning of wings." He flew around her again, replicating the pattern of light pulsations emanating from her skin. "The pulsing of your body might be some type of communication," Axel guessed. "Your hair…Now that is truly splendid."

"Splendid?" Beth asked, embarrassed by his appreciation.

"He means you can move your hair independently. It is an old characteristic lost to our race." Goren automatically reached out to grasp Beth's hair again. Axel blocked the Guardian's hand, resuming his role as Beth's protector. Still, a single strand of hair coiled around the Guardian's thumb for a few seconds.

"A chimera of your type," Goren resumed his explanation, after moving a short distance away, "possesses genetic material that allows you to assume characteristics imprinted into each DNA strand. The degree of transformation available is unique in each chimera. We have identified genetic strands in you from four extremely advanced species, including my race. This is the reason we let your group into the Treasury.

"You have great value to us, Beth." Now Goren's voice pleaded and, despite her obvious anxiety at his proximity, moved closer. "Through millennia, my race has lost the qualities that promote a thriving civilization. Our scientific applications have inadvertently diminished our biological vitality. When we systemized reproduction, we lost the very randomness that allows leaps in genetic mutations necessary for evolution. Our science has eliminated challenges that might have strengthened our resilience and fueled our thirst for innovation.

"You could help us regain some of what we have lost. Your DNA is young and vital. It shows none of the refinements we have made. You could reconstitute my race, maybe even allow us to return to our home planet. This would be a priceless service to my people."

"So what happens to me?" Beth hated to mention something as small as her hopes for her own life. But saving a race was just too big to take seriously. No one person could do such a thing. "Will I stay like this now?"

Goren pointed at the mirror. "Look."

Beth glanced in the mirrored wall and saw that her hair had turned back to its usual honey color, and the strange bits of genetic alteration were gone. Although her skin still glowed, it had stopped pulsing. She had not connected the strange tingling sensation to her returning human characteristics.

"Obviously, physical contact with me triggers your Guardian DNA. You were showing our real appearance altered by your human form. Without some effort on your part, it seems you revert back."

Beth felt a deep sadness at the implication of his words. The only reason he had touched her was to force her to transform. There had been no real connection between them outside of this freak show. Tears came unbidden into her eyes. Impatiently, she wiped them away, frustrated with her own stupidity. He had told her this was what he had been trying to do. But somehow the experience had touched her heart.

Somehow Goren seemed to understand the reason for her sudden change of mood. "It's true that your morphogenesis was my motive for letting you and your people in, and it was also my motive for trying to get close to you," he admitted reluctantly. "But, Beth…" This time Goren walked around Axel and pulled her around to face him. "My ruse has trapped us both." Goren set his arm against hers, and their glowing skin began to intensify. "Axel is right. This is a form of communication. When two Guardians are ideally suited to produce an exceptional child, a bioelectric synchronization is triggered. You must have noticed?"

Beth nodded. She dared not speak in case her voice broke and gave away her emotional vulnerability.

"When I triggered your transformation, you became in all particulars a Guardian. In this state the connection was made, and we were matched, even though you have no desire to stay here."

Beth was humbled by his accurate appraisal. Despite her attraction to the Guardian, she was eager to continue her mission on the *Aries*. The obstacles that stood between them loomed, seemingly insurmountable. Basically, he was an alien with his own agenda, and she was a human captain just beginning her adventures in space. Chris might want to share her space journey with a husband, but Beth did not. Besides, whatever personality she had credited to Goren was based on her experience as a human, not the actuality of his life as a Guardian. Recognizing the reality of their situation, Beth did feel better.

"The transformation reverses on its own," Goren reminded her, "so you'll soon be restored to your original state."

"So how does this benefit your race?" she asked. "I mean, if the change is temporary…?"

"We believe the length of transformation can be controlled by you. I was hoping, if you come back, we might investigate your unique abilities. It could take as little or as much time as you allow." Goren held up the ring. "Will you accept?"

The advantages of gaining Goren's friendship were tempting, but Beth viewed her assignment on the *Aries* as a promise that all her dreams would be realized. Transforming into one of her chimera identities had been harmless so far. Goren's investigations might not be so innocuous. Beth remembered Sarah's warnings. But in the end, the chance for Guardian allies made her choice.

Beth held out her hand. He dropped the ring into her palm, and she slid it onto her finger. "You must visit our Quanta soon. They'll be delirious with joy."

"I'm a ring call away," Goren quipped, before assuming a more serious expression. "Right now, I think you might want to rescue your friends."

"What!" Beth sputtered, seconds before Mark's voice boomed through her ear transmitter. His stress was audible.

"Urgent. Beth, please respond. Our planet teams are in trouble."

"This is Beth. Mark, what's happening?" She exposed her wrist, revealing Mark's worried visage.

"I've received SOS calls from both Citron and Sentara. They need immediate assistance. Can you return right now?"

"Of course. What's wrong?" Beth couldn't understand why Mark was being so elusive. Then she remembered their security protocols. He had to get permission before revealing any sensitive information. "Captain Beth Griffin, all clear. Please speak openly,"

Beth repeated their code. "Now what is wrong with the ASH and BESS?"

"On Citron, the ASH's captain, Andre Solski, has died, and Christine has started showing the *same symptoms he had*." Mark's voice cracked on the last few words. Death was the most crippling event for any survey ship. "Lena and Mitchell are in comas. They have no leadership or medical personnel other than their Quanta.

"They don't believe Chris has long to live, and Malcolm wants me to come immediately. They have not been able to identify a cause, propose any cure, or offer relief." Mark's voice sounded haunted as he described the extent of Citron's dire situation "Andre's death confirms the worst possible scenario. Mac is helpless. He's demanding the *Aries*'s more advanced technical and medical resources."

"And what of Sentara?" To call on the *Aries* so soon after planet fall could only mean that they were up against their own destruction as well.

"Nicole has been charged with murder, and she's being held by the authorities. The planet's council chairwoman Cragon says the rest of Rose and Amy's team is infected by an illness the Sentarans thought had been eradicated. She won't let them speak to us or leave the planet. We've been trying to communicate directly with Rose and Amy using their ear transmitters. Rose started a transmission that was cut off abruptly. They probably let us hear a few words to increase our panic and their bargaining position."

"What were the words?" Beth asked.

"'Please come,'" Mark said.

Beth felt a fierce loyalty to the small band of people who relied on her for protection. She would have liked to ask Goren to help, but something held her back: a feeling, an instinct, a foreboding.

"How does this work?" she asked Goren, pointing at the right diamond on her ring.

"In precise detail, imagine where you want to go and touch the stone."

Beth touched the appropriate jewel and at the same time imagined the pilot seat on the shuttle they had left in the slot canyon before the planet had regenerated. A black whirlwind rose around her, freezing her skin and stealing her breath, before transporting her instantly to the cruiser's cabin. Dizzy and nauseated, she would have fallen if she hadn't already been seated.

Miraculously undamaged, the little ship was floating on a pristine mountain lake. Almost in the same moment, Axel popped in and hovered over the copilot seat. Beth started the engine and scanned for the dampening electromagnetic field that had created trouble upon their arrival. Goren must have turned it off. The small cruiser easily lifted above the water and headed out of the planet's atmosphere. When they were in range, she scanned ahead and eventually spied her beloved *Aries*. She signaled that she was ready to begin landing protocols.

Impatiently, Beth swung into the port docking bay, disembarked, and ran to the bridge. Her crew was at their stations ready to leave. Only Axel gazed back at the planet. From the ring, she heard Goren whisper a soft farewell. Despite her best intentions, a shiver rippled down her back. "Good-bye," she whispered back.

Beth slipped into the navigation chair ready for Axel's signal to begin.

"We go to Citron first," she informed everyone. "Their need is more urgent." She buckled the heavy straps and extended her awareness into the ship. Seconds after she felt the familiar disorientation, the space around her blurred, and then they were a few parsecs from Citron.

Mark flipped on the communication node, and immediately a recording of Mac's weak voice delivered a message of doom.

"*Aries*, this is Malcolm. Please stay away. I repeat: do not land on this planet." His words were slurred, and a soft wheezing shadowed his breathing. "All of the landing party is now infected. I don't know how much longer I can hold on, so I'm setting this message on automatic. This illness is extremely infectious and always lethal." The recording was interrupted by a racking coughing fit. For several moments, all they could hear was his frantic struggle for oxygen. When the words continued, they were slower, interspersed with gurgling breaths. Beth sensed his hopeless despair. "Chris is showing signs of organ failure. She can't survive much longer. Please don't jeopardize yourselves by trying to help us. We're already lost." After several moments of silence, the message repeated.

Shock clouded everyone's features, and no one spoke during the second transmission.

Axel raced around the bridge, deliberately breaking the silence and drawing the attention of the stunned crew. "Captain, the Quanta can visit the planet without risk and get samples from the ASH surveyors for analysis. We will call upon our nexus to do intensive studies. If we put the ASH crew into deep comas, it might slow the disease's progression. We need to contact Siri and Ella."

Abruptly Beth darted to her command station and remotely halted the repeating message. Then she signaled the planet. "This is *Aries*. We're in orbit. Please advise us on your current status. "

Connor assumed a protective position near Beth. His manner had lost all traces of duplicity and arrogance. "I can go down in an AV suit," he volunteered. "It should protect me sufficiently."

"As far as we know," Beth said. "Our greatest peril is that we don't know what the landing party is actually facing." She spoke gently, mindful of Connor's new demeanor. "I do appreciate your offer. First, let's get some concrete information. We have to make contact with the landing party."

"This is *Aries*," Beth repeated. "We're ready to offer rescue services. Please respond."

Several moments passed with only static. Beth tried again, this time demanding a response.

Sharp clicks indicated someone's movements, and Siri's mechanical voice interrupted the static on the intercom. "Mac is attending to the other patients. He is acting outside of normal human perimeters. He keeps…singing."

"What is your status?" Axel asked, circling Beth's communication console. His eye stalks had become nervously entangled.

"I am unaffected so far. Ella's systems are malfunctioning. We have completed several joint diagnostics. We do not detect any biological invaders. I have instructed Ella to continue internal monitoring. So far, she has no new information."

Axel beeped in a worried fashion. "Captain, request permission to join Siri?"

There were a handful of Quanta who had achieved leadership status in the nexus hierarchy. A candidate had to demonstrate superior reasoning adeptness, as well as distinguishing behavior in the field. Axel was one of these. Beth worried about sacrificing one of a very valuable group, but she knew that if she didn't provide a good reason using superior reasoning adeptness, Axel would go anyway. Permission was a courtesy, not a requirement.

"I need time to think," Beth pleaded. She would not rush headlong into a decision that could kill her entire crew, including the Quanta. "Axel, give me an hour. Please."

"Very well."

Beth detected his obvious reluctance. She could only hope he would keep his word and wait.

Turning back to the communication panel, she addressed Siri. "May I speak to Mac?" Silence greeted her request. Quanta didn't always understand the subtle niceties of conversation. She would've liked some indication of his intentions.

"This is Mac," Malcolm said after a few moments.

"Thank God," Beth replied. "Give me your report." She used an official directive, hoping this might override his unpredictable behavior.

"Chris is the worst, and Lena is close behind. Symptoms include high fever and difficulty breathing. White particles collect on their skin and in their blood. Their joints harden until they can't move, and their major organs begin to fail. During the progression of this illness, patients can have wild hallucinations. All the afflicted eventually fall into a coma.

"Look, Captain Griffin," Mac's voice grew stronger as he made the assertions that would condemn his entire team. "We've reached the point of no return. The chance that you might find something useful before we die is slight. I can promise that you will become infected and most likely die with us if you come down."

"Don't give up yet," Beth implored. "Send us all your medical data. Maybe I can find some pattern that you missed and infection can be avoided with Hazmat suits. How are you feeling?"

"For some reason, my symptoms aren't as severe as everyone else's," Mac admitted, almost jovially, a surprising reaction when everyone else was on the verge of death. "I don't know why I haven't lost consciousness. I should've when Mitch did."

A sudden increase in restless moans came across the communications link. A Quanta beeped urgently on the planet. Beth heard Sarah curse under her breath.

"I've got to go," Mac said vaguely. "I'll leave communications open in case something changes." The node went quiet, and even background sounds became muted.

"I need to think. I have to be sure before taking measures that are irreversible. I'll be in my office." Beth left the bridge, desperate to find a way to save the ASH. Nervously, she rotated her ring as she climbed the stairs to her office. Once there, she pressed the appropriate stone. Goren answered instantly.

"How are your planet teams?" he asked at once.

"You heard that our Citron detachment is very sick. They've warned us to stay away or die with them. I can't leave them, even if it means sacrificing one of us. We need to know what's attacking their systems." Beth's voice shook with her increasing anguish. "I was hoping you might know of something that could help."

"What are your options?" Goren's voice was calm and reasonable.

Beth took a deep breath to help focus her thoughts and began to list her choices. "I can bring the ASH surveyors to the *Aries* under quarantine. I'd be taking the risk that whatever infected them will infect the rest of my crew. I could send Axel down to help Siri, but he might become infected like Ella, and he is one of an elite group of sophisticated Quanta. I could bring Chris up and subject her to a harsh decontamination. I just don't know if this procedure would kill the virus and her at the same time." Beth's voice trailed off as her helplessness began to scramble her thinking. She needed some guidance from a powerful source.

"What is likely to produce the best information, with the smallest risk?" he asked.

Apparently, Goren didn't provide answers. Rather, he acted as a sounding board, helping her discover her own solution. She was reminded of an old proverb: Give a man a fish and you feed him for a day. Teach a man to fish and you feed him for a lifetime.

Beth decided that bringing Chris up for further study while keeping her under strict isolation was the best compromise with the greatest measure of safety. Siri could implement isolation protocols and then transfer Chris to Axel in deep space. She had just signed off with Goren, when she heard a knock on the door.

"Captain, we need you back on the bridge. Something has happened," Mark called through the door.

CHAPTER 17
THE CITRINALS—CHRIS

Chris deftly wrapped Andre in a sheet before enclosing his corpse in an air-tight bag. His body was strangely light, as if something vital was already gone. The odd white particles had completely leaked out of his body after his death. Chris stood for a moment over Andre, murmuring a prayer of good-bye. She wanted his passing to have some of the gravity and tradition of his people back on Earth. She mentally bid farewell to the dreams they had created together, dreams that had been doomed from the start. Finally she nodded, and the two Quanta lifted the body between them and popped out.

Chris had expected to feel nothing for Andre. After all, he had gone too far. Unexpectedly, grief consumed her, producing a torrent of tears. She took a few steps toward the dressing room, finding each foot as heavy as a lead weight. Waves of exhaustion flooded her body, making her bones ache. Fighting a growing dizziness, she sagged into a nearby chair. When the Quanta reappeared and returned to monitoring Lena's progress, Chris forced herself to stand and walk normally to the isolation room exit. Once in the dressing room, she removed her protective clothing with mounting difficulty, wiping her eyes when her vision grew blurry with tears.

Once she had finished changing, Chris shuffled to the sink in the main medical bay. Consumed by an overwhelming thirst, she selected an oversized water bottle from the cupboard above the sink and filled it with cold water. She quickly drained the bottle and then refilled it impatiently. This time she forced herself to take small sips only to find it empty again after a few moments. Refilling it a third time, she carried it outside. On her way to the main cabin, a second wave of exhaustion hit her, and she stumbled. Andre's old quarters, a few feet away, beckoned invitingly.

Time stretched out as she hobbled the short distance to his fancy cabin. After what seemed an eternity, she turned the knob on the outside door and swung it open. Clinging to her water bottle, she headed directly to the bedroom, crawled into the bed, and burrowed into the crisp cotton sheets and downy pillows. The bed's soothing comfort lulled her into a deep sleep.

Chris lost track of day and night as she drifted in and out of consciousness. On some level, she knew she was in trouble. Initially, she fought against the blanket of darkness and forced herself to wake up long enough to take sips of water to slake her terrible thirst. Still, she grew weaker and weaker. Facing the inevitable, she surrendered to her sickness. When she stopped fighting, she began to hear the strangest sounds. At first they were faint, like the echo of music playing in another room. As they became more distinct, she recognized them as a replay of the songs she and the twins had been singing on the beach. Before she could make out any other details, she fell back into the dark void.

Later Chris found herself sitting on a moss-covered log, smelling the thick fragrance of forest humus and hearing the patter of rain falling through the evergreen canopy. She was enveloped in a damp fog that settled on her skin and made her shiver. She could distinguish the roar of falling water in the distance. Nervously she started humming the songs she had heard earlier, as a sort of talisman of protection. The twins appeared on the log next to her, revealed by the shifting mist. They started to sing along with her. She accepted this strange tableau until she realized how impossible it was. Wasn't she sick? Wasn't she dying?

"Let me talk to you," she pleaded urgently. In response, the singing got louder. The figures, who she had assumed were Mitch and Mac, stood and began walking down the beach, the fog evaporating before them. Not wanting to be left behind, Chris ran after them. "Stop," she called, reaching toward the departing figures. The twins kept getting farther and farther away. "Please don't leave me." She tried to run faster, but she began to sink into the pink sand.

She clawed for solid ground, gasping for air. Then a woman's voice began to sing. "Sleep, young one. Soon all will be well again." She stopped fighting then and slipped into the familiar darkness.

Chris woke up to the discomforts of lying on a hard cot and was assaulted by the familiar sights and sounds of the infirmary. Unexpectedly, she felt a deep-rooted sense of well-being.

Mac looked a wreck. Even though his joints were swollen and his skin was a dusty gray, clear signs of the infection, he was hobbling around with a makeshift cane, trying to offer whatever comfort he could. She could tell that every movement was painful because he paused periodically to brace himself for his next exertion.

Mitch and Lena were lying unconscious on nearby cots. Their vital signs joined hers in a cacophony of beeps and flashing lights. Mac was monitoring the progression of the disease in all of them simultaneously, so he hadn't noticed when Chris's vital signs returned to normal.

Chris sat up silently and swung her legs slowly over the side of the bed. She slid off the cot, crouching, trying to conceal her movements from Mac. She needed time to consider their situation before being beset with questions.

Chris gradually noticed her new heightened senses. As she crept toward the open door, she could clearly see the swirling colors of the inlet water and the vibrant shades of green in the encroaching forest. Fish swam just under the surface, their faceted scales blinking in the refracted sunlight. She distinctly heard Mac's soft muttering, despite the monitor's loud beeping. Her tactile sense reveled in the suppleness of her old clothes.

Chris caught a quick movement out of the corner of her eye. She turned quickly to spy an alien creature flying above the beach. Before she could slip outside to investigate, her reprieve from Mac ended.

"Chris? My God, how are you?" he whispered, his voice as gravely as an old smoker's. He looked at the monitor that showed her vital signs. Chris had kept her wrist sensor on to circumvent the alarms.

"I've recovered, Mac," she reassured him. "We're all going to recover."

Mac's eyes brightened with hope, and he stood straighter. Then he glanced at the transmitter. "The *Aries* is here," he told her. "They want to come down."

"Absolutely not!" Chris rushed past Mac to the main infirmary's communication node and opened a channel to the *Aries*. With everyone sick, the isolation's universal precautions had been abandoned. "This is Chris, commander of the Citron mission. Acknowledge?" she insisted.

Axel responded, chirping with relief. "This is Axel. Chris, are you OK? You sound OK."

"I've recovered, Axel, but I need to check everyone's status before giving a full report. Please stand by."

Chris returned to the sick room, grateful to see Lena and Mitch awake and their vital signs improving. Malcolm, on the other hand, had collapsed. He had submitted to the illness only when he knew the others were safe. Gently Siri carried him to an empty cot, and Chris connected an IV to dispense fluids, nutrients, and electrolytes.

Lena had risen to sit on the edge of her cot and was stretching stiff muscles. The physical abnormalities of the alien infection had vanished, leaving her skin a healthy pink. Gingerly, she set each foot on the floor before shifting her full weight onto her legs; she then stepped away from the bed. Lena looked up to find Chris studying her.

"Chris!" she cried, rushing forward impetuously. Her feet tangled in her haste, and she crumpled into a heap on the floor. Looking up sheepishly, she shrugged.

"Lena!" Chris shook her head, delighted that her friend was back to her old self. Since Lena had protected her on more than one occasion, she considered her more a sister than a colleague. "I've been assured that we'll fully recover," Chris revealed recklessly.

"Assured? By whom?" Lena pressed.

"How are you feeling? Do you remember how you got sick?" Chris tried to cover her inexplicable comment. Silently, she cursed her slip of the tongue. She really wasn't sure why she knew they would be OK.

"I feel pretty good." Lena jumped to her feet. "Ready to go. As to how I got infected, your guess is as good as mine. I've been helping Mac retrieve samples from deeper ocean depths. Mitch's drones are only good in low pressures."

At Mitch's name, Chris looked for her right-hand man, only to find the other cot empty. "Mitch?" she called, scanning the room.

He was standing at the doorway, gaping at something outside. He waved them over. "You're not going to believe this," he promised, twitching with excitement.

Lena hurried to the door, towing Chris. Mitch grabbed their wrists and pulled them outside and onto the beach. Chris twisted around in astonishment. Surrounding them were vast swarms of otherworldly creatures flying in every direction. There were countless species hidden in the ceaseless motion of numerous indi-viduals. Some were fragile and gossamer-webbed, and others were large and formidable. Long lace tails trailed off delicate fins. She could see amazing details, so beautiful in their intricacies. The creatures circled them, their huge eyes pools of voiceless appeal. But most disturbing was that they should have been bright and full of color. Instead, they were shades of gray, shades of gray that flew.

"Can you understand us?" Chris implored.

The creatures just turned away. Defeated, Chris was distracted by her amplified senses. She could hear layers of sound, some close and some far away. Within the cove the water rustled like shuffling cards, while beyond the breakwater the wind roared and churned the water into choppy white waves. Breezes delicately tickled her skin and lifted her hair to caress her neck. An increasing chill brushed her lips and cheeks with biting bits of ice, as the sky dark-ened. She could tell a storm was approaching.

Tiny shouts coming from the communication node, back in the infirmary, finally caught her attention. She ran back to the of-fice, letting Lena and Mitch follow more slowly.

"*Aries* calling Alpha team—please respond," Beth called.

"This is Chris," she interrupted. "Things are evolving quickly, Beth. Lena, Mitch, and I have recovered with no noticeable nega-tive side effects. We need to continue our investigation. I would like a few days to explore possibilities. Until then, all humans should keep away."

"And what of Andre? Your message said he died," Beth asked, sounding suspicious of their abrupt recovery.

"Yes, Andre is dead. He must have had a special vulnerability. The Quanta have already disposed of his body."

"This apparent remission could be temporary," Beth warned, frustration and concern spilling through the speakers. "Since we could become infected, and since the BESS is also in serious trou-ble, I'm going to hope you can find answers on your own."

"Rose and Amy are in trouble?" Chris asked, alarmed. So many problems in so little time did not bode well for any of them.

"Yes. It appears that the Sentarans lured our people to their planet under false pretenses. Now they claim our comrades are too sick to talk—as if we'd believe such nonsense. I don't know what they want or, more to the point, what we can do about it.

"I really shouldn't get into this over an open line. I'll give you particulars when we can meet. Hopefully by then we'll both have good news. Either way, the next time you see me, I'll be coming down. Call us if things get worse," Beth confirmed.

"Acknowledged," Chris returned and terminated the connection.

Chris jumped when moaning erupted from the sick room. Through the open door, she could see Mac tossing restlessly. She entered the room to find the physical signs of his illness fading.

"Ella told me of the creatures flying outside," Siri said, pointing toward Ella floating near the doorway. "I was able to view them only after trying several different ultraviolet frequencies. You are able to see them unaided?"

Chris nodded. "I believe it's a side effect of our condition."

"Have Ella's systems begun to improve like the rest of us?" Lena asked hopefully.

"No, she has no link to the nexus," Siri intoned ominously.

Mitch whistled sympathetically, and Lena patted Ella, whispering words of encouragement.

The nexus, Chris knew, referred to the link between all Quanta. They could operate as a single consciousness sharing resources. Alone, Ella would be at a great disadvantage. Chris noticed that when the little computer moved toward them, her lights began to dim. When she stopped next to Siri, he attached an auxiliary power cable to her to recharge her power core. Despite possible risk, he connected a special data cable between them, so Ella might feel a connection to her lost kin through him.

While Siri and Ella were trading information, Mac revived, full of spunk and banter. "Why am I hooked up to these confounded machines?" he protested, struggling into a sitting position. "I was just trying to take a short nap." He scrutinized Chris, the Quanta, Lena, and Mitch, eyebrows twitching, looking like a muzzled clown in his medical mask. Finally he shrugged and tossed the stifling face gear away.

"How can you have recovered already?" Mitch exclaimed, huffing in disbelief. "The rest of us had to endure a long period in pain before falling into a coma."

"It must be my robust genes," Mac said and grinned.

"Actually, I think it was just the opposite," Chris countered. "Do any of you remember anything?"

"I remember a black void: thick and suffocating." Lena shuddered, her voice falling to a whisper. "There were images and sounds."

Mitch stared at Lena pensively. "Images and sounds," he repeated softly. "Yes, I remember that. Wait, there was something..."

"An ocean cove...flowing rocks...forms that kept changing," Lena went on, as if Mitch had never spoken. She looked out the door. "We must go." She walked outside and headed for the bay's breakwater.

"Yes, we must go," Mitch repeated. Instead of following Lena, he walked stiffly toward the rear of the camp.

Chris stood on the main stoop, confused. She watched as Mac ran after Lena, and Mitch headed toward the airstrip. He opened the larger cruiser's hatch and boarded. She wanted to follow him, but her concern for Lena and the others kept her frozen. To her relief, once Mitch had taken off, her trance broke. She ran nervously after Lena and Mac. The Quanta followed her.

Mechanically, Lena went to the breakwater and climbed onto the pile of rocks that formed a natural barrier between the bay and the ocean. Today, the protected bay was smooth as a mirror, and in the channel, black waves thrashed as the wind whipped them furiously. Chris could taste salt on her lips and smell the distinctive brine of the sea. Fighting a growing sense of unease, she let the others go ahead.

Initially, a solid dirt path made walking easy. Eventually, however, teetering rocks replaced the level trail. The Quanta followed closely behind Lena, unimpeded by the terrain, while Chris slipped and stumbled over the irreverent rocks, grumbling at their lack of cooperation. The black stones would wobble just when she needed them to remain stationary. Chris envied the Quanta, who glided above the jagged path. Soon she was covered with bloody scratches.

When at last the party arrived at the end of the rock pile, Lena climbed up on a large boulder that stretched out over the water and cocked her head, listening. The ocean breeze splashed ice-cold water onto Chris, soaking her clothes. Rain burst from the rolling cloud cover, making a bad situation even more intolerable. She was shivering uncontrollably by the time the rain stopped and the water returned to a smooth mirror.

Chris was about to demand they return for dry clothes when Lena pointed toward the horizon. "Do you see?" she asked. "They are coming."

Chris heard the mental echo of Andre's identical words, adding to her growing sense of doom. She spotted a shimmering light beneath the surface of the water, out in the channel. As the disturbance came closer, she could see swirling ribbons of light forming rings of color. The light changed from dim flickers to a spinning glow to a bright beam, shattered by the channel's ceaseless motion.

Right in front of Lena, the water gathered into a bubbling cascade that mushroomed into a fluttering flower silhouette. Chris thought the form was made of ocean water, but upon closer inspection she could see that it was actually composed of a dense, transparent element around a core of twisting lights. The petals shifted shape from short and thick to long and thin. The stem was as narrow as a blade of grass and then as thick as a man's arm.

Finally the liquid being solidified into a form akin to the crystal flowers in the cave. The core patterns of light swirled ceaselessly, mesmerizing Chris as they had before. Before Chris could break her trance, Lena turned stiffly to face the entire group and, in a voice not her own, began to speak:

"We are called Citrinals. We are natives of this planet. In order to communicate, we've joined with this life-form. This bond has allowed us to learn your language and history by accessing its memories.

"We need your help," Lena droned, in the same dead voice. "You can now see the flying visitors that live on our planet. Because we're animated mineral, our race is able to travel to other dimensions where physical laws are different. We found races enslaved by oppressive regimes, anxious to escape. So we offered them sanctuary. Too late, we discovered that there is a terrible price for transporting and sustaining them here. Our life force is failing.

"Although we have taken individual forms, our race began as a single consciousness in this planet's ocean. When the silver mind found us, it showed us the benefits of individualization, and we began traveling the cosmos. Periodically, we must return here to regenerate in the silver. Otherwise we revert to immobile minerals locked in silence."

Even using Lena's voice, Chris could hear the alien's revulsion. This must be the Citrinals' version of hell.

"We were unaware of the weakening silver until the consequences were devastating," the Citrinal admitted. Even though Lena's voice was flat, her eyes darted from face to face. "We don't have the power to return the refugees to their own dimension in time to save ourselves. Soon we will be entombed in this ocean, trapped in a waking sleep.

"By accident, we learned that your race has a power that regenerates us. Our curious children were drawn to your camp against strict orders to stay away. They would approach as part of the waves pounding along this beach. When they were carried back into deeper water, they could move independently again. More and more of us visited your camp, and soon many were individualized again. We must discover your secret before we're imprisoned in the ocean once more.

"In exchange for access to this planet's resources, we want the chance to learn how to replicate your power and the opportunity to join with those humans who wish direct dialogue with our kind. You have already formed an alliance with the Quanta, so we thought you might be willing to consider one with us. If you refuse, we must ask you to leave." Lena stood painfully rigid, her expression grim.

"I have questions," Chris stalled instinctively. Despite the threat, which in all honesty was their right, her internal alarms were ringing wildly. Something was terribly wrong with their so-called joining. Chris reasoned that this joining must be the illness that had overwhelmed her people. So far, Andre was dead, Lena was acting like a puppet, and Mac might require some serious time in a padded room undergoing intense therapy by sympathetic professionals. Right now, he was talking to an invisible friend and giggling, his strange giddiness more than a little disturbing.

When the water figure nodded, Chris felt overwhelming relief. Maybe she could learn something useful. "What is the exact nature of this joining? What are the side effects?"

"Your race is new to us, so we haven't discovered all the consequences of joining. It seems that the joining is permanent. Severing the link will result in death for both parties. We want to assure you that we are not parasites, physically sharing your bodies for some selfish purpose. We seek a partnership with those able to handle such an intimate connection. However, there is always the possibility of bad results, a failed joining."

"A bad result is putting it mildly," Chris mumbled, as she watched Mac pantomime baseball to an imaginary audience.

"Your people are isolated in physical shells, experiencing connection only through words and touch," the Citrinal continued. "Our people are always connected and share their experiences with many. We live as a linked community, and our collective consciousness is quite resourceful. Joining would give your people access to all that we have experienced and imagined.

"Through this host you call 'Lena,' we've learned that your people are acquiring unexpected gifts from our bond with you. You now have magnified senses and enhanced mental acuity. We think many benefits will come from blending our societies," the Citrinal declared triumphantly.

"I vote for the alliance," Lena chimed in.

Even though Lena sounded normal during this last comment, Chris knew she was still different. Her expression was confrontational and suspicious, so unlike her usual demeanor. Chris was reminded of Lena's strange actions when she'd become sick. The implication was painfully clear. She couldn't tell where the alien stopped and the real Lena began.

"We need time to consider the possibilities and consequences," Chris insisted. She needed some basis for a decision other than this alien's word. Then she remembered Mitch. He could provide the necessary delay that was so essential. "We have to consult Mitch."

"Where is Mitch?" the Citrinal hissed. The cascade shot up thirty feet and sprayed the entire group. A rigid Lena scanned the immediate area. The two Quanta beeped questioningly. It was clear they hadn't noticed Mitch was missing.

Chris guessed that the alien wasn't happy that not everyone had been compelled to meet them. "He had other errands," she explained, covering for him. She really didn't know what his gig was.

"May our friends come here without becoming infected?" Chris asked, distracting the bubbling figure with more questions. This was more important than Mitch's location. Beth would return soon and want to land.

"While we wish others for the joining," the living mineral admitted, "we'll wait for permission."

"We'll need two days to make our decision." Chris hoped this would be enough time to learn the whole truth.

"Agreed. We will meet back here." Without further ado, the Citrinal disappeared. Where once there had been a living fountain, there were now swirling waves. The flickering play of light beneath the surface headed for deeper water. A mound of water, displaced by the alien, marked its progress. In a matter of seconds, the water settled back into quietly lapping waves.

Chris wasted no time in useless arguments with Lena, who seemed bent on supporting the Citrinals. Chris didn't trust her, and Mac was…well…er…occupied. Her first priority was to find Mitch. Stumbling over the rocks in her haste to get back, she swore profusely as her arms and legs acquired new scrapes and cuts. It took a painfully long time to reach the dirt path. When she arrived at the first buildings, Chris saw Mitch's cruiser far out over the Crystal Mountains. He was returning.

CHAPTER 18

CAVERN CRYSTALLINES—CHRIS

"**W**hen do we contact Earth?" Lena asked, skipping up alongside Chris. Without waiting for an answer, she brought up several more topics as easily as a baby bird pecking at seeds. "Linking with the Citrinals is phenomenal. Look at those deer hiding in the trees. I can almost smell their soft fur. Those flying fish have ruby scales." Lena pointed to the center of the channel. "Can you believe our luck? We make first contact with a sentient species and end up new and improved. We need to send requests to the alliance immediately."

During this barrage, Siri had offered no analysis or opinion. Chris, covertly glancing at her floating friend, hoped for some insight. Unfortunately, the Quanta were, as usual, inscrutable.

Chris let Lena chatter without interruption as she walked toward the airstrip and brooded over the strange conversation with the Citrinals. All their arguments hung together with perfect logic. Maybe that was the problem. Everything was too perfect. The Citrinal had given no downside to the joining, and there was always a downside.

And just why was Lena so ready to jump on their bandwagon? Lena was usually their most cautious team member.

"Really, Chris, I can take care of all the arrangements," Lena offered. "I'll contact the *Aries* as soon as Mitch agrees."

Wait. The word was faint, hardly discernible. Chris felt a thrill of fear. "What?" she asked, looking around. The voice was nearby.

"Did you say something?" Mac asked, catching up with the two women.

"I said I can contact the *Aries* as soon as Mitch agrees," Lena repeated louder, with a smile that never quite reached her eyes. She looked at Chris, puzzled. "Something is wrong. I should be able to contact your host by now."

Chris laughed nervously. Lena's unrelenting crusade was exhausting and unnerving. "Nothing's wrong. *Relax.*" Chris looked directly at Lena, making the last word a command.

The noise of the cruiser made further conversation impossible. Everyone watched as Mitch glided in, skillfully touched down, and shut down the vehicle's systems. In the welcome silence, the hatch swung open, and he hopped out.

"As to contacting the *Aries* or anyone else…" Chris faced Lena with a stern expression. "You will wait. There will be no action until we all have time to consider. You'll keep your opinions to yourself unless asked. Siri, I trust you to secure all communications until we reach a consensus. Agreed?"

With a mutinous expression, Lena gave a barely visible nod. Siri beeped in a singsong tone that sounded like "OK." Satisfied, Chris headed back to the main cabin.

Mitch needs to speak with you alone, a soft whisper said. Chris tripped involuntarily but quickly recovered, feigning an embarrassed expression.

Who are you? Chris thought, feeling silly. Talking to a voice in her head was not a good sign.

Remember the cove and the cave. Remember Andre's attack.

Images crowded into Chris's mind. She saw beautiful crystal flowers swaying in the cove cave. She stumbled again when images of Andre's attack triggered reflexive panic.

Wait, she pleaded silently. *I can't listen right now.* Chris refocused her eyes, forcing her feet to keep moving forward. The mental scenes vanished instantly. She prayed that Lena hadn't noticed her confusion and discomfort. But why should she get lucky now when this whole mission had been one disaster after another?

Lena reached out a steadying hand. "Chris, maybe you should lie down. I can give you a sedative. I am, after all, responsible for your mental health." Chris recognized the one way Lena could gain control of their situation: declare her unfit.

"That won't be necessary." Chris affected her old confidence. "I just need some quiet time."

"Chris, may I speak with you?" Mitch interjected.

"Of course," she replied too quickly. Any way to get away from Lena was welcome.

Mitch touched Lena's shoulder and smacked his lips suggestively. "I really would love dinner. Lena, would you mind? You're such a good cook."

Lena had made frequent excuses to cook, so she couldn't gracefully refuse now. She stormed away, refusing to be dismissed quietly.

"Was it me?" Mitch asked impishly.

"I don't think she has ever fully recovered. She took us to the breakwater to meet with this planet's aliens, the Citrinals." Chris sighed heavily.

"They were afraid of this." Mitch guided Chris back to the cruiser. "It's imperative that we talk out of the range of the sea beings. I'm surprised you haven't already been detected."

Confused, Chris allowed him to take her into the cruiser. Mitch jumped into the pilot's seat and lifted off as soon as the hatch locked.

Chris checked the camp below before they were out of range in time to see Lena waving frantically. "We have an objector." She pointed out the window.

Mitch called the base's central communication node and smiled when Siri responded. "Chris and I are going to examine some new crystal readings. Tell Lena not to worry."

"Understood," replied Siri.

"She'll just have to wait until we get back," Mitch said before setting the cruiser to full speed.

"I'm going to wring her neck," Chris raged, as soon as they were some miles away from camp. "Lena can't stop insisting that we lure our entire planet here as hosts. I'm not ready to give away the entire farm, and I can't understand why she is. I must assume that Lena is under their complete control."

"Tell me what happened," Mitch recommended sympathetically. After engaging the autopilot, he led her back to one of the comfortable couches.

Chris ran her fingers nervously through her hair, trying to soothe her agitation. She began pacing the narrow space, gesturing with her hands as she spoke. Mitch escaped back to the pilot's seat, out of her way.

"After you left—mysteriously, I might add—Lena took us to the end of the breakwater, and an alien appeared in a cascade of water. Using Lena as its voice, it told us that they had infected us in order to communicate with us. The flying creatures we saw are refugees they saved from other worlds. They want to form an alliance with us, like the Quanta. But something feels very wrong. I don't believe it's safe to bring a large contingent of imperfect humans here. We might end up like the refugees: floating helplessly in another galaxy.

"But you left on your own. Do you know something about what is happening?" Chris asked hopefully, finally plopping back on the cushioned seats.

Mitch took the seat opposite and leaned forward confidentially. "Chris, we all have symbionts: living mineral that attaches to our brain centers." He placed his big palms over her fidgeting hands. "Ella and I were infected when we found one of their caves in the Crystal Mountains. You, Ella, and I have symbionts from the caves. They're called Crystallines. Lena and Mac were infected by the children of the water: Citrinals. They must have been exposed when they ran tests on the ocean.

"The Crystallines summoned me back to your cave near the waterfalls. They told me what happened when Andre found you. They infected him to save you. Unfortunately, he continued to fight against the joining, and they couldn't prevent his death."

"Lena tried to help him. Her symbiont must have known what was happening."

"It's likely that Andre's symbiont was never strong enough to make its presence visible." Mitch leaned closer to show her his face. "Look," he said, putting his eyes directly in her line of sight.

There were sparkling specks dancing around his pupils. Chris could see the Mitch she knew, along with the lively being that had joined with him, peeking out of his eyes. These tiny lights conveyed, in their complex motion, an orderly intelligence that yearned to be known. If eyes were the windows to the soul, then she could see both souls.

Chris moved to a small mirror hanging on the wall. In it, she could see the swirling flecks of her own symbiont. The blue and green chips suggested youthful gaiety and playfulness. Chris smiled back, until she remembered Lena.

Lena is not as you once knew her. Now released, this inner voice spoke in a sweet, lilting tone. *She is totally under the thrall of her symbiont. Let us tell you our story in our way. Also, we can bring you up to date on Mitch's discoveries.*

Images flooded Chris's mind. This time she could relax back into her seat. The room around her faded, superimposed with a night view of the river base. The evening bonfire provided a warm circle of home to the otherwise alien landscape. In the images, she could see the crystal flowers hiding in the underbrush surrounding the camp. The silver ran just below a layer of soil, allowing them complete freedom to roam. They had cleverly followed behind Mitch's probes, outside the view of their cameras.

Then Chris began to receive scenes from Mitch's experiences. She saw events unfold as if she were Mitch. She knew his thoughts, felt his emotions, saw his perceptions, and understood his decisions. The day he went to the Crystal Mountain range unfolded.

"I have found an alien energy signature," Ella informed Mitch, pointing.

Mitch's eyes followed Ella's gesture to a canyon filled with giant crystalline pillars. The formations were not shaped in the expected haphazard fashion of earth crystals, but instead had precise rectangular faces. Mitch was reminded of New York skyscrapers made entirely of perfectly faceted glass. Inside each pillar, cords of energy curled into helix patterns before intertwining with other strings. These fused strings gradually brightened until they exploded and filled the pillars with brilliant blinding light. Then the light would fade, and the process would begin again. When Mitch flew close to one of the strange energy fires, his cruiser looked like a child's toy beside the huge crystals.

Mitch turned on his digital recorder and released three specialized probes. Instantly, Chris recognized them as ones designed to measure different wavelengths of light: infrared to optical to ultraviolet. This data would tell Mitch what elements and chemicals were used to fuel these strange conflagrations.

Followed by his team of probes, Mitch flew up and down the crystal towers using his ship sensors to measure particle emissions. He looked rather like a mother goose leading her chicks, except that Echo, his smallest chick, kept lagging behind and getting lost, either that or Echo just wanted to go its own way.

After several hours, Ella popped into the cruiser, startling Mitch. He glanced up to find the sun low on the horizon. He signaled for his three probes—Red, Ultra, and Echo—to return. Immediately, Red and Ultra hurtled through the open hatch, knocking over equipment before crashing onto the couch. Mitch laughed at their ludicrous antics, not surprised by the damage. These probes were programmed prototypes, so haphazard flying was to be expected. He spent many late nights repairing and reprogramming his little creations.

But Echo hadn't returned. Mitch scrutinized the canyon patiently and found Echo circling the three largest pillars, stopping briefly at the apex of each and buzzing loudly. Mitch increased the volume on Echo's receiver and gave the emergency command to return. With a sigh of relief, he saw Echo spin around and head back. As it approached, it weaved unsteadily.

Ella had returned to the open door. She had jerked out of range when Red and Ultra had bounced off the door, snorting at their clumsy entrance. She was not impressed with Mitch's ingenuity and seemed embarrassed by the airbots' inelegance. When Echo entered, she immediately hooked him on one of her appendages and attached a data storage device to the little probe.

The images stopped, and Chris looked questioningly at Mitch.

"These pillars are the oldest crystal structures on this planet," he offered by way of explanation. His eyes gleamed with suppressed excitement. "Echo recorded a strange transmission coming from the largest pillars. Ella and I were unable to decode these signals until my symbiont could finally speak to me. He said it was a second

SOS sent into space, a call for anyone to come help them escape the return of their terrible prison caused by the Citrinals' efforts to save alien refugees.

"The first SOS was sent many centuries ago when the Crystallines were alive and intelligent, but trapped in these mineral pillars, a frozen existence. Their efforts seemed futile, until the alien spores came. They call themselves the 'silver mind,' and they used their power to shatter the crystal matrix that held the Crystallines trapped. The newly freed crystals could take any shape, so these silly creatures chose flowers. You see, they loved the flowering plants on their planet that were as immobile as the Crystallines themselves. The multitude of colorful minerals provided a vivid palette for their new shapes.

"Now because the Citrinals are draining the silver mind's energy, the crystal flowers are dying. They hoped we were their saviors. They didn't realize we couldn't hear their call for help."

Chris nodded, momentarily overwhelmed by the story of these exotic crystals. Before she could ask questions, her inner vision blurred again, and the scene at the breakwater appeared. These images came from her memories.

I am with the one you call Mitch. A low masculine voice filled her thoughts as she watched a replay of the alien dialogue on the breakwater. *I was the one who urged him to come to us. We did not realize that Lena and Mac were already claimed by the Citrinals.*

This time when Chris studied the breakwater speech, Lena's silent struggle was obvious. In her twitching jaw and stiff, straining body, Chris saw the tiny signs of Lena's rebellion. She was not nonchalantly letting the Citrinals speak through her; she was fighting to reclaim her own body. So the Citrinals could take control. The first lie had been uncovered.

Lena tried to break out of its thrall, but her symbiont was too savage, Chris's symbiont snarled, obviously offended by the counselor's mistreatment.

When will the Citrinals know that we are not infected by them? Chris asked mentally.

In the early stages of merging, the symbiont is hidden. The group mind does not instantly make contact, Mitch's symbiont explained. Chris liked his low, resonant mind voice. *You are a new species, and they might suppose that the merging is taking longer. As you saw, each union has its own timetable.*

What of Lena? Chris asked, her voice trembling. *Do we all lose control? Can you drive us around like a car?* Her team had already been infected and bound to any and all consequences. It was alarming to be totally at the mercy of what might happen next.

Each pairing achieves its own balance between host and symbiont. My equilibrium with Mitch, wherein each can speak, is common. But your race is new to this type of mingling and therefore has not experienced the final settling. Logically, if the mind of the host is weak, then the symbiont will exert more influence over the body. If the host is strong-willed, like you, then they may override their symbiont. The body's first loyalty will always be to the host, not the new tenant.

Chris, you have already established your dominance by ignoring your symbiont. We called you, along with Mitch, but you didn't come. As you saw, Lena is struggling for domination. Your race is strong; many would prevail. Regrettably, the Citrinals' involvement complicates everything. If they discover that you hold Crystallines, you will be killed.

Chris felt a stream of uneasiness, which she knew came from her symbiont. The lilting voice of her new companion spoke. *They have offered you an alliance. We would like an equal opportunity to create an official relationship with your race. You have not been fully informed of all relevant facts.*

"We have arrived at the preprogrammed destination," interrupted the ship's autopilot.

Mitch ducked his head sheepishly. "We've already arranged a meeting. We can't risk discovery before we hear from the Crystallines." Ella popped into the seat next to Chris. "We've called

Ella here for the meeting. Did you have any trouble?" he asked the little computer.

"Nothing we couldn't handle," the computer assured him. "I think Lena is gaining a measure of success at subduing her symbiont."

Mitch nodded, slipped back into the pilot seat, and flipped the switches that restored manual control. Chris looked out the window, expecting a view of the familiar meadow and waterfall. Instead, Mitch descended into an incredible hidden valley. The trees formed a canopy of thick foliage filled with crystals, hiding the central river from view. This amazing river was not water. It carried the thick mercury-like fluid called the *silver mind*. It sparkled as it surged into a complex of caves nearby. Chris could see the familiar glow inside the cave entrances.

She waited impatiently, as Mitch cautiously landed in the unfamiliar terrain, before bounding through the open hatch and into the large central cavern. She longed to see the extraordinary world of the living crystals again, for nothing could match the firsthand experience.

Inside the cave, silver flowed everywhere, creating waterfalls around limestone pillars and against cavern walls. Chris recognized her favorite glasslike blooms playing in the swift currents of silver. She watched as they surfed over the falls, dove through the pools, and climbed back up the walls, before running the same route again. They swerved dangerously close to stalagmites and stalactites, undamaged and unconcerned. The crystal flowers' antics drew her laughter, while the massive crystal beams that framed several geodes stole her breath away. Before Citron, she had never expected to see brilliant faceted gems the size of buildings.

In the center of the cave, a cleared arena offered makeshift benches obviously intended for Mitch and Chris. Rivulets of silver crisscrossed this area, providing a means for the crystal creatures to come close to the benches.

Chris wandered through the great amphitheater, fascinated by each new alien feature. She could see isolated passages leading to glowing rooms that hid unknown treasures. Ella was documenting the more fabulous displays. Chris wondered if Ella's symbiont was providing her with the companionship her nexus could not.

Several tiny versions of larger flowers were cradled in the silver like dozing infants and others were tossed into the air, trilling like laughing toddlers. Chris marveled again at the way the silver could expand and contract, taking on whatever solidity it desired. Sometimes it flooded like water; other times it was as hard as metal. Periodically, intriguing streams of gold light flashed through the fluid.

A new, expectant rustling grew in the cavern. Crowds of floating crystal began gathering around the cleared arena. Increasingly complex patterns of gold light rippled across the floor, and the flowers began their characteristic swaying.

Chris heard her companion's familiar voice translate mentally. *All parties have arrived. We are ready to begin.*

Mitch, Ella, and Chris were directed to the center benches by their companions. Chris felt self-conscious and nervous as she settled herself on a bench next to Mitch. From one of the isolated passageways, several towering violet creatures crossed to the humans. Apparently, they weren't being assisted by the silver rivers. Clumsily, they lurched forward on slender stalks.

"What in the world?" Chris exclaimed. "I thought—"

That we could not get around without our silver. The nearest purple crystal quivered. *We who rule have this mutation.* The voice they heard was eloquent, musically modulated, and obviously the mental voice of the amethyst ruler. *It seems that our discovery of your special ability has been duplicated by our water cousins. They have also used the ancient practice of joining to infiltrate your group. So we must hurry. Please come with us.* The ruler waved an amethyst stalk toward the back of the cavern.

The tall amethyst crystals led the humans to an elaborate archway. Two gold pillars, with veins of silver coiling down the length of each, framed the entrance. The door was as high as the ceiling, and the small group entered a vast chamber that gave access to a network of hallways filled with cubbyholes. Within each hollow nestled a snow-white, oval cocoon. These globes glowed with an iridescence similar to that projected from the cave walls.

This chamber is the heart of our community. These orbs contain mineral lattice bathed in our living silver. The silver mind is the power that animates us. It gives us our freedom to move independently and the ability to express ourselves. Our children are born here, and our adults come here to be regenerated.

You see, we don't die in the same manner as your race. After a predetermined period, those of our race just renew their life force. All must come to this chamber. But as you can see, something is dreadfully wrong.

The tallest flower waved toward the rear of the chamber.

Chris scanned the numerous rows of regenerating hollows until she could see the back area. A distinct foul odor assailed her nose. She peered deeper into one shadowy hallway and spotted large sections of dead crystal. These cracked, blackened hulks spilled smoking decay.

"What has happened?" she cried miserably. At some point, like a baby duckling, Chris had imprinted on this beautiful race.

Our living silver is failing. The power to transmit intelligence does not regenerate as quickly, or in the volume necessary, to sustain our population because the Citrinals use it to capture their refugees.

Chris shivered at the word *capture*. The implications were obvious. So here was lie number two.

The silver river sustains all creatures on this planet, the mental voice explained bleakly. *When the sentient silver fades, our population dies also. We have warned our ocean cousins that they are destabilizing the silver by trying to support so many aliens. We think they use the refugees to travel deeper into other dimensions and now can't return them when their own survival is at risk. In response, they have diverted more of the silver mind to regenerate their own people, with no concern for the rest of us. We were fortunate they lost the ability to leave the planet and couldn't draw more energy from our silver mind.*

Then your people came. Some believed that you came in response to our SOS. But when it became clear that you couldn't hear it, those few believers had to abandon this hope. So we planned to stay hidden until you completed your survey and left. Our planet is toxic to many alien life-forms due to the high concentrations of minerals in the water and air. If you had persisted, we could have used the silver mind to increase particle concentrations, so you would have had to leave.

While we waited, your race serenaded us with your beautiful singing. We rejoiced that another race shared our love of sound. Your music stories beckoned our young and, miraculously, awoke our silver. The little ones' renewed vitality was soon apparent to everyone. We tried to contact you using our crystal sounds, but you didn't understand. So we spoke in the rustling wind and the crashing waves. We pleaded through the crackling fire and the squeaking branches. Still, you didn't answer. So we took the risk and used the ancient gift of joining. This is the greatest sacrifice a Crystalline can make, surrendering its will to another life-form.

The mental voice's cadence echoed in such a haunting way that Chris felt a profound sympathy. Tears came to her eyes.

By the greatest stroke of luck, you brought a way to save our silver mind. We had called to the Guardians for help, but they didn't answer. Their silence seemed to condemn us.

"You know about the Guardians?" Chris asked, a new excitement gripping her. "We have only rumors."

On Earth, all information about these gatekeepers came secondhand from the Quanta. Here was a unique opportunity to expand their knowledge from an independent source. Fortunately, the leader of the Crystallines seemed in a mood to talk.

Do you know the science behind the Guardian portals?

Chris shook her head. Humans had been so happy to find a way to travel through space that nobody had asked too many questions.

We discovered the time-space portals quite by accident, the amethyst ruler explained. *We believe that black holes are formed when massive gravity wells tear the membrane of our universe. These black holes create the familiar shape of spiral galaxies by pulling stars through the tear like water falling through a funnel.*

As these super black holes accelerate away from the center of our universe, they leave a trail of holes behind, allowing travel to locations in space otherwise too far away. We believe that space is not flat like a piece of paper, but wrinkled like a rumpled sheet.

We think dark energy keeps these tears stable enough to use as doorways. The trick is gaining access to these windows, which of course is how the Guardians police violent races.

Chris held her breath, fearing any sound might stop the alien's story. Mitch, too, seemed spellbound, holding himself rigid and unmoving.

The Crystalline's mental voice grew solemn, as if he was about to impart some closely guarded secret. *The real secret is not everyone can pass through these portals safely. Since the portals exist outside space-time, travelers must be able to sustain their forms when they move through. One way is to use intelligent resonance. Consciousness, when properly manipulated, can create a bubble of protection. On this planet, Crystallines and Citrinals have to use other methods that your science hasn't yet discovered.*

But time is running out, and we want to demonstrate the great value you have to us and to the Citrinals. If you will sing one of your story songs, you will see what we have just discovered. The leader bowed then, in a manner that conveyed high esteem. The tall creature's movements were so graceful and precise that the gesture was utterly disarming.

A new group of emerald flowers carried two musical instruments through the group. They handed both to Mitch. How the

Crystallines had retrieved them from their ocean camp, under the noses of Lena and Mac, would remain a mystery.

Awkwardly, Mitch handed over the keyboard. Chris considered several songs before beginning one that had a wide range of high and low notes. Mitch copied the melody faithfully before weaving in harmonic variations on his guitar. Chris repeated the spirited chorus a second time, and the nearby Crystallines started to quiver in a sympathetic rhythm, creating a musical reverberation that echoed through the nursery.

When the song reached its dramatic crescendo, telling of the final union of the young lovers, the crystal world responded. Magically, the silver river fused into spherical globes that rose in the air. These floating balls of intelligence, so like mercury, began to coat the burned-out cocoons, and soon many were glimmering with dim light. Chris maintained the high note for as long as she could. Finally, she had to take deep mouthfuls of air, grasping Mitch's shoulder for support. Surprised, Mitch stopped playing, and the silver dropped back into the rivers.

Despite the abrupt end to the song, Chris saw that several of the dark orbs continued to shine and finally blazed with self-generating intensity. The silver river itself sparkled with brighter luminosity, splashing playfully around the musicians, rushing down the corridor, through the door, and out into the main chamber. They had indeed regenerated the precious silver mind.

Mitch, beaming with delight, lifted Chris into a great bear hug and swung her around in circles. A cooling wind of flapping mineral petals filled the nursery. Chris's symbiont relayed to her that this was the Crystallines' way of celebrating the success of their experiment. For all the amethyst leader's seeming confidence, the aliens hadn't been entirely certain that this demonstration would work.

Chris sobered when an image of Lena flashed through her mind. The Citrinals had warned her that tampering with the joining would mean death. She prayed that, in this at least, they had been lying.

"Our friends are being held under the thrall of the Citrinals. Can you help us?" she asked the leader.

There is an ancient toxin that can force the Citrinals out of your friends, he responded. *It is dangerous and carries great risk. It is possible that neither symbiont nor host will survive.*

"Mac would never accept a life of servitude," Mitch hissed, so full of anger he was shaking. His eyes narrowed, and he pressed his lips together. "I know what my twin would want us to do."

"Lena doesn't want this joining," Chris pointed out, remembering the girl's silent struggle. "We must help her fight them."

The leader nodded and motioned the humans to follow. He led them back through the main cavern and down various passageways until they arrived at the mouth of a remote, dark tunnel different from the rest of the cave complex. As soon as Chris crossed the threshold, she left the lighted world of living crystals and entered a dismal, dank shaft hewn into dense rock. A river of silver followed the group, very much like an interested parent.

Soon, hot steam obscured their path, making all their forms indistinct. The air grew heavy and oppressive. Chris stumbled in the half-light and caught Mitch's steadying arm for support. Without warning, they found themselves standing in front of a heavy granite door.

In a world of dancing crystals and precious minerals, this door stood out like a wound. Solid and unyielding, the ominous slab could have shielded the end of the world, and, for Citron, it did just that. It opened to a barren room. Against the walls, dirt had been piled high, adding a layer of protective insulation. The room was empty except for a pool of bubbling, malodorous brown sludge in the center of a dirt floor. A granite cover, similar in composition to the door, had been pulled askew, so a sliver of the pool was visible.

This substance will make your systems toxic to the Citrinals, Chris heard. *The symbionts in your friends will be forced to exit their bodies or die. We don't know what it will do to humans.*

Chris acknowledged lie number three. Citrinals didn't die if separated from their hosts.

The Crystalline leader chosen to speak for its race pointed toward the middle of the room. In response, the silver river flowed through the dirt like a mythical snake and pushed the cement cover further open. A fetid odor overwhelmed the room. Chris covered her nose and mouth with her hands and swallowed deliberately to calm her uneasy stomach. She had a horrible premonition that they might actually be required to drink the foul stuff, and, sure enough, the leader's next statement confirmed her fears.

You must consume this substance diluted by two parts water.

The leader lifted a small quantity of dirt to indicate the amount of one portion. Luckily, it was about a teaspoon.

It will be difficult, but it will achieve your goal.

Ella collected several doses from the bubbling pool.

Chris turned to Mitch, one eyebrow raised questioningly. "Do you want your companion gone?"

Mitch tilted his head and pursed his lips thoughtfully, considering her question for several long moments. Then he shook his head.

"I came to space because I wanted to find the future, what I like to call 'tomorrow's treasures,'" he admitted with a faint smile. "My companion offers me a way to experience life that is impossible on Earth. As twins, Mac and I have always been close, so I'm used to sharing my thoughts. Joining is the next logical step. My one concern is whether a companion can leave this planet for extended periods." Mitch looked at the amethyst leader.

The leader beckoned to a transparent flower waiting at the door. The newcomer brought a strange bracelet of silver fluid to the leader, who handed it to Mitch.

Your companion is willing to travel with you. But he requires regular exposure to the silver, so we have prepared this container. The bracelet will fill his needs for three Earth years. Then you will have to return, so he can regenerate. The bracelet will also allow you to communicate with us. If ever something happens to your companion, the silver will know and send word.

Much to Chris's astonishment, she too realized that she wanted to remain joined. With her companion, everything was brighter and more intense. Returning to her original state would mean seeing the world through muffled senses and being truly alone for the rest of her life. Even if she remarried, a prospect that was currently intolerable, she would never know this degree of intimacy.

Chris felt a thrill of fear as she recognized the seductive power of this race. Once joined, no reasonable person would want to go back.

But Ella had no use for a mineral stowaway. She wanted to reconnect to the Quanta's nexus. Because Ella was, in fact, a machine, the companion was able to leave under its own power. Chris watched as a glimmer filled the edges of Ella's panels before pouring off her body as a cascade of mineral dust. This sparkling dust combined with the silver river and then reappeared as a small clear crystal. The river rose under the little fellow, and the crystal surfed from the room, making a sound very much like "Whee!"

"Our superiors will be coming to Citron," Chris admitted. "Can they avoid infection without drinking this ooze?" She doubted Beth would jump at the chance to drink a smelly brown sludge upon landing.

In order to become infected by one of us, we have to make physical contact, the amethyst leader warned. *If you are already carrying a symbiont, you can't be infected again. Keep your friends isolated, and they will be safe. If anyone shows signs of infection, you can always inject the brown death. Just increase the water dilution.* With a demeanor that might have suggested a mischievous grin, the ruler added, *You don't have to drink it.*

Chris smiled sheepishly and winked. "That's good news for Mac and Lena."

The leader led everyone back to the cavern entrance. *If you have trouble with the Citrinals, your symbionts are the fastest way to contact us.*

Chris felt a flare of animation from her usually quiet companion, followed by fear at the amethyst ruler's next words. *We don't know what kind of reception you will get when you return to your base. Be prepared for anything.*

"We will, and thank you for the antidote," Chris said.

Chris and Mitch collected their instruments and headed for the cruiser. She gazed regretfully at the beautiful valley. Even in danger, she wished she had more time to explore. Like Mitch, she marveled at their good fortune in finding a planet with such an exceptional alien race. Citron had both vast mineral wealth and fantastic natives—a mineral race. What other secrets lay hidden in those glinting mountains?

Chris spent the time flying back feeling thrilled as she imagined a life on Citron with the Crystallines, and then dreading how far the Citrinals would go to acquire human hosts.

CHAPTER 19

IONE CRAGON'S PLAN—ROSE

The cat must be out of the bag, Rose decided. Whatever grace Amy had hoped to achieve had, all too soon, run out. Amy faced Ione squarely, her arms akimbo, feet planted. Her eyes burned with a coiling ferocity, prompting Ione's guards to move closer to their leader.

"Talia—her name was Talia Sarin. She was our microbiologist. She was sweet and shy and wouldn't have hurt anyone—that is, until your *guards* got a hold of her," Amy hissed. "They killed her."

"They?" Ione repeated, uncertainty muddling her arrogance. "Who are they?"

"Jared," Amy hissed, her loathing stark and seething.

"Why?" Ione repeated, with obvious disbelief.

"Because she was trying to protect me from his *second* attack!"

"Why was Jared attacking you?"

"Because I wouldn't sleep with him."

"Where were the other guards?"

"Helping him."

"Where are they now?" the chairwoman demanded.

"You'll have to ask them," Amy spat with disgust.

"They let you leave?" Ione became more intense. She wouldn't accept vague answers.

"The last time I saw the three men was at our forest camp," Amy answered truthfully.

Rose knew this was the best strategy. The truth was easy to remember and most likely to be accepted without more questions. But Amy needed to change her role in this cross-examination. Ione had seized the role of interrogator, which would soon put them all at the tender mercies of Sentara's legal system. So Rose wasn't surprised when Amy took over the role of questioner.

"What's going on? Your goon squad is acting all temperamental. Did your men get lost?"

Rose could feel Amy's fear riding just beneath the surface of her friend's bravado.

"Jared, Justin, and Jeffrey have gone dark," Ione answered, throwing an accusing glance at both Amy and Nicole.

"And you think we had something to do with it," Rose said. "We are weak humans. How could we overcome your elite guard?"

"Enough! Until we can locate them, all of you will be confined here." Ione gestured to her guards. Eight men surrounded the humans, blocking all exits. Three others strode out the front door. "These three will investigate your forest base. I want to talk to you alone," she demanded, turning to confront Rose. "You're their leader, so you'll answer for their actions."

Rose wondered at Ione's persistence in isolating her. It was Amy who had commanded the forest group. Rose guessed that it might be because she was the one able to use telepathy. Maybe Ione thought Rose was the only real threat. Iona took her arm and propelled her toward the door. This time, Rose didn't resist.

Out of the corner of her eye, Rose saw Amy launch herself at the guard who was blocking the side exit. She jumped on his back and used her forearm as a vice around his neck to try to incapacitate him. When two other guards moved to stop her, the Quanta immediately intercepted them. Human flesh might succumb to the Sentarans' superior strength, but metal cylinders would not. So the men, who would've easily stopped Amy, battled futilely against the floating computers. The Quantas' outrage was evident in their tangled eye globes, flashing lights, and aggressive beeping. The little droids held them off long enough for Amy to knock the guard aside and escape out the door.

When the remaining guards foolishly rushed to subdue the Quanta, Nicole confronted Ione.

"You're not taking her away from us," she snarled. "We stay to-gether until the *Aries* comes." Then Nicole shoved the chairwoman away from Rose.

In response, Ione's angry eyes focused on a point above the struggling crowd, and she whispered one word: "Stop."

Instantly, everyone, including Rose, froze. Her shields hadn't protected her. Even the Quanta were still. As Ione touched each of her men, they broke out of their trance and came to attention. She instructed two of them to carry Rose out, and the other guards took control of the humans and their computer allies. The last thing Rose saw was her team being led out of their quarters in chains.

Rose was whisked away in a vehicle that looked very much like an automobile. Quinn had told her there were only a few on the entire planet. She might have been impressed except that they had tied her hands and feet, making her status as prisoner plain. The windows were tinted, keeping her plight a secret from watching bystanders. Every time they hit any irregularity in the road, Rose collided painfully with the side of the conveyance. She knew she would have dark bruises as evidence of Ione's tender treatment.

They stopped in front of a courtyard of official-looking build-ings. Rose could hardly credit the similarity of their architecture to Earth's. The columns of pale marble were identical to those found in most major cities on her planet.

A coarse-looking soldier, who didn't have any of the dazzling features of the council's private guard, opened the car door and brutally pulled Rose out. He was a dwarf, barely reaching five feet. The man had dull, bruised eyes, a broad, protruding brow, and sallow skin. Any hope she had of appealing to his better nature vanished when he smiled, revealing rotting teeth. This man experienced constant pain as a regular part of life. His large calloused hands held her in a painful vise, while Ione leisurely exited the car and led the group down a long portico.

The sun, which was dim only a few hours each morning, burned Rose's white skin and blurred her vision. Ione and her men put on special sunglasses. Rose just closed her eyes, forcing her guard to drag her in the right direction. When they were inside, the soft, cool breeze of the air conditioning offered Rose some comfort. She opened her eyes to a large marble foyer. She and her brutal companion were alone.

Her guard hauled her down a hallway into an executive office with hardwood floors and stiff-backed chairs. Rose heard the loud cyclical tick of a pendulum wall clock. The guard thrust her into one of the chairs positioned in the center of the room and facing an immense desk. Using a thick prickly rope, he tied her wrists to the arms of the chair. He bound her waist with several more coils. Hobbling her ankles guaranteed she was powerless to defend herself. This new guard kept eerily quiet throughout the whole procedure. She heard the door slam as he left the room.

Rose struggled to get free, but the ropes were unrelenting, and her efforts resulted in raw wrists and ankles. So she scanned the room for some avenue of escape. Despite its starkness, there were still feminine touches. In front of her was a desk made from fine-grained polished wood. Next to it a globe of the island planet turned slowly in its brass stand. Two tinted windows flanked the desk, letting in filtered sunlight. In its quiet way, the room was elegant. Rose had expected a sterile torture chamber.

After a period of tense waiting, Ione entered the office, went directly to a concealed cupboard, and poured herself a drink. Even though Rose was the one tied up, the chairwoman was the one who looked uncomfortable. Ione settled behind the desk and slowly leafed through several bound reports. Rose wondered how many bleeding prisoners had sat here before her.

Rose considered possible ways to unsettle the grand chairwoman. She was in no hurry to match wits with Ione Cragon. Her power was clearly greater than Rose's, even with her childhood training. She reasoned that all of them had to be infected, to some extent, by the alien spores. Why weren't the surveyors' powers growing?

The blistering sun began its brief descent, and warm dappled colors touched the room.

At last, Ione spoke to her. "We know that Amy's guards are dead, and we believe that Amy and Nicole killed them."

"Then you would be wrong." Rose spoke with such conviction that the truth of her words was unarguable. "Surely your justice system requires proof."

"Normally." Ione leaned back in her chair, pressed her fingertips together, and studied Rose.

As time stretched on, Rose realized Ione was using silence as a weapon to unsettle her. If ever they were going to escape this nightmare survey, Rose was going to have to show some teeth.

"We know everything," she challenged. Maybe she could get Ione to disclose what was really going on.

"You know what?" Ione replied carefully. She wasn't going to be drawn out easily.

"We know that you've acquired enhanced mental powers from living on this planet. We know that your race is in danger of extinction. You knew we would discover the dangers on Sentara and refuse your offer. So why bring us here?"

Ione was visibly shaken by the extent of Rose's revelations. Rose could see the chairwoman struggling for a new offensive tactic.

"Well? Why bring us to a planet that will ultimately kill us?" Rose pressed her momentary advantage.

"You're not going to die," Ione scoffed, adding, "if you help us. You don't have the important answers. We need an alliance with your people to restore our technology, not to overcome some lethal characteristic inherent to this planet. When we landed on Sentara, we were overcome almost immediately by brutal weather. All our equipment and instruments were lost, and when we were able to take stock again, we had little left to help us rebuild our technology."

"Then why try to seduce us? That was our guards' intention from the first moment we landed, an intention you had to have approved."

"To make you stay. We knew, of course, that you would discover the challenges of living here and run like rabbits back to your safe planet. We had to keep you here long enough to help us."

"And you thought that liaisons would keep us here?" Rose asked, finding this explanation unbelievable.

"In our law, a baby is owned equally by both mother and father. You wouldn't have been allowed to leave." Ione seemed quite pleased with this plan.

Rose laughed. "Well, your efforts were worse than useless. Don't you research your schemes? Human women control their own fertility until they're ready for babies. We don't get pregnant by accident." Rose was appalled at the utter futility of everyone's loss. The Sentarans' stupidity had cost Talia, Justin, and Jared their lives.

"Your authorities didn't tell us that," Ione sputtered, looking very foolish. In a surprisingly childish gesture, she picked up a cup of pencils and threw it across the room. She punctuated her next words with impatient hand gestures. "We studied your species in great detail before inviting you here."

"Our reproductive practices are not a matter of public record. We don't reveal everything—just like you didn't inform us of your real situation." Rose forced her voice to sound conciliatory. She desperately needed to get her people off this planet, intact.

"We will have those children," Ione vowed, finally revealing the real reason for this whole charade. "We will send our spies to Earth to find the drug that restores your fertility." Ione had abandoned any pretense at civilized behavior. She came around her desk, her face twisted with rage, and viciously spit in Rose's face. "We have you, and we have your ship. We will learn your science from your equipment and use it to find a way to thrive here—without giving up our powers."

"Do you think we came here without safeguards to protect our people? We have already informed Earth of our survey results."

"According to what we have communicated to the *Aries*, your team has succumbed to an incapacitating illness and will be unable to leave. Your survey obviously missed vital data." Ione seemed satisfied that the women, along with Sam, were effectively trapped.

"Why?" Rose cried shrilly, overwhelmed with frustration. "We would have helped you without any tricks."

"We couldn't take the chance that you would make an unacceptable recommendation. Earth could relocate our population, removing the danger caused by our close sun. But we won't leave, so we are forced to lure others here, using them to infuse our population with healthy children."

"You deny your people the chance for healthy children because you hang on to this empty power," Rose jeered. Even when Ione pulled her head back in retaliation and bursts of agony blurred her vision, Rose still confronted her. "The most convincing explanation for this selfish blindness is that you gain the most from this planet's enhancing properties." Then Rose took a gamble that would either set them free or incarcerate them permanently. She had one chance, while Ione was willing to give her some credibility. "And you, of course, will bear the heaviest price."

"What price?" Ione dropped her hair abruptly. She put her face close to Rose's, digging her fingers into the surveyor's shoulder, trying to use pain to intimidate her into talking.

Talking, whether of the truth or not, was just what Rose had in mind.

"The alien spores that have given you extrasensory perception have a terrible side effect. You see, it isn't the sun that heightens your perception, it is another life-form, which are the true natives of this planet. Sam detected these curious spores when he dissected the bodies you so generously provided. He couldn't figure out how these people had died until he examined their brains. As your power increases, the number of spores needed increases. Your desire to be the greatest and most powerful Sentaran on your world might require enough spores to fry your brain and—"

Rose stopped abruptly, leaving the rest to Ione's imagination. If she pushed too hard, the chairwoman might not believe her.

Ione stomped away from Rose and then turned to glare at her speculatively. She obviously didn't trust her. Rose felt the intrusion of her probing thoughts, like a sledge hammer attempting surgical incisions. She had already set her shields strong.

Meticulously, Rose created an elaborate matrix of fabricated memories. One way to keep Ione from learning the truth was to fill her mind with scenarios that supported her claim. If she was successful, Ione wouldn't be able to tell what was true from what was invention.

Fortunately, Rose knew it was common for people to create an elaborate scenario of what they called truth. They started with facts and interpreted them in light of their own experience and beliefs. What "truth" Ione Cragon had learned from her subjects in the past might have contained this conjecture.

Rose's intense concentration was disrupted by the sound of crashing glass. She never knew how long she had kept Ione distracted with her mental mazes. The chairwoman had persisted in trying to penetrate Rose's defenses to discover her innermost thoughts. It was Ione's greed to know all her secrets, not just the spore information, that allowed Rose to detain and deceive her long enough for her friends to arrive.

She felt the chairwoman stiffen as a loud commotion filled the room. Even as Ione jerked around, someone was dragging her away. Ari, Mirim, and Evan looped a heavy white cord around her and tied her to the other wood chair. Rose flinched away from a new, irritating high-pitched buzz. Ione was grimacing.

Amy cut the ropes holding Rose, pulled her to her feet, and enclosed her in a reassuring hug.

"How did you find me?" Rose asked, touching Amy's face to confirm her presence. She didn't want this unexpected rescue to turn out to be some sick trick of Ione's devious mind. But Amy was solid, and Sam touched her shoulder with a real hand.

"Ari created a link with you using the increased energy of the Quanta nexus. Our allies are full of surprises," Amy admitted. "Ari told us where they had taken you. The problem was in trying to neutralize Ione's power. I found a way, Rose. It was so simple." Amy laughed with nervous excitement.

"After I escaped, I headed back to the ship, hoping to call for reinforcements. And then it happened!" Amy's eyes shone with a new brightness. "I could hear them, Rose. So many voices…

"At first, it was hard to make out individual conversations. I tried to find Ione's mental signature. I had to know what she wanted from you. The funny thing was I could hear you almost immediately. It must be our friendship that makes our connection so strong, and the ship is very close to these buildings.

"When I arrived at the ship, I tried to call the *Aries*, but the connection was jammed with ear-shattering static. We weren't getting any help from Beth. Then it hit me." Amy's smile got wider. "Maybe all the voices are transmitting on one frequency. If I could find a way to disrupt this connection, I could create a diversion big enough to rescue you. I programmed the main converter on the BESS to produce a handheld disrupter that could broadcast on any frequency. The problem was in finding the right frequency. So I rotated the wavelength until the voices in my head were replaced by the buzz. You should have seen it, Rose. The guards dropped like overripe apples." She demonstrated with hands. "I had already toned down my own receptivity, so I wouldn't be incapacitated. Then I went to rescue our team. I figured I would need reinforcements to confront the council. Luckily, Ari was still connected to our ship."

"We had already released the Quanta and were ready to go find you, when Amy arrived," Sam supplied. "She told us about the disrupter. We didn't know how long the guards would be out of action, so we sent Sophie and Nicole to the BESS to move the ship closer to here. I'm anxious to put this planet and its shenanigans behind us."

"If you knew the truth," Rose murmured. A coldness penetrated her bones, and she shivered. "Ione was planning to keep us as permanent guests, even if she had to create a plague to do it."

Sam guided Rose to an open window with a view of an undeveloped field. The others crowded behind. Sam pointed to the far trees. "The BESS is there."

Rose struggled awkwardly through the window and then dashed across the field toward the tree line, the others behind her. All too soon, alarms began blaring. Soldiers came around the side of the building in time to see the small group running across the field. Rose cursed their bad luck and prayed for a glimpse of the BESS.

When the clamor of the soldiers got closer, Rose ran with renewed vigor. Then a shot rang out, and hot pain tore across her cheek. Blood ran down her face. Another shot, and a second crippling sting in her calf threw her forward. She scrambled for balance. Ari appeared under her arm, offering support and preventing her fall. The guards were shooting at them. It seemed that Ione would kill them before she would let them escape.

Rose tensed in anticipation, imagining the next bullet, which could drop her like an exposed deer. Her heart beat violently, her stomach clenched, and her leg throbbed. But instead of the searing pain of another bullet, she heard the unmistakable ping of metal against metal. Briefly, she caught sight of her three computer friends shielding the surveyors, giving them the few extra seconds they needed to reach the ship. Ari fell behind when Rose leaped through the open hatch into the safety of the BESS. Ari and Evan, supporting a wheezing Sam, came through next. Nicole, with Mirim shielding her, entered last.

The hatch closed with a reassuring click just before several bullets pinged off the hull. The ship trembled as Nicole engaged the roaring engines. Then it lifted off the ground, and the group gave a cheer of victory. Rose laughed with relief, because she had secretly feared they would never leave Sentara. Everyone, except Talia, was on board and heading for the safety of outer space.

But when they neared the edge of Sentara's atmosphere, Rose felt the ship bump hard against an invisible barrier. The engines roared uselessly, forcing Nicole to disengage forward thrust. Several satellites surrounded their ship and broadcasted an ominous message: "You will not be allowed through the planetary defense shield, which was activated as soon as you entered Sentara's atmosphere."

Rose realized there never had been a way to escape.

CHAPTER 20

THE CITRINALS' ANSWER—CHRIS

Lena greeted them wearing a happy turtle apron that mocked the harsh expression on her face. Her jaw was tight; her eyes, hard. They had been gone so long that the sun was falling behind the horizon.

"Where've you been?" she demanded rudely. "What crystal readings could be important enough to keep you out so long? Our hosts grew suspicious when they saw you leave again. They couldn't contact your symbionts."

Lena peered intently into Chris's face. But Chris's companion had already withdrawn from her eyes, leaving the symbiont blind and Lena still in the dark about the companion's true nature.

At the Crystalline cavern, Chris and Mitch had agreed to keep up the subterfuge until they could free Mac and Lena from their symbionts. But now, facing a suspicious Lena, she knew she had to confess the truth. It was time to find out how the Citrinals would react.

"We went to visit the other beings that live on this planet. Mitch and I discovered their caves after we built our river camp. They call themselves Crystallines, and they're the ones who infected us."

"So that's why we couldn't reach you," Lena retorted, her eyes narrowing malevolently.

"We're ready to meet with the Citrinals now," Chris offered, despite Lena's hostility. They couldn't avoid this confrontation, so she might as well invite the lions into their den.

"Not tonight," Lena said. "We want to gather our leadership for the meeting. We wait until morning."

"Have you contacted Beth?" Chris was testing Lena. If the Citrinals wanted more hosts, they would have to reach her people off planet.

"I was able to get around your guard dog, if that's what you're asking, and I did reach Beth. I told her we have a unique opportunity that we can't pass up. After our first conversation, that stupid Siri managed to remove a piece of the transmitter node and flew off to hide his prize before I could stop him."

"Did Beth say anything about your plan?" Chris didn't need to hear Lena's side of the conversation. She'd repeated it enough times.

"She wanted to talk to you, of course. I told her you had gone off without a word. I said I was concerned about your mental health and advised her to insist you get counseling to help you process Andre's traumatic death." Lena's smile was a horrible caricature of her natural one. Her companion was enjoying its power. For this race, domination and deceit came as easily as breathing.

"I emphasized the many advantages of joining with the Citrinals. I described, in great detail, the wonderful perception and strength enhancements we've all experienced. I explained that the Citrinals would share Citron's vast mineral resources and their unique science.

"I urged her to contact Earth to start the colonization process. I'm sure there are many who would jump at the chance to live in the luxury available to all who live here."

"So when do they arrive?" Chris asked, innocently.

"I don't know," Lena admitted. "Beth insisted on speaking to you first. Then she started asking irrelevant questions."

"Irrelevant? Like what?" So Beth had not swallowed Lena's fish story completely.

"She asked how I got joined," Lena grumbled. "I told her I didn't remember exactly. Then she asked about the length of my illness and whether the Citrinals offered a reason for Andre's death. I told her that his death was an accident, and I promised that all other questions would be answered when she arrived."

Chris had steered Lena into the cabin under cover of their conversation. Mitch was already sitting at the long wood table, examining his laptop. Ella was mixing chemicals in the adjacent lab. Mac was outside preparing an area for the upcoming meeting. Siri was missing.

Lena busied herself straightening items in the kitchen. She rubbed her noise absently and opened the window over the sink. A fresh breeze cleared the cabin momentarily of the foul odor of Ella's preparation.

"And?" Chris asked.

Grudgingly, Lena continued. "Then she pressed me about how the connection works. Does the symbiont ask, or does it just act?" Lena paused to fill a glass with water. Her hands were shaking, and water sloshed onto the counter. Swearing softly, she wiped up the spill before returning the dish towel to its hook. She slowly drained the glass before speaking again. "She wanted to know how the Citrinals communicate. Do they speak to my companion, who speaks to me, and then I repeat it, or do they just talk through me?"

All at once, Lena was consumed by a paroxysm of coughing. She swayed and caught herself on the counter. Then she froze, her expression blank, her eyes staring past Chris.

"What is it?" Chris asked uneasily. It occurred to her that Lena might be in real danger, especially if the Citrinals decided to shut her up. They wouldn't want the Crystallines to know the extent of their power over the humans.

"I don't know." An expression of unholy fear lit Lena's face. Tears filled her eyes. "I can't remember how I was before two days ago." Her voice was small, like that of a child who is afraid to look under the bed.

Slowly, Lena sank to the floor and began rocking back and forth. When Chris gently arrested the manic motion, Lena started to tremble instead.

Sobbing hysterically, she cried, "Help me, Chris. I can't stop them."

All at once, her eyes turned back into her head, and she fell over, unconscious, her silky black hair falling around her body like a shroud.

Urgently, Chris motioned to Ella, who brought over a large syringe of brown fluid. Chris fumbled back Lena's hair, slipped the needle into her carotid artery, and injected the fluid directly into the blood supply to her brain. Chris watched in horror as Lena's skin began to turn black and her breathing rattled. Holding the empty syringe, she prayed for some sign of improvement. Ella deftly reclaimed the needle and hid it in one of her smaller compartments, an instant before Mac burst into the room.

Malcolm didn't waste time on words. He launched himself at Chris, and they both crashed to the floor before Chris could kick him and scramble away. In the seconds before he hauled her back, she saw Mitch race for the converter. He punched several buttons before pulling out a heavy, suffocating blanket. Chris's symbiont communicated what her role was in Mitch's plan to subdue Mac. Once they'd immobilized Mac, Ella would inject him with the antidote.

Chris went wild kicking and scratching until she managed to escape Mac, giving Mitch an opportunity to throw the blanket over his twin. Then Chris landed on one side of the blanket, and Mitch held down the other. Mac roared with a ferocious rage and continued to struggle in spite of being smothered.

In the end, Mac's emotionally fueled strength proved extraordinary. One of his arms snaked free and struck out blindly, hitting Chris, but she hung on stubbornly. Changing tactics, he bucked violently, which hurled Mitch off the other side of the blanket. When Mac turned his attention back to Chris, Mitch retrieved a sturdy wood chair and brought it down on his brother.

Instantly, Mac sagged under the heavy cover and lay deathly still. Chris lifted the blanket off slowly. At first she couldn't detect any signs of life and recklessly leaned closer to see if he was breathing. Silent bubbles of saliva burst from his lips when he took a long shuddering breath.

Chris waved Ella over. The Quanta brought an extralong, round syringe completely full of the brown sludge. The amount of drug in the barrel looked to be three times greater than Lena's. The little computer must have reasoned that Mac would require a larger dose to eradicate his symbiont. Chris chuckled to herself at the obvious nervousness of the professed logical computer. She extended her hand for the needle, carefully inserted it into Mac's neck, and injected all of the fluid. Ella wasn't the only one who wanted to make absolutely certain that Mac didn't wake up in another maniacal rage.

Chris rechecked Lena and found her still unconscious, breathing shallowly. Luckily, her symptoms had not worsened. Mac was still down for the count.

Chris was still waiting for some sign of the expelled Citrinals when the front door slammed open, sending fragments of broken window glass crashing to the floor. Siri hurtled into the room, his eye globes spinning wildly.

His usual quiet voice cracked with strain. "Millions of Citrinals are coming."

Chris and Mitch raced to the front door to witness a force of such number that they froze in wonder and terror. The cove, the channel, and the ocean beyond bubbled with endless cascades of swirling, transparent silver.

"My ever-loving God," Mitch gasped. "We'll never escape. We are going to die."

His words finally catalyzed Chris into action. If she was going to die, she would go down fighting. "We have to transfer our survey reports to flash disks and destroy any equipment of value."

"I have already moved the Alpha subsurvey hovercraft next to the backdoor and loaded the important equipment," Siri assured her. "When you and Mitch returned, the water in the bay showed the telltale signs of returning Citrinals, a lot of returning Citrinals. I concluded that a quick retreat might become necessary."

This news offered a measure of hope for the small group alone on a planet set against them.

Chris and Mitch frantically completed the last critical tasks necessary before they could leave, trying to ignore the gathering army outside. Their heightened senses identified ocean waves breaking around an immense force. Thousands upon thousands of sounds flooded the cabin, indicating thousands upon thousands of beings approaching their shrinking port in the storm.

Finally the ASH team was ready to leave. Mitch, Ella, and Siri picked up their fallen comrades, Mac and Lena, and Chris opened the door. Outside, as far as the eye could see, armies of aliens stood ready to descend. Inexplicably, there was a clear space around the cabin and their subsurvey cruiser. Mitch placed his body between his brother and the menacing army and backed out. Ella carried the slight frame of Lena, whose skin was so black that Chris feared she was already dead, and followed.

The Citrinals watched, motionless. It seemed to Chris that they should have attacked as the surveyors ran to the ship. It was at this point that they were most vulnerable.

Chris waited for Mitch and Ella to carry Mac and Lena aboard the cruiser. When the engines roared to life, she dashed the short distance and jumped through the open airlock. The door snapped shut behind her with comforting finality.

Mitch cursed at the controls. The vessel shuddered, refusing to lift. Chris scrambled into the copilot chair and lifted her gaze to look outside. Waves of aliens were crossing the short distance to the ASH. Their exotic, flying refugees had vanished completely. Chris could sense their terrible rage through her symbiont. This alien army had one purpose: destroy the newcomers. They had covered the struggling hovercraft and solidified, making the cruiser too heavy to take off.

Frantically, Chris tried to open a link with the *Aries*. The familiar noise of the wireless searching for the appropriate wavelength was missing. Their communication device was dead.

"What's happening? Why doesn't this stupid thing work?" Chris slapped the impervious console, frustrated and desperate.

"I disabled it when Lena called Beth," Siri confessed desolately. "The device is missing the central capacitor. In the confusion, I left it behind. I will retrieve it," he promised.

"Are you mad?" Chris shouted, pointing through the windshield. "You can't go out there."

Siri was already gone.

He reappeared on a hilltop some distance behind the Citrinal horde and began thrashing through a small cluster of bushes. It was lucky for him that the water crystals had such singleness of purpose; they didn't seem to notice him.

Chris extended the ship's shield over the hatch to prevent the Citrinals from penetrating farther into their ship. This also prevented Siri from returning. Since the Quanta had created these shields, they were effective even against their own peculiar method of popping in and out. The shields had been one of their first innovations implemented after they built interstellar space vehicles.

The shields were their one defense, and the *Aries* had the most advanced version. No alliance ships carried large-scale weapons. Any offensive technology was too dangerous and too tempting. One slip, and space travel was over. Besides, they were explorers, not soldiers.

For the moment, the shield was holding. Unfortunately, the hardening aliens would soon block their view of the outside.

Without warning, a high thrumming filled the clearing. Chris scanned the hills, hoping for a miracle, and found one. The Crystallines burst over the last rise in numbers to rival the Citrinals. Waves of silver carried the jeweled creatures toward the besieged ship. Their strange thrumming roared through the cove, creating a sympathetic reverberation in the water entities. Where there had once been solidified Citrinals, there were now waves of water crashing back into the ocean.

We have to act now, Chris's symbiont urged. *They can't maintain that destructive pitch for long.*

"Siri! We can't leave without Siri!" Chris shouted and powered down the shield emitters.

"We must leave while we can," Mitch yelled over the din. "Siri will have to find his own way home."

Without waiting for her consent, Mitch engaged the engine, and the vessel rose. Inevitably, the disruptive vibration of the Crystallines began to falter and then faded away to a perilous silence. A new montage rose below them. In the main channel, beyond their small cove, riding on the backs of the flying refugees, was a troop of Citrinals.

"Oh my God, I don't believe it," Chris squeaked as she stared out the window. "We're trying to leave. Why won't they just let us?"

Then two things happened simultaneously. The ship escaped the planet's atmosphere, and Siri appeared behind the pilot seat holding the capacitor.

CHAPTER 21

THE GUARDIAN'S FIRST LAW—BETH

Beth thoughtfully reset the navigation to head for Sentara, reluctant to leave her best friend, Chris, to the mercies of an alien disease.

Central Alliance had forwarded all the survey tapes from Rose's Quanta Ari. She now knew about Talia's tragic murder and the enhanced abilities of the Sentaran guard. Somehow, Beth had to locate her lost team and get them off that dangerous planet.

As soon as the *Aries* had completed the portal shift to Sentara, Beth wriggled out of her suffocating navigator chair and shook off the usual disorienting sensations.

"Status?" she asked Mark.

"I've opened a channel to reach Rose, but an energy field surrounding the planet is blocking our transmission," Mark admitted grimly.

"Try to send a message to their government council," Beth suggested. "The field is theirs, so they should be able to penetrate it. I have to hope that they still want a relationship with our world."

Mark talked his way through several levels of protocol before finally reaching the Sentara council chairwoman. The link was limited to audio.

"This is Ione Cragon, director and chairwoman of the planet Sentara," said an apologetic voice. "We're experiencing communication interference from solar-flare radiation. It might be easier if your captain came down to our planet for a face-to-face meeting."

Beth glanced at Mark skeptically. He had detected a shield he said was blocking their transmission, not radiation. What was this Cragon playing at?

"This is Beth Griffin, captain of the survey ship *Aries*. We would like to talk with our people first. Is Rose with you?"

"I'm afraid that your people have been infected with what we thought was an eradicated disease," Ione objected. "They're suffering from hallucinations and violent fits. Any communication with them would only alarm you. If you would come down, we can show you their condition."

"Our team found nothing to suggest there was any contagious disease on your planet. Can you explain?" Beth asked, suspiciously.

Why was this woman pressuring her to come down? If this disease was real, she would be putting Beth in harm's way. If not, she would be adding her to the list of possible hostages. Did this chairwoman really think Beth was so easily lured into a trap? Cragon had obviously not read Sam's, Rose's, or Amy's reports. They had not been muddled. They had shown a precise application of the methodical survey procedures. Beth felt her rage growing, fueled by her own powerlessness to take immediate action.

"Easy." A soft voice hummed like fur against her ear drum.

Beth recognized the unique tones and resonance. "Goren?" she breathed, equally as soft. Her ring became warm on her finger.

"What?" Ione asked sharply. She had heard Beth.

"We'll have to be quick," Goren warned. "The Sentarans have exceptionally perceptive telepathy, and Ione is dangerously self-serving. She has Rose and her people hostage. If I had known beforehand, I would have warned you about Sentara," he lamented. "When I realized your team was already there, I kept hoping you might gain valuable insights from contact with an outpost of your own species.

"Sentara has only enough technology to send scanning probes through the portals. We've reluctantly allowed this because they have been struggling to survive. They must have started luring other races to their planet under the guise of needing help. With you, they have finally crossed the line," Goren growled protectively.

"We thought the plague was extinct," continued Ione. "All our people have acquired a natural resistance. Unfortunately, your people are showing recognizable symptoms of this illness."

Both conversations overlapped, and it took Beth a few moments to realize that Ione was answering her earlier question.

"We have isolation facilities available," Beth offered, determined to try reason first. "We have been instructed to collect our team and return home. Our Quanta are ready to coordinate a safe transfer of Rose and her team."

"We'll need to speak with you in person first," Ione persisted.

"Why? Anyone coming down to your planet will be at risk of becoming sick."

"Because we will not release your people otherwise," Ione declared, all pretense at civility gone. "You may take the appropriate measures to ensure your safety. You have one hour to comply." A loud click was followed by silence.

Beth stared bleakly at the dead receiver.

"I don't believe her," Mark snarled, breaking the poignant silence. "She's not going to release our people, now or ever. Sam's reports said they could find no evidence of disease, any disease. This is just a ruse to keep our team—and maybe some of us as well. A navigator captain would be a powerful bargaining chip."

"Cragon can't be trusted," Connor agreed. "You can't go down there!"

"Meeting Cragon on her turf is obviously not an option," Beth conceded. She would never put herself at this woman's mercy. "I want each of you to come up with ideas for saving Rose and her team. We'll meet in my ready room in twenty minutes. It's foolish to make snap decisions without collaborating."

Beth needed privacy to continue her conversation with Goren, and the *Aries* needed whatever insights he might reveal. So she went to her ready room ahead of the others.

"What does she want?" she asked abruptly, when she knew she couldn't be overheard.

"Ione is taking a terrible chance trying to keep your team," Goren confessed. "We have already given her one warning about her use of the portals to lure in other races to do her bidding. She knows she risks our wrath by threatening other species. But she needs women with high ESP potential, so she'll try to trap as many navigators as possible. Look, Beth, I've decided to help you rescue your crew. I've been on Sentara, and I've already found Rose's cell."

"Are you sure you want to get involved?" Beth asked generously. "I mean, this is our mistake, and we should be the ones who find the solution."

"Normally, I would agree. But we knew about the alien spores native to this world and didn't warn the first explorers away. When the floods stranded these people, we didn't intervene. When these new Sentarans became more and more infertile, we didn't help them. We hoped they would quietly find a solution to their problems or die out naturally. Instead, they trapped innocent explorers. It would be unacceptable if any of your survey party were killed, even accidently, by our inaction. This is a violation of our first law. Nobody may use the portals to further a murderous agenda."

"But how will you explain your presence to my crew?"

"You, my girl, have a Guardian as your new best friend. You can explain to the others that we met unexpectedly on the rogue planet. I didn't leave a clear memory of everyone's exact movements when I sent your crew back to the *Aries*. But we need to bring everyone up to speed at the same time. I think they're all still on the bridge."

Fortunately, the ready room was just off the bridge, and Beth went directly to her captain's chair unnoticed. Everyone was busy studying monitors and making notes.

Without warning, a strange static-electric heat began racing along Beth's skin, and a woman's form appeared next to her. She jumped back.

In the next moment, a blaze of green light flashed to a point in front of her, blinding everyone on the bridge. The first thing she saw, when the black spots cleared, was Goren reaching for Ione. At first it seemed as if he were touching solid flesh, but when his fist closed, it encountered nothing more than a projection of light.

Ione registered the sudden appearance of Goren by turning a sick shade of gray, and then vanished.

"A hologram," Goren cursed. "She certainly has been busy." Goren lifted Beth's hand to access her ring. "We need to act fast, now that Ione knows I'm here. She won't leave your friends alive for long. They are evidence that might bring terrible consequences to her race. Sometimes it works to our advantage to have a deadly reputation; sometimes it doesn't."

Goren pressed the appropriate jewel, and both he and Beth vanished from the bridge in another flash of blinding green light. The force of the translocation left Beth dizzy and shivering. She slumped to the floor after they rematerialized.

"Damn shield," Goren muttered.

Beth had time to recognize Rose sitting in a dirty cell, before angry shouts erupted from the other side of the door. Beth saw, to her dismay, two dirty bandages on her team leader. One was on

Rose's worried face, and the other was visible through the bloody tear in her pants. She had barricaded the door with the few meager pieces of furniture in the room, a bed and chair. It would take the guards only a few precious seconds to break through.

"Time to go," said Goren, grabbing Rose's wrist and pulling Beth to her feet.

This time the three translocated to the council room. It was filled with alien devices that could easily be retracted into convenient hollow spaces, leaving no sign of their existence. With her back to the room, Ione was turning knobs on a lighted panel. When she jumped to an adjacent lighted pedestal, she caught sight of Beth, Rose, and Goren.

"Going somewhere?" Goren asked unnecessarily.

The machine glowed brighter, and the pedestal began to crackle. Ione smiled in triumph. In a third flash of green light, Goren appeared beside her on the pedestal.

"I don't think you'll be wiggling out of this one. It seems you've been up to trouble once too often, Ione." Goren grinned devilishly.

He picked her up and carried her off the machine, tossing her roughly into a corner. After powering down the device, Goren returned to Ione, shaking his head in disappointment.

"I thought your race stayed out of other people's affairs," Ione retorted, her eyes bright with panic. Apparently, she didn't even try to use her psychic traps on Goren. It seemed reputation could influence events.

"That is usually true. You have managed to create an exception."

A commotion at the door drew everyone's attention. Beth watched uneasily as Amy, Sam, Sophie, and Nicole, connected by ankle and wrist chains, were led into the room. They were each assigned their own jailer, in every case a slovenly, squat brute with rotting teeth and yellow skin.

"Good, my surprise has arrived." Ione looked directly at Rose, her eyes sparking evilly. "You'll notice that your Quanta couldn't make our little gathering. We're studying them more thoroughly. Our earlier examination was so rudely interrupted." She glanced around and caught Goren studying the newcomers with an intense, measuring gaze. "I would be careful, Goren, before you try anything nasty."

Beth's stomach flipped uneasily. Her connection to her own navigation partner, Axel, was profound. She couldn't imagine what they were doing to Ari and the others. Whatever it was, it couldn't be good.

Unexpectedly, Goren returned Ione's smile. His next words caught Beth completely by surprise. She'd been convinced that the tides had turned against them. It now seemed that everything was progressing favorably.

"Good, now that everyone is together, I can settle affairs with you once and for all. Your greatest flaw, Ione, is that you've always overestimated your own power and underestimated everyone else's.

"The reason the Guardians haven't interfered with Sentara before now is because the spores that are responsible for your amplified senses had taken responsibility for you. You see, they are actually the most intelligent native life-form of this planet. But you have left us with no choice. Violent races cannot act without consequences in our sector of this galaxy."

Then, in a manner that was right out of an old B movie, Goren raised his arms. A low hum echoed through the large room, growing in volume. The windows began to vibrate and ultimately broke in a series of crashing explosions. Roaring flames of power consumed the form Beth knew as Goren.

"No, wait," Ione squeaked, her supreme confidence gone. She ran to the blazing light that had been Goren and fell to her knees, her hands clasped together, sobbing uncontrollably. She seemed to have some idea of what was coming. Beth sure as hell didn't, and, from Ione's behavior, she was sure she didn't want to.

The floor rumbled and shook, and the doors and window frames melted, leaving raw holes to the outside, even though the room remained cool. The inferno that was Goren danced around the room and blasted every piece of alien technology. Then he surgically targeted and destroyed the chains that held the BESS crew. The guards backed away, terror distorting their features. A translocation green flash signaled the return of their abused Quanta. Having a Guardian on their side definitely cut through a lot of red tape.

Then Beth heard a strange weeping, which grew louder by the second. At each opening in the room, amid the melted wreckage of glass and concrete, dozens of creatures whined, wailed, sniveled, and yowled. The weight of their numbers pushed the nearest inside, and the humans were crowded to the center of the room. As far as Beth could see, animals crawled, hopped, and slithered into the council room. It was a display unmatched by any she had ever seen.

Some of the creatures so closely resembled Earth animals, Beth couldn't tell the difference. Others had extra parts that made them distinctly Sentaran. All of them were facing the bright flames that receded back into the form of Goren. Although no one spoke, Goren gestured as if in heated conversation. Then, noticing the blank faces of the humans, he waved, and Beth could hear the dialogue.

"You can't interferrrr," a small voice beseeched.

Beth studied the group of animals surrounding Goren. To her surprise, it was one of the smallest that spoke. She wondered what distinguished this one from the others, until she heard the creature's persuasive appeal.

"We, on Sentara, are many species who live as one community. Would you really kill all of us for the actions of the chairwoman and her guards? How can you use violence to condemn violence?"

Beth was confused. Was Goren really going to kill everyone on Sentara? Is that what had scared Ione?

"Ione and her men have acted independently of the decisions of our conclave." The small creature's voice conveyed a desperation that touched Beth's heart. "She said the humans would help her race overcome their terrible deterioration. We didn't know she intended to imprison them against their will. She will be dealt with, and the humans will be allowed to return home."

"I want to stay, at least for a while." Sam came forward with several small animals perched on his shoulders and in his arms. "Sentarans and humans are genetically the same race. We could learn things of incalculable value from their experiences here. The unique community on this planet could be preserved. Cragon and her people can be restrained, given the proper inducement. If the alien spores allow us to stay, I would like to make contact with them. They must be a remarkable race."

A favorable rustling greeted his request.

Goren shook his head sadly at Sam. "The animals can't control the humans, or they would have already. Ione and her supporters, on the other hand, will overpower you and try to use human technology to contact other susceptible races. They need to pay the price for their actions."

Again the humming began, and again the animals' cries rang out.

During this discussion, a kernel of an idea had taken root in Beth's mind. She dashed to Goren's side and reached through the flames to stop his transformation. She knew she had more influence over Goren than the others did. Maybe he would listen to her.

"What we need is a policing agency for the Sentarans," she suggested meekly. "We could act as watchers, who would live on Sentara after acquiring the same enhanced abilities and who would warn outsiders away. We could use Earth volunteers, individuals who have already sired children or who don't want any. Meanwhile, our scientists could research the Sentarans' unique deterioration. If we could find a solution, then the Sentarans wouldn't be a problem for anyone anymore. All we are asking for is time, Goren, time to help a race in trouble, time to help a race of ancient humans. Admittedly, they have acted terribly, but we have faced this dark side of our nature for centuries and have achieved some measure of success at building an honorable society."

"We can imprison the chairwoman Cragon where she can do no further harrrm," reminded the small speaker for the rising tide of creatures.

Goren finally relented. "If the humans are willing to act as security and guarantee compliance, I will put you all on probation." He stumbled over the unfamiliar word and then smiled and winked at Beth before turning to face the larger group.

She heard his voice whisper in her ear. "It worked. Sometimes the illusion of lethal consequences is more effective than actual violence.

"Remember this day," Goren intoned. "For if I come again, there will be no stay, and whoever is on this planet will face a shared fate." Goren looked directly at the other council members, who, drawn by the commotion, had entered the crumbling council room. "The Earthlings will have equal standing with the Sentaran humans. Since they are accepting the responsibility for monitoring you and for the consequences of failure, they deserve some standing."

Raising his voice so everyone in the room could hear, Goren declared his conditions.

"In this capital, you will erect a monument documenting this day. A video will run showing your leaders signing the treaty that holds you to this planet with human watchers. The treaty will be available for anyone to read. I will include a hologram of what I was about to do. For those who do not know the terrible wrath of the Guardians, you will see it now. You can be certain we will carry out our promise should you resume your criminal activities."

Goren waved his hand, and above the crowd appeared a completely alien landscape. The sky was green, and the water brown. A city pushed out the natural world like a nest of soldier ants consuming all life in its path. The inhabitants were short, square, scowling creatures who wore metal instead of cloth. The image left Beth unaccountably queasy.

A figure who was obviously kin to Goren raised his hands and spread his arms wide. He transformed into a roaring column of fire whose flames dripped bloodred sparks. The natives watched the Guardian scornfully, unprepared for the devastation to come. The flame coiled and slithered, touching the bold soldiers, who were standing close by. These foolish beings vanished instantly, replaced by a blackened hole. The rest of the doomed audience, realizing their peril, shrieked horribly as they ran back toward their city. But the fire couldn't be outrun, and it slid through the city, stopping to consume many more of the running soldiers.

"Remember," Goren stated with a cold, ominous finality. Then he vanished in a flash of green.

Beth hid her smile. Goren sure did know how to put on a good show.

CHAPTER 22

THE CITRINAL SPHERE—CHRIS

Siri hastily reinstalled the capacitor, and Chris laughed with relief at the welcome, familiar buzz. Beth immediately responded to her call for help.

"Chris, what's happening?"

"We're being attacked by the Citrinals, one of the native populations on Citron."

Beth's surprised cough briefly interrupted Chris's desperate explanation.

"I think we may have started a civil war," Chris cried. "We need you here as quickly as possible."

Chris glanced at the ship's rear camera and saw, to her horror, a mass of specks speeding directly for them. The Citrinals were riding their refugees like horses. That this was possible in the vacuum of space was terrifying.

"They're following us. We're about to be attacked," she shrieked.

The *Aries* appeared seconds later. Their home ship swung in front of the smaller ASH cruiser to shield her from the advancing aliens.

The Citrinal horde swarmed the human ships and then solidified into thick sheets of dense ice, forming a spherical prison that encapsulated the *Aries* and ASH. Layer upon layer of ice was laid down until it completely blocked out the light.

In the back of Chris's cruiser, Mac and Lena began to thrash restlessly. Until now, her two infected friends had remained unconscious. Then Chris heard Lena cry out in pain.

"Why isn't that stupid antidote working?" Chris snapped, frustrated.

They had risked everything on the hope that it would cure Mac and Lena. Apparently, once the Citrinals knew their human hosts had been injected with the brown sludge, they had launched their attack against the surveyors. Chris headed to the back to offer comfort to her friends. She could do nothing about their new prison. All the ASH had was shields.

As if matters weren't gloomy enough, wild electrical sparks suddenly jumped along the ceiling and walls, very much like those in the ice forming outside. At the same time, silver alluvium began to ooze from Lena and Mac, causing them to cry out in a rising crescendo of piercing screams before they collapsed again. The Citrinals, after escaping from their bodies, reformed into balls and flooded the cabin with more electrical current.

Mitch was attacked first. He had time to scream once before he slumped into unconsciousness. Chris tried to reach the transmitter to warn Beth of this new threat. Even as her symbiont wailed in helpless fury, the electricity focused on her, and she sank into a cramping darkness that allowed no argument.

CHAPTER 23

QUANTA SECRETS—SIRI

As soon as their humans were rendered unconscious and vulnerable, Siri and Ella flew into action. Siri extended a funnel-shaped device toward the Citrinals inside the ASH. Despite a renewed flurry of electrical bolts aimed at them, the Quanta deflected the danger unaffected. They had erected personal protective shields using the same technology as those installed in the ships.

Then Siri activated the funnel. It generated enough suction to pull on anything not tied down. Every loose object in the small ship flew toward him. The mineral beings resisted fiercely. Inevitably, however, they were sucked up the funnels into specially shielded compartments. Then Siri popped out, to reappear outside the growing ice structure.

With a beep of satisfaction, he spat Lena's and Mac's Citrinal symbionts out into space, ridding the humans of the pesky, persistent invaders. Giving the Citrinals no time to react, he vanished again and reappeared inside the ice prison a few feet from the *Aries* and the ASH. The five other Quanta—Axel, Ari, Mirim, Evan, and Ella—were already floating there at predetermined positions.

With the arrival of Siri, they formed a complete circle around the stranded ships.

Then they began spinning, blinking in and out of visible space. Siri lost all sense of himself as a separate and distinct entity. He was one with a greater wholeness that extended throughout the nexus. Every exploration spaceship and many establishments on Earth had at least one Quanta, and he could see them all. With each blink, he and the others were replaced with their twins, no matter how far away they had been stationed. Physical space could not separate a Quanta pair. A shuffling blackness emerged, resembling the black spots one sees after staring at the sun. These spots grew into larger and larger pockets of darkness that expanded to surround the Quanta and both ships.

This strange behavior drew the attention of the hostile aliens, and they stopped building their unique ice prison. The Citrinals that were still individualized rode away from the sphere, which began to spark and crackle more aggressively. Webs of electrical current crisscrossed the ice structure, expanding to cover more surface area. When the entire Citrinal sphere was blazing with waves of sizzling power, a beam as wide as the *Aries* itself erupted and headed straight for the two vulnerable ships.

But it didn't destroy the *Aries* and ASH. The Quantas' envelope of blackness absorbed the bolt of energy and reflected it back on the Citrinals. The beam burned through the ice cage and splintered the structure into millions of slivers. The resulting ice chips continued to spark with electricity, which fed the beam until it found its way down to Citron's surface. As soon as it hit the planet, the beam vanished. Obviously, the Citrinals would not allow their weapon to damage their home.

Siri and his Quanta kin had created a singularity intrinsic to their quantum nature. The black phenomenon was a gravitation well so dense that all matter and energy were thrown back from it. Unfortunately for the Citrinals, the Quanta weren't done. Siri and the others reversed the direction of their spin, this time moving so fast they were an unearthly milky blur. The blackness collapsed and was replaced with a huge deadly maw. The Citrinal droplets, in the midst of converting from ice into their normal form, were pulled relentlessly into the vacuum of its impenetrable darkness. The droplets desperately combined into bigger and bigger structures as they tried to use their collective power to pull away from the vacuum. Every new drop that crashed into the growing ball of multiple aliens slowed the structure's fall into the maw.

After a final herculean surge of power, the Citrinals' forward motion came to a shuddering halt. They reversed direction and began struggling ferociously back toward their home. In response, the speed of Siri's quantum circle increased. This time they were spinning so fast they vanished entirely, replaced by the whisper of acceleration. The resulting magnetic force was just too great to resist. One by one, the Citrinals were pulled off the ball and yanked into the black orifice. If water drops could scream in the emptiness of space, in that moment, they would have.

To Siri's horror, the vanishing Citrinals called to their brothers on the planet, begging to be rescued. Millions more of their race rushed out into space, clinging to the last of the refugees, in a last-ditch effort to save their brothers. Their efforts only threw them into the path of what was voraciously devouring their comrades, and they too evaporated into the nothingness created by the Quanta.

Realizing they were about to annihilate an entire alien race, Siri and the others screeched to a halt, hoping to save the last of the Citrinals and their refugees, who never stopped fighting to escape. But the maw collapsed too slowly, and when at last it was gone, so were all the Citrinals.

CHAPTER 24
STRANGE REQUEST—BETH

Both the ASH and BESS were safely docked back on the *Aries*, ending Beth's current mission for all practical purposes. Two teams combining Quanta and human mediators were heading to Citron and Sentara in order to negotiate treaties with the locals.

Nicole had effectively ended her career with Central Alliance when she had turned on Amy, so she was being escorted back to Earth. After Talia's death, she had lost her usual enthusiasm anyway. Sam had managed to obtain permission to bring a sample of the strange alien spores back to the ship. Mac and Lena were returning to Earth for examination and rehabilitation. They were suffering from post-traumatic stress brought on by their brief bond to the Citrinals. Obviously, losing a symbiont was not an easy adjustment. Chris and Mitch would be staying on the *Aries* until their symbionts' bracelets ran out of silver-mind fluid and they had to travel back to Citron for regeneration.

Beth had assumed that the *Aries* would also be returning to Earth for new staff and new orders. But the alliance had kept her out in deep space. She had been instructed to continue her astronomical studies while replacement crew were cleared and sent to a rendezvous location.

So she instructed Axel to set a heading for the mysterious and intriguing Dragon Nebula. Their musical engines had just begun their acceleration melodies, signaling the initial phase of a portal shift, when Goren's voice jerked her out of the early stages of her trance. It was unsettling, to say the least.

"Beth?"

Quantum shifting took complete concentration and delicate maneuvering, so his interruption meant they would have to start again. Axel disengaged the ship's drive after hearing Goren's call, and the ship rematerialized back in normal space-time.

"What is it?" she snapped. She wished she could have some warning before he spoke, like a ring or a bell. She wanted the choice to refuse his call in case she had to, for example, finish climbing a steep cliff or battle aliens or make a delicate portal shift.

His next inquiry left her speechless. Of all the things he might have said, this was not even on her list of possibilities.

"May I join your crew? I would greatly increase your chances of finding galactic curiosities," he coaxed. "I find your race's enthusiasm contagious, and I would like to partner with you in the same manner as your Quanta. We've isolated ourselves long enough."

"What about the Treasury?" Beth asked, after closing her gaping mouth.

"The Treasury progresses at its own speed. It doesn't require constant attention. My mechanical assistants handle all maintenance issues. This detour is no different from other expeditions I have taken to collect artifacts. Time passes differently for us. It's that long-lived thing," he teased, reminding her of their earlier confidences.

Beth couldn't even imagine what fabulous assignments a Guardian member would gain the *Aries*. She could hardly believe their good fortune.

"It seems we have a new member of our crew," she announced without further preamble. "He is the Guardian, Goren. Some of you met him on Sentara."

Mark whistled, Connor growled, and Axel just twirled in excitement. With a flair for the dramatic, Goren appeared on the bridge wearing an *Aries* uniform and a pair of large black-framed glasses. The crew eyed their new member speculatively.

"Let's get out of here. I believe we have a date with a dragon," Beth quipped, winking at Mark. She turned back toward Axel. Sometimes it was best to avoid questions.

ABOUT THE AUTHOR

Carol Johnson enjoys a rich history of personal and professional experiences that animate her tales. As a CPA, she has learned the intricacies of navigating government and legal systems. As a prolific photographer, she has discovered the wealth of beauty hiding in the countries around the world, inspiring the landscapes in her novels.

As an eager adventurer, she has lived in the beautiful Alaskan wilderness for three years; spent a memorable month long vacation visiting the temples of Athens, the caves of Crete, and the pyramids of Cairo; cruised the exotic islands of colorful Puerto Rico, St Lucia, Barbados, and St. Marteen, and climbed the snowcapped volcanos and hidden woodlands of Washington State.

9 780996 132206